DEAMHAN
DEAMHAN CHRONICLES

ISAIYAN MORRISON

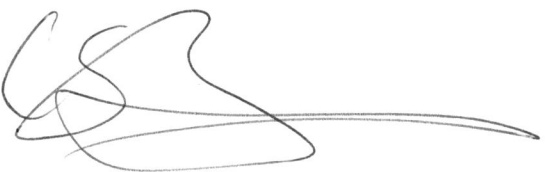

Rainstorm Press

Rainstorm Press
PO BOX 391038
Anza, Ca 92539
www.RainstormPress.com

ISBN 10 − 1-937758-40-0
ISBN 13 − 978-1-937758-40-0

Library of Congress: 2013947563

Deamhan
Publisher: Rainstorm Press
Copyright © 2013 by Rainstorm Press
Text Copyright © 2013 Adebusola Adesiji

Interior book design by −

The Mad Formatter
www.TheMadFormatter.com

Cover Design by: John Cosentino

Special Thanks

To the Adesiji family. Thank you for believing that I could do this! I love you all!

To the Haskins family. Thank you so much for being there for me and believing in my ideas. I miss you guys and promise to visit soon! Tomika, Alexis, Sina . . . you gals are too wonderful and I'm blessed to have supportive friends like you.

To my boyfriend. You've been my rock and have always had my back. I love you! Here's to a promising career! Keeping my fingers crossed.

DEAMHAN

PROLOGUE

The rain carried the yellow-imbued blood down the sewer drain behind Caroline Austin, leaving an uncanny trail. The water fell like sheets from the heavens, blinding and suffocating her while she ran down the empty Minneapolis streets. The small, open wounds on her breasts throbbed in uncontrollable pain. Caroline swiped at the seeping blood in an attempt to dilute her trail, wishing the dark liquid would mix with the rain and disappear.

Caroline heard the heavy footsteps closing in behind her. Her legs buckled, and she fell to the pavement, the dirty rainwater sloshing into her eyes, blinding her. Her mind raced with sordid thoughts of death. She didn't want to die, not here, not now, but her body froze in fear, and she couldn't move. She closed her eyes, focusing on the image of her daughter that glowed for a brief moment in the darkness. The image gave her unusual strength, and she shoved her body upward, forcing herself to stand. The sound of approaching footsteps snapped her mind back to reality.

In front of her, a bum sprawled on the sidewalk, was sound asleep. She ran toward him, opening her mouth to scream, to wake him from his drunken stupor. Yet no sound would come. The sudden, cold draft of death from behind kept her running. She turned the corner and there was Lucius.

She tried to catch herself, to turn and run the other away, but she slipped and fell in front of him. Looking up at his figure before her, she wondered how anyone as old as him could be so fast. Lucius leaned against the building, his brown hair falling gracefully behind his back. His smooth, oval face shone, his concerned gaze releasing some of her fear. His eyes could lock even the most nonsubmissive Deamhan and bring them to their knees. She had never been this close to him. She always believed she never would.

He took slow steps toward her, holding out his hands. Surely he knew of her strong interest in him. She'd written detailed articles and biographies about him. These same writings were influential in her organization's understanding of the Deamhan. Before her, not much was known about his origins. She'd uncovered the rumors and silenced speculations without invading the privacy he had left.

He took another step toward her, and this time she moved back. It plagued him that she feared for her life. She noticed small droplets of rain glistening off his face in delicate drops.

Caroline turned to run, but he again appeared in front of her, blocking her way. She stumbled and fell to the pavement, her breath coming hard. His cold hands scooped her into his arms without effort, brushing her wet and matted bangs from her pale forehead. Her eyes gazed away, unable to stare at him while he brushed his cold hands against her right cheek.

He noticed a fresh, wet bloodstain above her right breast. Pulling back her shirt, the Deamhan found a small, jagged wound. Deep.

She was dying.

The stranger held her close to his chest and turned to carry her to safety. *How dare they not follow his decree!* He'd been clear: they weren't to harm or attack her. She was protected. One of his own had disobeyed the law, ratcheting up the tension between the Deamhan groups.

He placed her ear next to his heart, hoping to keep her awake.

She opened her mouth to speak, but he silenced her, touching an icy finger to her lips.

"Sleep, Mrs. Austin." His voice was soft. "You are safe here . . . with me."

CHAPTER ONE

Veronica Austin stood in line behind a tall woman with long black hair, her blonde roots clearly visible in the streetlight brightening the corner. A circular tribal tattoo of jagged black lines decorated the base of the woman's neck between her broad shoulders.

Dad never liked tattoos.

He didn't like the idea of Veronica returning to Minneapolis after twenty years either, but that didn't stop her.

A huge neon sign hanging above the entrance glared "Dark Sepulcher," with the "L" blinking in rapid succession. Black paint peeled from the brick walls, now discolored from years of treacherous Minnesota winters. Posters of upcoming concerts and events lined the wall. Veronica wasn't interested. At a glance, you'd mistake the building for an old factory, but Veronica knew better. She'd been told that the building housed secrets—dark secrets—and she planned to discover each one. This was the starting point in the search for her mother.

She cleared her throat and the woman glanced back, giving her a half-smile. Instead of real eyebrows, the woman had drawn severe black swathes with an eyeliner pencil, and she'd colored her lipstick line above her upper lip, giving her mouth a full, yet abstract look.

Two bouncers stood at the front entrance dressed in black T-shirts with "Security" printed in white letters. Veronica handed the taller bouncer her California driver's license and waited while he studied it under the glare of his bright flashlight. She sucked in breath, preparing herself for questions about why she'd come and what she wanted with Dark Sepulcher. Instead, the bouncer flicked the license back to her and motioned for her to enter.

Veronica slid a five under the steel bars of the cashier's window, who snapped up the bill without a glance as she bobbed her head to the beat from her earphones. Veronica thought she recognized the chorus of "Devil Went Down to Georgia" by Charlie Daniels escape from the girl's earphones, but it drowned under the bass coming from behind a thick, dark curtain blocking the venue's entrance. She stepped forward, sucked in another deep breath, and pulled the curtain back.

She wondered how her mother felt, walking into this same mysterious environment nearly twenty years ago. The question repeated in her head like a broken record. She needed an answer. Her mother had always been a quiet and loyal wife. What could drive the woman to go against her husband's wishes and visit Dark Sepulcher? Could it be the same force now thrusting Veronica to follow in her mother's footsteps?

No one in her father's bastardized organization—The Brotherhood—had the balls to question her mother's disappearance. No one except for Veronica. Her father buried all photographs and mementos of her mother and he sent Veronica to San Diego to live under the care of The Brotherhood. His actions had since festered inside Veronica's wounded heart. He'd sold family heirlooms, pawned his wedding ring. He'd destroyed family pictures—the frozen moments that captured family outings, picnics, and celebrations.

Now, Veronica remembered only one picture of her and her mother standing in front of a rollercoaster on a hot Saturday. Her mother wore white shorts with a black fanny pack, white sandals, and a pink short-sleeved shirt. Veronica wore her favorite white dress decorated with butterflies and flowers. Though she'd been only five at the time, she remembered the moment as if it happened yesterday. They'd stood in line at the water park, waiting for their turn on the "Wet Excursion." They'd just finished a bag of sugar doughnuts. Her father could throw away the photo, but nothing he could do would fade the memory of that day.

She'd become a threat to her father who now had the title: President of the Midwest Division. The Brotherhood had split America into three divisions long ago with each division answering to the Head Master—the overall leader of the organization. During the time of her mother's disappearance, her father held the title of Region Leader, a step below President, and his duties included handing out orders to the researchers under his control, one being his own wife; Veronica's mother.

Veronica trusted The Brotherhood (humans who studied and documented the Deamhan from afar) as much as she trusted words from a politician's mouth. They were known throughout the Deamhan world as humans who watched but never interfered. But something happened during the time of her mother's disappearance. Somehow they had intruded on the Deamhan and for this; the President of the Midwest Division was killed. The Minnesota Chapter disbanded, her father was promoted and the researchers scattered to the Eastern and Western Divisions, leaving Minnesota. Afterwards, the Deamhan grew stronger in numbers and without the eyes of any human on them, they also grew more violent.

When her father heard she planned on moving back to Minnesota, he warned her to not reopen her mother's case. In the past, Veronica had believed whatever Daddy said to be was the honest-to-God truth. If he'd told her the earth was flat, she'd have thrown out her globe. Parents never lie. Her daddy never lied.

Not until her mother disappeared.

Now, Veronica had no clue what she might encounter in Dark Sepulcher. As she pulled back the heavy curtain, her eyes jumped frantically back and forth as they tried to adjust to the darkness. Life-sized macramé figures hung from the ceiling. White smoke spewed from fog machines and drifted ghostlike toward the crowded dance floor. Writhing bodies moved in trance-like motion to throbbing music blasting from massive speakers surrounding the floor. Veronica felt an unexplainable euphoric vibe circling the club with the fog. It enthralled her.

This wasn't the scary Dark Sepulcher from the story told to children at bedtime to frighten them from misbehaving. *"If you act up, the scary Deamhan will get you!"*

No, this is party central.

Or so she thought.

Veronica focused her stare on a small stage standing erect to her left. A wooden beam hung horizontally above the stage with a woman tied fast to the beam. She was topless except for small pieces of black tape covering her nipples. A short man wearing a tuxedo stood before her, alternately caressing and slapping her stomach with a wooden paddle. Her face cringed and relaxed with each slap. Her eyes rolled to the back of her head and her tongue darted out, glazing her lips.

A small crowd had gathered around, watching the public display of foreplay. Veronica felt the erotic tension of the group increase with each slap of the woman's stomach. The group began to sway, slithering and smiling by the controlled fiasco.

Though mesmerized, Veronica moved on, passing a row of silver-tinted booths next to the wall. A group of boys and girls, none appearing older than eighteen, huddled in the corner booth talking over a small lit candle in the middle of the table. They laughed aloud, shouting over one another until their voices became a jumble. The music changed to a faster rhythm and they fled the booth, pushing past Veronica in their rush to reach the dance floor.

Much to Veronica's relief, everyone looked human. None of the clubbers possessed traits of the Deamhan: the sharp fangs, the dark hollow eyes, the pale, ashy skin. She'd expected them to ooze from the woodwork, romping around like drug addicts looking for their next high.

The speakers pulsed with beats of industrial music. She felt the bass thumping and vibrating each inch of her body. She'd been to raves and dance clubs in San Diego before, but the music had never been this loud.

Of course, The Brotherhood had an explanation for the loud music. Before she left, Veronica raided their files, discovering what information she could about the club. A vampire, quite different from the Deamhan, owned Dark Sepulcher. To Veronica, vampires and Deamhan were one and the same—evil, foul and wretched, yet they also had differences. While vampires lived off the blood of humans, Deamhan lived off the psychic energy generated from humans in different ways.

11

Their loud music drowned the screams of victims held in torture chambers below Dark Sepulcher. They perfumed the air with strong, sweet incense, covering the smell of rotting flesh and tainted blood. Of course, Veronica hardly believed everything The Brotherhood said about the Deamhan, but she remained on edge, just the same. How could she not? She'd lost her mother here. Still, her body couldn't help but move to the pounding beat. The fog-filled room, the gyrating bodies, the electrified air, it all combined to assuage her worries. Despite herself, she felt her lips part in a seductive smile.

And that's when she saw her first Deamhan.

In the writhing crowd, a woman tossed back her head and laughed. She twirled her pale hands above her head as she danced, her long brown hair bouncing around her shoulders. A true professional at mimicking human movements, she'd made a flawless attempt to hide her true identity. The darkness hid the most visible signs, but her razor-edged teeth could not be masked. "She's a Deamhan Ramanga," Veronica whispered into the deafening din. Even as she said the words, she felt her heartbeat pick up its pace.

A baby-faced guy dancing with the Deamhan seductively snaked his arms around her tiny waist and ground his pelvis against her. *Is he crazy?* The boy had to see those teeth up close and personal. He had to know she could sink them into his tender flesh at any moment. *Why didn't he run?*

Every child who grew up in The Brotherhood knew the tales of the Deamhan. Teenagers in the organization played pranks and blamed their stunts on these creatures, whether or not they believed in their existence. Every tale described the Deamhan as being bloodthirsty as starving wild dogs. These ruthless creatures didn't think twice about killing anyone, including researchers and those they sired. They maintained their secrecy by hiding, remaining unknown to the world around them. They weren't as old as the vampires but even the vampires feared them. But here they stood, in a vampire club, doing what they wanted without anyone to tell them otherwise. They walked, talked, danced and conversed with their human food.

Alert to their presence now, Veronica scanned the crowd. Deamhan, it seemed, popped up everywhere. Many danced in groups, though some danced alone. Others danced with a single partner, human and Deamhan alike. Yet fear didn't exist, except in Veronica's fluttering chest. No one else cared.

The cities of Minneapolis and Saint Paul had turned into a breeding ground for the Deamhan. The cities had to deal with progressive but painful development stages, and Veronica had noticed these changes immediately upon her return to the city. The downtown skyline had undergone transformation by skyscrapers. Condominiums had popped up on any land that could support them. The Mall of America—an oversized mega-center supporting the habits of shopping addicts who could spend a month's salary in a day—had expanded in the years since she'd left. As if it needed to be bigger. The new attention the city earned also affected the Deamhan. Minneapolis no longer fit its moniker of

"Mini City." The Deamhan adapted to its growth and changes to survive. Dark Sepulcher served as an excellent example of how well—and fearlessly—they'd adapted.

Still, one thing about Minneapolis remained the same. Its seasons never changed. Always—forever—would come winter, spring, summer, and Veronica's favorite, fall. Autumn brought relief in cooler weather, longer nights, and colorful trees spreading their blanket of decaying leaves across the ground. A sudden memory of her mother raking the yard, stuffing leaves into orange bags painted with jack-o'-lantern faces sprang into Veronica's mind. She remembered how they decorated their house with cardboard cutouts of Frankenstein, ghosts and vampires. Now here she stood, walking among their kind.

"Yep. Minneapolis has definitely changed," she whispered to herself again. "And so have I."

She pushed the recollections to the hindmost part of her mind. She had to focus, couldn't let her guard down, even for a moment. This place was theirs. Here, the Deamhan walked without fear.

But so did the humans.

To her right, a large crowd had gathered at the bar, cheering on a man who chugged a full bottle of vodka. A cadaverous woman with blonde dreadlocks stood behind him, caressing his shoulders with red-tipped fingers. Her formal black dress accentuated svelte curves, and her crimson lips formed a perfect "O" as she cheered on the drinking man. Even from several yards away, Veronica could see the bright white contrast of the woman's spiky teeth.

When the man downed the bottle's last drop, fists and shouts pierced the air, and the bartender passed another bottle to the blonde Deamhan. She suggestively licked the neck of the bottle, revealing her pointy canines and passed the bottle to the man, who thrust it over his head, then resumed his guzzling.

Veronica shuddered and turned away, immediately spotting two Deamhan males. They ogled the dancing crowd with lusty eyes as they moved like liquid throughout the club, indifferent of being known and unhindered by any repercussions it might cost them.

Veronica felt a gentle tap on her right shoulder and jumped. She whirled around, coming face-to-face with a young waitress with a tray tucked under her left arm, her right hand perched on a pillar.

"You want anything?" she screamed above the music.

Veronica only shook her head, startled by the woman's bizarre appearance. She wore a black wife beater, faded black pants, and her mascara was smeared and smudged. She winked and smiled a welcoming smile, then turned on her heel and disappeared into the crowd.

The music thundered even louder now, and Veronica returned her attention to the dance floor. Two dancers clad in sheer white shirts, micro-minis, and fishnet stockings gyrated on a raised stage in the center of the dance floor, while the horde of men below them at floor-level clawed at their feet. One of the dancers

13

placed the spiked heel of her knee-high boot against a man's forehead and shoved him backward. Like shamans in a ritual trance, the men and women twirled their hands and moved their hips from side to side.

Veronica stared at the performance until the rapidly blinking dance lights caused vertigo to set in. Feeling nauseous, she turned and leaned against the railing that separated the dance floor from the rest of the carpeted venue. She swallowed back bile, resisting the urge to regurgitate the ham and cheese sandwich she'd wolfed down earlier.

The tiny hairs on the back of her neck danced. She felt the waitress standing behind her and stiffened. Veronica knew it was vital to hide her thoughts from the Deamhan, and she did her best to make her mind a blank slate by imagining a brick wall.

She'd heard the stories from her best friend Sean Fechin about researchers in The Brotherhood having their thoughts invaded by a Deamhan. It was just one of their various abilities. They couldn't control humans like vampires could with the sounds of their voices. Instead they forced themselves into a human's brain, scouring it for any information they desired. Each of the researchers told Sean it hurt like hell.

"You okay?" The waitress tapped Veronica on the shoulder.

Veronica slowly turned around, trying to envision a blank wall.

"You sure you don't want anything?"

A bottle of Jack popped into her mind. "Whiskey."

"Whiskey?"

"Yeah, just whiskey."

The waitress twisted her mouth into a wry smile. "Whiskey it is, then." She headed for the bar.

Veronica turned back to the dance floor, appreciative that the music had changed tempo and volume. A slow song oozed throughout the club. One of the dancers left the stage, men trailing behind her like hungry pups. She stopped just outside the bathroom door, and the men jammed into one another like cars at a traffic light. The dancer graced them with a sultry smile, blew a kiss, and closed the door behind her. As if the spell she'd held over them had broken, the men glanced at each other in confusion, then each headed back toward the dance floor.

The waitress seemed to appear out of nowhere again, and she placed a shot of whiskey on the table in front of Veronica.

Veronica handed her a five. "Keep the change."

"Thanks." She folded the bill between her fingers with one hand, and tucked it in her cleavage. "Anything else I can do for ya?"

"Yeah. How long has this place been open?" Veronica glanced around, feigning awe. She didn't expect hiding her thoughts to be so difficult.

The Brotherhood had Goliath-sized manuals about dealing with the Deamhan, if you encountered one. All new researchers were required to read and study

14

the book prior to their first honorary mission into the world of the Deamhan. But Veronica refused. Instead, she took the route of the non-professional. She practiced the "How to Control Your Mind" exercises from *Dummy* books she'd loaned from the library in San Diego. Sean also helped by smuggling copies of affidavits from field researchers that explained how they'd reacted when they were in the presence of a Deamhan. She relied on these stolen copies to help her survive in this new world. Now, she hoped she'd studied enough.

The waitress rolled her coal-rimmed eyes to the ceiling and tapped her chin. "It's been here forever." She shrugged.

"It's always packed like this?"

She smiled. "Oh, yeah. Everyone comes here. There's nothing else to do in boring Minnea-snore-a." She gave Veronica an once-over appraisal. "You here by yourself?"

"No, I'm with a friend."

"Well, have fun. It's a kick ass club." She waved and walked away.

Veronica tossed back the whiskey and gagged as it stung the back of her throat. The volume of the music increased again, and the crowd's jollity changed with it. They cheered, pumping their hands at the DJ booth in unison. The DJ whistled into his microphone in response, nearly deafening Veronica.

She finished the rest of her whiskey, sipping slower this time, as she scanned the crowd. Her stomach gurgled a complaint against the harsh liquor. She sought the bathroom door again and noticed a crowd of women pushing in. *Better go get in line. This could take a while.*

Veronica excused herself through the crowd, passing another group of scantily dressed teenagers. Her eyes settled on an older couple nestled quietly in a corner booth. Their arms wrapped around each other in a quiet embrace, watching the dance floor. *How odd.*

Cautiously, Veronica pushed open the bathroom door. A group of women stood in various poses in front of the cracked and broken mirrors near the far wall. She stepped over the clumps of matted hair and wet, crumpled toilet paper on the bathroom's white-tiled floor, noticing the wet garbage lining the sinks and stalls. The toilet in the last stall overflowed, spilling its nasty contents onto the floor. The bathroom's filth contrasted the rest of the club. Dozens of different conversations overlapped one another, and the sound of the running toilet grated Veronica's nerves. A few of the women glanced up, then continued pasting on make-up in blotches of cherry, amber, peach, tan, purple and black.

Not all of them were human. One woman, particularly ghostly, applied a heavy layer of face powder to give her skin a normal hue. She painted her eyes, lips, and cheeks to eliminate her Deamhan markings. Veronica saw the dancer, now standing in front of the mirror brushing her hair. She chatted freely with the Deamhan woman, giving her tips on what kind of makeup appealed to men.

A chill snaked up Veronica's spine.

The dancer shoved her hand into her red backpack and pulled out more cosmetics to add to the many bottles and tubes littering the sink.

Veronica approached the sinks, her steps tentative. The dancer watched Veronica's silent approach in the mirror. In one swift motion, the female Deamhan scooped her belongings into an oversized handbag and pushed her way out the door. The other women followed, leaving Veronica and the dancer alone.

Veronica adjusted the water temperature to cool and prepared to splash her face, but was afraid to take her eyes off the dancer. She knew she should say something, but "Hello" might sound bold. "What a nice night" seemed silly. "You're a really good dancer." Nah. The woman would think she was hitting on her.

"You have to wait a minute," the dancer said as she stared at Veronica's hands.

Veronica glanced down and then jerked her hands from the milky water gushing from the faucet. In a moment, the water ran clear.

"Thanks," Veronica said. "I nearly put that on my face." She noticed a healing scar above the dancer's collarbone, slightly discolored. A scab wound extended from the middle of her back down to her cleavage, stitched together with dried blood. Healed bite marks covered her neck.

The Brotherhood called them *minions*—humans who spied and reported to their Deamhan owners the details of who, what, when and where. They were mentally unstable, dangerous, and they vied to be sired by serving their masters well. They dreamed of becoming powerful and immortal like the vampires they'd seen in movies or read about in books.

"How did you get those?" Veronica asked, pointing to the dancer's scars.

The dancer glared. "That's really none of your business."

Veronica dropped her head and murmured an apology. She snatched a paper towel and dried her hands. "Sometimes I don't think before I open my mouth," she added.

The dancer's shoulders relaxed and she returned to brushing her hair. "It's okay. You aren't the first person to ask."

Veronica knew she wouldn't be the last, either.

The dancer turned to her again. "I've never seen you here before. You a first-timer?"

"It's obvious, huh?" Veronica appraised her own clothing in the mirror. Her faded black shirt revealed its age and tiny holes. Her blue jeans were ripped at the knees, but that was fashionable, right? She looked down, noticing the fraying cuffs and her scuffed shoes. Fashion had never been her thing.

The dancer coughed a laugh. "No, not really. Anything goes at Dark Sepulcher." She struck a pose in the mirror, pursed her fire engine red lips, and blew herself a kiss. "See ya, toots."

As she strutted out the door swinging her tote behind her, two women rushed in, nearly knocking the dancer down, but she never spoke up nor broke stride.

The two shoved into the nearest bathroom stall together, slamming the stall door behind them.

What the hell?

A loud bang echoed from the stall, rattling the adjoining booths in domino effect. Following loud and furtive whispers, a fit of giggles erupted from behind the wooden door. A leg covered in bruises and welts jutted from under the door.

As Veronica tiptoed to the exit, the stall door flew open and slammed the wall. A tall, dark-skinned woman stood up, straightening her black leather mini skirt. Completely naked from the waist up, her small breasts sported erect nipples. She grinned knowingly and lifted her skirt, flashing Veronica with black, boy-cut underwear with the word "sexy" glittering in red.

Stunned, Veronica froze.

The other woman squatted over the toilet with legs spread, her underwear tangled around her left ankle. Her tight red shirt bunched above her full breasts, revealing pale, perky nipples and a tight torso. As she stared at Veronica, her lips twisted into a half-grimace, half-grin, and then she let her legs fall farther apart, proudly showing Veronica her shiny, bright pink tissue.

The African American woman inhaled deeply.

"Mmmm." Her eyes bored into Veronica's. "Your scent is intoxicating." She curled her upper lip into a snarl and jerked her thumb toward the squatting woman. "Better than this whore." She cocked her head back, closed her eyes, and sniffed the air again.

"You're a virgin," she cooed. "Untainted."

When she smiled again, Veronica noticed the blood on her lower fangs. She took a step back toward the door, her hand hidden behind her, frantically searching the air for the knob.

"Hey," the squatter snapped, crossing her legs. "She's mine." She wrapped her arms around her bloody-toothed partner's waist, and pulled her back into the stall.

Veronica slid another step backward. The door loomed in the corner of her eye. It seemed a million miles away.

"Tell her, tell her you're mine," the woman demanded as she jumped to her feet. "Tell her!"

"Shut up." The African American woman's command immediately silenced her lackey. She turned to Veronica. "What's your name, honey?"

Her voice felt sensuous in Veronica's ears, and her eyelids felt heavy. Veronica could feel her inching closer, and though she knew she had to move, part of her wanted to stay. The woman opened her mouth as if to smile, and her tongue languished out, slowly licking the blood from her teeth.

Veronica's fingers grasped the doorknob; she jerked open the door and fled into the club.

"Where're you going, baby?" the throaty voice called behind her.

The slamming of the bathroom door silenced her laughter.

Veronica rushed back to her table, her heart pounding out a cadence in rhythm with her hurried steps. What she learned on her own about the different kinds of Deamhan ran through her mind again now, in an effort to calm herself.

For centuries their kind went unnamed. They were called demons, hell spawns, and even vampires. Centuries ago researchers in Ireland finally settled on the name Deamhan, due to their licentious behavior. Based on their feeding habits, they then split the Deamhan into the Ramanga, Lamia, Metusba, and Lugat.

Through blood and with sharp teeth, the Ramanga drained every drop of blood from their victims. Being the only Deamhan with retractable fangs, they relied on the psychic energy within the blood to survive. The Brotherhood labeled them as the strongest of the Deamhan.

Considered sexual whores, the Lamia fed by draining the same energy through the mouths of their victims. They had no need for fangs. All they needed was a viable opening and a willing or non-willing participant.

The Metusba, the quiet of all the Deamhan, fed off the psychic energy contained in their victim's auras. They stood in the crowds without the need to be up and close with their victims and they drained only what they needed, nothing less and nothing more.

While the Metusba walked among the crowds, the Lugat slithered, feeding off the leftover psychic energy by using their hands. They could feed off of almost anything; where a person sat, what a person touched.

Though they differed in feeding habits, they all died the same; beheadings, staking, starvation, and sunlight.

"Hey!" The waitress again appeared in front of Veronica, stopping her in her tracks.

How does she do that? Veronica glanced toward the bathroom, afraid she'd be followed. Her chest heaved and beads of sweat collected on her forehead. *Maybe she'll think I've been dancing.* The air around her felt thick and heavy.

"You okay?" the waitress asked.

"I need a drink."

"Another whiskey?"

Veronica nodded, and the waitress disappeared into the crowd. Veronica held her breath to calm her rapid breathing in hopes the adrenaline coursing through her body would dissipate. The pulsating bass emanating from the speakers grew louder and more intense, causing her to rub her temples. The dancer from the bathroom had returned to the stage, now even more scantily clad in a short skirt with white electrical tape X'ed over her nipples, dancing in gymnastic gyrations.

The crowd's movement grew violent, with patrons pushing and shoving. The throng morphed into a mosh pit, and Veronica wondered how long it would take before someone was crushed. Fog machines released a steady stream of mist from above the crowded dance floor, giving the huge room an ethereal atmosphere. The lights dimmed, and Veronica could hardly make out the waitress as she returned, carrying a shot of whiskey.

"Here ya go." She handed Veronica the drink.

Veronica gulped her drink and wiped her mouth with the back of her hand, this time thankful for the sensation of the amber liquid searing her throat. She preferred vodka, but at this moment, any liquid running down her gullet was good enough.

"You want another one?" she asked. Veronica nodded, and the waitress left. Veronica dropped her face to her hands, trying to readjust. *Damn, this is harder than I thought it'd be.* Her mind raced: *hide your thoughts, don't show fear, stick to the plan.*

She felt a tingling sensation deep in her forehead. In seconds, it had increased to the extent of a migraine. She looked up squinting, the pain becoming more intense with each passing moment, and she knew.

Someone is reading my thoughts.

The waitress returned with two drinks. She placed them in front of Veronica.

"Uh, thanks?" Veronica couldn't recall ordering two whiskeys, but she pulled out a ten.

"It's already paid for." The waitress pointed to a man sitting at the opposite end of the bar, his long brown hair slicked back in a ponytail. He wore black jeans and a long black see-through shirt, revealing pierced nipples and a six-pack. Beautiful.

He stared at Veronica with deep brown eyes and smiled, his pale skin resembling a Deamhan at its finest. She felt the pain in her forehead ebb and flow, subsiding a bit each time. Veronica turned to the waitress, but she'd again disappeared.

Muddled, she downed the whiskey and slammed the empty glass on the table in front of her. She shut her eyes and concentrated on emptying her mind. The pain diffused into a mild tingling.

Veronica snapped her eyes open when a male voice told her to not be afraid. She whipped around, but no one was near.

The voice came from within her head.

"It's okay," the voice said.

She looked at the man, who still fixed her in his stare, and he slid from his seat and headed her way.

She dropped her head and stared at the counter. She fought the urge to fling her glass at him and run. Leaving Dark Sepulcher wouldn't answer the questions about her mother's disappearance. *Don't think of Mom.* She quickly visualized the brick wall.

"Your thoughts stick out," the man said, taking the empty stool next to her.

His penetrating stare caused Veronica's head to tingle again, but the tingle stopped as quickly as it started. She'd clouded his attempt to rummage through her mind.

Veronica cupped the whiskey glass and stared into its glowing liquid.

19

"Beautiful women like you shouldn't drink whiskey."

What a line. His respectful approach did nothing to impress Veronica. The Deamhan were naturally devious.

Veronica remained quiet. The stranger smiled and reached for the glass, grasping it from the rim and placing it front of him.

"I'm trying to start a conversation," he prompted.

From the corner of her eye, Veronica saw him examine her. His eyes roved her short, formal straight brunette hair, her face, and finally her hands. Even over the din of music, she could hear him inhale her virginal scent. She tried hard to block her thoughts from him, but the tingle told her she was failing.

"You should know it turns me on when you do that," he said.

She glanced at him, making eye contact for a second and then quickly looked away. He mumbled something, but his voice was too low for her to hear over the blaring speakers.

Veronica's thoughts caught his attention again, and he leaned back on the stool, studying her.

Veronica understood now how a woman could fall for a man like that. Most of the men in Dark Sepulcher were attractive, but this man was *hot*. She stole a covert glance from under her eyelashes. Tall, medium build, long, glossy hair— *stop it. Stay off that bandwagon.*

His full lips broke into a smile. "Sorry I intruded on your thoughts. But I gotta admit, I like what I see in there."

Veronica felt heat rise in her chest, neck and face. *Busted.* He offered his hand, another trick she wouldn't fall for.

"I'm Remy and you are?"

Remy. The name sounded too familiar. Veronica recalled the name listed somewhere on the documents she'd stolen from The Brotherhood. His name was just one of the many that stuck out to her but at the moment she couldn't remember why.

She fixed her thoughts on her napkin, staring at the condensation ring left by the wet glass. Still her mind wouldn't quiet. *What Deamhan type is he?* Until she knew which, she couldn't be sure of his level of threat. She couldn't get too close.

Despite herself, she stole a quick look in his direction.

He flashed a ready smile.

Teeth aren't sharp and pointy. He's not a Ramanga. She stared again at her drink, wiping the droplets of water from the side of her glass.

"Am I scaring you?" Remy's voice interrupted Veronica's thoughts. She shook her head and remained silent.

"Do you talk?"

"Not to strangers." She immediately regretted her gutsy remark, knowing it would intrigue him further.

"Maybe you should." He traced the rim of the glass with a slender, pale finger. "You're new here."

Veronica wanted to check him out but knew she should avoid his eye. She looked over her shoulder and then at the ceiling. She glanced at the sticky floor and studied the woodwork on the bar.

"Nervous?"

He'd read her like an open book. She felt a tiny tingle as he tried again to read her thoughts.

"Your thoughts. They come to me kinda like a movie: sometimes clear, other times fuzzy." He chuckled. "Right now, they're crystal. Do you really find the bar's wood grain that intriguing?"

Veronica couldn't help but grin.

"Do you smell that?" His voice dropped to a loud whisper. "I smell a vampire."

Remy's eyes fixated over Veronica's shoulder.

The dark woman from the bathroom sashayed over and leaned against the bar on the other side of Veronica.

Veronica hardly recognized her. She now wore the professional attire of a business woman: grayish slacks, a red blouse, and a gray suit jacket. She'd styled her hair into a chic ponytail and glossed her lips in red.

Remy and the woman locked eyes.

Veronica felt a fierce, electrical tension emanating from the two, and glanced back and forth between them. The woman smirked, and Remy smiled nonchalantly.

"She's mine, Remy," she said. "He said I can have her."

Remy revealed his even, pearly teeth, his finger still tracing the rim of the glass. "Already tired of the other one?" he asked.

Unable to stand the crackling air between the two, Veronica slid from the stool.

The woman placed her hands on her hips, blocking Veronica's escape with her elbow. Remy smiled. "Not every female who strolls into Dark Sepulcher belongs to you, Alexis."

Veronica made a mental note of the vampire's name.

"But this little catch is stirring up the attention." Her lips puckered.

"Oh, that's it," Remy said. "You just want to be the first to take her."

Veronica eased sideways. They were playing a game to see who would be the first to have her. Well, she wasn't going to be "had" by anyone.

"Please sit." Remy respectfully motioned to Veronica. "Don't let Alexis scare you."

Leaving again entered Veronica's mind. *If I ran, would they stop me?* Alexis seemed to be the more violent of the two. Remy appeared relaxed and comfortable in the mini-altercation. Veronica wondered how easy it was for them to sense her discomfort. She decided to leave.

"Excuse me." Veronica slid past Remy, intending to walk away.

Remy reached out his arm, blocking her path. "But we haven't talked yet, researcher." Remy tapped his index finger on the counter.

His comment stopped Veronica in her tracks.

"Researcher?" Alexis visibly cringed at the mention of the word. "Well, then. You can have her." She snarled her lip in distaste. "I don't like researchers. Their blood tastes funny."

A cold chill blew up Veronica's spine. Try as he might, Veronica couldn't allow herself to be associated with The Brotherhood. She was not a researcher, her father made sure of that. He kept her away from it, shielding her just enough to tell her what she needed to know. Even if her father wanted her to follow in her mother's footsteps, Veronica wouldn't allow herself to be used in the way that her mother was. The bad memories of The Brotherhood were fresh in the execrable minds of the vampires and Deamhan alike. She couldn't risk allowing Remy to peg her with the title of "researcher", thus immediately black-listing her in the club—and in the city.

"I'm not a researcher," she blurted. *Not like my father.*

"Then who are you?" Remy asked, fixing her with his penetrating stare.

She buried the important pieces from her memory like names, cities, places, and the reason why she came to Dark Sepulcher from her mind.

"What? What is it?" Alexis asked Remy. "What do you see?"

Remy smirked. "Nothing now."

"That's why she interests you?" Alexis rolled her eyes. "Because she knows how to hide her thoughts unlike the whores you prefer?"

Remy tilted his head to the side, still studying Veronica.

"That should make you want to kill her even more." Alexis turned her body toward Veronica, gloating over the fear she saw in her eyes.

"Now, now, Alexis," Remy said softly, "let's give Veronica a chance to explain."

Veronica again felt the tingling sensation. He even knew her name. This time, it hurt.

Remy persisted.

Veronica ran toward the front exit. She plowed through the crowd, knocking past people and Deamhan alike. The sensation continued until she passed the security guards outside. Her heart thumped in her chest, and she drank fresh air in huge gulps.

As she reached the corner and turned in the direction of her apartment, she slowed her pace. When she neared the end of the block, she paused and checked the street behind her.

Sloppy. Mother would never have acted like that.

As she continued her walk home, thoughts about her father's warning before she left San Diego repeated over and over in her mind. He'd said she wasn't ready to come back to Minneapolis. Nonsense.

She had to be.

The full moon filled the night sky. Veronica zipped her jacket as the wind picked up. She turned her face to the wind and inhaled, letting the crisp air fill her lungs. Fall was the best time of year in Minnesota. She shoved her hands into her pockets and mounted the steps to home.

CHAPTER TWO

A loud slapping sound woke Veronica, and she jerked upright on the couch, startled. She cocked her head, listening for the arcane sound to repeat itself but nothing came.

Moving her head from side to side, she stretched her neck. A sharp pain in her back reminded her why she should have slept in the bed last night.

The apartment building, Palm Oaks (once a shoe factory that fell victim to a wave of new development) sat facing the bank of the Mississippi River. She'd considered a larger apartment, but the river view kept her there, despite the fact that in only a few days, she felt she'd outgrown the tiny space.

Since childhood, Veronica felt a weird attraction to water. Watching vast amounts of it rush downstream, caught her attention as a child. The Mississippi River was her favorite. She marveled at its course and the history behind it thanks to Mark Twain's majestic adventures.

She released an audible breath as she turned her head to look out of the window. The leaves on the trees that banked the edge of the river were in the middle of changing colors. Her gaze drifted near the red asphalt bike path to the old gazebo. Now weather beaten, its white paint cracked and peeled at the edges. Its once-detailed walls were nonexistent, destroyed by the harsh Minnesota weather.

Yep, I'm in a great location.

The apartment building was also located near many of the dance clubs and bars littering downtown Hennepin Avenue. The area seemed perfect for her. At night, the street came alive with tourists and Minneapolis citizens crowding the sidewalks along with young adults who bar-hopped to relieve themselves from the job pressures of corporate America.

Hennepin Avenue ran the length of two miles from east to west, beginning at the bank of the river and ending near the freeway. Its warehouse district rested near the eastern edge, close to Dark Sepulcher. With huge, boarded-up vacant buildings, the district felt desolate and quiet until nightfall; except for the occasional police sirens in the distance. It agitated her that many of the buildings, part of original downtown Minneapolis, were shamefully left to rot in disrepair. Finally, the city decided to renovate half of the buildings, turning them into condominiums and businesses instead of tearing them down.

Veronica stretched her arms overhead, then reached for the remote control on her coffee table and flicked on the TV. In her still-groggy state, she paused on a breaking story about a house fire near the warehouse district. The camera crew panned on the ruins of the destroyed home behind the newscaster. The report showed a crowd gathering across the street from the fire, watching smoke escape into the sky from smoldering pieces of wood and debris.

A newswoman dressed in a bright red shirt with short, carrot-colored hair, spoke into the microphone about the fires. The news surprised Veronica. Before coming to San Diego, she thought she'd researched all there was to know about the state of Minneapolis until her best friend, Sean warned her about the fires. Crime wasn't high but from the news report, anyone else not knowing about the city would have thought differently. She didn't know what this had to do with her search, but the news report gave the impression that the fires were frequent and out of control.

The camera panned right to left, filming the other homes on the block. Old Victorian homes with bright green lawns and brick lined porches came into view. Tall red oak gates separated the properties and expensive cars parked on the streets and driveways.

Sean told her that the Deamhan in Minneapolis now violated their Dictum—basic rules laid down by their ancestors centuries ago on how to survive in the human world without risking your privacy. Now the Deamhan of today in Minneapolis released their transgressions on each other. Besides the fires, they killed each other by the hundreds. Veronica knew about these dangers. And Remy and Alexis' reaction to her last night proved that the creatures remained unstable.

Still, the Deamhan had turned a total one eighty from their Dictum. Some of its rules were simple, yet explicit: maintain secrecy, dispose of human remains, and respect the Ancients, the oldest of the Deamhan. Something caused them to sway from those rules decades ago and Veronica blamed that *something* on her father and The Brotherhood. Her father declared the city an off-limit zone for all Brotherhood members, right around the time she boarded her flight. It was typical Brotherhood behavior.

Veronica finally pulled herself from the couch. The bright sunlight crept through her window and blinded her. She twisted the window blinds to block the rays and smiled to hear and see the birds chirping outside her window. When she opened the window, the smell of wet leaves and dew entered her nostrils. Below, the sidewalk came alive with cyclists and rollerbladers. The Jubilee Coffee shop across the street spilled its patrons onto the sidewalk. The clear blue sky showed nary a cloud.

"This is the Minnesota I remember," she said to the robins beneath her window ledge. *The Minnesota that surprises me when I least expect it.* A beautiful state with breathtaking scenery, lavish forests, and ten thousand lakes.

And Deamhan and vampires.

Little did its residents know what lurked in the city and slithered from the burrows at sunset.

She sat back on the couch, wiping the morning sweat from her forehead. The smells and the scenery made her think of her mother and her childhood. Reliving her childhood without the tragedies became her one thing she wished for in her teenage years. Just the thought of her mother coming back home from her assignments felt like needles puncturing her skin. One Saturday evening, at the age of five, Veronica used bright pink crayons to scribble a *Welcome Home* sign for her mother while she sat on the dining room floor of her parents' shabby two bedroom apartment in south Minneapolis. Her father paced back and forth in the living room, puffing on his tobacco pipe.

On her piece of construction paper, below her child-written words which read "Welcome Home," she'd drawn three stick figures in black of mom and dad with her in the middle. In the foreground she attempted to draw a pyramid. She'd never seen one before but from what her mother told her, it was a huge triangle with four huge and uneven bricks.

The front door creaked open and she had jumped to her feet. With her drawing in hand, she raced to the door and collapsed into her mother's arms. The smell of wet leaves emitted from her brown wool jacket. She watched her mother reach into her purse and pull out a sandwich bag filled with dirt and small pieces of limestone.

Veronica took the bag and ran back to her safe spot on the dining room floor. The beautiful limestone and rough speckles of sand sparkled. She poured a small amount in the palm of her hand but her excitement was short lived when she heard the deafening sound of her father's hand hitting her mother's cheek.

Veronica didn't remember if her father had really slapped her mother's face, or if the abundance of the memory caused her to think he had.

She rubbed her eyes with her fists to erase the vision.

On the other hand, she felt thankful that her mother still appeared so lovely and fresh in her dreams and memories. She knew her mother believed in what she was doing, but Veronica had never understood the reason she'd involved herself in The Brotherhood. It wasn't like her father's side of the family, who had a history with the organization. Her mother started at the bottom and, over time, she'd moved up in the organization's status to researcher and she was good at it. The Brotherhood's historical research department in San Diego often sought her mother's opinion on the Deamhan. The staff and administration admired and respected her mother at the same level which they feared her father. Veronica remembered being forced to play with the other kids whose parents were also researchers. She was home-schooled and she attended high school as a teen.

Veronica remembered the McKenzie twins, Joseph and James, the nerds of the group. They excelled in academics, but sucked in athletics. Kelli Simpson, a pudgy blonde girl, had a crush on Joseph, but he claimed she had cooties and broke her heart. She loved to drink Kool-Aid and once claimed to a teacher that she was allergic to prune juice. All three of them became researchers and they were moved to the Eastern Division with its headquarters based in New York.

Her thoughts moved to Sean Fechin, her best and only friend in The Brotherhood. He was the only person she could trust. With her own father hardly at home, he became her adopted brother and he stuck his neck out for her. His family also had ties in The Brotherhood, except that his parents both retired early and didn't force their son to follow in their footsteps. It was Sean who secured the secret documents about the Deamhan for her. He supported her decision to go to Minneapolis.

And then there was Kenneth Dearhorn. Even now, sitting alone in her apartment, Veronica sighed to think of him. Kenneth Dearhorn was smart, athletic and handsome for his age. She could still picture his hazel eyes and smooth skin. He claimed Native American and Irish ancestry. He was also cocky, arrogant, and fickle. Every girl in school had a crush on him—including Veronica. At the time of her mother's disappearance, his father, Peter, was the President of the Midwest Region with Veronica's father serving under him. He trained his son rigorously to one day become a researcher and take his father's place as President. Unlike Veronica's father, Kenneth's father didn't shelter him from the Deamhan. Instead, he allowed his son to marinate with them. When Kenneth's father was killed, Veronica's father sent Kenneth along with her to San Diego to continue his training. Now he had the job of lead researcher of the Western Division. Soon, he'd be President.

The pressures of representing the Austin family name became a burden to Veronica. Her father expected Veronica to be like Kenneth and to not question but to remain silent, but she proved to be nothing like him. The Brotherhood was engrained in her family genes. Her grandparents and her great grandparents both worked for The Brotherhood. It was her mother who had no family ties in the organization and who also viewed any teachings of The Brotherhood to be propaganda and argued that no child should be exposed to it by force.

Veronica paced the floor. A morning of reminiscing caused her to yearn to hear Sean's voice. She pulled the cell phone from her coat pocket and dialed his number.

"So now you call," he answered.

"It's only been a couple of days, Sean," she replied.

"Three, to be precise. Besides, you told me as soon as you arrived in Minneapolis you'd call."

She remembered. Their short conversation about her trip became clear as though it had happened yesterday. "Well, I had to get settled first." She headed for the kitchen. "I still haven't unpacked everything yet."

"What do you have to unpack? It's not like you're staying there forever."

"So now you're my self-appointed protector." The noise of rustling papers and Pink Floyd's *Dark Side of the Moon* rebounded from the ear piece. "I thought you didn't like Pink Floyd?"

"What makes you think that? I've always like Floyd." He grunted. "So, how is it up there?"

"So far, so good"—she opened the door of her fridge to retrieve a carton of orange juice from the top shelf—"I guess."

"And Dark Sepulcher? Was it like I said it would be?"

"Uh, I went last night." Veronica heard his audible gasp across the miles.

"I thought you were going to wait a couple of weeks."

"I was, but I changed my mind." She heard more clattering in the background.

Sean lowered his voice. "So, what happened in there?"

"They were everywhere." Veronica pulled an empty glass from the cabinet. "You should've come with me, Sean. It's unbelievable."

"I'm sure it was," he replied, "but you know I don't have the stomach for that."

Veronica knew all too well. Sean didn't plan to head out into the field as a researcher. He avoided danger like the plague. He was most comfortable sitting behind a desk at The Brotherhood headquarters in San Diego.

"You know I don't want to be anywhere near them, Veronica."

"Yeah, you don't have to tell me twice, Sean." Veronica heard the twinge of excitement in his voice. She pictured him sitting in a dark enclosed office, his back to the wall, his hand cupping his mouth, and his eyebrows raised in elation. "Well, I really didn't think they'd let me in."

"They? The Deamhan?"

"And the vampires."

"Well, did anyone recognize you?"

"One Deamhan accused me of being a researcher"—she poured herself a glass of juice from the pitcher in the fridge— "so yes, I think they recognized me."

Everything she knew of Dark Sepulcher came from Sean's excellent ability to obtain secret Brotherhood files. He'd taught her that the building that housed Dark Sepulcher had been through many facelifts in the past: a bar, a theatre, a hotel, and even a house of ill repute. Its vibrant history placed the building and surrounding structures in the historic district of Minneapolis. The building still maintained the look of an old two-level warehouse, complete with a small upper level and fire escape stairs on the outside of the building. It had been Sean's suggestion that she begin her research there. He'd told her it was common knowledge that no researcher had stepped inside the venue since the day the Chapter left the city. While there, they'd avoided the building at all costs.

"You think so? Who was it? What happened? Were you hurt?" Sean shot questions as fast as pellets fired from a gun.

Veronica sipped from her glass. "I should've been more prepared. I should've studied the documents you gave me."

"You didn't read over them?"

"Yeah I did, but not enough to remember everything."

"Veronica, you promised me you would." His voice grew solemn. "You need to be more careful and more prepared."

"I'm fine." She heaved a sigh. "But I think I'm going to need some more information."

"What kind of information?"

"One of them, the Deamhan who accused me, went by the name of Remy. I recognized the name but I was wondering if you could find more information on him."

"Like his history?"

"Yes, his history, anything you can. I'll gladly take."

Sean hesitated. "It's—it's not going to be easy. They're revamping the archives here and moving the majority of the files to a secured location until they're done."

The Brotherhood archive was the most impressive part of the San Diego headquarters. It housed old researcher accounts about the Deamhan in the western hemisphere and other relics from past centuries. She reserved to comment, knowing her father used his position as President of the Midwest Region and his influence to keep every information they had secretive and hidden. It boggled her mind. Of course, it wasn't coincidental that they decided to revamp the library just when she needed access to the information.

"But that's where you come in, Sean. You can get almost anything."

"Well, that might change," his voice softened to a whisper.

"What—what do you mean 'it might change'?"

"Nothing. Never mind. Let's see. Remy, right?"

"And Alexis. She's a vampire."

"A vampire." He blew out pent-up breath. "A vampire and a Deamhan at a club together? I thought they couldn't stand each other."

"Well, they can't, from what I saw."

"Yes, of course. I'll get started." Sean's voice suddenly took on a pleasant, professional tone. She heard more muffled sounds and the muted voice of a man in the background.

"Veronica, I gotta go," Sean whispered. "Let me in on the inside scoop when you call back. You are going to call me back tomorrow, right?"

"Yeah, of course."

"And Veronica," Sean said softly, "keep your cell on and be careful."

"I will."

"You should stay away from that club for a few days at least."

Veronica glanced at the television. "Yeah, I have some sanctuary hunting to do. Bye for now." She snapped her cell phone shut and sipped her OJ.

* * * *

29

"Who was that?"

Sean rolled his brown eyes and he looked away from Kenneth Dearhorn.

Kenneth wasn't being curious. His actions came off as crude. Sean refused to say Veronica's name. He knew that Kenneth wasn't that much of an idiot. Moreover, eventually he'd find out anyway.

Sean replaced his phone in the cradle, turned down the volume on the radio, and leaned back in his leather office chair, a gift from Veronica's father.

"I came here to tell you to not worry about Rick's eulogy." Kenneth leaned against the edge of Sean's desk and he picked up his electric pencil sharpener, examining it.

"Why not?"

"Because *I'm* writing it."

Sean gripped the Styrofoam cup in his hand and brought it to his lips. The coffee had turned lukewarm. His eyes fixed on Kenneth's tall medium build body and the mischievous smile overshadowing his hazel eyes.

"I want to know how you managed to get Mr. Austin to approve for you to write an eulogy," Sean asked, "especially since you didn't even *know* Rick."

"No, you can't know."

Sean wanted to smack Kenneth's smile off his face. Scattered papers and desk-memos about the recent increase of Deamhan activity in San Diego, and a report about the recent death of Rick Sorfield littered his large office desk. Rick's body was found underneath the inner pass of the Interstate 5 freeway in Chula Vista. Large fire ants had eaten away his eyes, and larva filled his ears. His throat had been slashed, and his body was drained of blood. They'd identified him by dental records because his face was unrecognizable.

Sean knew Rick. Unlike majority of researchers, Rick didn't have family in the organization. After being viciously attacked and nearly killed by a Deamhan, he'd decided to join The Brotherhood. He and Sean had competed for the more lucrative desk position after their formal graduation. Sean had landed the job, and Rick ended up as a field researcher. He'd only been on the job six months before his murder.

The last time he saw Rick, he was wiping coffee stains off his white shirt and cursing under his breath. The Deamhan could smell a human from half a mile away, and the smell of coffee mixed with his human scent increased Rick's chances of being discovered. Sean had patted him on his shoulder, joked about how the coffee stain matched the brown stripes on his white tennis shoes, and told him not to worry; at least he wasn't holding up a sign with "Researcher Here" in bold letters.

Rick had joined in on the laugh.

Now, Sean blinked hard and blew air through his pursed lips. *Rick didn't deserve to die like that and this asshole has no right to write Rick's eulogy.* Still, it was better than being turned into a Deamhan for the organization to research.

Sean breathed heavily. "Congratulations, I guess."

"I came here to see if you have any ideas on what *should* be in Rick's eulogy."

Sean's eyes darted to Kenneth. "You can't be fucking serious."

"Rick was Brotherhood. He was family." Kenneth stood up and he walked around to the other side of Sean's desk. "I might not have known him as good as you may have. However, I want to do my best in representing his legacy, if you know what I mean."

Sean exhaled. There wasn't anything he could do except agree. Kenneth held the lead researcher and he was the personal favorite of the President of the Western Division, Kurt Luzier. Disagreeing or failing to participate meant disobeying Mr. Luzier's orders and nothing was worse than working in the backroom, filing paperwork and handing out mail for the remaining of his career. He had to play along, for now.

He forced himself to smile. "If I think of anything, I'll let you know."

"Good." Kenneth placed his hands on his hips. "Also, after the funeral, Mr. Luzier has advised me that you're to stay. Mr. Austin has asked to speak to you privately."

"Me?"

Kenneth nodded. "So be on your best behavior, Sean." He leaned over and whispered, "I know you were talking to Mr. Austin's daughter."

Sean placed his fingers on the back of his head and he leaned back in his chair. "Now, why would she call me, Kenneth?"

Kenneth laughed. "Why wouldn't she call you? You're her best friend. You know I'm going to find out anyway so you might as well tell me now . . . Sean."

"Tell you what?" Kenneth stood his ground.

"What would Mr. Austin think if he knew you were helping his daughter?" Kenneth straightened his jacket. "Come to think about it. What would Mr. Luzier think about you disobeying your Brotherhood oath by helping Mr. Austin's daughter?" Kenneth smiled and he gracefully walked out of the room.

Sean rested his head on his desk. He tried to clear his mind. He knew the way Kenneth worked. He'd already told his superiors about Sean's involvement and that message was sent to Mr. Austin. After Rick's funeral, he would be reprimanded and relieved of his duties. Still, it couldn't be that bad. Wherever he ended up wouldn't get in his way of getting the information Veronica needed. "Remy" wasn't a name he'd heard frequently, but The Brotherhood's Deamhan Database was always adding new additions.

Damn.

He wished he had the courage to be there with Veronica, in the mix, delving into hands-on research, coming face-to-face with a Deamhan. He yearned for the experience but his fear of the environment dampened his desire.

Veronica had confided in him about her dissatisfaction with her father over her mother's disappearance. Sean knew there'd been a strong effort to sweep the unusual circumstances under the rug—to bury it—and so he'd called Mrs. Austin's disappearance one of the risks that researchers took when they agreed to work in the field. Sean made sure he'd been there to back Veronica when the rumors flared up about her mother's disappearance battering Veronica's memories. Now he found himself becoming the coward he hated, and this hatred ran deep and festered inside his soul. Nevertheless, Rick's death and Mrs. Austin's disappearance caused Sean to worry about Veronica, his little sister. He couldn't bear the same thing happening to her.

Better Rick than Veronica.

Sean turned up his radio, catching the intro of Pink Floyd's "Comfortably Numb." He could relate. From his office window, he watched the cars rushing down the freeway below. However, the sun had escaped the horizon and the moon sat visible and high in the sky. Sean raked his fingers through his dark hair and huffed. "She'd better call me back," he muttered to the empty room.

The sun's rays blinded his eyes. Another California day, gone.

CHAPTER THREE

After straightening her cluttered apartment, Veronica scoured the bottom of her duffel bag and pulled out a framed picture of her mother.

She tenderly ran her fingers across the photo like she'd done a thousand times, noticing its yellowing edges. The picture of her mother sat in her purse for years and, afraid she was going to lose it on her trip to Minneapolis, she had it framed before leaving San Diego. She kissed her mother's likeness and placed it in a position of honor on her dresser.

"Enough," she whispered. Turning from her bedroom, she gathered the bag of kitchen trash, stuffed it into a nest of cardboard boxes, and headed out the door for the dumpster. After she locked the door behind her, a creaking noise coming across the hall startled her, and she turned to see a brown-eyed man in his 30s toting his own bag of trash.

"Must be trash time for everyone," he said, a grin playing at the corners of his mouth. He wore a red shirt and faded, ripped blue jeans, and when he turned to lock his door, Veronica noticed he sported a short black ponytail.

"Yeah, I guess so," she answered.

"Did you just move in? I haven't seen you around before."

"Yeah." Veronica nodded. "Just a few days ago."

He dropped the bag of garbage near his feet, wiped his hands on the front of his jeans, and extended a smooth palm. "I'm Murphy Norton."

"Veronica Austin." She accepted his handshake, taking note of his firm grip and muscular forearm.

"Welcome to Palm Oaks."

Brilliant, even teeth. Nope! Not a Ramanga nor a vampire. And he is f-i-n-e, fine! "Thank you."

Murphy Norton nodded toward the boxes. "You finished unpacking, Veronica?"

"Yeah, finally." A giggle burbled from her lips, and heat rose in her face. *Quit acting like a little schoolgirl. He's gonna think you're desperate!*

She shifted the box of garbage to her hip and stared at the floor, feeling oddly nervous. The only time a man had ever made her feel this way had been when she was a teenager. That man was Sean.

She remembered how Sean commented on her furious blush when they first met. At the time, he'd been dating a cheerleader from public school in Mission Valley. The cheerleader often visited, flaunting her personal assets in tight-fitting shirts and short skirts. She'd popped her gum when she talked, and when she'd first met Veronica, she'd patted the top of her head like a dog.

To make matters worse, Sean had introduced Veronica as his "little sister." From that moment on, everyone in their neighborhood considered her as such. His words proved prophetic, and soon their relationship had taken on the loving, platonic vibe of brother and sister.

"Well, like I said, welcome. I think you'll like it here. It's a nice building."

"Thanks."

"You in college?"

"No. Are you?"

He nodded. "Yeah. I go to the Minneapolis Tech College down the street. Thought maybe I'd see you around campus."

"No, I just moved to Minnesota," she said.

He scratched the back of his neck and tightened his ponytail. "Where from?"

"California."

"I'm new to Minnesota, too. I'm from Florida. But I've always wanted to go to California."

There's that smile again. Veronica felt herself grow warmer.

Murphy awkwardly stepped forward. "Hey, sorry. Do you need help with that?"

A gentleman too! Veronica shifted the heavy box again. "Yeah, thanks."

He took the box from Veronica's arms as easily as if it were stuffed with feathers. "Trade ya." He nodded toward the small bag of garbage he'd dropped by his door. "Mine's light."

"It's a deal." Veronica picked up the white kitchen bag and followed Murphy down the hallway.

"Say, I'm having a get-together tonight. Small group, just a few friends. You're welcome to stop by."

"Oh, um, I'm going to a club tonight—but thanks."

"Really? Which one?"

"Dark Sepulcher," she answered. "Have you been there?"

He cocked an eyebrow. "No, I've never been, but I hear it's wild. Maybe I'll check it out sometime."

"It's not all that great," she said, trying to sway him, "I think it's overrated." Veronica couldn't help but notice the way his well-worn jeans fit the curve of his ass and thighs. The muscles in his upper back flexed as he shifted the box into one arm and turned, again extending his hand in her direction.

"I can take the rest from here."

"You don't have to do that. I've got it." *Besides, I like the view from back*

34

here.

He reached for the bag. "Really, I'll get it. I'm going to the store any way and I'm parked out back." He grabbed the bag and flipped it over his shoulder like Santa carrying his pack. "If you change your mind, just come on over. People should start arriving around eight or nine."

Veronica quickly stepped around him and held open the door.

"Ya know, that's college student time." He laughed when Veronica's forehead wrinkled. "You know, when you say something starts at seven, and people don't get there until later? They're my friends and they also go to college, so . . . ."

"Ah, college student time." She nodded. "That makes sense."

Murphy bounded down the steps then turned. "Hey, if you need anything, or if you want to hang out or something, just knock."

Veronica nodded and gave a little wave then watched as he disappeared around the corner.

She thought of her experience at Dark Sepulcher. "A get-together sure sounds better than that zoo," she murmured. She knew that returning a second night in a row would not be wise.

Returning to her living room, Veronica plopped down and flipped the TV on again. The news report of the house fire replayed. Maybe a party wouldn't be a bad idea, she thought, as she closed her eyes for a moment of rest. *Sure sounds better than spending another night hounded by a Deamhan.*

* * * *

A whisper tickled her ears. Veronica slowly opened her eyes, squinting against the white glare that lit up the room. She covered her eyes then shielded them and tried to peer out again. The room was white, vacant, and empty except for the bed she lay on in the middle of the room.

As her eyes adjusted to the light, she glanced around. *This isn't my room! This isn't even my house!* She swung her legs off the bed and stood, feeling icy tile beneath her bare feet. After running her hands over the soft, silky gown she wore and marveled at its texture, she touched her face and her hair, which was slicked back into a tight bun. *I must be dreaming.*

Just then, a black door manifested to her right. It opened, revealing a dark gloominess. From the darkness, a faint image of her mother appeared.

Veronica tried to call out, but she couldn't speak. The air around her turned frigid and, though she could faintly hear the wind, the room was eerily silent.

The image of her mother moved away from Veronica, slowly floating down the dark hall.

Veronica moved as if through water, her feet slowly sliding along the floor until she reached the doorway. A cold breeze swept across her face, carrying her mother's voice to her ears. *"Veronica."*

35

The voice was soft, and Veronica strained to listen.

Her mother's image floated farther away and grew fainter until it disappeared like smoke in the wind.

Her call went unanswered and she took another step through the dark doorway. She'd lost her mother before and there'd been nothing she could do. Now older and more aware, Veronica felt she had control—something she hadn't felt since she'd left San Diego. *I won't lose you again!*

Feeling braver, she took another step. Suddenly, the hard floor gave way beneath her feet. She frantically reached for the doorframe, her nails snapping against its wood. The floor fell away and her body tumbled forward. She flailed her arms then plummeted, finding nothing but dark emptiness surrounding her.

Veronica screamed and this time found her voice, loud and clear. She opened her eyes wide in terror to find a commercial on TV, and the sound of sirens in the distance emanating from her living room window.

Sitting still for a moment, she reoriented herself as her heartbeat slowed to a normal pace. From outside her front door, she heard men laughing, a door open and close, and footsteps running up and down the stairs.

Veronica turned off the TV and groggily lifted herself from the couch. Curious about the raucous in the hallway, she peered through the front door peephole. Three men stood in the hallway outside Murphy's open door, sipping from red plastic cups. They appeared to be typical college students dressed in jeans and Ts, and ready to party.

Veronica sighed and leaned heavily against her door, feeling envious of their college experience which she'd been denied. She'd wanted to study archeology like her mother. She'd dreamed of exploring ancient lands that had shaped the future of the world. She still remained curious about Egypt, was anxious to see the Coliseum in Rome, and Stonehenge mesmerized her. The history of the Deamhan and their past intertwined in these ancient sites, captivated her.

Her father had scoffed at the idea. To him, it was a waste of time. He'd told her there was nothing to be gained by higher education, except the incurrence of student loans. Still, the thought of college crossed her mind now and then, and it flared brightly now as she spied again on Murphy's friends. Their college life, though intimidating, intrigued her.

Murphy appeared in the doorway, jokingly pushing his friends back into his apartment. "Get inside! You'll scare the neighbors."

Veronica jerked her eye from the peephole as he stared at her door. When she peeked again, he'd disappeared, closing the door behind him.

Deflated, Veronica returned to the couch, her mind drifting from Murphy to her dream. She'd often dreamed of her mother, but never like this. This dream frightened her. Her mother had tried to warn her. It wallowed in her gut.

She punched a throw pillow and stared at the now-dark TV screen. Taking a deep breath, she closed her eyes. *Come back, Mom. Let me dream of you again.*

CHAPTER FOUR

The next morning brought cool winds to the city of Minneapolis. Veronica zipped up her yellow hooded jacket before stepping out from her apartment.

Students jogged and pet lovers walked their dogs on Mississippi Drive—a two-way road, resurfaced from its aged red bricks to asphalt pavement located behind Palm Oaks. Puffy clouds littered the skies and small streaks of sunlight occasionally peeked through them. The apartment building resided in a college-oriented community complete with bike racks, coffee shops, and used clothing stores. A man no older than Veronica stood on the street corner, playing his guitar to an audience of a few passersby.

This is the Minneapolis I remember.

Compared to the abandoned buildings of the warehouse district, the surroundings seemed serene enough to give Veronica a sense of belonging. She stopped a local jogger and questioned him about the district, learning that the area grew rampant over time with city police when the fires first started.

The jogger frowned in distaste. "You wouldn't catch me there."

Unfortunately, I have to go there. Veronica thanked the jogger and they parted ways.

Veronica signaled a passing taxi to take her to the house fire. Upon entering the taxi, the smell of old cigarettes and wet upholstery snaked up her nostrils. She gripped the back of the driver's seat when the taxi sped off. In the rearview mirror, she watched the driver meticulously twist the ends of his handlebar moustache with his right hand and tap on the steering wheel with his left. He whistled along to the music on the radio. The taxi sped through multiple intersections and only at Washington Avenue and Tenth Street did he decrease his speed.

"Are we there yet?" Her body reeled from the driver's inability to drive in a straight line.

"No, no, I tell you when." The driver's broken English confirmed Veronica's uneasiness. The taxi came to a screeching halt at a stoplight. Veronica's eyes shifted to the left at the cemetery. She recognized the area from her childhood. Wilkes Cemetery was protected by the Minnesota Historical Society, making it just one of the oldest and rarest locations in the city. She recalled her mother's admiration for its weathered, sunken headstones and unkempt plots. Veronica still remembered the path of perfectly positioned bricks leading to the gravesite of one of Minneapolis's founders.

She also recalled the gravesite of a little girl located near the back, surrounded by a rusted fence. Veronica's mother used to pluck the weeds and remove dirt from the weathered tombstone, which read:

Sarah Anderson.
Born 1852
Died 1860.
8 years.
Sleep little Angel.

The taxi continued down the street. The scenery turned from storefronts to Victorian homes and towering brick buildings. Again, the taxi screeched to a halt at a stoplight.

"Drop me off right here."

"House is down there. I drop you closer."

"No, it's fine. Right here."

The driver parked the taxi and laid the back of his hand on the top of the passenger seat. "Fifteen dollars and twenty cents."

Veronica handed him a twenty-dollar bill and exited. The taxi sped away, leaving a cloud of exhaust, which engulfed her. She looked up at a green street sign that read "29ᵗʰ Avenue." She was only one block east from her desired location.

Cold wind stung the tips of her ears. Veronica trembled and her thoughts switched to her cozy apartment. Dried and dead leaves raced along the sidewalk in miniature tornadoes. The area was uncanny and a little quiet for what she expected. She wrapped her arms around her body, taking baby steps while reading bright yellow and orange graffiti covering the walls of the building next to her. They were unique and some of it was unreadable. From what she could decipher, the bubbly images read "Ramanga."

She was in Ramanga territory.

Veronica headed east until she reached the intersection. Across the street, charred remains of the house were clearly visible and sectioned off with yellow police tape. A group of people stood across the street gawking at the destruction. The only part of the house standing was a burned back wall. Black and gray smoke floated from the middle of the home while firefighters combed through the remains.

Sean was right.

This was just the first of many destroyed sanctuaries Veronica would witness and she had to prepare herself for it. The Deamhan were burning each other out of house and home!

Veronica joined the group of onlookers.

An older woman with brown and gray intermixed hair turned to speak. "Isn't it just horrible?" The woman folded her arms across her chest. The corners of her mouth dropped in discontent. Flaccid wrinkles stifled her face. "The police has to do something about this. It's ridiculous."

"I saw it on the news last night," Veronica replied. "How many homes have burned now?"

"A dozen or so." The old woman's focus remained centered on the burned ruins. "Thank God no one was hurt." She exalted. "It was a lovely home. I just can't imagine what the couple and their children are going to do."

"A family lived there?"

"Yeah. And those poor kids." The old woman turned to Veronica again. "It was a home for at-risk youths."

"At-risk youths?"

"Of course, I'm sure." The woman lifted her head and smacked her lips. "Those kids had medical issues. I spoke to their adoptive parents, God-fearing people." She paused then continued. "They stayed up into the wee hours of the morning sometimes, helpin' those children." She pointed to the opposite street corner. "See that lot over there?"

Veronica followed the woman's gaze.

"Another house went up just last week." The woman's voice dropped to a whisper. "It's them juvenile delinquents. They have nothing better to do." She then pointed at a gray windowless van parked halfway down the street. "And that van drives up and down this street daily. I've called the cops about it, but they don't do anything."

Veronica realized that nothing fit the stereotypical sanctuary Sean warned her about. The old woman mixed gossip with reality. There was no way Deamhan would sire children. It was against their own rules to do so.

"Hoodlums are turning this neighborhood into a war zone," the old woman stressed."Was there anyone home at the time of the fire?" Veronica asked.

"God, I hope not." The woman grasped her chest. "The poor, poor children."

Veronica doubted the woman was that hurt or even cared as much as she let on. Veronica scanned the crowd of housewives and older women. She overheard their conversations; mainly gossip and accusations, which didn't help her investigation. They had no idea about the real horrors happening in the city. And didn't want to fathom what could happen if they did know.

Her eyes caught sight of a short, thin woman standing alone near the edge of the crowd. She appeared unconcerned at the gossip, instead staring at the ruins. The young woman looked up and her eyes met Veronica's.

"This city needs more cops," the old woman continued on her rant.

Veronica turned back to her, nodded, and then returned her gaze to the mysterious young woman. Her smooth blonde hair was pulled back in a ponytail and her clear blue eyes remained fixed on Veronica. She wore a brown leather jacket, a white shirt, and blue jeans—definitely too young to blend in with the "house-wives" in the crowd. She didn't belong.

"Are you new to the neighborhood, sweetie?" Again, the older woman swayed Veronica's attention. "I hope this doesn't influence your opinion about the neighborhood." She placed her hand on Veronica's shoulder. "Most of our families have lived in this area for generations."

"That's cool." Veronica neglected the woman's stare. Her eyes remained glued on the mysterious woman, watching her pivot slowly. The woman walked down the street, glancing over her shoulder a few times at Veronica.

The sound of a cop car's sirens broke the air.

"Is your family from Minneapolis?"

Veronica ignored the question. Following her hunch, she took off after the mysterious woman.

The woman disappeared around the corner. Veronica picked up her pace and turned the corner. She stopped. The woman was gone.

"Hello," Veronica called out. Baffled, she turned back to the crowd. Her thoughts raced. For once she felt calm, thinking that the woman was a research-er, but what could be relaxing about that? The thought crossed her mind of com-ing back later that night to investigate the burned house. It was closely followed by the nightmarish fact of being out alone at night. Waiting wasn't a bad option either, yet the longer she waited, the more impatient she became.

The fires would have to wait . . . for now.

CHAPTER FIVE

Despite the charcoal sky, the polished oak casket gleamed under the funeral tent. Raindrops sparkling on the silver cross adorning the casket caught Sean's eye. He cursed under his breath.

"Of all the days it could've rained."

Sean tilted his head at the bloated gray clouds. He'd never seen a southern California downpour like this and it came on a day that deserved the sun's warmth more than any other.

His friend Rick wasn't a high-ranking member of The Brotherhood. Yet the casket he laid in told otherwise. Thousands of dollars from Sean's own pocket—plus donations—paid for it. Not a dime came from Presidents of the Western, Midwest, and Eastern Divisions or the Head of The Brotherhood. Sean dropped his head, pretending to be in prayer. He covertly scanned the mourners from behind his dark glasses. As best he could tell, all of them were researchers from the local Chapter.

A fresh onslaught of uninvited tears coursed from behind his dark glasses. He felt so angry and so helpless. This funeral shouldn't be happening.

The priest closed his Bible. Sean joined the line of mourners, each carrying a bright red rose to place atop the casket. He stared at the rose in his hand and huffed. Rick hated red roses.

"Sorry, buddy," he said as he placed the rose in the pile. "I'd have preferred a lily, too." He stepped aside and watched Kenneth Dearhorn place a rose on the casket, mumble a prayer, and step away. The President of the Western Division, Kurt Luzier, followed Kenneth. Sporting a dark suit and tie and dark glasses, he approached the casket and placed his own red rose on top of it. Behind him and the last one in line, stood Veronica's father. Gripping the handle of his black cane, Mr. Austin hobbled forward. He placed the largest and darkest rose atop the mound of flowers.

One by one, the mourners dispersed, but Sean lagged behind in covert surveillance of Kenneth's conversation with Mr. Austin and Mr. Luzier. He'd give anything just now for one of those high-tech eavesdropping devices he'd seen on the Internet. He wondered what lies Kenneth spoke in their ears. He didn't doubt that Kenneth would do anything to secure his position as the next President of any Division. He loved power, just like his dead father.

Disappointed and downhearted, Sean ambled back to his car and waited until Mr. Austin was ready to call on him. Images of Rick's well-dressed, motionless form pierced his mind. The mortician's expertise made it possible for the funeral to be an open casket. It was hard to believe that just days ago, Rick's face was unrecognizable.

He glanced down the hill at the flower-strewn casket, and observed the intimate way Kenneth held Mr. Austin's elbow as he guided him back to his limousine. Kenneth's hands tightened into fists. It still incensed Sean that Mr. Luzier chose Kenneth to give Rick's eulogy. The way Kenneth pretended to mourn . . . hell, Kenneth didn't know Rick at all. Not like he did. The tribute had been so generic, so common, and so impersonal; Kenneth could have pulled it from a handbook.

Rick deserved better.

The Brotherhood took responsibility for the grand funerals and interments of its members, insisting that employees were actually *family*. That's what the name "Brotherhood" meant. They were brothers and sisters, by oath and loyalty. Well, that's what they were led to believe.

Of all the coffins Sean saw emblazoned with The Brotherhood's cross, his own great-grandfather's had borne an extraordinary gold cross, not like Rick's silver-embedded casket. When Sean's great-grandfather died at the age of a hundred and one, The Brotherhood hired the area's best-known caterers, and the grieving family members were handed rare orchids and exotic flowers to place atop the casket in lieu of red roses.

Sean rubbed his chin. He unlocked the driver's side door when he heard Kenneth's voice behind him.

"Hey," Kenneth called from halfway up the sloped hill.

Sean sighed and looked over his shoulder. Kenneth approached with a smile on his face. Water droplets fell from the ends of his light brown hair.

"Why the long face, comrade?"

"It's my friend's funeral, Kenneth."

Kenneth still grinned. "Mr. Austin is ready for you."

Tense, Sean exhaled.

"No need to get nervous, Sean." Kenneth slapped him on his shoulder. "It's just a talk."

Mr. Austin limped up the hill with the support of Mr. Luzier. A recent hip surgery forced Mr. Austin to rely on his cane as temporary support. Though frail, Mr. Austin could still invoke nervousness into any researcher.

Sean's throat tightened as he waited for Veronica's father to speak. Instead, the old man greeted Sean with a firm handshake.

"Good afternoon, Mr. Austin."

"Any time of day during a funeral is not good." Mr. Austin gazed at the sky.

"But we need the rain." He raked his fingers through his wavy dark hair. Sean noticed no signs of gray; parallel wrinkles banding his forehead being the only telltale on his face that signaled his age.

"Yes, sir," Sean replied. "Much needed rain."

"Oh, please, Sean. Call me Samuel when away from work."

"Ahh, Samuel. Of course." Sean nodded. *I knew that.*

Mr. Austin turned to Mr. Luzier. "Thank you for your help, Mr. Luzier."

Mr. Luzier nodded and he took the umbrella from Kenneth and placed it in Sean's hand. "If you need anything, Mr. Austin, please don't hesitate to ask."

Mr. Austin motioned at Sean to follow him. "Walk with me for a moment, Sean."

The walk. Sean cursed the thought. *This is about Veronica.*

Sean measured his steps to match Mr. Austin's hobbling gait as the two ambled deeper into the heart of the cemetery, passing weather-beaten monuments and new headstones. The older man's silence weighed heavy on Sean. His palms dripped with perspiration. He wiped them on his shirt, tipping the umbrella to one side, exposing the older man to the rain.

"I'm sorry, Mr. Austin."

"I told you to call me Samuel." Mr. Austin stopped, hooked his cane over his forearm, and pulled out a pipe and a pouch of tobacco from his overcoat.

"Sean," he said, returning the pouch to his pocket and pulling out a small box of matches, "I'm sure you understand why I'm concerned about Veronica."

Sean suppressed the impulse to heave a deep sigh. "Yes, sir, I'm well aware."

Mr. Austin struck a match and lit his pipe. "Are you also aware of her intentions?"

Sean nodded.

"I know she updates you on her progress."

"Mr. Austin—er, Samuel—I'm just as concerned as you are about her being in Minneapolis."

Mr. Austin held his pipe steady between his teeth and snatched the umbrella from Sean's hand. "No, you're not." Smoke billowed from the side of his mouth.

The rain dissipated, turning into a light drizzle. Droplets still covered the leaves and grass, causing their color to appear brighter than they were. Mr. Austin's presence provoked Sean, and he knew Sean had to choose his words carefully. Being in the presence of the President of the Midwest Division and the overseer of all the local Chapters in that region was intimidating. He had to think before he spoke.

Mr. Austin sucked hard on his pipe, expelling smoke while he spoke. "I heard she went to Dark Sepulcher."

"Yes, sir. I begged her not to go, but she went anyway."

"It's obvious she isn't listening to you." He fixed Sean in his gray-eyed stare.

"But, you see—"

"You're a valuable asset to this organization, son. More than that, Veronica likes you." He turned his pipe upside down and smacked its stem against the side of his hand, knocking ash onto the ground. "I spoke to Mr. Luzier and we both agreed that you're perfect for the task."

"Yes, sir, I know, but—" Sean paused. "Task? What task?"

"Mr. Luzier has agreed to promote you to field researcher," Mr. Austin replied. "And you're to go to Minneapolis and bring my daughter back unharmed."

"Sir?"

"My daughter trusts you."

Sean shook his head. He didn't want any of it. A field researcher? Just the thought created a mild pain in his chest. "Sir, she's only called me once. I mean, I'm grateful you decided to choose me, but I'm not right for this."

"You can make her listen." Mr. Austin's voice grew louder. "Kenneth informed me and Mr. Luzier that you acquired documents for Veronica. You violated your oath by acquiring these documents and giving them to someone who isn't a member of The Brotherhood."

"Sir, I—"

"What you did by helping my daughter is punishable, Sean." Mr. Austin puffed on his pipe. "Do you understand?"

Sean quickly zipped his mouth shut and he nodded.

"But I persuaded Mr. Luzier to hand you over to me in exchange for dropping the charges against you and bringing shame to your family."

"Yes, sir." Sean stared at the ground but forced himself to nod.

Mr. Austin again reached into his pocket, this time pulling out a folded manila envelope. "You will leave tomorrow." He placed the envelope in Sean's hand. "And you won't tell anyone where you're going."

Sean stared at the envelope. "Sir, I appreciate what you've done for me but I have no experience as a field researcher."

Mr. Austin held up his hand. "Your parents were loyal members of The Brotherhood, Sean. Being charged with treason will bring shame on your family name." He grabbed the umbrella from Sean and he walked forward. "After you arrive, you will report to Kenneth via email. He's now the new Region Leader of Minnesota."

Sean looked over his shoulder at Kenneth who stood against Mr. Luzier's limousine. Kenneth waved at him and a feeling of anger ripped through Sean's mind. *That bastard.*

"You won't inform my daughter that you're coming," Mr. Austin continued. "You will keep in contact with Kenneth Dearhorn via email and phone. You will sway my daughter away from Dark Sepulcher. Any information from here on out will be about the sanctuary fires and that alone. Do you understand?"

"Yes sir," Sean replied in a defeated voice. "I do."

Mr. Austin nodded. "Don't mess up this opportunity, Sean."

Tentatively, Sean unfolded the envelope and peeked inside and found a short stack of bills and a small piece of paper topped by a single plane ticket to Minneapolis.

CHAPTER SIX

A line filled with provocatively dressed young men and women wrapped around the block which led to the front doors of Dark Sepulcher. Veronica froze, shocked to see how the line had grown since her last visit. Perhaps they'd scheduled a special performance for tonight? Had the club's popularity blossomed so quickly? She took her place in line behind a tall man wearing a ruffled white shirt, black pants, and long artificial nails. Amused, she watched him press his fingers against his fake vampire-style teeth, trying to make them adhere to his natural overbite.

She surveyed the crowd, finding it difficult to separate Deamhan and vampires from humans. Deamhan meticulously disguised themselves with make-up and clothing. And with so many wanna-be humans dressed like vampires, she couldn't tell one from the other.

The line inched forward. Veronica eavesdropped on several conversations until her gaze met the eyes of two women in line behind her. Except for their height, they looked identical—long brown hair and deep brown eyes. The shorter of the two wore a white mesh shirt revealing a black bra and a white miniskirt. The other wore purple leather pants and a pink tank top.

Twins, Veronica thought. *Great.*

"Aren't you cold?" the taller twin asked Veronica.

Surprised, Veronica pointed at herself. "Me?" She knew she wasn't dressed for

Minnesota weather, but neither were they. She no longer owned gloves or a scarf. She sacrificed warmer clothes for club apparel. She shivered then nodded.

"I've never seen you here before." The taller twin's eyes roved Veronica's body.

Not again. Veronica wanted to stop the conversation before it started. She turned her back on the twins and stared straight ahead.

"Don't scare her, sister, especially on her first night here."

Veronica cringed as they conversed behind her.

The line crept forward and when she reached the front door, the bouncer waved her through without checking her ID. Veronica walked through the curtains and into the stodgy air and interior of Dark Sepulcher. She pushed her way through crowds of contorting dancing bodies, trying to create distance between herself and the Deamhan twins. Music thumped throughout her body.

"You're back," a familiar voice said from behind Veronica.

She turned to find the waitress who'd served her the night before.

"You ran out in a hurry the other night," the waitress stated as she placed a napkin on a nearby table.

"Oh yeah, I-I lost track of time. Sorry about that." Veronica had no idea why she apologized. She looked over her shoulder. Realizing the twins weren't following her, she caught her breath and relaxed.

"Wow, you look like you just saw a ghost," the waitress said.

"I'm fine." Veronica slicked back her hair.

"Can I get you anything?"

"No, nothing right now. Thanks."

"You look like you need a drink." The waitress ignored Veronica's answer. "I'll tell you what. We have a new drink. It's on the house." The waitress playfully slapped Veronica on her wrist. "It's called Sensual Appetite, and it's delish!" She patted a chair next to the table. "Sit and relax." She leaned toward Veronica and whispered, "My name is Chelsea. If you need anything else, just holler."

Before Veronica could refuse, the waitress pushed through the crowd and disappeared. A fresh burst of fog spewed from a machine above, engulfing the dance floor. The gyrating crowd cheered in approval.

Veronica's eyes moved to the back at a small room nestled in the corner directly above the dance floor. A rowdy cheer to her left caught her attention. A group of scantily dressed men and women hovered around a circular table. The light flickered above them. Veronica recognized Alexis; her arms draped around the neck of a man sporting a business suit and red tie. He sipped from a chalice and pointed to the crowd on the dance floor.

Chelsea returned and placed a clear plastic cup on the table in front of Veronica. The dark red drink had no ice, but a hint of blue had settled at the bottom of the cup. "Here you go," she said, tucking the tray underneath her arm.

"I'm not thirsty." Veronica pushed the cup away.

Immediately Chelsea latched onto her wrist and pulled Veronica's hand toward the cup. "Nonsense." Chelsea's eyes narrowed in on Veronica. Her eyes turned black and her mouth opened slightly, revealing her fangs. "Now drink up, researcher. Don't let a good drink go to waste."

Veronica looked to her left then to her right. The club music seemed low-set as all eyes in the vicinity were on her, including Alexis'. Chelsea released her grip and waited for Veronica to drink.

Veronica grasped the cup, lifting it to her lips. She closed her eyes, paused, and then tipped the cup. When the liquid touched her lips, she opened her eyes. The Deamhan now encircled her, standing close enough that Veronica felt Chelsea's breasts pushed against her forearm.

"Drink," Chelsea whispered, "or I'll drink you."

Veronica took a long, deep swallow; thick liquid slid down her throat. The wretched taste of iron and blood made her choke, and she dropped the cup onto the floor, gagging. The Deamhan laughed.

Veronica shoved a napkin to her mouth as the liquid circled in her stomach. Her eyes filled with tears and her mouth frothed. She rushed to the bathroom, elbowing her way through the crowd. Her stomach gurgled and heaved. A sudden gust of air pushed her forward, and cold hands grasped her arms and yanked her into the bathroom.

"Please struggle." The voice of the taller twin tickled Veronica's ear.

"Yes, please." The voice of the shorter twin tickled Veronica's other ear.

With the bathroom door slammed shut behind them, the twins pushed Veronica to the cold, dirty floor. She winced as her ribs smacked the tile; pain shot through her stomach and into her back. She stole a glance under the stalls before she raised her head. They were alone. Bare fluorescent bulbs flickered overhead, giving the room an ominous glow.

The taller twin gripped Veronica's arms in her powerful grasp. She easily lifted Veronica to her feet and violently slammed her against the bathroom wall. Breathless, Veronica made a dash for the door, but was shoved back. The taller twin wrapped her fingers around Veronica's neck. Veronica clawed, trying to break free, but the Deamhan was too strong.

Veronica stared into the twin's dark, menacing eyes. Her vision twisted in and out. The bathroom floor rippled as if water suddenly covered the floor. Veronica's head swooned and fear dissipated. The drink flowed through her veins, intoxicating her.

It was a high she hadn't felt since she smoked weed for the first time in her teenage years. A sense of invincibility and relaxation overtook her. She tried envisioning a brick wall in preparation for the Deamhan twins to invade her thoughts, but the tingling sensation never came. Instead she drifted into the furthest part of her mind where she kept sacred memories of her mother carefully hidden from human and Deamhan alike.

"I told you, sister." The tall twin licked her lips. "She's ripe." The Deamhan twins knowingly locked eyes and giggled.

With a handful of Veronica's hair in her grasp, the taller twin pulled, yanking Veronica's head violently to the side. She opened her mouth and her canines protruded from her pale gums. "Her scent is strong, Brandy. And her skin," she said, sniffing Veronica's neck, "is so soft." She stuck out her tongue and licked Veronica's neck from her ear to her collarbone.

Veronica shivered from the trail of wet spittle left on her skin.

"What to do with her." The tall twin increased her grip around Veronica's throat. "She doesn't have the markings of a minion."

Brandy stepped away from the door. "But, Branda, I heard she is protected."

Her mouth opened, exposing sharper and longer fangs than her sister's.

"What Deamhan would be stupid enough to give a researcher protection?" Branda scoffed. "Especially one as stupid as her."

Protected? Veronica struggled to keep her eyes opened. Darkness toyed at her periphery, and she thought she might faint from lack of oxygen.

"I want her first, sister." Brandy's eyes widened. "Oh, can I? Can I please have first bite?"

"Sure." Branda slowly released her grip.

Veronica gasped, her lungs searing as they engulfed fresh air.

"But don't get greedy."

Brandy replaced her sister's stance and shoved Veronica back against the wall. She sniffed the side of Veronica's face and chortled as Veronica struggled against her. "I like it when they fight." Brandy closed her eyes and swayed her head back and forth as she spoke in a singsong voice. "Like a fly, caught in a spider web, about to meet its maker."

"Protected." Branda huffed, her nostrils flaring. "What a crock of shit."

A strong wind manifested, and Brandy instantly released her grip. Her head jerked to the bathroom door as it flew open on its own.

Veronica's legs crumbled. She fell to the floor gasping for air. She looked up in time to see a fuzzy image of the Deamhan twins running out of the bathroom with Deamhan speed and the door slamming shut behind them.

Whatever scared them away had impeccable timing.

Veronica leaned against the wall, coughing up phlegm. She rubbed her tender neck and lifted herself to her feet. Veronica shuffled over to the sink and turned on the water. The euphoric feeling from the drink had subsided. Her hands now trembled. She splashed warm water on her face. Her breathing relaxed. She examined the red and purple bruises on her neck in the mirror.

"Shit," she said, her voice hoarse. "But I'll be damned if I'll let these freaks run me out of Dark Sepulcher again."

She touched the wall to steady herself. The Sensual Appetite ravaged her body. The drink's stimulating effects returned with a punch. Veronica hurried out of the bathroom and to the main room.

The club walls swirled around her. White and gold streaks trailed behind the patrons dancing on the dance floor. Afraid to walk any farther, she rested against a pillar and dropped her head into her hands.

Who would protect me?

She knew what it meant. If a human or even a Deamhan was said to be *protected* it meant that someone claimed them as their own. They were off limits, untouchable. To achieve this status, the one being protected was usually a minion or claimed their loyalty to a very strong and old Deamhan. But she wasn't anyone's to claim and she wasn't any Deamhan's minion. Her curiosity grew. Who protected her and what was she being protected from?

Veronica lifted her head from her sweaty palms. Flashing strobe lights semi-blinded her; however, she found her vision acquired more depth. She could see into the darkness and make out shapes, people, Deamhan and vampires she hadn't noticed before. Noise from the crowd grew quieter, more distant. The drink was altering her senses!

Just as the thought occurred, her vision became crystal clear. Immaculate. She now could single the Deamhan out in the crowd. They looked taller, darker. Their fluid movements, their hardened skin. When provoked by one of their own or a vampire, the Ramanga threatened with their fangs. White light pulsated from the Lamia's mouth and the Lugat's hands, and there was a weird glow around the body of the Metusba. They fed indiscriminately in the crowds with Deamhan speed, only taking enough from their human victims to not notice. Blood dripped from Ramanga lips. Lamia embraced their victims in intimate kisses as they sucked the life from their mouths. Veronica watched in horror as a white streak of light flowed from the mouth of a pretty young blonde into the mouth of a muscled Lamia. Victims dropped to the floor, their energies weakened by the Metusba. Desperate Lugat on the dance floor swiped their hands on railings, disposed cups and napkins—anything to get a psychic taste of their victims.

And that was the Deamhan. Vampires were just as repulsive.

"Now you see what we see." A voice caressed Veronica's ear.

Veronica quickly turned, standing face to face with a jubilant Alexis, dressed in a short and shiny black pleather dress. She sported a pink wig, the hair cut into a short bob.

Alexis snaked her cold hand up Veronica's arm and moved in closer, standing inches from Veronica's neck. "It's a funny drink, isn't it?" She dropped her hands to Veronica's hips and sensuously slid them up her stomach, over her breasts, and to her neck.

Electric vibrations ran through Veronica's body and she found herself unable to move, unable to struggle.

"What did she give me?" Veronica's breathing raced. "Vampire blood? I'm dying?"

Alexis threw her head back in laughter. "You researchers aren't the sharpest tools in the box." Her body swayed with the pulsating beat of the music, and her hands caressed Veronica's face. "To be made a vampire, researcher, you'd have to be drained of your blood and have it replaced by vampire blood. It's a simple process which takes only a night." She curled her fingers into Veronica's hair, tilting her head to the side. "To be made Deamhan, your physic energy needs to be drained and replaced by the energy of a Deamhan. A somewhat complicated process that takes several days."

"Then what did she give me?"

"It's not for you, you know," Alexis answered. "But it's so entertaining watching a human on it." Her mouth engulfed Veronica's in a passionate kiss.

Veronica stiffened, feeling Alexis' tongue slide past her lips, her own tongue, and down into her throat. Her gag reflex repressed, and a warm, acidic liquid regurgitated from her stomach. Her entire body shuddered as Alexis suckled violently, sucking out the contents of Veronica's stomach into her own mouth.

Oddly, Veronica experienced total relaxation when Alexis released her.

Alexis leaned to the side, spitting red liquid onto the floor. "There. All better." She wiped her mouth with the back of her hand and licked her full lips.

"Wh-what did you do to me?" Veronica's buzz slowly faded.

"Nothing much." Alexis grinned then grabbed Veronica's wrist and placed a small envelope in her palm. "He wants you to come back."

"Who?" Veronica stared at the envelope. By the time she looked up again, Alexis was gone.

Veronica wiped her damp forehead. Her body felt loose and weak. Her senses returned to normal. As she gawked at the small puddle of red liquid near her feet, she felt a tap on her shoulder.

"Veronica?"

She turned and stood face to face with Murphy.

"Murphy?" She willed her eyes to focus, surprised he was there.

"Are you okay?" He pulled a handkerchief from his pocket and dabbed at the sweat on her forehead. "You look sick."

"What are you doing here?"

"I thought I'd check this place out." He wrinkled his forehead. "You don't look so good."

He shouldn't be here. Still, she welcomed his presence even if his form-fitting blue jeans and loose white T-shirt made him stick out in Dark Sepulcher more than she did.

"Were you leaving?" he asked.

Veronica nodded weakly. "Can you get me out of here?"

"Yeah, sure." He took her hand and led her toward the exit.

The floor felt uneven to Veronica's steps, and she fought symptoms of vertigo as Murphy led her through the heavy black curtains and out the front door. A cool breeze rushed against her face and up her back. Overhead, the sky glowed with an orange haze, and she wondered if it was pollution or the streetlights that lit up the city.

"Feeling better?" Murphy asked.

She tensed at a loud buzz and looked up then sighed in relief when she realized the sound originated from an airplane heading to Minneapolis International Airport, which wasn't far away.

"Veronica?" His voice drew her eyes back to his face.

"Yeah, I'm sorry. Let's go."

"Did you drive or walk?"

She looked behind him at Dark Sepulcher in the distance. "Taxi. I called a taxi."

He pulled out his cell phone.

51

"No, don't."

"Are you okay to walk back?"

"Yeah, I could use the fresh air."

He nodded and put his phone away.

Veronica leaned against his body while they walked down the street. She held on to his arm firmly. Every so often she looked over her shoulder. She didn't know who would come for her. She expected Branda and Brandy to finish what they started. Maybe walking back to Palm Oaks wasn't the smartest thing to do after all.

They walked down the street and passed a group of men dressed in dark clothing. Veronica looked over her shoulder, watching them walk into Dark Sepulcher.

"What's wrong?" Murphy asked as he removed his arm from Veronica's side, forcing her to stand on her own.

"It's nothing."

"Well, are you feeling better at least?"

"A little. Thank you." Veronica put her hand to her head, suddenly embarrassed.

"You still look tired. What happened?"

"I ordered a drink that was too strong for me," Veronica lied. She carefully excluded the name of the drink. It contained something that gave the drink a magical element. Whatever it was, she didn't want Murphy to try it.

"That place is kind of weird," he continued. "Just as I walked in, I saw this guy and girl biting each other. Are all gothic clubs like that?"

"Dark Sepulcher is, well, special," she answered, resting her fingers around his forearm. "It's creepy."

Veronica and Murphy crossed the deserted street and headed down Hennepin Avenue. They passed boarded up stores and vacant facades. "For sale" signs lined the windows of several empty buildings, and an odor of urine lingered in the cool air.

Murphy made small talk, chattering about his family and life in the Florida sunshine. He explained that his mother worked as a receptionist, and his father was an electronics technician. Veronica half-listened as she repeatedly glanced over her shoulder, looking and listening for the unknown. Tiny hairs on her neck danced and, despite Murphy's proximity, she still didn't feel safe.

"What is it?"

"I just want to get home." She forced a weak smile.

"Yeah, me too," Murphy replied. "My warm bed sounds good about now. So um, what do your father and your mother do?"

Veronica quickly changed the subject. "What did you say you're majoring in at college?"

"I'm taking generals now," he answered. "I haven't declared a major yet. I'm thinking maybe engineering or criminal justice. My father wants me to become an engineer, but I don't know yet. What do you think? Can you see me as an engineer or a police officer?"

Just ahead, two dark figures shadowed the street at the end of the block.

Murphy stared at her, waiting for an answer.

She pressed his arm and halted, nodding her head toward the two in front of them. "Who's that?"

"Where?" He squinted, peering down the street.

Orange streetlights bathed the two in shadows, but from the length of their hair, Veronica knew exactly who they were.

"Quick. Let's go this way." She gripped Murphy's arm to spin him around.

"But the apartment is that way, Veronica." He pointed down the street in their current destination.

Just as they turned, the two figures quickly appeared in front of them.

Before Veronica could react, Brandy grabbed Murphy by the neck, lifting him several inches off the ground. Branda spun Veronica around and wrapped her forearm around Veronica's neck.

Murphy gasped and his eyes bulged.

"Now, where were we?" Branda whispered in Veronica's ear.

Murphy balled his fist and stuck Brandy across the chin.

She smiled. "Oh, he's a keeper, sis. I love a fighter!"

Murphy swung again, but she caught his fist in her palm.

"What the fuck?" Murphy's eyes swelled from the pressure of Brandy's grip.

"All the things I can do to him, sister." She slapped Murphy across the face. Even in the shadowy night, his cheek burned red with her palm print.

A surge of pain shot through Veronica's already-sore neck. She tried to fight, but her strength was no match for Branda.

"What do you think, sister?" Brandy's eyes scanned Murphy's head from head to toe. "Do you think he'll like me?"

Branda sighed and rolled her eyes. "I don't care. As long as I get to play with her."

Brandy's smile slowly dissipated. "You never care about what I want." As if he were an afterthought, she abruptly released Murphy. He dropped hard to the concrete, coughing and rubbing his throat.

"Of course I do." Branda's gaze didn't leave Veronica who continued to struggle.

"Then why don't you care?" Brandy stood next to her sister. She placed her hands on her hips. "If you care, let me have her first."

Branda quickly eyed her sister. "You have him, Brandy."

"But . . . I . . . want . . . her!"

In a flash, Brandy's eyes shifted away from her sister and down the street. Then she looked over her shoulder and back to her sister. Veronica noticed her alarmed gaze. Dread was the last thing she'd ever expected to see in the eyes of a

Deamhan.

The sound of breaking glass broke the air. Something or someone was there.

"Brandy, what is it?" Branda asked, exposing prolonged canines.

A gust of warm wind blew past them. Branda's grip loosened. Veronica fell to the pavement. She quickly crawled toward Murphy.

Dark blood oozed from a slit on Branda's neck. It rained down her chest, splattering the ground in front of Veronica and Murphy. Branda reached for her neck, rubbed her gash and examined the reddish black fluid. Blood spurted from every orifice from her face; like a jet stream, it poured out her nostrils, mouth, ears, and eventually her eyes. The skin around her ear-to-ear wound turned black. Like intricate spider webs, the discoloration spread until it covered her skin.

Her head hit the pavement, followed by her body. It crumbled into little pieces before finally disintegrating before their eyes. Murphy jumped to his feet and pulled Veronica back to avoid the cloud of dust and pool of blood.

Brandy screamed and, with Deamhan speed, dashed across the street, disappearing around the corner.

"What the—what the hell was that?" Murphy coughed and gagged as the wind picked up, blowing ashes across the street and into the air. "Veronica, what the hell was that!"

How could she explain? At that moment, no words could describe what they saw. I guess this was what being protected meant.

"We need to go." She pulled a wide-eyed Murphy down the street toward Palm Oaks, clutching the crumpled envelope to her chest.

CHAPTER SEVEN

Alexis straightened her shoulders, jutted her chin, and yanked opened the door. She strode past a makeshift cross nailed to the wall holding a gagged and tied human woman. She stopped short, inhaled the scent of blood seeping from the lacerations on the woman's breasts and stomach. Tiny razor blade cuts covered her legs. The victim breathed erratically. The wounds weren't deep, but effective to cause pain.

"This one is dying," Alexis called out. "She'll need food soon."

More human bodies laid scattered in the back room. Some were in the first stages of decomposition while others were passed that. Near the back wall, five Deamhan held down a scantily clad woman. She kicked valiantly, fighting against her handlers. They pinned her arms and legs to the floor and they sunk their teeth into her soft flesh. An amused smile tugged at Alexis' lips. The victim's sobs and whispers fell on deaf ears.

One of the Ramanga bit into her wrist hard enough to cause an audible crunch. The human shrieked in pain. Moments later, her writhing slowed to a stop.

Alexis rolled her eyes. *How many Deamhan does it take to kill a human?* Their kind never ceased to annoy her.

The scent of fragrant incense masked the odor of fresh blood. She hated coming back here especially with the Deamhan around. She reminisced about the times when it was just her and Lambert, surrounded by dozens of humans to pick and feed from. They picked and chose their meals in their own hell bent paradise.

Now, Lambert invited the Deamhan to the back room to gorge on their hapless, helpless victims. He accommodated them while ignoring his own kind. He never invited vampires to the room anymore, and she didn't understand why. He loathed the Deamhan as much as she did.

Sniffing indignantly, she walked past the bartender and a Deamhan who acknowledged her presence with a nod. She passed the remains of a human nailed to the wall, his intestines exposed and hanging from his abdomen with his heart and his lungs nailed to the right of his body. His scrotum was stuffed in his mouth.

She recognized Lambert's artwork.

Lambert loved to use some of his more unique kills displayed as a fine still life. He used the remains of his victims, contorting their broken limbs and insides as an effigy to the human body. He found the human body to be intricate and complex.

Impressed, Alexis moved on. She found it a waste of time examining the decaying, misshaped bodies of humans. Besides, she didn't want to press her luck by keeping Lambert, her maker and her lover, waiting any longer. He hated waiting.

She pushed aside the red silk curtain that sectioned off the octagon-shaped feeding room, filled with tastefully placed black beanbag chairs. A nude, hard-bodied man lay atop a long black table in the middle of the floor. It surprised Alexis that vampires, not Deamhan, surrounded the body, picking at it in feast.

Behind them, observing the melee with a gleam in his brown eyes, stood Alexis' lover for centuries, Lambert. His shoulder length brown hair, pulled back in a ponytail, hung over his left shoulder. He licked his slender lips, revealing his sharp pointed fangs (not as long as the fangs of a Ramanga, vampire fangs proved to be just as sharp.)

Lambert, his arms folded across his chest, raked his eyes over Alexis' body. In his hand, he held a white, blood-spotted handkerchief and the silky black robe from the night before. Alexis smirked, remembering the naughty, decadent things he did to her in that robe.

Lambert clapped his hands, grabbing the attention of the bloodsuckers away from their meal. "A time alone with my woman."

The dejected vampires exited against their will, leaving the pulsating man softly moaning in pain. Alexis slinked toward Lambert, provocatively swaying her hips from side to side as she darted out her tongue to wet her lips.

Lambert opened his arms, accepting her into his embrace. She felt the warm blood on his lips. He kissed the top of her head and he yanked off her pink wing. He grasped a fistful of dark brown hair, yanking her head back and revealing her long, dark-skinned neck.

He dropped the wig to the floor. "Did you give it to her?" he whispered.

"Yes, she has the note." Suggestively, she stuck out her tongue and curled it upward.

Lambert wrapped his lips around it and sucked violently, causing her to spasm in pleasure.

Tingling heat rushed between her legs and, as if sensing her deep need, Lambert slid his hand into her pants, slipping his forefinger between the throbbing lips of her vagina. A moan escaped from deep within her chest. She didn't want him to let her go but he did just that, pushing her to the floor.

"You're losing your edge," Alexis said through panting breaths. "I remember the time when that used to hurt a little. Now you're all pleasure; no pain."

She lifted herself from the floor and straightened her shirt.

The human moaned, and Lambert quickly covered his mouth.

"The way this one moans," he said, shaking his head in disgust, "it annoys me." He moved his hand over the victim's nose and looked back at Alexis. "And I really enjoy moaning. Maybe I am losing my touch?"

Alexis let out a deep-throated laugh. "You can always make him your next artwork masterpiece."

"No. No, that's been boring me lately," Lambert replied. "Humans nowadays don't take care of themselves like they used to. They fill their bodies with drugs, they eat fatty foods. Their blood tastes like processed garbage. So this researcher. What do you think of her?"

"Guileless but interesting."

"Yes, interesting. She keeps coming back even though it's not in her best interest."

"Chelsea gave her Sensual Appetite. You should've seen it!" Alexis shivered in contentment. "It was so much fun sucking it right out of her."

The victim's body jerked violently under the pressure of Lambert's cold hands.

"Fun to watch too." Alexis closed her eyes. She relived the moment, recalling the smallest details like the bead of sweat that trickled down the side of Veronica's neck when Chelsea had given her the drink and the look in Veronica's eyes, thinking that she had somehow been sired.

"Get rid of the waitress." Lambert pressed harder. The victim's thrashing turned to twitching, then a final shudder.

"Why?" said Alexis, raising her voice.

Lambert removed his hand from the victim's mouth and licked the blood from his palm. "She disobeyed me. I told all of them, vampires and humans, that the human is protected by a Deamhan. She's not to be touched or harmed."

Alexis huffed. "And since when do the Deamhan tell us what to do? They can't even follow their own rules."

"Not our concern." Lambert wiped the remaining blood on his hands with his handkerchief and tossed it to the floor.

"Fine. I'll give her a warning. Tell her not to do it again." Alexis lowered herself on the couch. "Or if you want I could flog her." A mischievous grin appeared on her face.

"You'd like that, wouldn't you?" Lambert walked behind the bar and grabbed a small shot glass from the shelf. He opened the small cooler underneath, pulling out a metallic flask.

"I would like that," Alexis agreed. "Very much." Her mind drifted to the plethora of floggings she and her lover had committed through the centuries. Not once did they bore her, except for the bootlegger they'd caught trying to sell his moonshine in their Speakeasy back in the day. He didn't scream. Not even once.

"Do what you want," he said with a lazy shrug. "My only concerns are for my club and for you. The last thing I need is unruly Deamhan threatening my already crepuscular atmosphere." He twisted the lid off and poured the liquid in the shot glass, filling it to the rim.

"Let me kill her." Alexis repositioned herself on the couch with her legs spread open. "I promise, I'll make it quick."

"No." Lambert downed the shot then poured himself another. He walked back and sat next to Alexis. "Did you not hear me when I said she's protected?"

Alexis pouted. She didn't like the way Lambert acted around the Deamhan now. This wasn't the Lambert she fell in love with. Even as a human, his mercenary lifestyle made him hard, unremorseful. Orphaned as a young boy, he was raised in a mercenary camp and lived his life as a mercenary for hire. Along with his tribe of Celtic headhunters, he raided small villages of his enemies, killing the men and boys, and raped their women and daughters. He beheaded his victims, tied their heads to his horse as in accordance with his religion. Sometimes he offered the heads to the Roman commanders who paid him for his bounty work. Scars from his human life still littered his back and his chest. Only when his teacher was killed by a vampire and Lambert went to seek him out, did Lambert lose his first and last battle as a human.

Of course Lambert loved to battle, to fight. He was born a warrior and he had a warrior's heart. He also loved the art of torture. He once cut off the hands of a Lugat he had captured and watched as the Deamhan slowly withered away, unable to feed due to the loss of his hands. When Alexis met him for the first time on York Plantation in upstate New York during the American Revolution, he had just stepped off a British ship in the harbor as an immigrant and was in the process of buying his own plantation. He tortured the slaves he bought but when it came to her, she found herself lucky. She enjoyed the pain and the suffering. Maybe she felt this way because of her screwed life as a house servant. Without Lambert, she would've never experienced what life had to offer.

Now she had to beg him if she wanted to slaughter any human or Deamhan in Dark Sepulcher. He thought twice about killing and maiming. He was preoccupied with making money than making enemies. It wasn't the Lambert she grew to love, but she'd do anything for him still. She'd follow him into the bowels of hell if she had to.

"Please, Daddy." She rubbed her hands on his chest. Calling him "Daddy" usually made him see things her way.

"I told you. She is protected. Someone has claimed her." He handed Alexis the drink.

"Since when do you follow a Deamhan order?" Alexis devoured the drink. In moments she felt it absorb into her flesh, spreading throughout her body. She closed her eyes and leaned back. "I've never understood why you decided to cater to them."

"You don't have to understand them, sweetheart." Lambert lightly kissed her cheek. "You and I both know that the best way to survive in this city is to remain neutral and not get involved in their squabbles."

"You mean Kei's squabbles."

"That too." Lambert kissed the tip of her nose. "Let them burn each other out of house and home." He dug his nails into her cheek and she gasped, gripping his chest with her hands. "We play it safe and smart, Alexis. That's what we vampires will do."

Thin trails of blood flowed from tiny pinholes in her cheek. Lambert dabbed his fingers in her blood and sucked it from his fingers, one at a time.

"What about your human friend, Lambert? The one that lives with the Deamhan?"

"What about him?" Lambert touched her wounded cheek with his finger and gently placed it over her lips.

"You confide in him about The Brotherhood. Does he know that they have returned?"

She slid out her tongue, tasting her own cold salty blood.

Suddenly, Lambert shoved her back, and she fell on top of the corpse. The body was still warm and for a minute Alexis felt her primal instincts surface, urging her to drink any remaining blood in his body. But that meant death for any vampire. His blood was now unhealthy. She watched as Lambert let his silken robe slide to the floor, exposing his rock hard penis and his defectless upper body. He stood over Alexis, straddling her.

"Right here?" Her sultry smile revealed her approval. With patience that made her ache, Lambert laid his body on hers and slowly, slowly, he entered her.

"Just like the first time." His fangs dropped as he continued rocking back and forth inside her. "1777. Oriskany."

"Outside under a clear night sky," she said, panting between thrusts, "the smell of gunpowder, mixed with blood . . ."

"Screams of dying men." Her fangs dropped and she bit into her lower lip in pleasure.

He slammed his hips against her. The pressure tore her open and she convulsed as he reached new depths.

"Oh, yeah," she moaned. "Only without the hot pokers."

He slid his hand under the table and pulled out a knife with a long, sharp blade covered in blood.

Her eyes grew wide, and an innocent giggle escaped her lips.

"I have a replacement for that." He twirled the knife in his hand, like a baton.

CHAPTER EIGHT

By the time they reached Palm Oaks Veronica agreed for Murphy to spend the night at her apartment.

He questioned her the entire way back. His fear disappeared, replaced by a natural curiosity to know what was going on. He sat on her couch, fidgeting his fingers. Veronica locked the front door, checked it, and then checked it again. It didn't matter how comfortable and safe she felt. Unlike vampires, Deamhan didn't need to be invited to come into her apartment. She walked over to the window and peeked through the blinds.

"What the hell was that, Veronica?" He jumped to his feet. "She exploded! Well, not like exploded but she turned to ash, right in front of us! Have you seen anything like that before?"

"You should spend the night, Murphy." Veronica walked to the kitchen. "I'll make you some coffee." Still groggy from the drink Chelsea gave her, she filled the coffee pot with water, poured it in the coffee maker, and turned on the power. She leaned against the kitchen counter, mentally unequipped to handle another barrage of questions.

"Are we in trouble?" His eyes widened and his eyebrows lifted. "Should we call the police?"

"No!" she answered, loudly and hastily. She caught herself staring down at Murphy. She leaned her forehead against the cool stainless steel fridge, just slightly out of his view. It wouldn't hurt to tell him about the Deamhan, she reasoned. He had every right to know, especially since he lived in a city filled with them. Telling him would better prepare himself for what was out there.

Would it?

"Why not?"

"They can't do anything, Murphy, believe me." Veronica walked over to the living room and she sat across from him. Nonchalantly, she pushed the envelope Alexis gave her at Dark Sepulcher off to the side of the coffee table.

"What do you mean they can't do anything?"

"Trust me. They can't."

He sat back, looking defeated. "That girl was so strong. I nailed her and she took the hit like a man." He winced as he rubbed his red bruise. "Better than a man."

"That's because she's not human. They're strong, even the newly sired ones."

"All I saw was a shadow, and then the girl holding you started to bleed everywhere. And then the other girl took off"—he snapped his fingers—"just like that!"

"Murphy"—Veronica leaned toward him—"I'm going to tell you something that you might not believe or want to hear. Just promise me you won't freak out."

He nodded.

Veronica took a deep breath and she began to explain the Deamhan.

She talked for over an hour, telling him what she knew; the types of Deamhan, how the city was their haven, how they died, and how they were turned. Yet anything about The Brotherhood she purposely skipped.

She told him the real reason why she came back to Minneapolis and how important it was to her to find out what happened to her mother. When she'd finished her spiel, she shrugged, realizing she had nothing left to say. It was now up to Murphy to handle what she just revealed.

Veronica returned to the kitchen for two cups of coffee, giving Murphy a moment alone to process what she'd told him. She filled the sugar bowl from the canister and she watched him stare down at the floor in thought.

When she looked back again, his expression morphed from confusion to concern.

Finally, he turned toward the kitchen. "So those two chicks, were these Deamhan creatures?"

"Yeah."

"And they're immortal. They live forever?"

"Pretty much."

"Stakes can kill them?"

She couldn't suppress a grin. "They can also die from exposure to sunlight and be beheaded."

"Like vampires who also live in the city?"

"Yeah."

"What about garlic?" A look of hope appeared on his face.

"No." Veronica peeked out from behind the wall separating the two. "Garlic doesn't work for vampires either."

"Why not call them vampires?"

"Because they aren't vampires. They're Deamhan," she answered. "They're different. I mean, I look at them as like distant relatives or cousins of vampires. But they're different. Even siring a Deamhan is a totally different process than siring a vampire. There used to be tons of them. So many different types. One time, they actually outnumbered vampires."

61

"What happened?"

Veronica shrugged. "I don't know. I just know that now they're like an endangered species. It's just the Ramanga, Lugat, Metusba and Lamia now."

"There used to be more?" His eyes widened.

She took a deep breath and muttered, "I believe so. I heard that there were eight clans in total but now, only four."

"These creatures hang out at Dark Sepulcher?"

"Not all of them. Majority of vampires hang out there."

"And the main reason you came back to Minneapolis is to look for your mother, right?"

"Yeah." Veronica walked from the kitchen carrying a coffee, sugar, and cream on a tray.

"Oh." Murphy soaked up the information like a wet towel. "That explains a lot."

Veronica stood in front of him. "What do you mean?"

"The people I saw at the club doing weird shit to one another." A look of confusion returned to his face. "I'm sorry."

"Sorry for what?" Veronica said as she handed the cup to him. "I wouldn't be here if I didn't believe there was a chance."

"I don't know." He sipped the coffee and cradled the cup in his hand. "I guess I'm sorry for what you have to go through."

Veronica opened her mouth to speak, but he quickly interrupted.

"I always thought this city was a little weird." He chuckled. "Boring, but weird."

"Well, every city has its secrets." She drew a long sip from her mug; the hot, sugary coffee warmed her chest on the way down.

"If you need my help with anything, Veronica, I'm here. Unless you want me to kill one of them and—well, I'd have to sit that one out."

Veronica watched as doubt clouded his face. "Oh no." She laughed, and he smiled sheepishly, his eyes crinkling in a way that warmed her as much as the coffee. "I wouldn't do that, Murphy. I'm not here to hunt them."

"What if your mom is one of them?" he asked. "What if they sired her?"

Veronica swallowed hard. The thought never crossed her mind. She didn't have a plan if she found her mother sired. The thought of it made her cringe. It wasn't possible. Her mother was still alive, somewhere in Minneapolis.

"She's alive. I know it." She patted his leg.

Veronica stared into her mug, watching the cream swirl into the murky darkness. The attack at Dark Sepulcher wasn't a setback. She still had to move forward, starting with checking out the burned house again to see if it could have been a Deamhan sanctuary, but she couldn't leave Murphy in her apartment by himself. She looked at him again as he sipped from his cup then stared down into it. How his beautiful eyes lit up when she described the Deamhan to him and the way his tongue had a sexy way of peeking through his teeth when he pronounced the *"th"* sound.

"You listening to me?"

Veronica flinched. "Y-yes. I'm sorry."

"You drifted off there. Where did you go? Are you okay?"

She cleared her throat and felt heat rise into her face. "You can sleep on the couch." She stood up, took a few steps down the hallway, and then stopped. "I was just thinking. I—I have to go somewhere tomorrow. Want to come with?"

"Deamhan search?" he asked.

She nodded slowly. "Something like that." She chewed her lip then straightened her shoulders. "So you want to come?"

* * * *

Murphy drove his beat up Toyota Corolla down the Hennepin Avenue, heading straight for the ruins in the warehouse district. The car's left tail light was shattered, and a rope tied to the bumper held the trunk closed.

Driving by Wilkes Cemetery, Veronica looked out the passenger side window quietly, noticing a pile of dirt next to a freshly dug hole. *A new grave. Interesting.* Before leaving San Diego, she learned that the famous Minneapolis cemetery was already at maximum capacity.

Murphy parked his car across the street from the ruins. He turned down the radio volume and leaned toward Veronica to get a better look at the burnt ruins.

"This it?"

She nodded and opened the door. They exited and walked around to the front of the car. Murphy leaned against the rusted hood.

Veronica crossed her arms, staring at the police tape surrounding the area. The strong stench of smoke burned her nostrils. A pile of blackened wood and small patches of scorched grass and earth in the front yard emitted white wisps of smoke. The site wasn't grand nor was it anything special.

"This place must of burned good." Murphy examined the area. "So this was a sanctuary?" His upper lip curled in disgust.

"That's what I'm trying to find out." Veronica sighed, realizing she probably shouldn't have brought him along. She couldn't forgive herself if Murphy got hurt. Most importantly, Sean would never forgive her bringing another person into her mess. By dragging Murphy along, she disobeyed one of The Brotherhood's policies, one of the only policies she believed in. However, she wasn't part of that organization so why should she even care.

"What are we looking for?" Murphy glanced up and down the street before slowly approaching the sectioned off area.

"Anything that might prove this was a sanctuary."

He ducked under the yellow police tape and picked his way forward, observing the ruins.

Veronica remembered the chattering old woman and glanced around to see if she and Murphy were being watched. She expected to see the nosy neighbors eyeing them through the curtains of their home, but the streets were usually empty at this time of day. She checked her watch. Just past four in the afternoon. They had to be quick and leave in a few hours before sunset, or nosy little ladies would be the least of their worries.

"I don't know how you can pick out anything in this mess." Murphy picked up a piece of burnt wood. "What are we looking for?"

Veronica ducked under the police tape. He was right. Besides already knowing the ruins used to be a home, nothing else around them proved it was anything other than that. Nothing stuck out to her; no remnants of a coffin (if the Deamhan even used a coffin). No sign of hidden compartments. Just charred pieces of wood and furniture.

"Be careful. Some of the wood is still hot." Veronica fanned her blouse as the heat emanating from the ruins warmed her skin.

"What kind of stuff would you find in a sanctuary?" Murphy's eyes flitted from the debris to the neighborhood and back again.

"Holding cells, lots of extra beds, maybe coffins. A sanctuary is like a Deamhan safe house." She stood in the center of the rubble and turned in a circle as she carefully scanned the neighborhood and quiet streets. "If we're lucky, maybe some remains of their victims." A lone squirrel ran into the road, paused, stood on its hind legs, and stared at them before it ran and disappeared behind a tree.

Murphy nervously jingled his keys. "The cops don't know about them?"

"No. The Deamhan keep their lives secret, remember?"

"How do you know then? Your mother?"

The Brotherhood. But Veronica didn't want to tell him about that. "My mother," she confirmed, turning to walk back to the car. "Would you've believed me if you hadn't seen for yourself, Murphy?"

"No."

At least he was honest.

"This is some paranormal shit," he said. "Like the Men in Black or Roswell. Stuff like that."

The squealing sound of tires pierced the air. A blue windowless van rounded the corner at breakneck speed, racing down the street. It swerved uncontrollably from left to right before coming to a screeching halt next to Murphy. The van seemed oddly familiar to Veronica. She froze and she locked eyes with the driver, a white male, who glared back from under a black baseball cap.

Veronica rushed back to the car and she screamed at Murphy to follow her. She stood frozen, transfixed on the driver. He obviously wasn't a Deamhan or a vampire. He didn't look like a researcher and to her knowledge, there were no Chapters in the city anymore.

A minion?

He didn't look like a minion.

She screamed for Murphy again but her words drowned under the roaring of the van's engine.

Veronica heard the van's passenger door open and footsteps running around the front of the vehicle. She snapped out of her trance. Instantly, she remembered the last time she'd been at this site. She saw the van before, down the street the other day.

Murphy ran to the car, unlocked it and they jumped in. He started his car, yanked it into gear, and sped off.

Three men in white ski masks and blue sweat suits appeared in front of the van carrying crowbars, chains, and knives.

"Holy shit!" Murphy's neck craned as he looked over his shoulder, then to the rearview then back over his shoulder. "Who the fuck are they?"

Veronica paced her breathing and finally replied in a short breath. "Minions, I think."

The old Corolla whined as Murphy maxed out the RPMs before he rounded the corner and changed gears. "Minions?"

"Lackeys, minions. Same thing." Veronica turned around to see if they were being followed before she spoke. "Human servants of the Deamhan."

"Human servants? You didn't mention anything about servants, Veronica!"

"No, I didn't." She leaned her head back against the headrest and exhaled. Her arrival in Minneapolis was no longer a secret. First Dark Sepulcher, now this? It wasn't a freak coincidence. The Deamhan knew she was in their city.

However, next time she told herself, she wouldn't run. Next time she'd be ready, armed, with a stake.

CHAPTER NINE

Veronica awoke feeling unsettled and fatigued. She squinted against the bright morning sun and rubbed her head, hoping to erase her awakening thoughts of yesterday's insanity—and of Murphy. She glanced at her bedside clock. I hope he's still asleep, she thought. Lord knows, he'd need the rest, after their harrowing night. She felt the need to protect him, to remove him from danger. Not just for his sake, but for her own.

She stretched her arms over her head, arched her back, and then swung her legs off the bed. The high-pitched voice of the perky morning newswoman caused Veronica to scowl. She'd left the TV on last night, feeling the need for human company, even if it came from an LCD screen.

On unsteady feet, she wobbled toward the TV to silence the bubbly news anchor. No one should be so energetic at this hour, she thought. As she dodged the coffee table, an envelope propped against the remote control reflected the sunlight. A lump swelled in Veronica's throat, and the taste of sour bile filled her mouth. With everything that happened, she forgot about the envelope Alexis had given her. Her hands trembled when she picked up the envelope and turned it over. A red wax emblem sealed the flap. She slid a fingernail beneath the wax and popped the seal. The envelope contained one small square of parchment. She stared at the handwritten words in disbelief:

"11 pm, Saturday. Dark Sepulcher
– Lambert"

Veronica swallowed hard.
Today is Saturday.
Her hand flew to her neck, her fingers fluttering. Finally, she would come face to face with a person—if he was a person—who could help her. And at his request. She felt her heartbeat accelerate.
Hmmm.
Wait.
It seemed too easy.

66

Why would Alexis, a vampire who drained the fluid from her stomach, give her the opportunity? The fact that Alexis didn't like her kind played fresh in Veronica's mind. But then, it probably was Alexis who saved her from the Deamhan twins in the bathroom and again on the street. Now, she'd been invited to go back. Tonight. On the busiest night of the week.

She grabbed her cell phone from the kitchen counter, anxious to speak with Sean.

He answered on the first ring. "Sean, speaking."

His voice thrilled her. "Sean!" She heard the phone fumble.

"Veronica?" He'd lowered his voice to a whisper. "How're you doing?"

"I'm fine. Why are you whispering?"

"You called me on my cell at the office."

"Oh . . . Are you in a meeting? Am I interrupting something?"

"Don't worry about it." The tension in his voice relaxed. "You sound tired. Are you alright?"

"I'm fine." *Two close calls with the Deamhan, my search for information is stalling, and now I've involved Murphy. Yeah, I'm dandy, all right.*

"Are you sure?" He sensed her shaky voice. He knew her better than she knew herself at times. He was always able to read her just by the twitching in her voice.

She yawned and scrunched her nostrils to the smell of morning breath entering her nose. "I guess so. I went to the burnt home yesterday."

"Did you find anything?" Excitement colored Sean's voice.

"We didn't find anything that could help me."

"We? Who did you go with?"

Veronica felt Sean's instant cooling through the phone.

"Well," she said, fidgeting with her nails. Her eyes locked on the broken red seal of the envelope lying on the coffee table. "Oh, no one. It's not really important."

"What do you mean, 'It's not really important?'"

"Really, it's not."

"Veronica, what happened." It wasn't a question.

Veronica let out a deep breath. She quickly regrouped, told him the details, careful to not place Murphy anywhere in her recap.

"I took a taxi," she said, crossing her fingers behind her back. In no way would she tell him about Murphy, at this point. As she continued her story, the lies compounded; the taxi driver waited while she searched the burned ruins, the blue van never appeared, and the men in black masks never existed.

"So you went with the taxi driver?"

She held her breath. Had he heard anything she'd said after that?

"Yeah." She mouthed a curse and covered her mouth. She hated lying to Sean, but she didn't want to listen to his sermon just now. Besides, he really didn't want to know the truth—not this truth—even if she was in the wrong.

67

Finally, he broke the silence. "So what happened when you reached Dark Sepulcher?"

She told him about the waitress and the bathroom incident, but lied again when she said she'd been alone when attacked outside of the club. She finished her deluded recap with the note from Alexis. She also decided to keep her protection status a secret, for now.

"Don't go back there," Sean said immediately.

Veronica expected his response, as her encounters always exploited his overprotectiveness.

"You can't go back there, Veronica. You almost got yourself killed."

"But I didn't."

"Alexis could've killed you."

"But she didn't. She actually helped me."

"No vampire or Deamhan ever helps a human. It doesn't happen, especially now. I warned you about this before you left San Diego."

"Don't you think I know that, Sean? But what was I supposed to do? Refuse her help? I could've died."

"Look, they can't be trusted," Sean argued. "Not now. Not since they don't follow their Dictum and their rules anymore." He took a deep breath, and she knew he waited for her compliance.

"That's only a Brotherhood theory," Veronica contested.

"No, it isn't. It's reality. If you don't believe me, ask Rick's parents."

"Rick?"

"Rick Sorfield."

"What does he have to do with it?"

Sean sighed. "He was buried the other day."

"Buried? Sean, what happened?"

"He was killed by a Deamhan."

"What? Rick?" What little Veronica knew about Rick came from Sean. They'd only had the most distant of acquaintances; she'd recognize him if they passed in the hallways of The Brotherhood's office in San Diego, or they'd wave at company picnics. She wasn't close to him like Sean was, but she knew him from their brief encounters. She didn't know him like Sean knew him. Not even close.

"Look, Veronica, it's dangerous out there. I'm not kidding. The Deamhan have basically given up on their own rules. They kill everyone and anyone, including their own kind."

"But Sean, I only went to Dark Sepulcher because you told me it was vital to my search."

"I know, but . . ." Sean's voice trailed off.

"I'm sorry, but I can't back away now. I'm so close I can taste it."

"Just be careful, please. You know I'm behind you, Veronica. I'm always behind you."

An uncomfortable silence filled the phone lines. Veronica heard Sean's frustrated huffing and sighing.

He once told her about the Deamhan's Dictum and how they followed it and respected its rules religiously. The Brotherhood called it "The Deamhan Ten Commandments" and like the Ten Commandments from the Christian faith, it laid rules issued by the Ancient Deamhans centuries ago, during a time in which they were nearly driven to extinction. It favored secrecy; protection of sanctuaries; no killing or betraying your own kind; outlawed siring a Deamhan at a young age and feed only when necessary.

Now they acted as if these rules never existed.

Sean broke the stillness. "Your father spoke with me at Rick's funeral," he said. "He warned me about helping you, saying that my actions could cost me my position here."

"He did, did he?" Veronica felt heat creep into her face.

"Yeah, well, the air is starting to get thick around here, anyway." He chuckled. "I wasn't worried. I just took it all in with 'yes sir' and 'no sir.' "

"He hasn't changed."

"Oh he has, believe me," Sean replied. "I was thinking, Veronica, that maybe I should come out to Minneapolis to help you."

"What!?" Veronica replied in a high pitched voice. "Why would you? I thought you wanted to avoid any type of field research."

"Yeah, I do but I just think that maybe I can help you more by being there."

Veronica paused. "You can't just leave The Brotherhood like that, Sean. They won't let you go."

"I know," he replied. "Frankly, I don't care."

Veronica propped her fist on her hip. She knew she couldn't stop Sean if she wanted to. She considered him her carbon copy minus the fact he was male. Even so not once had he encountered a Deamhan. He'd never done field research because his parents were avidly against it. He was still a noob in progress. Still, something hounded her about his suggestion. It didn't feel right.

She chewed her lip. Why was he so curious to come see her? "Sean, The Brotherhood is the only thing you know," she said sternly. "And besides, I need you there. Who else can I trust besides you, to get me information when I need it?"

"I just don't want anything to happen to you. Just thinking about everything you've been through since you got there made me realize that you're not safe."

"You forget how well I know you. Being afraid for me can't be the only reason you want to come here?"

"What other reason should there be? If you go back to the club, I'm flying there. I mean it."

"Look, I don't need a bodyguard," she snapped. "If that's what you're suggesting, you can forget it."

"I never said that."

"I don't think you could help me if you were here." She laughed to ease the tension between them. "I simply can't see you fighting a Deamhan."

He chuckled. "Yeah, I can't, either. I could see myself running from a Deamhan, though."

"I can see that too."

"I never mastered the art of kick ass like you," he joked back. "Remember when you beat up that jock in history class?"

She grinned, remembering. "He deserved it."

Besides arguing with her father, she recalled her teenage years filled with arguments and fights at The Brotherhood. She wasn't a fighter. In fact, she loathed confrontation to the point that she rarely voiced her opinion if a student made fun of her. She held her anger, and eventually it gathered inside her, releasing itself on a boy a little older than her, who tried to steal her lunch. It was her first fight, and she barely remembered punching him. Afterwards gossip circled around her high school. Suddenly she was the girl that others were afraid to mess with.

"You laid him out flat, Veronica." Sean laughed. "Two hits. You hit him, and he hit the ground."

"Yeah? Well, he had it coming. Was his name John or Don?"

"I don't remember."

She giggled, then grew serious. "This isn't school anymore though, and the Deamhan are much stronger than a pimpled-faced jock."

"Knowing that, do you still intend to go back to Dark Sepulcher?"

"You'd go back if you were in my shoes?"

"Probably."

Veronica could hear Sean holding his breath. "Oh, you know you would, Sean."

"I would." Sean's words were slow, uncertain.

"Why are you so adamant that I stay away from there?" Veronica asked. "Besides the obvious, I mean."

"I know you're curious, but just—just be careful, okay? I worry about you being alone there."

"This time I'm invited back, Sean," she said. "This may be the break I've been looking for." Veronica scratched her forehead. It occurred to her that their conversation had swerved off track, veering dangerously close to the fact that Murphy accompanied her. She changed the subject. "What about that information I wanted you to get for me?"

"Still in progress," he answered. "Truthfully, I'll be surprised if I find a piece of scratch paper in their archives that hasn't been lined out in permanent black ink."

A quick knock at her front door interrupted their conversation. She turned to look, seeing dark movement through the tiny space underneath the door. The shadow moved right then left.

"What's that?" Sean asked.

"Someone's at my door." Veronica walked toward the door. "Hey, can you look up something for me?"

"Yeah. What?"

"A name."

"What's the name?"

"Lambert. It's the name on my invite." Veronica looked through the peephole. "And I don't know if he's a Deamhan. He might be the vampire who owns Dark Sepulcher." She saw Murphy through the peephole, staring at the floor, patiently waiting.

"Okay." Sean sounded unsure.

"And one more thing. . ." Veronica smoothed back her hair and moistened her lips.

"Sure."

"I remember you mentioned something about sanctuaries being burned and that The Brotherhood speculated they were Deamhan sanctuaries. Do you think you can find the locations of other sanctuaries in Minneapolis?"

"I can check."

"Thanks, Sean. For everything." She put her hand on the door's chain guard, rattling it so that Murphy wouldn't leave.

"Yeah," he said. He sounded nervous. "No problem. Almost all of the files here are secured so it might take a while. The new archive location your father commissioned to be built years ago is heavily guarded."

"They're no longer accessible?" Veronica's hand halted on the doorknob.

"I can still get them," Sean said, with an egotistical edge to his voice. "It just means that now I might have to do some late night rummaging."

"Thanks. I owe you tons."

"You're the one that's in an off-limits zone, sweetie," he replied. "You need to be careful." Murphy quickly knocked on the door again, grabbing Sean's attention. "You got company?" Sean asked again.

"Just my next door neighbor."

"Hmm, you want some information on him, too?" he joked.

"Shut up," Veronica joked back. "And call me back this afternoon."

"What about tomorrow night?"

"No, this afternoon."

Murphy knocked again. "Veronica, are you okay?"

She heard his muffled voice through the door.

Sean chuckled. "You'd better answer, Veronica."

"I'll talk with you later." Veronica snapped her cell phone shut and opened the door.

Murphy immediately looked up at her.

"Hey, I'm sorry for disturbing you." He smiled.

Disturbing me? His sudden appearance thrilled her but she viewed her uncombed hair and morning breath being far from looking her best.

"Oh, no, I just woke up." She covered her mouth. "I haven't had time to brush my teeth. What's up?"

"Oh." His eyes jumped from her face to the floor. "Sorry. Want me to come back?"

"What's wrong?" she asked, concerned.

"Oh, nothing." He looked into her eyes and smiled as a hint of red crept into his cheeks. "I just came to check in on you, see if you're okay."

"I'm fine." Veronica felt a flutter in her stomach. "How did you sleep last night?"

"Good"—he nodded, as if trying to convince himself—"better than I thought I would." He nervously scratched the back of his head. "Yesterday was intense, huh?" He cocked a half-smile. "It's weird. I know I'm going to be looking over my shoulder if I leave my apartment at night."

"Everyone should."

"Only if they knew. Well after yesterday, I was curious, and I looked on the Internet for the Deamhan."

"The Internet?" Veronica felt her eyes bulge.

"Yeah," Murphy said, nodding. "Did you know that Deamhan means demon of the air in Irish tradition. In English it means evil and of course demon."

"No, I didn't know that." Veronica slowly smiled and her brow scrunched. She didn't know where he was going with the conversation.

"I also looked up Lugat. Did you know that a Lugat was a creature that people considered harmless? They only feed on victims for a short period of time. Yeah . . . well these Lugats in Minneapolis seem far from harmless."

"Yeah, I know." Veronica leaned against the doorway.

"Why would they call them Lugat?" he continued. "Those Deamhan don't resemble a Lugat."

"Why call them Deamhan?" Veronica offered. "I don't know, Murphy. Hey, ummm, I have some stuff to do and—I don't mean to cut you off."

He nodded, staring at the floor in thought.

Veronica guessed his curiosity was natural, especially after last night, but she didn't want his interest and research on the Deamhan to go any further. He had no idea of the danger he could face.

He stole a sheepish glance at her and smiled. "Yeah, I have some things to do myself. I just wanted to see if you were okay."

"I'm fine. Thanks."

"Okay, well, I guess I'll see you later." He turned away, then turned back to face her. "Do you have any plans for tomorrow night?"

"Plans?"

He reached into his pocket and pulled out two tickets. "I have these two tickets to a comedy show in downtown Minneapolis. My friend chickened out at the last minute. Do you want to go?"

He handed the tickets to Veronica and she glanced over them. Two front row seats, sixty-nine bucks each. She felt it again, this falling feeling. It felt like rocks tickling her insides. Her face flushed. *A date?*

"Too much caffeine on an empty stomach," she said, feeling a foolish grin spread across her face.

He's so cute, so sweet, so—stop it.

She didn't want the romance. She didn't need it. Not now, maybe not ever. Yet, she felt drawn to him.

"Sure," she said, more brightly than she'd intended.

So much for doubtful thoughts.

You sound like an over-eager schoolgirl.

His face brightened and, for a brief moment, it glowed. "Great."

"Sounds like fun. Besides, I could use a few laughs."

Murphy nodded. "After maybe we can hit a bar or something. Unless you don't drink."

"I drink sometimes."

His expression turned serious. "I don't drink as much as my friends."

Veronica shrugged. "Well, I've really gotta go. I'll see you tomorrow then?"

"Okay, yeah. See ya." He flipped his hand in a brief, childish wave and turned toward his apartment. He opened the door, glanced back with a silly grin, then stepped inside and closed the door.

"I'm not the only one who's as giddy as a schoolchild," Veronica whispered, then shut her own door and collapsed against it in a fit of giggles.

CHAPTER TEN

It was shortly after sunset when Veronica realized Sean wasn't going to call.

She hailed a taxi to Dark Sepulcher. The warm weather seemed to draw the inhabitants from their homes and out to the clubs and bars to enjoy the Minneapolis social night life. Before leaving her apartment, the weatherman predicted a slight chance of rain after midnight.

Veronica didn't let the meteorologist on the six o'clock news deter her invite. The short cab ride felt like hours to her, and she stared at the tiny dots of water collecting on the windows. In her head, she reviewed the different scenarios of what she was going to expect. Maybe it was a trap. Maybe Lambert personally wanted to kill her. Maybe the whole meeting was conjured up by Alexis and Remy to get her where they wanted her. She thought of what Sean said. Maybe going back wasn't her best option.

However, this opportunity gave her the chance to question her mother's disappearance, and she accepted the risks. Veronica took a deep breath and exhaled gently. If things didn't go as planned, she had a backup. She patted a small wooden stake concealed in the inside pocket of her brown jacket. She wasn't going into Dark Sepulcher without it.

She arrived at a line of club-goers waiting along the wall to get inside. She walked past them all, grabbing the attention of some and receiving a gallant stare from others. She approached the front door and showed the bouncers her invitation.

"Right this way." The bouncer handed the invitation back to her. She followed him through the front door, past the black curtain, and into Dark Sepulcher. They cut through crowds of drunken people dancing to the thumping music. The bouncer forcefully pushed people out of the way to create a clear path. They made their way near the coat check in the back corner, and he stopped in front of a black door that slowly swung open. Alexis stood in the doorway, her arms planted firmly on her hips and with her lips extended in a wide grin.

"She's expected," the bouncer said to her. He walked away, and Alexis continued to stare at him until he disappeared in the crowd.

"Feeling better?" Her eyes scanned Veronica from head to toe. She flicked her long, black ponytail to her back. Her short, black mini-skirt and a small T-shirt showed off her curvaceous figure. Small scars covered her upper chest and her arms. "We haven't been formally introduced." She held out her hand.

"No, we haven't," Veronica replied. From Alexis' clothing, she accepted Alexis had a taste for less fanciful clothing. She loved wigs, short skirts, and shirts that revealed her flat and toned mid-section. Maybe she preferred to look like a whore.

Alexis paused, her handshake completely ignored. "I'm sorry about that." Alexis shifted her arm to brush Veronica's bangs from her forehead.

Veronica stepped back.

"You smell sweet." Alexis sniffed around Veronica's face. Her eyes fluttered in response.

Veronica watched Alexis catch herself by stepping back.

"Sorry. The urge to sink my teeth into your flesh is a little too strong to handle."

Discomposed, Veronica covered her neck. "I guess I'm nothing but just a meal with legs to you."

"Somewhat," Alexis answered. "You're little miss untouchable, for now."

Veronica adjusted her jacket and in a quick second, Alexis sighted a circular tip of a wooden object.

"What's this?" Her movement was quick and she reached for Veronica's jacket, pulling out the wooden stake. "Wouldn't want you to hurt yourself." Alexis analyzed the sharp piece of wood before tossing it aside.

Veronica kept note that her movements were quick, just like the Deamhan.

"Well." Alexis rubbed the corners of her mouth in an unhurried motion. "I wouldn't mind seeing a little blood here and there." Her eyes drifted to the darken balcony above. "He might, though."

She turned and began walking, disappearing into the dark hallway.

Veronica wasn't eager to follow her. She felt Alexis' distaste for her, and it thickened the air around her. But she couldn't ignore the moment and her need to take it.

For Mom, Veronica thought as she stepped into the shadowed hallway.

"This way, researcher." Alexis turned and motioned for Veronica to follow.

Veronica held her arms to the side, using the walls as her guide. The dark foyer gave off an odor of iron, possible dried blood. The smooth walls rubbed against her fingertips. The little information she obtained from The Brotherhood about vampires didn't mention anything about what to expect when a researcher finds themselves in the presence of a vampire. She knew that Deamhan relished in torture chambers and blood baths. Maybe vampires did too.

Her eyes slowed to focus, and she was able to distinguish the outline of Alexis' body in front of her.

Ahead, a loose hanging bulb from the low ceiling flickered. The path split into two flights of stairs; one headed up to a red lit hallway, and the other down into obscurity.

"This way." Alexis ascended the stairs. "Our private rooms are down those stairs."

"Private rooms or torture chambers?" Veronica asked as she followed.

Alexis turned and snickered inauspiciously. "Private rooms."

Veronica reached the top step. A red incandescent light now brightened the hallway. A long red carpet covered the floor. Along the walls, painted pictures of landscapes and people hung in perfect symmetry. Veronica looked at small, circular red sofas positioned in the middle of the hallway. The faint thumping of music vibrated the walls. Again, Alexis motioned Veronica to follow her. The area had an elegant vibe compared to the chaos happening below. Apparently, Lambert was a sophisticated vamp.

"Where are we going?" Now feeling undaunted, Veronica questioned their route.

"Here." Alexis approached a thick brown door decorated in carved circular etchings resembling ancient calligraphy. She knocked then turned the knob slowly. She pushed the door open and stood aside, allowing Veronica to enter.

The flames of white candles stationed on wooden ledges throughout the room gave the space a disenchanted glow. The air smelled of Indian incense. An immense glass window towered over the dance floor with a thick red curtain draped over its edges. A glass bowl filled with grapes sat on a glass table arranged between two black leather couches covered in red and blue velvet pillows. A black curtain blocked the far wall of the room. Veronica awed at the room's splendor. It was absolutely beautiful and not what she expected of a vampire.

It was far from stereotypical. She expected to see filth and remains of dead or dying victims scattered throughout. She'd prepared herself for the smell of blood and decomposing flesh covered in pure orifices of human decadence. There was none of that. Unlike a Deamhan, Lambert valued luxury over secrecy. Veronica's curiosity surrounding him grew.

"Would you like a drink?" Alexis walked over to the bar near the black curtain.

"No."

She grabbed a glass from the counter and pulled back on the tassel. The curtain drifted to the left, revealing an unsettling image.

Veronica gasped, covering her mouth. Two wooden beams in the form of a cross held a woman who looked to be near death. Metal bracelets covered both her wrists and ankles, keeping her stationed on the cross with only a small, wooden platform for her bound feet. Totally naked, bite marks, welts, and other bruises peppered her skin. Bloodied thread sewn her lips shut. Her eyes remained closed with her head tilted to the side.

Veronica watched Alexis press a white button located on the wall. The woman's body jerked. Her mouth opened slightly, and she let out a muted scream. The metal bracelets constricted and blood seeped from a tiny hole in them, dripping to another opening located on the bottom platform, beneath the woman's feet. She pressed the button again and the woman wailed. The flow of blood continued, and Alexis placed her cup beneath the window near the floor, under a small spout where it emptied. She stopped pressing the button and gently sipped the blood from her cup.

"Ah." She snickered at Veronica's horrified response. Underneath the bruises and dried blood, the woman looked oddly familiar to Veronica. She'd seen her before in Dark Sepulcher, but she couldn't place where. Her ponytails were disheveled. It took only seconds to finally realize where she'd seen the woman before: in the bathroom with Alexis on her first night in Dark Sepulcher.

The curtain whisked back into place, hiding the malicious view. Suddenly the environment didn't seem as luxurious as Veronica believed it to be. It masked the dark side of Dark Sepulcher and it gave a fooled sense of contentment to its victims before they were devoured. Just like the victim behind the curtain, drained whenever Alexis wished it. This was the Dark Sepulcher Sean warned her about.

Alexis walked past her and toward the door.

"Is this what I came here for?" Veronica's question did little in aggravating Alexis.

"Who? Her?" There was no remorse in Alexis' voice. Still grasping the cup in her hand, Alexis licked her lips. "She's just another bipedal on the food chain. Like you." She closed the door behind her.

Veronica walked to the couch, slowing sliding into the cushioned seats. She buried her head in her hands to rid the image of the woman from her mind. She thought of the pain of sharp incisions on her wrists and ankles every time that button was pressed, her wounds kept open and being kept alive for as long as Alexis wished.

Being a witness to another human's suffering tampered with Veronica's reason in accepting her invite. Feeling powerless to stop the woman's pain and suffering—was this going to be the norm? Veronica mentally prepared herself for this. But why did the woman's plight haunt her?

"Focus, Veronica," she whispered to herself.

Her hands tottered slightly and she grabbed a grape from the glass bowl. The urge to run out of the room to the nearest police station flew from her thoughts. They wouldn't believe her anyway.

She popped the grape in her mouth and took another from the bowl. She placed her hands underneath her legs to control her shaking. Her eyes scanned the room's decorations: a huge flat screen television, cordless phones, a DVD player, computers, printers, a microwave, massive stereo equipment—all overshadowed by artifacts littering the walls.

An ancient double battle mace weapon, complete with two mace heads covered in long spikes laid next to a desktop computer. Near the flat screen television she saw a chain mail armor suspended above a long table covered in a red silk table cover. A warrior's helmet sat in the middle, surrounded by small knives and miniature candle holders.

Hanging above the computer, Veronica saw an old oil painting of a man in chain mail armor and a helmet. His deep, dark brown eyes beamed at her. His brown hair fell gracefully over his shoulders. He sat in a chair decorated in jewels and small carved statues of dragons.

She stood up from the couch and slowly walked over to the glass window. Below, the club seemed alive with movement. The thick and insulated glass kept out the music, yet it thumped to every sound of bass.

"Veronica Austin." A voice called out behind her. She turned around facing the man behind the voice. He shifted his fingers through his thick brown hair. He wore a black turtleneck shirt with black pants. The candlelight tricked Veronica's eyes, and she observed his irises changing from brown to hazel. His prominent jaw line and his pointed nose completed his smooth and seemingly ageless face. Her eyes shifted to the portrait, then back to him. It was him but from a different time period. The picture didn't do his guise any justice.

"It's a one way mirror," the male announced. "Don't worry. No one can see you up here."

Veronica looked back at the mirror. "I don't know if that's a good thing or a bad thing."

"Depends," the male replied. "I'm Lambert." He bowed his head slightly. In his hand, he held a chalice similar to Alexis'. "That picture is of my other life. Not the best portrait of me, but I prize it nonetheless." He walked over to the couch. "Are the grapes good?"

"They're good. Thanks."

"Well, I thought about getting more for my human guests." He studied Veronica's stiff and rigid posture. He lowered himself on the couch.

"I still remember what good grapes tasted like." Lambert sniffed the bowl. "Not that it'd do me any good anyway, right?"

Veronica pulled out the invitation from her pocket. "Is this a trick?" She tossed it to him.

"No." He caught the note and placed it in his pocket. "I sent it to you for a reason."

"I'm here." She walked over to the couch.

His face crinkled, and a wide smile appeared. "That you are."

"So, you're a vampire."

"Yes." Lambert crossed his legs. "I thought you were aware of this."

"Alexis' actions kinda reminded me."

"Ahh, Alexis." Lambert tilted his head to the ceiling. "My little darling. My soul mate. You know, she was my minion before I turned her. You do know what a minion is?"

She nodded, aware of the generic term. "Minions are human servants who are owned by a Deamhan. But you're not a Deamhan, you're a vampire."

"True, but I couldn't pass up the need for a minion of my own."

What The Brotherhood knew of minions Sean passed onto Veronica. She knew them to be extremely dangerous but very useful to the Deamhan. Like servants, they did whatever their Deamhan owners wanted them to do. They ran errands, watched other minions, and kept tabs on researchers in the city. Some went as far as killing for their owners with the promise of being sired after years of loyal service. Their numbers increased in recent years due to the overwhelmingly popularization of the vampire in American culture. They jumped at the chance at becoming immortal, even if it meant killing other humans.

"The Dictum prohibited human servants unless it was necessary for the survival of the Deamhan." Veronica recanted one of the rules in The Edict.

"I'm a vampire. I don't care for their Dictum." Lambert waved at her reply. "And apparently, they don't either. Please sit."

Veronica hesitantly lowered herself on the couch across from him.

"I love the term 'minion.' I wouldn't call her that to her face; she'd stake me." He smiled devilishly. "But enough about my darling; what about you, researcher?"

"I'm not a researcher. I've attempted to make that clear."

"Not everyone thinks so. You successfully hid your thoughts from Remy. No human affiliated with The Brotherhood is able to do that. And you came here armed with a stake."

"It was for my own protection," Veronica answered.

"What if you miss the heart of a Deamhan? Do you trust your aim researcher?"

"You know I don't have to aim for their heart to incapacitate them," Veronica replied. "But as for a vampire . . ."

He stared at her and tilted his head slightly. "Something you learned from that obstructive organization you claim you aren't a part of?" He pushed the bowl of grapes toward her. "Did they teach you how to lie as well?"

"I'm not lying," Veronica replied in a raised voice. He pushed her into a position that she didn't want to be in. Instead of interviewing him, he was interrogating her.

"Yet you know things that most humans don't know." He stood to his feet and walked over to the black curtain.

Before he pulled the tassel back, Veronica said in a shaky voice, "P-please. . ."

He smiled innocently. "Please?"

"Do you have to do that now?"

"Do what?"

"Eat."

He dropped the tassel. "No, I guess not." He paced back to the couch. "I'm sorry about Alexis. Dealing with the Deamhan daily is making her cranky." He gently sat on the couch. "As you know, they're a rough bunch."

"Like vampires."

"Yes, like vampires." Lambert huffed and smiled. "I own Dark Sepulcher. I cater to the Deamhan and vampires alike. It makes my venue more—how can I say—appreciated? I don't discriminate. Everyone's money is green to me, even yours."

Veronica gazed into his empty and soulless eyes. "But I didn't come here for that."

"So why did you come here in the first place?"

Veronica opened her mouth, but she found herself speechless. This is it, she thought. Now or never. She didn't lose sight of him and she watched him rub his hands together, feeling his rugged stare while he waited for her explanation.

"Curious about our kind?" he suggested.

"No, not even close."

"You were probing my venue, Veronica," he affirmed.

"I wasn't." She paused. Yes, I was, she thought briefly, before relaxing her thoughts then suddenly realized there was no need to hide them. Vampires were incapable of reading minds, but they were good at deciphering body language.

She continued. "This is the only place in Minneapolis that vampires and Deamhan socialize."

"And the only place in Minneapolis that has two for ones for only a dollar and fifty cents." His gaze didn't quiver. "Oh c'mon, researcher, you have to do better than that."

"Like I've said before, I'm not a researcher."

"Then why are you here?" His voice rose, and he leaned forward. "And who sent you here?" His voice shook her and she slightly jumped back.

She gathered her wits. "I have a couple of questions to ask you, Lambert."

"I ask the questions, researcher."

"Would you stop calling me that? I'm not a researcher." Her voice screeched. No way would she tell him about Sean and her father. They were irrelevant. But she was curious on how much he really knew about her.

He was losing his patience. His eyes narrowed and she caught a glimpse of his fangs that had now dropped.

Veronica took a deep breath. "I'm looking for someone important to me."

"Well." He leaned back. "That's all you had to say."

"I'm looking for my mother. Her name is Caroline Austin."

"Are you?" He placed his arms on the back of the couch.

"My mother and my father worked for The Brotherhood, and the Minnesota Chapter that disbanded right after she disappeared." She waited for his response, but he remained quiet. "I'm just trying to find out what happened to her."

"Your parents were researchers?"

Veronica nodded.

"And you're not." He slowed his speech, emphasizing each word that came from his mouth.

"I was raised in The Brotherhood because of my parents," she said slowly. "But I didn't follow in their footsteps. I'm here on my own."

He smiled. "Ah, now we're getting somewhere, my curious sleuth." He clapped his hands, and Veronica jumped at his odd behavior. "You're here to find your researcher mother."

Veronica sighed in relief. She could move on from defending herself to learning about her mother's disappearance, or so she thought.

"You say you're not from The Brotherhood, you're not a researcher, and we all know you're not a minion. This just makes you a nosy human who knows too much."

"Look." Veronica slammed her hands on the glass table. She immediately regretted her outburst, and she lifted her hands and stepped back. For the first time, Veronica wished vampires could read her thoughts. "Do you know any-thing about my mother?"

"Sassy." He grinned. "I like it. Have another grape, my dear." He pushed the bowl of grapes to her.

Her body grew stiff, and her hands were tightly curled into fists. "Do you know her?"

His eyes scanned her, again making her feel uncomfortable. "Your heartbeat is fast. I can smell your sweat. Are you angry?"

"What?" Dumbfounded, Veronica shook her head.

"Alexis was right. You smell so sweet, like cotton candy." He smiled and this time his fangs showed. "Please, eat."

"I'm not hungry," she replied. "Please, do you know anything?"

He exhaled. "As you might already know, The Brotherhood hasn't been in Minneapolis for decades, so I doubt your mother is lurking around. If she was, it would've made vampire headlines a while ago."

There was something unique about him, which Veronica couldn't figure out. His face held a smirk only noticeable when she looked into his eyes. His witty and quick comments. He was a thinker, and from the prosperity of Dark Sepul-cher, she surmised that he was also a good businessman. She couldn't believe he didn't know anything about her mother. The Deamhan and vampires knew all researchers in their cities. She suppressed her doubts and began to explain.

"I'm not here to interrupt your lifestyle. I don't like coming to Dark Sepul-cher as much as your customers don't like seeing me here. I know this place was here when The Brotherhood was here. I also know that you're the type of person who knows everything that occurs in Minneapolis."

"Never heard of her." He smirked. "But I do remember when the research-ers left." He placed his right elbow on the edge of the couch, in a comfortable position to think. "You come here in need of answers . . . why don't you ask The Brotherhood?"

His attack made Veronica a little hesitant to reply.

"They didn't tell you, or they couldn't tell you?" He moved his head to the left and rubbed his chin.

Veronica lowered her eyes to the floor. "They wouldn't tell me."

"Interesting." Lambert nodded. "And your father?"

"We aren't on speaking terms."

"Your father is still a member?"

"This is not about my father. This is about my mother."

"Answer the damn question!" Lambert jumped to his feet in breakneck speed. He loomed over her, his eyes dilated and his mouth opened. Veronica couldn't help notice that his sharp canines extended further than even the Ramanga twins.

She gripped the side of the couch, taken back. The couch's springs dug into her rear. "Yes, yes, he's still a member."

He stepped back and closed his mouth. His fangs retreated and he straightened his shirt. "Excuse me. Sometimes I do get carried away. But a daughter at odds with her father. How cliché." He drummed his fingers together. "And what would your father think of his daughter associating with vampires?"

"I think I made a mistake coming here." Veronica disregarded his question. "It's obvious you don't know anything about my mother." She stood up from the couch and turned to walk to the door when Lambert opened his mouth to speak.

"Your father is the president of the Midwest Division." His words stopped Veronica in her tracks. She turned and watched him stand. She expected him to lash out, to bite her and suck every ounce of blood from her body just in time for Alexis to appear at the door and finish her off. Instead he stood, watching her. This revealed piece of information turned his smirk into a defined smile, and Veronica felt a need to defend herself.

"I know how it sounds."

He raised his hand to interrupt. "I do admire your courage to waltz into my venue and start digging for info, but I suggest you question your father about such matters."

"I can't."

"I suggest you find a way."

"I wouldn't be here if there was another way."

"There is always another way." Lambert approached her. "You don't know the resources your father has at his disposal." He threw his head back in an earsplitting laughter, which caught her off guard. "My dear, you really don't know much, do you."

Veronica folded her arms in displeasure. "Apparently I don't," she said in a monotone voice, "so why don't you tell me?"

He reached out his hand to touch her cheek and she moved back.

"Humans are so cocky, so authoritative these days." He lowered his hand. "And so clueless." His eyes attenuated themselves on her. "You'd make a great vampire. I can see you committing many talented atrocities."

"I don't have a desire to become a vampire."

"A moment alone with me and I'll have you begging me to be your maker."

"No thank you." Veronica lifted her head high. She held her ground. She didn't want Lambert to sense any fear from her. Vampires craved it. So did the Deamhan.

"Are you just gonna keep on trying to scare me?" she asked. "Or are you going to tell me what you know?"

Lambert's lips stretched to a wide grin. "Sure." He sighed, releasing the last of his laughter. "Have you heard of a Deamhan by the name of Lucius?"

The name didn't sound familiar to her.

"He was the oldest living Lugat in Minneapolis during the time your parents were in the city. He kept order and made sure that all Deamhan followed the Dictum. He disappeared around the time the Chapter left. Most Deamhan believe he was murdered by his consort, Kei." Lambert's eyes began to dance in excitement while he continued the story. "And many Deamhan believe The Brotherhood was involved. His consort is now the most hated and dangerous Lugat in the city."

Sean didn't mention anything about Lucius and Kei to Veronica and the documents he provided her didn't mention him at all. Her eyes lit up to the new information, but she didn't know what they meant in regards to her mother's disappearance.

"How do I know you're just not making this up?" Veronica questioned Lambert.

"You don't." He held out his hands in front of him as if he waited for her to embrace him. "But if I'm lying, strike me down."

"I'll keep that in mind. Is this Kei person still in Minneapolis?"

"That bastard has never left." Lambert rolled his eyes in disgust. "Can't blame him. Can you imagine your reputation if you killed your all-powerful sire? Lucius wasn't any Deamhan; he's one of the oldest on this continent. He was an Ancient. He was respected."

An Ancient? Veronica's thoughts tumbled around the phrase. Ancients didn't live in Minneapolis. Why would they?

She continued her questioning. "Why would they believe The Brotherhood had anything to do with it?"

Lambert gave her a look of suspicion. "Are you defending them?"

She quickly replied no. She couldn't defend an organization that didn't explain why they left the city without her mother, an organization that claimed to know nothing. Now she knew why things became unstable when they left. It didn't match the story her father told her and what Sean was telling her. They didn't leave because the Deamhan were out of control. They left because they had involved themselves in the Deamhan's personal affairs.

"Lucius was no ordinary Deamhan. He ruled the Lugat in the city with an iron fist. He kept other Deamhan in line. No Deamhan and vampire were strong enough to take him out." Lambert paused. "But a Deamhan with the backing of The Brotherhood . . ."

"So you're telling me that my father worked with Kei to kill Lucius?"

"Your father's organization placed that lunatic on a pedestal." He sneered. "Why? No one knows. Now Kei summons his Gatherings for the riff raff who slither from their dens. He kills any Deamhan, vampire, or human who stands in his way. He burns sanctuaries for his own pleasure. He's violent and uncontrollable." He paused. "Don't get me wrong, I like a little violence in my life, but they're creating unwanted attention and that's the last thing we vampires and Deamhan need from the humans."

Veronica found his descriptions of Kei antipathetic and full of distaste. He hated him more than he hated her being inside Dark Sepulcher. "What kind of benefit would The Brotherhood get for helping Kei?"

Lambert shrugged. "Again, that's a question you should ask your father. What I do know is that Lucius is gone and Kei rules in his place."

Veronica didn't know if Lucius or Kei had anything to do with her mother's disappearance, but it had to be of some importance if Lambert was telling her. What he told her didn't seem far from the truth and if what he said was true (and she trusted him as much as she trusted her father), it exposed a level of The Brotherhood her father purposely hid from her.

She whispered, "So where can I find Kei?"

"You don't want to find Kei," Lambert said. "Believe me, human. You don't."

Veronica felt a rush of unwanted adrenaline pump through her, increasing with anger toward her father. She wanted Lambert to tell her more.

"I'm not leaving Minneapolis until I know what happened to my mother and if I have to find Kei to get answers, then I have to look for him."

Lambert shook his head. "Stubborn, human." His eyes drifted from amusement to annoyance. "You wouldn't survive another week looking for Kei. Your protection status won't help you."

Protected. It was the second time she'd heard that word. She didn't know exactly what it meant.

She heard a loud grumble echo from his stomach.

He walked over to the table grabbing his cup, and he continued to the window. He glared at the crowd below. "Go and don't come back."

"What?"

"Go and don't come back," he repeated. "Your protection can only take you so far."

She approached him. "I keep hearing that I'm protected. What does that mean?"

"It means exactly what it means." Lambert patted his toned stomach and ignored her question. "Now, if you'll excuse me. I'm hungry."

She gulped loud enough for the noise to echo. She knew the vampires became extremely unpredictable when it came down to a good, easy meal. If he attacked her, she'd know how to deal with it, but there wasn't any sunlight around nor any sharp objects. She missed her stake.

Veronica watched him grab a bottle of bourbon from behind the desk. He poured himself a shot and he quickly downed it. Like Deamhan, vampires were capable of consuming liquids and digesting human food, opting for regurgitating it later. Alcoholic beverages proved necessary for the vamps who liked being in a drunken state, even if the affect was not as potent as it would be in humans.

"Relax," Lambert said in an impatient voice. "You're not dinner." He looked at the black curtain.

"Is it because I'm protected and that you can't hurt me?" she questioned again.

"You wouldn't be protected if you didn't belong to anyone." He slightly turned his head over his shoulder. "Someone, a Deamhan, has claimed you as their own."

"But I don't belong to anybody—"

He raised his hand to interrupt her. "Be careful where you tread, my dear." He slowly lowered his hand. "It would be wise to belong to somebody in this city, especially if you place yourself in their world. And even so, being protected doesn't mean much." He walked over to the curtain. "If Kei wanted to, he'd have his followers kill you." His voice was deafening to her ears. With every step he took, his voice grew louder and filled with anger. "He kills without remorse. He bathes in tubs of blood and flesh." He stopped for a moment, in thought. "That sounds pleasing: a bloody bubble bath." He quickly returned to his statement. "He'll kill you on sight or maybe make you his bitch." He stopped in his tracks; his eyes had widened, and he balled his fists, breathing deeply. "Now, what kind of morals would I have if I just told you where you can find him? It's like signing your death warrant." His voice seemed cold as ice.

"Morals? Vampires don't have morals."

He wrapped his hand around the tassel. "We like to believe we do." He pulled back and pushed the white button. Veronica looked toward the door, seeing Alexis standing in the doorway. She heard the victim whimper and moan. The horrid contraption went to work again, and the grips tightened. Blood flowed from the spout and into his cup.

He walked over to Veronica, holding the blood-filled cup. He closed his eyes and sniffed the liquid, reopening them while he drank it. Veronica heard the door open behind her and she turned to watch Alexis walk into the room and slowly approach Lambert. She placed her arms around his waist and licked his neck until he finished his meal. He gently rubbed the side of her head in euphoria. They were completely engulfed in their diminutive blood ritual.

Alexis turned her sight on Veronica. "Can we kill her now?"

Lambert wiped the blood from the corners of her mouth. "No, Alexis. We can't." He placed the empty cup on the counter. "I'm sure you know the way out,

Veronica."

Veronica didn't wait and hurried out of the room and down the hallway, repeatedly looking back.

She watched Lambert grip Alexis in a kiss of extreme passion. He embedded his fingernails into her back and slowly began to scratch, drawing blood. She moaned, letting her head drop back freely. He brought his nails up to his mouth, sucking the thick, rich blood from them. He locked eyes with Veronica as she glanced back from the hallway. He grasped Alexis again; biting into her neck with such force that her legs became flaccid and he became her only support to stand.

CHAPTER ELEVEN

Veronica rushed down the stairs. The music blasted from the speakers shaking her eardrums violently. She excused herself through the crowd, heading toward the exit. She felt a cold grasp on her wrist that twisted her around by force. Remy stood in front of her. He wore a black leather jacket with a black button T-shirt and dark blue jeans. He placed his other hand on her waist, pulling her closer to him. Veronica tried pushing him off her but she felt helpless in his grip.

"I've missed you." A devilish smile appeared on his face. She attempted to pull away again, but he increased the pressure on her wrist.

"Let go of me." Veronica tried to push him away.

"We didn't get to finish our conversation from the other night." His grasp only became stronger. The beats streaming from the speakers snuffed her screams for help. The patrons continued to dance around them. They swayed back and forth in a dance too slow for the music. He stood taller than her. She looked up, and his eyes stared back into her own. She felt her body beginning to melt within his grasp. The more she struggled, the more she belonged to him.

Her heartbeat increased and he stroked his hawkish fingers over her smooth skin. "You smell like a vamp."

Veronica cleared her head free from thoughts and waited for the burning sensation to start but it never came. Instead he placed his finger in front of her mouth to quieten her.

"Shhh," he said in a faint whisper that she heard underneath the music. Their dancing tempo increased while he dragged her along the dance floor.

"Let me go," she pleaded to him.

"Do you think I'm going to hurt you?" he asked her in a soft voice. "And I thought I made a great first impression on you."

She remained quiet.

"Would you care to join me at the bar? They have two for ones." His brown hair was still pulled back in a ponytail. The smell of his new black leather jacket and expensive cologne radiated from him.

"Care to join me?"

"What do you want?"

They continued to dance across to the opposite end of the floor. He placed his hand behind her head and gently pressed her face in his chest. She felt his hard and cold body through his shirt. Her head began to throb slightly, and his words dilated sensually in her brain.

I want you.

What she wanted was to run from him, to break free through the crowd and toward the exit.

"I just want to get to know you more," he replied. "You ran out unexpectedly."

"I don't like being threatened," Veronica said.

He pulled her along the dance floor, spinning her around. He placed his hands back on her hips, and they continued their dark jig. "Sorry if I made you feel uncomfortable. That wasn't my intention."

"Then what is your intention?" she questioned.

He moved her in closer. "Like I said, to get to know you." His body was lean, tight, and his muscles flexed when he moved his arms. "If I thought you were such a threat, you'd be dead already." Small, loosened strands of his hair dangled, slightly touching her forehead.

Veronica suddenly felt infatuated with him. *Concentrate, Veronica.* He looked into her eyes, and she tried to look away. She felt her eyes drift to them and she wanted to rub her hands over his chest and up to his face.

Everything she knew about Deamhans disappeared from her mind. She left herself open to him, voluntarily pressing her face into his chest. She closed her eyes and opened her ears, hoping that he would exhale just once. He appeared different from her; not human. He became all she knew and all she wanted. No fear, no Deamhan, no Dark Sepulcher, and no search.

Yes. There was a search.

She blinked her eyes, refocusing back on reality and distancing herself from Remy's orchestrated trance.

"You're not scaring me." Veronica's lower lip quivered.

He chuckled slightly. "I'm not the one you should be scared of." His grip began to wane. They stopped moving and she took a step back, free from his hypnotic restraint. He turned and walked away casually through the crowd. The rhythm of the music changed, and the dance floor started filling with people. She watched Remy sit on a bar stool and she glanced around, sensing her vulnerability while alone.

She followed him to the bar.

"I know how you Deamhan act." She stood behind him. "And I know I can never trust a Deamhan." Her mind reverted to the woman at the burnt home. *Maybe he was working with her?* Remy soon picked up on her thought.

"No." Remy turned around and ordered a drink from the bartender. "I don't have any minions." He turned back to her. "If you want, you can be my first."

Confused, she shook her head no.

The bartender returned, placing a glass in front of him.

"You're right, you can never trust a Deamhan, researcher. I don't even trust Deamhan."

Veronica sat on an empty stool next to him. He continued to look forward and sipped the dark liquid from his cup.

He was a Ramanga or maybe a Lamia. Either way, he can't be trusted.

"I'm not a Ramanga," he replied to her thoughts. "But I am a Lamia."

Lamia. They had no sharp teeth like the Ramanga, but fed from their victims by mouth. *As long as I don't kiss him.*

"Do you always do that?" he asked her.

"Do what?"

"Let me give you some advice, researcher," Remy said slowly, "if you plan to hide your thoughts, you shouldn't think. You should just 'do'." He sipped his drink and he looked forward, observing a female waitress from across the bar staring back at them. Remy briefly waved at her and she nodded.

"You see her?" He nodded to the waitress. "She'll be my first meal of the night." He placed his cup up to his lips and before taking another sip he spoke again. "And the other human behind her, near the back standing alone. She'll be my second."

Veronica remained silent, still trying to figure out what Remy had in store for her. She wanted to make a run for the exit, just like the first time, but she didn't want to show any fear.

"I've been hearing stories about a researcher in Minneapolis, searching for her researcher mother." He sipped from his cup again, drinking the last drops. "A researcher who's bold, stubborn and stupid. Your name fuels minion conversations." His eyes drifted to the right at a man wearing a black hooded jacket sitting at the very end of the bar. "The Deamhan sent out their minions to spy on you, to figure out what your true agenda is." He then looked to the left at another man sitting at the opposite end, talking to a woman. "They use their minions instead of just approaching you and asking you straight, like I'm doing."

"Where are they?"

"They're everywhere." He looked over his shoulder at a short man wearing a black jacket and faded filthy black pants. The horribly dressed man stood near the dance floor, his brown eyes locked onto her. Remy turned back to order another drink.

Veronica slid off the stool and stood next to him. She immediately wanted to leave Dark Sepulcher, but Remy grabbed her wrist.

"Do you always run when you feel cornered?" Remy asked.

"Only if I have to," Veronica replied in a shaky voice.

"We can smell a human's fear easily," he whispered. "Your scent is so strong that I can taste it." His warm breath roasted her skin and it awed her. "Kei has his eyes on you." Remy watched the bartender place another drink on the counter in front of him. "And you don't want Kei to have eyes on you." He sipped from his drink again. He wiped his mouth with a small napkin, and he stood up from his stool. "But you have nothing to fear. They're just minions." He waved them off.

She felt him searching her thoughts again, seeing through her fake impression of fearlessness. With her hidden layer now exposed—she had every right to feel threatened. If Kei was this powerful then the Deamhan in the city had to know their place. But no Deamhan was untouchable in Veronica's eyes, not even Lucius.

"But I can protect you," he whispered to her. "We can protect you. All you have to do is ask." Remy's eyes briskly turned to a female Deamhan watching Veronica and himself from behind the bar. Veronica looked in his direction. The dark haired female didn't turn away.

The staring war between Remy and the dark haired female lasted for a few seconds more before Veronica decided to jump in.

"Who is that?"

"A friend." He quickly looked at Veronica before turning his attention back to the female. He nodded and tilted his head to the side. Veronica watched quietly. Sometimes the Deamhan communicated by reading each other's thoughts. Maybe that's what they were doing.

Remy nodded again and turned his attention back to Veronica. "I know a human that can help you."

"And why should I believe you?" Veronica's eyes focused on him.

"You shouldn't," he answered. "But if you're feeling interested, he lives in a sanctuary out of town called Blind Bluff Manor."

A human living in a sanctuary? It was unheard of. She couldn't imagine why a human would want to live in a sanctuary with Deamhan unless they were a minion. She continued to look at him in a bewildered gaze.

"You've heard of Blind Bluff Manor?" he asked.

Again she didn't respond.

He sighed and slightly shook his head. "They don't teach them like they used to in The Brotherhood anymore." He repeated the name of the sanctuary in an attempt to make her understand. "His name is Nathan Tiernan, and he has a sanctuary called Blind Bluff Manor."

"I'm not some inexperienced human that'll fall for your lies," Veronica replied. "There has never been a human who's owned a sanctuary."

"They really *don't* teach you researchers like they used to." He chuckled. "Back in my day, researchers were more stealthy, smarter, and harder to kill. Now, anyone can be a researcher."

"I'm not a researcher," Veronica insisted.

"Of course not." He slid off the bar stool and walked past her.

"I don't trust your kind. All you Deamhan do is lie."

"True." He continued to walk through the crowd. Not wanting to be left alone, Veronica followed him. Remy stopped and turned back around. "But what

I told you about Nathan Tiernan is true. He can help you." He raised his hand slowly and gracefully swiped her cheek. "And you need all the help you can get." Veronica noticed the minion Remy pointed to earlier slowly raise himself up from his stool with a blank stare.

Remy tilted his head to sniff the air. "I love that smell." He turned his head to look over his shoulder. "The smell of fear."

The minion raced toward the exit with Remy continuing to walk in a calm pace after him. The other two minions were now gone from the seats. Veronica ran after Remy out the front entrance. He was quick, and she'd almost lost sight of him until she saw him down the street, turning the corner.

She called out after him, running as fast as her legs could carry her. She passed the patrons standing along the wall, still waiting to get into Dark Sepulcher. She turned the corner and stopped. She saw him standing over one of the minions in the club. The minion kneeled on the pavement with his arms lifted in the air in fear.

The minion clasped his hands together and tears began to stream down his face. His mumbled speech about his wife and two kids fell on deaf ears. He pleaded his case and upon seeing Veronica, he turned to her, crying that he wasn't there to harm her, only to watch. He explained that his master was stronger than Remy and if any harm came to him, his master would avenge him. Still Remy didn't budge. He placed both of his hands on the man's shoulders and remained quiet, only smiling while the man continued his defense.

"Don't kill him," Veronica pleaded.

"Shhh," he ordered. "I'm trying to concentrate."

She watched while his hands rubbed the side of the minion's face.

"Are you reading his thoughts?"

"They're blurred," he answered. "Blocked." He increased his grip and the minion began to gasp for air. "But I guess that's expected when you serve Kei."

"What are you doing?" Veronica stood next to him. "You're killing him!" Even if she wanted to, even if she was able to, she couldn't force Remy to stop. She had no power to stop him. Remy's face filled with the thrill of this hunt and his smirk added to his haunting stare. He fed off of it; his dark aphrodisiac.

And his nature.

"I can smell Kei's scent all over this one." Remy wrinkled his nose in disgust.

The man frantically shook his head no. "Please . . ."

"Remy, please don't," Veronica pleaded.

Remy quickly turned to face her and he snapped. "This minion belongs to Kei. If he could, he'd kill you without a thought. Now, why would you beg for his life?"

Veronica opened her mouth but found her voice muted. She slowly moved back from him. His eyes turned from brown to a murky black. The veins underneath his skin began to pulsate.

91

Remy placed his hands around the man's neck, lifting him to his feet. The man screamed, and Remy placed his mouth over his. Veronica watched him sucking and gurgling while the man began to shake in his grasp. There was a moment when Remy pulled back and a small trail of blood dripped from the victim's mouth. He then went back in sucking the essence; the life force from his victim. The minion's body went limp and his bloodshot eyes remained open, staring into the heavens.

Veronica covered her mouth to hold in her screams.

It ended quickly. Remy released his grip and the minion's body fell to the pavement.

Remy's feet staggered and he placed his hands on a parking meter nearby for support. "Woah." He licked his lips ecstatically. "Always a rush." He turned to Veronica.

She stepped back again, not knowing what to do. She had just watched a Deamhan feed on an innocent human being. She had to do something.

"He's far from innocent." Remy stood up straight. His skin now glowed and his body looked healthy; anew. "He's killed plenty of humans for Kei. He's burned sanctuaries; he's tricked Deamhan to their deaths. Yes, he's far from innocent. Don't cry for the minion, Veronica. He wouldn't cry for you."

She didn't know if Deamhan avenged their minions. She prayed that the dead male lying on the pavement was just one of many minions Kei had to spare. Now, there was no turning off her fear. She was scared for her life.

Remy straightened his leather jacket. "Kei may be the most powerful Deamhan in the city, but he's not the oldest." He placed his hands in the pocket of his jeans and he turned to walk back to the club. Before turning the corner he stopped and looked over his shoulder. "Nathan Tiernan. Blind Bluff Manor." He snickered. "Perhaps I'll see you there?"

CHAPTER TWELVE

Veronica jerked awake to the sound of continuous banging on the front door of her apartment. Sweat dripped from her forehead and her eyes adjusted to the sun's rays illuminating her living room. The pounding continued, and she lifted herself from the couch with a sharp pain scurrying down her back.

"Veronica, are you there?" a familiar voice uttered from other side of the door.

Veronica hurried over to the door, wiping the sleep from her eyes. She flattened her disheveled hair and unlatched the lock on the door. Sean stormed in carrying two briefcases.

"Sean?" Veronica closed the door behind him.

He set the two briefcases on the floor in a loud thud.

"Oh my God." Surprised to see him, she wrapped her arms around his waist, hugging him tightly. "Why didn't you call?"

"I did." Sean gently kissed the top of her head.

"How long were you out there?" Veronica felt the dryness in her mouth as she spoke. She buried her face into his chest.

"Just a couple of minutes." His medium sized frame towered over her. Veronica noticed his dark slacks and his short sleeve shirt and his brown hair with blond highlights. His appearance was different from the last time she saw him. He looked more mature.

"When did you arrive in Minneapolis?"

"About an hour ago," he answered. "I know, I know. You told me to not come, but you didn't answer my phone call. I thought something was wrong."

"I told you I was going to Dark Sepulcher."

He stared at her for a brief moment before replying. "I didn't think you were going to go."

"What do you mean you didn't think I was going to go? You knew I was going to go."

Sean pulled back from their friendly embrace. "Never mind, Veronica. I'm just glad that you're okay."

"I'm fine." Veronica laughed slightly. "Are you okay? I mean, you're the one who flew all the way from San Diego because I didn't answer your call."

"Obviously I didn't come just because of that."

Veronica's eyes zoomed at a tattoo on Sean's left forearm. "When did you get that?" He looked at it and smiled. The tattoo as detailed as it looked, didn't fit Sean's personality. The last thing she thought he would do in his lifetime would be to get a tattoo of a cherub striking down a demon of Satan with a gleaming yellow electric bolt from the heavens.

"A couple of weeks ago."

"Sean!"—Veronica playfully slapped him on his shoulder—"I thought you were afraid of needles?"

"Who told you that?"

"You did silly," Veronica said. "Doesn't matter though." She hugged him again. "Oh my God, I'm so happy you're here." She released him. "Wait. How were you able to leave San Diego this easily? Did The Brotherhood let you go?"

"Never said it was easy." He looked away for a moment. "I'll tell you later. So, what have you found out so far?"

Veronica sighed in exhaustion. "Where do I start?"

"How about with Dark Sepulcher?"

"I spoke with Lambert."

"Lambert? The owner of Dark Sepulcher?" Sean's mouth jumbled with excitement.

"Yeah and oh my God, Sean, there was a lot. There's more going on in this city than I realized." Her eyes drifted down to his suitcase. "What's in there?"

Sean grabbed one of his suitcases. He popped the two notches and opened the lid. "I found some more paperwork in the library. I hope it helps." He pulled out a stack of papers. "I wanted to show you this before you decided to go back to Dark Sepulcher." He placed the papers on the table and leaned back on the couch, placing his hands over his forehead.

"Why didn't you just fax them?" Veronica flipped through them.

"I didn't have a safe landline."

The papers were heavily marked, and most of the information was lined out. They were directly from The Brotherhood's classified files."

The first stack of stapled papers had the name "Lambert" written on the top in cursive handwriting. His date of birth, sired date, and the name of his sire was missing. The paperwork stated he was a Celt, born in Gaul, abandoned as an infant and raised as a mercenary for hire—a headhunter.

The second stack had the name "Alexis" typed in the upper right hand corner. Her real name was Alexandria and her date of birth was listed as 1757 on a plantation just outside of New York City, called York Plantation. Her sired was listed as "Lambert" and the date, August 6th, 1777 at the Battle of Oriskany.

Veronica found the information regarding Remy to be more interesting. The paper listed his date of birth as 1830 in Paris, France. It also listed the date he was sired; 1849, and his maker's name, Julian of Endor. The information on the second page listed his human parents as Charles and Louise Durand and his younger sister, Marie Durand—all deceased during the 1848 Revolution.

"He's about 150 years old." She knew the expression that specified the amount of years a Deamhan lived after they were embraced. "Young" was never older than three hundred years.

Both Alexis and Lambert's paperwork was incomplete which didn't surprise Veronica, The Brotherhood mainly focused on Deamhan.

"You got them." Veronica hugged Sean.

"Sorry it took a while," Sean said. "I tried to steal everything that I could."

"Sean . . . what about The Brotherhood?"

"I know the risks, Veronica. I don't want what happened to Rick to happen to you."

"Well I'm glad you're here." Veronica smiled warmly. She placed her hand on his shoulder and kissed him on his cheek. She skimmed through the remaining paperwork that wasn't stapled. The jumbled phrases and words didn't stick out to her. A few times she saw Lambert's name but it was followed by more blacked out lines, blotching out details.

"They're hiding something." Veronica sighed. "This is worse than declassified U.S. documents."

"Yeah, I hear ya'. But it was all I could get at such a short notice. So, what did you find out at Dark Sepulcher?"

"Sean, I understand that you came because you're worried, but you didn't have to come."

"Veronica." He stopped her. "I don't care about what The Brotherhood might do to me." He smiled briefly. "Besides, I was getting pretty annoyed with that place anyway—too much bullshit and the pay isn't all that great."

"You just now realized that?" she joked.

"No, I just haven't been as vocal as you have about it."

"True."

"Plus, they're revamping the whole organization. They're cleaning house and I mean cleaning house."

"Do you think they're expanding?"

"I don't know. Whatever it is, they're keeping it under wraps."

"Well, it would make sense." From an early age, Veronica knew how guarded and sneaky The Brotherhood could be.

"If they're expanding, they're being really secretive about it."

"What other cities could they expand to, Sean? I mean, there's a Chapter in every major city in America."

"Almost. I would assume Denver, maybe Seattle. There's a huge population increase in those cities," he answered, "and don't forget other countries. I can see them in South Korea by the end of the year."

"South Korea?"

"Yeah, I wouldn't put anything past The Brotherhood." Sean sifted through his suitcase again. He pulled out a piece of paper and handed it to her. "I found some more information about another Deamhan. Anastasia." He pointed to it. "Does the name sound familiar to you?"

"No."

"Apparently, she's an older Ramanga who also lives in Minneapolis," he replied. "She seems pretty dangerous."

Veronica flipped through the paperwork. She caught the name of Anastasia's sire, Lucia, and her eyes lit up. "Is this a mistake?"

"I don't know. Why you ask?"

"Lucia sounds so close to Lucius. But Lucius isn't a Ramanga, right?"

Sean grabbed the paperwork from her and his eyes narrowed in on the information. "I honestly don't know." He read from the paperwork. "Date of birth, 1565. Sired date, 1592. Temperament, unapproachable. Avoid at all costs. Human father, killed by Lucia. Human mother, killed by Anastasia." His eyes met Veronica's. "Wow, she killed her own mother? Sounds pretty dangerous."

"She sounds like every other Deamhan." Veronica grabbed the paperwork from him and she placed it on the coffee table. "Well the good news is that I may have found out the Deamhan who could also be responsible for my mother's disappearance."

"Who?"

"Kei. He was sired by Lucius. Lambert told me that The Brotherhood was helping him get rid of Lucius."

"And you believe that?"

Veronica shrugged. "It's a start."

"Well, we have a lot of ground to cover then."

"We?"

"Yeah, you and . . ." Sean trailed off. "You and I," he quickly corrected. "I have someone from the inside helping me."

"Someone from The Brotherhood?"

"Don't worry." He smiled. "I'm not the only person in the organization that wants to see you succeed."

"Sean, are you sure?"

"Yep. Positive."

Veronica discontinued her question. She trusted Sean's judgment. Why wouldn't she? "I need to know everything there is to know about Kei. You think your contact can get that?"

"Yeah, unless there isn't anything to be found." He handed her a sheet of paper covered in writing.

"Another one?" Veronica glanced at the document. The top half was unreadable, and she couldn't decipher exactly what the information contained.

"Here's some more info on that Remy Deamhan guy."

Veronica thought back to the minion Remy had killed at Dark Sepulcher the night before. "Is he dangerous? Is he tied into my mother's disappearance?"

"Who knows? But this is the interesting part," Sean replied. "According to this"—he pointed at another piece of paper, again inundated with black marks—"he lives in a sanctuary outside of Minneapolis."

"Blind Bluff Manor?"

"Yeah." Sean squinted. "How'd you know?"

"He told me about it." Veronica's mind rushed back to the previous night.

"Whoa, what did he tell you?"

"He didn't say *he* lived there. He mentioned some guy named Nathan Tiernan lives there."

"Nathan Tiernan?" Sean's eyes bulged but he continued. "Are you sure he said that name?"

"Yeah." Veronica watched Sean slowly slide off on couch. "Do you know who he is?"

Sean leaned back in his seat. "I remember my parents talking about the Tiernan family separating from The Brotherhood. I thought it was a myth or something they used to persuade me from even thinking about leaving. The Tiernan family abandoned their oath around the time of your mother's disappearance. They were like the ex-researchers you had to hate. Vamp lovers, Deamhan lovers."

"Remy did say Nathan owned the sanctuary," Veronica replied. "That's really odd."

"Yeah, it makes no sense whatsoever," Sean commented. "A human owning a sanctuary and living with Deamhan?"

"Maybe he's not human? Maybe this Nathan Tiernan person was sired by a Deamhan?" She watched his eyes twitch and fill with concern.

"No, from what I remember he's still alive and he's human." Sean twiddled his fingers, instilled in deep thought.

"We have to assume," Veronica added. "Besides, we don't know if this person is related to the Tiernan family."

"Veronica, he was a researcher who worked with your mother and under your father who was the Region Leader at the time your mother disappeared," he replied. "When the Minnesota Chapter disbanded, he resigned from The Brotherhood. The Tiernan Family has been in The Brotherhood for centuries. This split was unheard of. The Tiernans, Dearhorns, Austins, Alvaros, Luziers, Pavels, are like the Kennedys of The Brotherhood."

"So you're saying that maybe Nathan Tiernan knows something about my mother?" Veronica tried to calm her nerves.

"I don't think it's a good idea to try to seek him out."

"Why not? He might know something!" Veronica's mind ran with the different reasons to go to Blind Bluff Manor. Yes, there was a slight possibility that he was no longer human however, the possibility of Nathan Tiernan knowing specific details about her mother and her mother's assignment when she disappeared was too great to pass up.

"We just can't jump into this without knowing," Sean continued. "Give me time to dig up some information on Nathan Tiernan." He searched the pockets of his pants for his phone. "Remy told me that Nathan could help me."

"And you trust him? A Deamhan?"

"Of course not."

"So we shouldn't overreact until we know for sure."

"We can assume that he's not human but we have to assume that he still knows something." Veronica pushed the issue further. "Maybe Remy was right."

Weary, Sean shook his head.

"Look, I know the risks I have to take, Sean," she quickly replied. "I know that I might have to do things that might put me in danger. But I'm prepared for that."

Sean's eyes sparkled and enhanced his excitement. "Are you sure?"

Veronica nodded.

Suddenly his face expression turned back to concern. "Veronica, I really don't know if you should just go in without further evidence."

"Sean, what more evidence do I need? I'm doing this even if you like it or not." She crossed her arms. "What's gotten into you? You're starting to sound like my father."

"I'm not like your father, you know that."

"Fine. So, any more information?"

"Fine." He sighed and succumbed to her deviant stance. "Lambert. He's a very influential vampire in Minneapolis and when I say influential, I mean influential. From what I've found when I read through researcher documents, he's been living in Minneapolis for a while. I'm sure he isn't content with what's happening in the city."

"He didn't seem happy about Kei either when I spoke with him."

"Why?" Sean asked.

"Kei's the head Deamhan in the city now, according to Lambert." Veronica scoffed that Sean didn't know anything about Kei. It didn't make any sense. She shrugged at his ignorance and continued with their conversation. "Lambert was hostile toward me. He told me that I couldn't go back to Dark Sepulcher."

"He didn't like you, huh?"

"No." Veronica sniggered. "I didn't know what to think of it."

"So you're still bent on going to Blind Bluff Manor." Sean's expression turned to doubt.

"Do you have the address?"

Sean looked at her.

"Of course you do." Veronica answered her own question.

Looking defeated, Sean pulled out another piece of paper from his briefcase, handing it to her. "The address is listed here. I still don't think it's a good idea for you to go there."

"I'm not enthusiastic with the idea either, Sean, but this could be something."

"It's a sanctuary. Remy won't be the only Deamhan we'll run into if we go there."

"We?" she questioned Sean. "You're coming with me?"

"Oh, don't play with me." He waved her off.

"The location doesn't seem far." Veronica pointed to the written address on the paper, circled with red ink. "How about tonight?"

"Deamhan roam at night," Sean answered. "How about in the morning?"

"Morning it is." She sifted through the papers in his suitcase.

"How was the sanctuary hunting, by the way?"

She slapped Sean's thigh. There was a lot of information she was willing to share, but not before she had her first cup of coffee for the day.

"Do you want some coffee?" She stood up and walked into the kitchen.

"Yeah, sure." He crunched his lips and his eyes began to wander.

Noticing his nervousness, Veronica asked him, "Sean, you okay?"

"Yeah, yeah. I'm fine." He straightened his posture. "So how about that coffee?"

* * * *

They spoke until early evening. Deciding to stay in, Veronica served grilled cheese sandwiches for lunch, and they sipped red wine throughout the afternoon. She revealed everything: the Sensual Appetite drink, her conversation with Lambert, and the lackey Remy killed. Sean showed interest by writing down the information on a notepad. His lack of knowledge about Kei became Veronica's utmost concern. How could he not know about a Deamhan whose influence in Minneapolis seemed more dangerous than The Brotherhood?

She continued with Lucius' disappearance and the uncanny timing. Occurring around the time when the Minnesota Chapter left the city, she believed that both events tied in together. Lambert knew more than what he revealed to her at the club and she wanted to go back.

"It's a quarter to seven." Veronica glanced out her window. Time flew by so quickly. The sun was deep in the horizon, and the first stars began to twinkle in the sky.

Sean sat across from her and looked at the clock on the wall.

"I have some extra sheets and a pillow in the closet." She pointed to her bedroom. "You can crash here if you don't mind sleeping on the couch."

"Cool. I bought a one way ticket." He stretched. "I might be here for a while."

Veronica sprung to her feet. "You're not going back?"

"Don't know," said Sean. "If I do, I won't be welcomed with open arms."

"Sean, don't do this because of me."

"I have my phone. I have a laptop. All I need is a wireless connection. I'm good."

His response didn't calm Veronica. They heard a door slam and deep, slow footsteps approaching the front door. There was a quick knock, and Sean looked at Veronica.

"Are you expecting company?"

Veronica approached the door, looking through the peephole. "It's Murphy."

"Who's Murphy?"

"My next door neighbor."

Sean leaned forward. "Is that a smile on your face?"

"Huh?"

"You're smiling."

Veronica stopped and chuckled under her breath. "People do that, Sean."

"Yeah, when they're interested."

She rolled her eyes and opened the door slightly. She moved to block Sean's view of the opened door. "Hey, Murphy."

Murphy smiled at her and didn't notice her unusual movement.

"Hey, Veronica." He wore a casual, long sleeve shirt with slacks. His brown hair was slicked back, and a mild odor of cologne entered her nostrils. "Are you ready to go?" He examined her.

"Go where?"

"The Comedy Club." A sense of concern overcame his face. "I invited you last night, remember?"

"Oh." She slapped herself on the forehead. "I forgot."

Sean approached them and placed his hand on her shoulder, grabbing her attention.

Murphy looked over her shoulder. "I didn't know you had company."

"Hey." Sean opened the door further. "I don't think we've been introduced." He held out his hand. "I'm, Sean."

"Murphy Norton." They shook hands.

"Wow." Sean pointed to Murphy's left wrist. "That's nice ink."

Veronica hadn't noticed Murphy's tattoo before. It was a circle tattoo in the image of a Yin Yang symbol with a darkened right section and a maroon colored left section. A coiled snake wrapped around an indecipherable symbol completed the middle area.

"Thanks." Murphy rubbed his tattoo.

"What is it?"

"Just an ancient symbol I found in a world history book," Murphy answered. "I don't remember what it means."

"It's nice work."

Murphy's eyes moved from Sean and to Veronica. "Sorry if I interrupted you guys."

"No, I just can't believe I forgot about the comedy club." She nudged Sean in his stomach.

"Oh." Murphy nodded and lowered his voice to a whisper. "Are you a re-searcher, too?"

Sean shifted to Veronica. "You told him?"

She smiled shyly. "I had to."

"Those Deamhan things attacked us," Murphy said.

Veronica whispered to Sean who looked away in disbelief. "Don't brood, Sean. I hate it when you brood."

"I can't believe you brought him into this." Sean didn't look at her.

"I was going to tell you. It's just that Murphy was with me when it all hap-pened."

"It was just her and me"—Murphy raised his hands in defense—"I swear."

Sean walked back to the couch. Veronica looked back at Murphy and shrugged. This wasn't the way she wanted to reveal it to Sean, not at all.

"I'm so, so sorry, Murphy. He came into town today unexpected and—"

"It's okay." Murphy smiled, reassuringly. "You're busy, I understand."

"Are you sure?"

"Yeah, it's fine, really. It'll give me more time to look up the rest of those Deamhan names."

"Deamhan names?" Sean questioned.

"Maybe we can do something another time?" Veronica suggested.

Sean crossed his arms and slumped over, shaking his head in disappoint-ment.

"Yeah, another time."

"Sure." Veronica looked back at Sean. She had to end Murphy's visit. "I have to go."

"Have a good night." He waved. "And it was nice meeting you, Sean."

"Same," Sean slowly replied back.

Veronica closed the door.

"You shouldn't have told him," Sean blurted.

"What was there to say?" Veronica approached. "'Oh, never mind the evil twin with the sharp teeth, Murphy. It's just a trick with the shadows.'" She sat next to him. "Sean, he saw it, and even if I lied to him, he would've figured it out anyway. I thought it was best to warn him."

"By telling him about researchers?"

"What's the matter?" She couldn't understand why he was upset. "If it's be-cause I didn't tell you earlier, then I'm sorry."

"It's not that. You haven't known him that long, Veronica," Sean explained. "Remember, you can't trust anyone here, including him." His words were a ghastly reminder of himself.

"So far you're the only one acting different around here."

"What's that supposed to mean?"

"Exactly what I said." She exhaled. "What's wrong with you, Sean?"

"Nothing. I just don't like him."

"You don't even know him."

"And it's in his best interest that I don't."

"Fine." Veronica reluctantly agreed. "Maybe I shouldn't have involved him, but it's too late now."

Sean stood up from the couch. "Then maybe we should get to know him." He scurried over to the front door and unlocked it. "Let's go."

"Go where?"

"Out."

"Out?"

"Yeah, why not." He opened the door. "We deserve some time to relax. You deserve some time to relax."

Veronica hastily agreed, not because she thought he was right, but because she needed the extra break.

CHAPTER THIRTEEN

Murphy joined Sean in humming along to the intro of "Renegade" by Styx that blasted from the jukebox. It was the tenth song that he had requested earlier in the night after their sixth pitcher of beer.

They clashed their filled glasses together in the air and raced to see who could finish their amount first. Veronica watched them in their act as drunken brothers, laughing and belching loud enough to carry over the song.

Being the only patrons at Bar 69, just down the street from Veronica's apartment building, gave them a legitimate excuse to sing at the top of their lungs. The small bar had four round tables, three booths, and three pool tables. Sean liked the fact that the cost for one song from the Jukebox was only seventy five cents and the beer prices didn't break his wallet.

With the alcohol traveling through his system, Sean found it easier to ignore the main reason he came to Minneapolis. He wanted to tell Veronica everything at her apartment. In the bathroom at her apartment, instead of using the toilet, he sat on it with his face in his hands contemplating if he was doing the right thing. He thought about what her father wanted him to do; give her false information about her mother. But he had already broken that rule. The paperwork he showed her was information he'd stolen. He couldn't bring himself to blindly follow what her father wanted of him, no matter if it was his duty as a member of The Brotherhood. Before he had left the office, Kenneth handed him an envelope stuffed with money and a small sheet of paper, pointing out his objective. Before Sean boarded his plane, he threw the paper away without reading it. He didn't care about the consequences. He wanted Veronica to find the truth and he believed he could help her while pretending to follow his orders.

The decision wasn't easy. If The Brotherhood found out he'd given her stolen documents, they'd come for him. In the meantime, he'd try to help her get as close as possible to finding out about her mother while playing the role of "spy."

Veronica cupped her empty margarita glass until Murphy filled her empty glass with beer.

"This is no fun if you don't drink," Murphy's voice slurred.

Veronica declined his offer, and Murphy refilled Sean's glass.

"Aw, c'mon, Veronica." Sean slapped Murphy on his shoulder like two buddies enjoying their drunken night.

"I'm fine," Veronica replied.

"She doesn't like beer." Sean leaned in close to Murphy's ear, but he yelled above the music. He felt his eyelids slowly closing. The ground swayed back and forth and he lost his footing for a moment, using Murphy as a support.

An unfamiliar song to Veronica replaced "Renegade" and Murphy bobbed his head to the beat. "I love this song."

Sean drank again, consuming everything including the foam that collected on the bottom of the glass. He wiped the excess from his mouth with the back of his hand and smiled drunkenly.

"I can tell." Veronica looked at the clock on the back wall. Two hours passed and Sean and Murphy were still embraced in their drunken shenanigans. She sipped the beer slowly through her straw and watched the bartender who was glued to a football game showing from the flat screen TV.

"How long have you guys known each other?" Murphy waved his hand back and forth between them.

"A while," replied Sean.

"It's a long story," Veronica added.

"I bet." Murphy belched then excused himself. "You guys must have some interesting stories about these Deamhan you're chasing."

"Pssft." Sean rolled his eyes. "We're not chasing them. We want to know what happened to her mother." He pointed at Veronica. Murphy's body slowly leaned to the right, followed by Sean, who still had his hand on his shoulder. Veronica chuckled and pulled the pitcher toward her.

"You both are pretty wasted." She slid off her stool. Sean watched her walk toward the bar, taking the nearly empty pitcher with her. She set it on the counter and nodded, thanking the bartender. He then heard the distinctive clinging of the front door open and he saw two women walk in.

He turned his head and watched the women approach the bar. Veronica returned to her barstool, and joined him in watching the Asian woman, wearing a sharp dress suit with high, heels walk up to the bar, followed by an African American woman wearing a white blouse and black dress pants.

"Thanks for inviting me out," Murphy said to Sean.

"Hey, nooooo problem." Sean turned back to Murphy. "God, those girls are hot."

"Go over there and say something to them," Veronica egged him on.

"Naaw," Sean replied. "They're not my type."

"I think they just winked at you." Murphy lowered his voice.

Sean turned to face them again. The Asian woman flashed him a look, winked, then looked away.

"Hey! Hey! They winked at me." A wide grin covered Sean's face.

"Did you wink back?" Veronica sipped from her beer.

From the corner of his eye, Sean saw the two women walking toward their table. He heard their sharp heels clicking on the floor and his eyes widened.

"Here they come," Veronica teased Sean in a whisper. The Asian woman placed her drink on the table. Sugar crystals covered the rim of her glass containing a yellowish-orange colored drink, topped with a small yellow umbrella.

"Hey." The woman looked at Sean. Murphy concealed his giggling by covering his mouth.

"I'm Amber, and this is Toni." Toni waved and gulped her drink.

"I'm Sean, and this is Veronica." He pointed to Murphy. "And Murphy."

Amber turned back toward Toni, who immediately walked back to the bar. Amber turned back, her face totally flushed. Her demeanor changed.

"I'm sorry." She stepped back and turned, walking away from them.

"Did I just get rejected?" Sean asked.

"I think you scared them." Murphy slapped Sean on his shoulder. Murphy stood up from his chair and stretched is arms over his head. "It's getting late. I think I'm gonna head back."

"Yeah, we should get back." Veronica brushed off the women's weird behavior. Sean slid off the stool and nearly lost his balance. He caught the edge of the table, but their empty glasses crashed onto the floor, scattering into shards.

"I think I might need a little help." He leaned against the table. He covered his mouth, feeling the alcohol regurgitating from his stomach. He rushed to the back of the bar to the men's bathroom. He pushed the door open and hurried to an empty stall.

The alcohol gushed from his mouth and his stomach convulsed. He stared into the toilet bowl and watched the yellowish liquid pour from his mouth. After the last chunks were expelled, he plopped to the floor, leaning against the wall of the bathroom stall. He wiped his mouth with the back of his hand and stared at the ceiling fan.

What am I doing? He again questioned his motive. A feeling of discomfort followed by the onset of jealously overcame his nausea. He didn't want to admit to what he saw in Murphy's eyes. *He likes her. He likes my Veronica.* However, something else confused him about Murphy, first starting with his tattoo. It was nice artwork, something he might consider. But it just wasn't right. Something wasn't right about him.

He heard the door to the men's bathroom open, and Sean immediately stood to his feet, checking his shirt to see if some of his bile had missed the toilet bowl. Satisfied, he flushed the toilet and opened the door.

He saw Amber standing in front of the door and Toni leaning against the only sink in the bathroom with her eyes slowly reverting to black. The two women remained fixed on him with Amber revealing her sharp prominent teeth. Sean paused and he picked up on the fact that they were watching, waiting to see what he planned to do.

The years of training in The Brotherhood, especially how to act when confronted by a Deamhan, ran through his head in a millisecond. Hide your thoughts and don't show your fear. Look for any weapon in your environment. Catching them unexpected was best, but what if they caught you unexpected? His training didn't cover that and it didn't cover what to do when confronted by two Deamhan in a men's bathroom.

Amber lunged at him first. He jumped back and slammed the stall door shut. He felt the door shake, and he heard her drop to the floor. Above, he heard snarling and he looked up, seeing Toni gripping the top of the stall. Suddenly his body began to feel weak. His legs wobbled from underneath him and his arms felt as if they weighed a million pounds. His head throbbed and his sight became clouded.

It didn't take long for him to realize what type of Deamhan Toni was; Metusba. She jumped on top of him, and he pushed her to the side. She landed, hitting her head on the bathroom seat. He opened the door and jumped over Amber.

Everything he learned about confronting a Deamhan from The Brotherhood kicked in. He searched the bathroom for any object he could use. He grabbed the hand sanitizer on the sink, but dropped it. He reached for a roll of toilet paper sitting on top of the paper towel dispenser, but he dropped that too. Finally, he grabbed the large waste can underneath the sink. He swung it at Amber, striking her across the face before she stood to her feet. He then raised it over his head and swung, striking her again. He continued his attack with each blow connecting, until he saw Toni walk out of the stall.

He swung the waste can at her but she caught it and she pushed him to the floor. Immediately Sean jumped back to his feet and he stepped back, readying himself for her attack.

"You're not as strong as they said you'd be." His liquid courage spoke for him. The men's bathroom door opened, and he quickly turned to look over his shoulder. Veronica stood in the doorway with Murphy behind her. She grabbed him by his shoulder and pulled him out of the bathroom. Murphy closed the door and reached for a broom, leaning against the wall nearby. He ran the broom through the door handle, bracing the door and trapping the two Deamhan inside.

Away from danger, Sean drunkenly smiled at Veronica.

"You see that?" He pointed to the door. "I took on two of them at once."

"You could've died!" Veronica screamed at him.

He stood silent then shrugged. Yes, he knew he could've died but not once did the thought cross his drunken mind.

Veronica wrapped her arm around him and hurriedly rushed him outside, with Murphy following slightly behind.

Sean looked at Veronica, who stared straight ahead. Not once did she look back.

* * * *

Sean didn't remember the walk home. He didn't see Veronica and Murphy, scared shitless, after his Deamhan encounter. What he did remember throbbed in his brain to the point that he felt like dying.

His throat cracked and his stomach growled when he rolled off the couch and fell to the floor. He stood up. It took him awhile to realize where he was. The sunlight peeped through the blinds, touching his skin.

Veronica stood in the kitchen with her back facing him. She looked over his shoulder, said good morning, and attended back to her coffee.

Hours later, fully awake, they headed to a local coffee shop down the street called "Jubilee."

Sean repeatedly apologized about what he called "the behavior of a virgin drinking college student." Veronica assured him that he had nothing to be sorry for. He agreed and popped four Tylenol before ordering a small hazelnut coffee.

The vast amount of voices echoing in the café around him didn't stop Sean's vigorous typing. The sunlight glared on the monitor of his laptop, and it blinded him for a second. He repositioned the laptop again in hopes that he could avoid the stinging after affect. Veronica sat across from him, watching his movements. He told her he had received information from his informant in The Brotherhood when in fact, he skimmed through an email sent from her father.

The email demanded a status update. Sean replied that everything was under control and that Veronica didn't suspect his true agenda. The email, filled with a list of demands, lacked brevity. On the other hand, it enforced loyalty. Sean read it over several times; once and awhile he shifted his eyes up to Veronica and curled his lips in a pleasant glance.

"What is it?" she asked.

"I don't know yet." He clicked on another email from Kenneth Dearhorn sent an hour after Mr. Austin's email. The demands grew more explicit in concern to Dark Sepulcher. He was to suggest to Veronica the possible correlation between the sanctuary fires and her mother's disappearance. He needed to persuade her to not go to Dark Sepulcher and that nothing could be found there. The email ended by stating that phase one was in progress and in Kenneth's signature was the title "Midwest Region Leader. The Brotherhood."

The Brotherhood was on its way to Minneapolis.

He brought his fist up to his mouth in thought. He still couldn't believe that somehow that jackass had kissed enough ass to be promoted to Region Leader. Sean had no intention of working under him. Somehow he had to postpone their arrival. Again he looked up to Veronica, thinking maybe just looking at her would help him decide on what to do but the cafe's menu had her complete attention.

Sean replied to Kenneth's email in the best way he could, giving them what they wanted to hear. He agreed to the demands, stating that Veronica was already moving her search in a different direction, away from Dark Sepulcher, and that he would be in contact if anything changes. He lowered his monitor. Maybe now was the time to tell Veronica that The Brotherhood was coming back to Minneapolis with Kenneth as their Region Leader. "I think that's it. I told my contact to get back to me before noon."

Veronica nodded and sipped on her mocha. "These drinks are so sugary."

"Now we wait again." Sean's mind went into thought. Along the streets, he noticed the parked cars and a few residents walking near the coffee shop. A group of bicycles strolled down the sidewalk, and a group of college students stood on the street corner, waiting for the light to turn green. "This isn't a bad city, Veronica. I could live here."

"With the Deamhan?" Veronica questioned.

"They're everywhere and in every city. No one can avoid that."

Veronica cupped her coffee. "What if your contact doesn't get back to you before tonight?"

"I don't know." He leaned back in his chair, positioning his hands on the back of his head. He knew Kenneth would send another email soon. But of what, he didn't know. He moaned and returned to his upright position. The Tylenol wasn't working, and his head throbbed just thinking about the chance of The Brotherhood returning to Minneapolis. "I think I want some more coffee."

"Don't get the white chocolate mocha unless you want a heart attack."

A group of businessmen nestled in a corner table, chatting raucously over their empty plates.

"Every time I look around, I can't believe Minneapolis of all places has one of the highest Deamhan populations in the country," said Veronica. "It's cold here half of the year and humid the other half. This city is small compared to Los Angeles, Chicago, New York, and Orlando."

"There are a lot of open spaces far from anyone here," Sean said. "Farms dot the landscape; your neighbors are miles from you. This is a perfect state if you want privacy."

He looked up at the ceiling, and his mind suddenly switched to Murphy. "Is your friend okay?"

"Murphy?"

"Yeah. He must have been scared out of his mind last night."

Veronica shrugged. "He took it pretty well." She paused. "Actually, really well. I was surprised."

Sean leaned upright in his chair. "I still don't trust him."

"Trust Murphy?"

"There's something about him that irks me. I don't know what it is. I just feel like he's hiding something."

"You should thank him." She sipped her coffee. "He saved you from the two Deamhan."

"I was doing all right." Sean smirked.

"Yeah, well, you were running out of weapons. Trash cans are useless against them, Sean."

"But it worked, didn't it?" Sean teased.

Veronica observed a special alert bulletin on the television behind Sean. The volume was low, and the picture of another home ravaged by fire loomed on the screen.

"What is it?" Sean turned to look.

"Another house fire last night."

No, not now! He watched the image of a charred home on the screen.

"I think I know where that is." Veronica's eyes danced. "South Minneapolis, just off the 35W freeway. Can you look up the directions?"

"We should wait and make sure it's a sanctuary and not some normal house fire."

"Wait? We all know the Deamhan are burning each other out of their own sanctuaries. Why would we wait?"

"It's not safe."

She gaped at him and he quickly stopped talking. "When is it ever safe?" Veronica stood up and yanked him from his seat.

Sean's mind raced quickly to think of another excuse but he came up empty.

"You could just wait in my apartment until I get back, Sean." Veronica gulped down the last of her mocha, which had turned warm.

"Yeah, right. You're not leaving my sight." He watched her eyes beam and her lips pull back into a smile. She placed a ten dollar bill on the table and she walked out of the coffee shop. He gathered his things, still trying to decide what to do. He wasn't good at spying and he didn't know how long he could hold out until Veronica finally discovered his true agenda.

CHAPTER FOURTEEN

The taxi pulled over on the corner of Cedar Avenue and Broadway. Veronica handed the driver a twenty-dollar bill, and she exited the vehicle with Sean just in time to watch the taxi drive off.

South Minneapolis was vastly different than the warehouse district. Two-story houses lined the vacant streets. They walked past an older couple moving debris and dried leaves from their front yard and a pre-school and its empty playground with swings drifting back and forth from the frequent gusts of wind. The sun had set and the air became colder. Veronica shivered and placed her hands into the pockets of her jacket. Sean unfolded a small piece of paper written with the address of the location and rechecked it.

"It should be somewhere up there, around the corner," he said to her. His lower lip shivered from the cold. Veronica grabbed his arm, and he placed it around her shoulders. Sean smiled and held her close. Any notion of his betrayal and the fact that Kenneth was on his way to Minneapolis, left his thoughts. He didn't want to think about it; not now. At that very moment, walking down the street with her, there was no other place he wanted to be.

They continued down Cedar; a one way street, near the main avenue of south Minneapolis. Two-story family homes secluded behind high wooden fences lined the streets. When they reached the corner, Sean stopped. He glanced to their left and right.

"This way." He pointed down a dark and secluded street. Veronica followed, and Sean picked up speed in his stride. Newly constructed homes adjoined the cul-de-sac. Halfway down the block, "For Sale" signs pitched in the front yards of finished homes moved in the wind. The charred remains of a home sectioned off by police tape, sat on the edge of the cul-de-sac between two empty lots.

"This is a perfect area for a sanctuary." Sean looked around. "It's quiet and less populated." Spools of grass stacked the front yards, ready to be rolled out at will. A distinct smell of burnt wood lingered in the air. Crumbled remains toppled upon one another. They stopped only feet from the ruins, staring at the implausible environment.

Sean awed. "Incredible."

"Do you think anything survived?" Veronica asked.

"Let's find out." Sean ducked under the police tape and stepped into the ruins. He slipped on the burnt piece of wood and held out his hands for balance.

"I can still feel the heat." Sean looked at Veronica.

"Be careful, Sean."

"I will," Sean replied. He watched her walk along the perimeter of the yellow tape, carefully observing the surroundings. He turned back to the remains and he started to remove the burnt pieces. He didn't know if anything remained from the fire. If any Deamhan died, their bodies would've turned to ash and scattered to the winds. But if any Deamhan survived, they sure wouldn't remain underneath the rubble.

"There's an empty hole over here," Veronica called out. "I think it's a basement or what's left of a basement."

Sean continued to dig through the rubble. His feelings about his assignment resurfaced and he tried to ignore them. He found it harder to block his own thoughts from himself than blocking his own thoughts from a Deamhan.

His hands moved over a smooth and burnt piece of wood. "I think I found something."

Veronica hurried back over to him. He tossed burnt pieces of wood to the side.

"What is it?" She waited for him to stop digging.

He cleared the remaining debris to the side, lifting up a piece of the blackened wood that stood taller than him. "A lid to a coffin," he said, turning the piece to the side, examining it.

"A coffin?"

"Yeah." His eyes fixed on the piece of wood. "It looks like it." He lifted it and placed it on his shoulder as he walked toward her. He dropped it on the ground in front of her and breathed in heavily, trying to catch his breath.

"It has to be." He couldn't believe his eyes. Beneath the layer of burnt residue, he clearly saw that the board had the shape of a lid. A small metal piece on the side of the wood further proved his theory. He continued to wipe away the smaller pieces of burnt chips.

She placed her hands on the burnt wood that was hardened and cracked from the fire. "I don't know, Sean. It's too burnt to tell what it is."

"It could be." He bent down over the piece to examine it. His mind wandered to the various possibilities. "We might have found an *actual* sanctuary."

Veronica placed her hands on her hips. "The coffin could still be down there."

Sean smiled. "If it is, then maybe the body is, too."

"I haven't heard that many stories of Deamhan using coffins, Sean."

"I read one report about a researcher finding a sanctuary full of coffins," he replied to her. Like vampires who used coffins to protect them from the sun during the day, Deamhan were also avid coffin users. But as time passed and their sanctuaries became more modern, they began to settle for beds and cubby holes, and basements.

"We should try to find the remains." Sean turned his attention back to the ruins. "They could be down there."

"And what if we find it? Then what?"

"This is your idea, Veronica." He lifted himself up from the ground. "You wanted to come here to investigate." The thought of discovering an actual Deamhan sanctuary rattled his brain. It was exciting yet at the same time terrifying. He wasn't cut out of field research and he worried about running into more Deamhan like the ones at the bar a few days ago. He also didn't want to admit the possibility that what he admired was nothing more than burned wood coincidentally shaped like the lid of a coffin. He rolled his eyes at his delusive theory and looked off into the distance.

"I know, Sean."

His demeanor suddenly changed as his eyes slowly protruded. "I thought you liked exploring the unknown and flirting with danger, Veronica?"

"Don't throw that back into my face," she barked back at him.

His eyes caught a glimpse of the house behind her. "What's that?" He pointed behind her.

She followed his stare to the wall of a vacant home. The writing covered the back wall of the home. Together they read the spray-painted construed bubbly-word "LUGAT."

"Is that what I think it is?" Sean squinted. "They tag their territories like this now?"

"Yeah. I saw something just like this a few days ago, Sean."

"Shit," Sean painfully whispered. He looked down at the ruins he stood in.

Veronica placed her hands on the graffiti. "So that sanctuary was a Lugat sanctuary."

Sean felt his cell phone buzz in the pocket of his jeans and the sound threw him back to reality. "Fuck." Sean looked up at her. "I have to answer this." He walked away from Veronica and he stared at his phone, knowing that Kenneth was on the other end.

"Hello," he answered.

Kenneth's voice echoed from the earpiece. "What the status?"

Sean's high-spirits vanished. He sighed, paused and then licked his already moist lips. "So far, so good."

"Good." Kenneth's robotic voice replied back. "How goes the mission?"

"We're at a sanctuary right now, Kenneth."

"Does she suspect anything?"

"Not yet, but she will."

"Well, as long as she doesn't now, we should be good," Kenneth replied. "Your email sounded rather disheartening."

"Really?" Sean cupped his hand over his mouth to hide the conversation from Veronica. "I don't see how. She's taking the bait. She hasn't been back to Dark Sepulcher. She believes the fires are directly connected to her research."

"Mr. Austin made his intentions clear, Sean. You are not to provide his daughter with any documented material."

"And I haven't." Sean felt a lump in his throat. He knew eventually they'd find out about the documents he'd taken before he left for Minneapolis, but he didn't think it'd be so fast.

"Are you sure about that, Sean?"

"Why wouldn't I be?" Sean replied. "Look, from what I'm experiencing here in Minneapolis, I don't see a need to restart the Chapter. Yes, The Deamhan are somewhat out of control, but bringing The Brotherhood back into this mess may do more harm than good."

"If Mr. Austin wanted your opinion, he would've asked for it," Kenneth interrupted him. "You are not there to access nor are you there to help her. Mr. Austin made that clear as crystal."

Sean nodded. "I understand."

"Good, because Mr. Austin isn't sympathetic to failure and he doesn't take second chances."

"I understand." Sean heard Kenneth sigh on the other end of the line.

"You were sent with a simple task, Sean and you failed by stealing more classified documents from the Library and the Archives. You've given Mr. Austin no other choice."

Sean remained silent, waiting for the phrase "you're fired." Instead Kenneth's reply turned into the last thing Sean wanted to hear.

"You are to immediately cease communications and all activities in regards to Miss Austin. You are ordered to check in at the Gathewait Hotel on Hennepin Avenue, Room 301, and stay there until I and several researchers arrive tomorrow evening."

"What?"

"You've been pulled from the assignment, Sean," Kenneth continued. "And do yourself a favor this time. Don't disobey Mr. Austin's orders again. I'll be in touch." Kenneth hung up the phone.

Sean stuffed his phone back in his pocket and he turned to Veronica. She had to know. No more secrets.

"Who was it?"

"We have to go now." He took Veronica by her hand and began to lead her down the street.

"Sean, what is it?" She struggled to keep up with his hurried pace.

"I'll tell you when we get back to your apartment. I promise." He increased his speed to a hasty walk.

"What's going on?"

"It's nothing."

"Was that your contact on the phone?"

"No," he blurted. "It's not that. It's—I'll tell you when we get back to your apartment." They reached the corner, and he cautiously looked down the street before proceeding.

"Who was it?" she asked him again.

He didn't answer.

She yanked her hand, breaking free from his grasp. "I'm not going anywhere until you tell me what's wrong!"

"Trust me, we need to get off the streets." He held out his hand.

Veronica heard the panic in his voice, and she saw his agitation. "Why?"

"I'll tell you when we get to your apartment." His breathing became erratic.

"Sean."

"Veronica, trust me. Please," he appealed.

She stepped away from him. "I trust you, Sean, but I'm not moving until you tell me what the hell is going on." Her comment blinded him. She never doubted him. This was a first.

She tilted her head to the side and crossed her arms in front of her chest. He released a tired sigh and deeply regretted coming back to Minneapolis. He wanted to relive the day when Mr. Austin gave him the stupid task. Saying "no" and refusing to spy on Veronica seemed easy enough. She had the right to know what was going on and he had no right to lie to her, as her best friend.

"Fuck it." He took a deep breath. "Veronica I—" He scratched his head, taking another deep breath. He looked over her shoulder in frenzy then he turned around, staring down the street. Again he looked over her shoulder before looking into her eyes.

"What, Sean?"

"Okay, fine." He conceded. "There's so much I need to tell you about why I came here but I can't tell you now, right here. I'm telling you, Veronica, it's not safe on the streets. I don't know if they're already here or not."

"Who? Who's already here?"

"The Brotherhood," he answered.

Her eyes widened. "Since when?"

"Since I arrived." He grabbed her hand, and they resumed their fast pace. "Kenneth might already be here, I don't know."

"Kenneth? Do you mean Kenneth Dearhorn?"

"He's the new Midwest Region Leader." He didn't look at her as she stared off into the distance, still taking in the information.

"Since when did he become the Midwest Region Leader?"

His shoulders drew back and his eyebrows arched higher on his face. "Before I left." They stepped off the curb and Sean waved his hands to signal a taxi. Veronica folded her arms, watching his frantic behavior. Cars drove past, including one taxi that totally ignored them. He looked down the street at a woman standing alone, underneath an orange street light, eyeing their every movement.

Were they already here?

114

Sean looked back at the woman again and Veronica followed his gaze.

"Sean, I've seen her before. At the other fire. Is she from The Brotherhood?"

"I don't think so." Sean looked at Veronica.

"Maybe a minion?" Veronica's eyes bulged from her sockets. "Lambert did tell me I was protected. Maybe this is what he meant?"

"We have to get out of here." Sean's panicked movements increased. He frantically waved his hands again at a taxi. Finally a white cab stopped.

Sean opened the door and hopped in the front seat. "Veronica, get in." He closed the door. She slowly opened the rear door and climbed into the vehicle.

"Where to?" The taxi driver pressed his foot on the gas pedal.

"Palm Oaks," Sean answered. Veronica leaned over to the other window. She watched the woman until the taxi turned the corner.

* * * *

Sean remained silent on the way to Palm Oaks. His eyes fixated on the scenery from the car windows while the taxi sped down the highway. Several times Veronica tried to make conversation but he didn't reply. Instead he nervously tapped his fingers on his knees.

His behavior was noticeable, and the taxi driver asked him if he was alright. Sean nodded, mumbled and continued with his erratic behavior.

It was only when they were inside Veronica's apartment that Sean began to release his frustration. He paced back and forth in her living room, undecided on how he could tell Veronica the truth without sacrificing their friendship.

Sean let out a weak laugh and ran his fingers through his hair.

Veronica took off her jacket. "Are you sure you're okay? You seem a little spooked."

He stopped pacing and looked at her. "They're coming, Veronica. Do you know what that means?"

"Sean, sit," she said as she pointed to the couch. "You're making me nervous."

He stared back at her and finally succumbed and sat on the couch.

"I don't care if The Brotherhood is coming back to Minneapolis." She sat next to him. "This isn't going to stop my search."

He tapped his feet rapidly on the floor. "That's not it." He leaned back and sighed.

"What is it?"

He didn't know where to start; The Brotherhood, her father, the real reason he came to Minneapolis . . . He couldn't bring himself to tell her everything just yet.

Before agreeing to his plan, Sean pieced the tiny remnants of what he could find together. He never told Veronica, but he'd always thought her mother had died. Killed, not by the hands of a Deamhan, but by the hands of her own father.

115

Everyone who ever worked in The Brotherhood during and after that time specu-
lated the very same dark scenario, but no one suspected and no one really knew.
When Sean tried to find out, his own parents warned him about digging into The
Brotherhood's dark history.

During his long work nights in his office at the San Diego headquarters, he
searched around, listening to the rumors being said about her father. He sifted
through old boxes filled with documents that smelled of old water in the building's dank basement. He hacked into The Brotherhood files, only to find that the
information he wanted was blacked out. He searched secret information before it
was moved in the highly secured and guarded library. His own parents told him
stories of their youth as researchers, unaware that their son was piecing together
clues. It was only a hypothesis, but he felt it was damn near close to the truth.
When Veronica mentioned the name Lucius to him, his brain lit up like a light
bulb.

"There's something that we're missing." His voice drifted as he thought.

"What?" The tension drove Veronica mad.

He lifted his head and turned slightly toward her. "Veronica, I'm sorry to tell
you this but, your father sent me here to spy on you."

Veronica gently placed her hand under her chin and she turned her head toward him. "What?"

"Your father sent me here to spy on you."

She raised her hand and he immediately quieted. "My father sent you here?"
Veronica didn't understand his comment.

"Believe me, Veronica; I couldn't say no." He hesitated.

She glared into his eyes, and he looked to the floor.

"You could've said no, Sean."

"You of all people know what happens when a researcher says 'no', Veronica," he replied. "I can't refuse your father. He's one of the three Presidents of
The Brotherhood. What would you expect me to do?" He expected her to push
away from him and to lash out like she used to when she became upset. Instead
her eyes began to fill with tears while she continued to glare at him. He felt her
body shiver in his embrace.

"I wish I could've told you sooner, Veronica." Sean continued. "I just
couldn't. I wasn't sure how to break it to you."

"You could have just told me, Sean," she whispered.

"I'm telling you now."

She cleared her throat and regained her posture. "What did my father want
you to do?"

He knew he had to tell her but still he held back and without thinking clearly, he replied, "Just to make sure that you stayed away from Dark Sepulcher and
if you found anything significant, to let *them* know about your progress."

"Are you lying to me now, Sean?" She pounced on his arm. The pain traveled to his shoulder blade like sharp pinpoint needles.

"No, I'm not," he exclaimed. "A part of me didn't want to say no too, Veronica. I mean, I want to be here to make sure nothing happens to you. I didn't want what happened to Rick to happen to you."

"I know the risks. I'm not a little girl anymore." She rested her head in her hands. "I know what I was getting myself into when I came back to Minneapolis." She stood up. "You of all people know that."

He nodded and startled by his lack of honesty, he quickly rose to his feet. So far, she absorbed his information better than he thought she would. He expected Veronica to throw him out of her apartment and to never talk to him again. But here he was, still in her presence. He waited for her response while his mind ran with wild thoughts. Finally, she pushed him away and stormed into the kitchen. He quickly followed her to the kitchen counter. She leaned back, glaring at the ceiling.

He tried again.

"Veronica, I know there's nothing I can say to make you feel better. But Kenneth is coming to Minneapolis with a few researchers. They're going to restart the Minnesota Chapter. You can't stop them."

"You don't understand. I don't care if they're coming, Sean. Let them come." She swiped back the brown strands of hair from her face, revealing a trail of tears running down her cheek. "What I care about is that you lied to me. You came here to spy on me."

He reached out to her and touched her shoulder. "I'm so sorry." She didn't respond. "If you want, I can leave now. I can walk out of that door and when they get here—"

"No," she interrupted and then placed her hands on her hips. "I don't want you to leave. I want you to come with me to Blind Bluff Manor."

"Excuse me?" He didn't expect that reply from her. "The sanctuary?"

"Yes. I'm going." She clasped her hands together. "I want you to come with me."

Surprised, he stepped back and watched her gather herself. She wiped her tears and for a moment, he saw a look of disillusion of himself in her eyes.

"Are you sure, Veronica?"

She nodded. "Positive." She placed her hands on his shoulders. "My father doesn't want me to go there, right?"

He nodded.

"Well, if my father doesn't want me to go there then it has to be important."

CHAPTER FIFTEEN

Winter arrived in Minnesota late that night. Veronica and Sean awoke to six inches of fresh snow on the ground with the air carrying thick and sticky snowflakes. The temperature dropped to below freezing with the wind burning any exposed areas of Veronica's face as they left her apartment and climbed into the backseat of a taxi. The taxi's tires spun over the black ice on the pavement, making the car move uncontrollably from left to right before it sped down the street.

The drive, an hour long, for the most part remained quiet. The Somalian driver tried to start a conversation with Sean about the weather, but Sean's bitty, apathetic replies killed it.

Veronica lost herself in her thoughts. A few times she looked at Sean from the corner of her eye, still wondering if he told her everything about why he came to Minneapolis. For the first time in her life, she didn't trust him and the Sean she knew before she left California was now lost to her. Part of her understood why he couldn't say no, but another side of her didn't understand why he agreed either.

She shuffled through the backpack sitting on her lap, pulling out her notes and some of The Brotherhood paperwork on Blind Bluff Manor (she also started to question the information Sean brought her as well.) The sanctuary, reportedly owned by a human and nestled far from the city, still didn't seem real to her. Images of what the place looked like flooded her mind. She expected it to be large, dark, overfilled with passageways and secret compartments for the Deamhan to rest during the day.

What she knew about sanctuaries she learned from her father and The Brotherhood. Deamhan sanctuaries were necessities in the time when the Deamhan were almost driven to extinction. Each sanctuary had an older Deamhan who acted as its leader with several Deamhan under him or her. They weren't mixed and each Deamhan type preferred to stay with their own. Some sanctuaries could be cramped, others not so much, but each sanctuary had its distinctive traits, depending on what type of Deamhan settled there. They preferred their locations to be further away from humans, usually in abandoned homes, farms, and even cemeteries, but that was not always true.

118

The Somalian driver weaved in and out of traffic. In the rear view mirror, Veronica saw downtown Minneapolis become smaller and smaller until it turned into just a pinpoint. The taxi meter read a little over five dollars. She expected the bill to round out to eighty. Nothing the driver said to them pushed on the conversation. Sean only replied when the conversation turned to the house fires. Another fire last night claimed a house in the Uptown district of the city. The police increased the reward to $50,000, in the hope to catch those responsible. This fire didn't make the news like the fires before it. Veronica assumed that the news reporters were already moving onto newer news.

Thirty minutes into the ride, the taxi driver blurted the name of the city. The taxi passed a green sign with the words: "Prudence Population 3,000" in white letters. Huge pine trees with snow collected on their branches grew on both sides of the road, standing tall and erect, creating a tunnel effect while the car moved. The freeway turned into a one lane paved road, surrounded by fresh, heavy snow.

"Excuse me, are you sure this is the right way?" Veronica decided to question the route.

"Yes, yes, yes." The driver's accent was thick as he spoke. "Your friend said you both want to go to Prudence, right? We are close now. Soon."

The taxi came to a four way stop with an abandoned gas station on the right corner. Veronica peered out the window, staring at the desolate land and its seemingly vacant scenery. The price of gas shown on its billboard still read ninety nine cents a gallon.

She nervously tapped her fingers on her leg. Just yesterday she considered the thought of coming to Blind Bluff Manor as something she had to mentally plan for. She envisaged her behavior in the city as gung ho. She needed to be. Now she believed that maybe her aggressive behavior turned against her. Blind Bluff Manor was no Dark Sepulcher. The secluded place worked against her. She tried to relax. She practiced for this moment and she feared those years of practice would fail her miserably. She couldn't afford to have her mind read— not now if not ever.

The taxi turned left and drove for ten more miles until it veered off on Lake Bend, another one lane road. Ahead, a black gate guarded off the remaining road. It stood about fifteen feet tall, and its metal gates were more than an inch thick. Above the gate, twisted in the black metallic frame, were the words "Blind Bluff Manor."

"I'll wait right here," the driver told them. Sean handed him the money, and they left the car. The air was chillier than in the city, and it carried a dust of snow. Veronica approached the electronic lock and pressed the talk button twice.

"This is secure for a sanctuary." Sean glanced around.

Veronica pressed the button again and noticed the icicles hanging from the edge of the electronic lock.

"They never described anything like this in the books," Sean continued.

"Hello, is anyone there?" Veronica raised her voice. She began to grow impatient, waiting for a response that she believed they weren't going to receive while standing in the cold. Up ahead, dim lights glowed behind a row of tall pine trees. Veronica pressed the talk button again and raised her voice to a banshee scream.

"Hello? Please answer me! Someone? Anyone? My name is Veronica Austin. Remy sent me here to see Nathan Tiernan."

Silence.

Sean tapped her shoulder and pointed off to their right and left. The length of a tall black steel fence stretched off into the distance on both sides. Like she predicted, Blind Bluff Manor sat on a large area of secluded land. The wind picked up, and their bodies gave out a quick quiver. The cold was beginning to affect them.

"Maybe no one's home?" Veronica whispered to Sean.

"Maybe." Sean approached the electronic box and pressed the button. "Hello, is anyone there?"

"Remy sent me here to speak with Nathan Tiernan," Veronica tried again.

Static exploded from the box followed by silence. Sean pressed the button frantically, becoming anxious to hear a voice. Suddenly the sound of static was followed by a man clearing his throat.

"I usually don't receive visitors at this time of day," the male voice replied. "May I help you?"

"Am I speaking with Nathan Tiernan?" Veronica asked. More static echoed from the box.

"Yes, I am Nathan Tiernan. It is cold out there, I can imagine."

Veronica and Sean strained to hear the voice.

"Please, tell the taxi to follow the road in to the front of my home."

Sean breathed a sigh of relief. "I guess that means we can go in."

Befuddled, Veronica looked around the area. "How did he know about the taxi?"

"Maybe there's a camera around here somewhere," Sean whispered. They walked back to the car.

"When the gates open, follow the road in," Sean ordered the taxi driver.

The driver shook his head, turning off his car. "You both walk rest of way." He spoke in broken English.

"What's wrong?" Veronica asked.

"Bad things about this place."

"What bad things?" Sean asked him.

The driver began to describe the superstitions that came with every unknown possibility to man: ghosts, demon worship, sacrifices, and paganism. Veronica wanted to confirm some of his superstition. Instead of explaining the situation, she reached in her purse and pulled out a hundred dollar bill.

The gates slowly opened, and the driver took the money. Sean and Veronica climbed back into the taxi and the driver started his car and proceeded to drive forward, taking his time approaching the house. He nervously looked in his rear view mirror, the side mirrors, and ahead. Reddish gravel and small, harmless rocks paved the road leading to the sanctuary a half a mile from the gate. Large trees empty of their leaves and brown grass sticking through the thick layer of snow completed the scene around them.

Veronica's fabricated picture of the sanctuary fascinated her inner curiosities. Blind Bluff Manor was the size of a mansion. Delicately beautiful, it had stained glass windows decorated with pictures of clouds tricked their eyes. Four windows lined the second story mansion sized sanctuary with a large balcony. The amber-colored front door itself stood towering over them. Overall, the sanctuary seemed secure, even with a small frozen pond near the front. Here, in this beautiful decorative palace, sat a Deamhan sanctuary.

Veronica comforted the driver one more time before exiting the vehicle. She and Sean walked up to the door. The porch creaked eerily with every step they took. The door opened slowly. A middle aged man, a little taller than Sean, stood in the doorway. His deep dark blue eyes met them at the edge of the steps. His neatly trimmed brown hair showed streaks of gray near his ears. He slowly took off his reading glasses, revealing crow's feet in the corner of his eyes, and he extended his hand with a smile, showing his gleaming teeth.

He moved aside. "Please, come in."

Sean and Veronica walked in cautiously, not expecting the inside to be more amazing than the outside. A long, elegant red carpet lay from the front door to a beautiful staircase leading to the second floor with a majestic balcony—a perfect place to view anyone walking into the home. Sean noticed a huge portrait of Queen Elizabeth II hanging above a fireplace in the far backroom illuminating its surroundings. Huge shaded lamps in the corners of the room illuminated the granite marble ceiling.

Besides the beautiful artistry that jumped at them from all sides, Veronica found the place to be empty and dark. She glanced up at the ceiling far from their reach, and her eyes rapidly found the next big thing to awe over.

Roman marble statues of gods and goddesses positioned on pedestals outlined the room. A replica of a Roman forum complete with a balcony for a Roman emperor completed the luxurious den.

"I guess you have an interest in Roman art?" The man noticed Veronica's interest in his statues.

"Almost anything historical, actually." Veronica turned to face him.

"Well." He smiled. "As do I." He stared them over for a couple of seconds before speaking again. "So, Miss Austin."

"Veronica, please."

"And you can call me Sean." Sean held out his hand.

"I'm Nathan Tiernan." They exchanged a handshake. "So, Veronica and Sean. What can I help you with?"

121

"Yes," said Veronica. "I have a couple of questions about the Deamhan in Minneapolis."

"Deamhan?" Nathan repeated. His eyes bounced to Sean.

"The Deamhan and The Brotherhood," Sean added.

Veronica continued. "I'm sure Remy has told you about me."

Nathan nodded. "Yes, Remy told me about meeting you at Dark Sepulcher but I'm afraid that's all he told me."

"I don't want to take up too much of your time," Veronica replied. "We just have a couple of questions, and then we'll be on our way."

"Nathan, please. Mr. Tiernan sounds so old. I don't look that old, do I?"

Veronica didn't answer. She noticed the deep dark wrinkles covering his forehead and his sagging cheeks. Obviously he seemed older and around the same age as her father.

"No you don't, Nathan." Veronica respected his correction. "Remy said you could help me with some questions that I have."

"I take it you had no trouble finding my home?" he asked.

"No."

"Uh huh." His enunciated reply sounded strange to Veronica.

"We mean no disrespect," Sean said, apologetically.

"Please." Nathan ignored his comment. "This way."

They followed Nathan to the illuminated backroom. A red velvet chair with a sunken impression sat in the corner. Next to it was a small dining table with a lone coffee mug on top of it. Sean and Veronica sat across from him in a twin matching couch, cushioned enough that Sean felt swallowed by it. Veronica felt they were invading his privacy.

"Excuse the mess," Nathan said. "I don't have visitors often, and this room isn't set up for anyone but me." He crossed his legs. "So, how can I help you?"

Veronica dug through her backpack and pulled out the paperwork.

"I came to Minneapolis to find out what happened to my mother." She spoke over the rattling of papers. "She was a researcher around the time the Minnesota Chapter was running in Minneapolis." She looked at Sean. "From what I was able to find, she worked alongside you and my father was the Region Leader. We believe her last assignment was to track a Deamhan by the name of Lucius."

"Yes, I do remember your mother and your father." His answer was quick. "But I'm afraid I can't recall what her last assignment was since the Region Leaders were the only ones who handed out the assignments."

"Do you know anything about Lucius?" she asked. "Lambert, the vampire owner of Dark Sepulcher, told me a few things but I can't confirm what he told me since I can't find anything on him from The Brotherhood."

Nathan's eyes locked onto the files in Sean's lap. "Of course you won't. They're really good at hiding secrets." He shifted his body onto his left side with his legs still crossed. "There were many members in those days that came in and out of Minneapolis and there were many Deamhan as well. At that time Lucius was the head Deamhan in the city— that I do remember." He eyed Sean. "Are you a researcher?"

Veronica looked at Sean, who didn't seem fazed at Nathan's question. Sean kept his posture, and his answer was quick. "No, not anymore."

Mr. Tiernan looked to Veronica.

"No, I never was," she answered. "I was raised around it, and my father is now the President of the Midwest Region."

Nathan sat upright, uncrossing his legs. A slight hint of a smile appeared on his face. "You remind me of your mother. She was a determined woman, always searching for the truth." He leaned back in his chair and continued. "She was also really protective of her family, more than your father." He grabbed the mug from the table and stood up from his chair. "Along with your mother, I openly questioned what your father was doing at that time, Veronica. Things were hectic and the environment unsafe. Many researchers lost their lives and the Chapter was on the brink of collapse.

"It was Lucius who kept things in order. He managed to control the Deamhan as long as we agreed to not interfere. Afterwards there was a calm period and no issues arose between us and the Deamhan. We were there to watch, to gather information, to understand them from a distance, like our ancestors did. However, your father had his own agenda and priorities." Nathan slowly paced over to his fireplace and leaned on the mantle, his eyes drifting over the files for a moment. "And things turned for the worse."

"What did my father do?"

"That's the problem. I never found out. No one in the Chapter knew until it was too late," Nathan answered. "By then your mother had disappeared and we had been attacked. We were forced to disband the Chapter and to leave the city in fear of our lives."

"But you didn't leave the city. Why?"

"No, I didn't." He sipped from his coffee mug. "Your father had me ejected from The Brotherhood and my parents, who had dedicated their lives to the organization, were cast out as well." He placed his coffee mug on the mantel of the fireplace. "But I can't say that I didn't see it coming."

"If you didn't know what was happening, why would my father cast you out of the organization?"

"History," Nathan answered. "Your family and my family have squabbled for power in The Brotherhood for generations. We are the only two families who never got along." He closed his eyes in thought. "The Dearhorn family stood on the side of the Austin family and the Pavel family stood on my family's side."

Veronica stared into the fire, caught in its hypnotic flare. It was the first time she'd heard of the conflicts between the families in The Brotherhood. There were so many questions and so many thoughts about what Nathan could reveal. She didn't know where to start.

"Hey," Sean whispered to her. "Are you okay?"

"Yeah." She nodded, snapping herself from her vertigo daze. "Yeah, I'm—I'm fine." She looked at Nathan. "My father never told me anything about this but that's not a surprise."

"I'm sorry that you have to hear it from me," Nathan replied. "After I was ejected from The Brotherhood I decided to stay in Minneapolis and further research the Deamhan on my own."

"Did you happen to find out what happened to Lucius?"

Nathan closed his eyes for a moment. "Lucius Valerius Pulcher. That was his birth name."

Veronica quickly glanced at Sean, who looked back with a confused stare. "His real name?"

"Yes," Nathan answered. "He's an old Deamhan; an Ancient is what they call them—Deamhan who are over a thousand years old. He was an avid follower of their Dictum and he believed in coexistence between humans, Deamhans, and vampires. It wasn't a popular stance among his own kind."

"Lambert told me that the Chapter was involved in his disappearance," Veronica asked. "Is that true?"

Nathan nodded. "Yes, and that Lucius was possibly killed by his consort. No one knows what happened to him. After he disappeared his consort, Kei, placed himself as leader in the city. Since then, the Deamhan have been out of control, killing each other, and burning sanctuaries."

Nathan walked toward the middle of the room and he stood in front of them. "I've been watching and documenting the Deamhan from my own home here. Those in support of Lucius are fighting against those in support of Kei."

"And where do you stand?" Sean asked.

Nathan paused before replying. "My stance is not important."

"But you live with Deamhan here."

Nathan nodded. "And their stance is not of my concern. However, Lambert seems to be more vocal when it comes to Kei."

The smell of hazelnut coffee drifted past Veronica's nose. "I could tell. When we spoke, I had the feeling that he didn't like Kei and he didn't like The Brotherhood."

"And he never will," Nathan answered. "Lambert has lived in Minneapolis for a long time. He is like the head vampire in the city. Most vampires shy away from the Deamhan but he has somehow found a way to incorporate them and tolerate them."

"And you want to go back to Dark Sepulcher?" Sean whispered to Veronica.

Ignoring his comment, Veronica continued to question. "Do you know where I could find Kei?"

"I don't." Again Nathan's response was quick.

Veronica glanced at Sean. Their eyes met. He probably had the same questions flopping through his brain.

"Do you know anyone who might know where he is?" She slowly turned back to Nathan. She watched Nathan fold his arms and exhale. His body language suggested that he wasn't thrilled about Kei, like Lambert.

"You don't want to look for him, Veronica." Nathan stepped in front of the glow from his fireplace. "You don't want to find him."

It was the same reply Lambert had given her at Dark Sepulcher. Instead of scaring her, it fueled her curiosity.

"Kei isn't known for his hospitality," Nathan added. "He is and has always been dangerous." Nathan clasped his hands together. His body language immediately changed from being open and inclined to being uncomfortable and unsettled. He stared past them, his eyes glassy and nervous. "He will kill you or anyone he thinks is a threat to him. He's killed humans, researchers, and Deamhan."

"He's the only one that knows what happened to Lucius and my mother was researching him around that time, then maybe he knows what happened to her as well?"

Sean reached over to Veronica. "It's not a good idea, Veronica." He lowered his voice. "You heard the man; he's dangerous."

"Eh." She snarled at him. "How ironic."

Sean pulled his hand back. "Veronica, please."

"It's not like I can find Lucius without him," Veronica raised her voice, getting Nathan's attention.

"Kei isn't hard to find." Nathan's eyes slowly followed a mosaic pattern of the Roman Goddess, Ceres, surrounded by pieces of fruit, on the floor of his study. "It's just that no one bothers to seek him out, especially a human. If a Deamhan like Kei can easily rid himself of his own sire, someone as old as Lucius—" He didn't finish his statement. Instead, he returned to Veronica. "Imagine what he could do to someone like you, Veronica."

"If I could find Lucius without Kei, I would, but I need to find out about my mother and what happened to her."

Nathan rubbed his chin. "Lambert was right. You're very determined."

"Damn right." Veronica held her head high. "Deamhan don't scare me." She spoke against her feelings. The Deamhan did scare her but her desire for the truth weighed more on her apperception. A glimpse of her father resonated in Nathan. He had the same attributes that most researchers learned from the organization, including Sean. He didn't take flak from anyone. He paid attention to her detailed statements. Many researchers from his time had to be. With Veronica's father sitting in an influential position, she understood his signs of caution.

"If it helps, I can look through some of my research I've accumulated over the years." Nathan's eyes drifted to the marble ceiling. "I might find something that can help you."

"Yes, that would help me a lot."

Nathan blinked and refocused his attention back toward them. "If you would like, we could meet tomorrow again to discuss these things."

"So you'll help her?" Sean asked.

"I can try."

"Tomorrow?"

Nathan nodded. "Yes, tomorrow at Dark Sepulcher."

Veronica's ebullient feeling halted when the words "Dark Sepulcher" exited his mouth. "I can't go back to Dark Sepulcher," she said in a panic.

"I'll talk to Lambert." He smiled. "I'll ease his worries about you."

"You have pull like that?"

"I wouldn't call it pull, Miss Austin. More like a favor." He reached out his hand, a gesture to end their conversation. "Tomorrow. A little after sunset."

Sean stood up without questioning and shook his hand. "Thank you for your time."

Veronica also stood up, surprised at Sean's quick submission to end the conversation. Nathan led them out from his study and to the front door.

"I will do all that I can." He opened the door, letting the brisk cold air into the foyer.

"Thank you again, Nathan," Sean spoke up. At that moment, Veronica felt a sudden glance from above. She looked up. A woman with medium black hair and strong brown eyes glared down at them from the balcony. Her stern and organized gaze made Veronica pause for a brief moment, causing Sean to look up as well.

She knew the woman was a Deamhan but who she was became a question for another day. The feeling of superiority and the sense that she didn't want them there at Blind Bluff Manor, oozed from the woman's pores. Her eyes, now pinpointed directly at her, scowled at them. The woman placed her hands on the balcony as if preparing to jump and squash them both under her feet. Nathan looked up at her, then back to them.

"Stay safe out there." Nathan looked back at them.

"Yes." Veronica agreed again to their future meeting. She glanced up one more time at the balcony, but the woman had vanished. They walked out into the cold and approached the taxi.

"Veronica, you seriously aren't thinking about going back to Dark Sepulcher," Sean said, pleading to no avail.

"Don't tell me what I can and can't do." She opened the taxi door. "I'm going. End of story."

"Do you really believe him?"

"I don't know, Sean. What I do know is that he's shown me that I can trust him. Something that you, my friend, haven't done." She looked back at the mansion one last time.

"Well I'm going with you, then."

"You can't. They'll read your thoughts before you even enter. Besides, I don't think my father would want you to."

"Don't." Sean sternly objected.

"No, I will. I don't know any more, Sean. I don't know what side you're on."

"I'm on yours."

"Sure." Veronica huffed.

* * * *

Nathan closed the door, and the silence of his sanctuary returned. He watched the taxi drive off his property and disappear down the road.

He remembered the day Caroline Austin disappeared. It happened to be on the same day Veronica's father ejected him from The Brotherhood. By that time, the stability of the Chapter edged toward breakdown. Lucius made it clear about how he felt when it came to The Brotherhood being in the city. He didn't like it at all but that threat didn't make Veronica's father budge. He insisted that if The Brotherhood ran from every threat, there would be no Brotherhood.

Lucius went out of his way to avoid violence. For a Deamhan his age, he'd somehow relearned the human trait of negotiation. Under his reign, researchers remained protected as long as they remained out of Deamhan affairs.

But it didn't last long.

In line to become the President of the Midwest Region at that time, Mr. Austin ignored Lucius' simple demands and his wife suddenly became the outspoken figure of her husband's undoing. She followed and researched on Lucius against his wishes, and when she finally came face to face with this dangerous Deamhan and survived, Samuel Austin had seen enough.

Nathan heard her footsteps behind him, and he didn't take notice. If the Deamhan he allowed to stay at Blind Bluff Manor wanted to creep up on him, they could easily do so.

"Lambert explained her situation." He chose not to face the female Deamhan.

The figure stood behind him. He felt her stare on the back of his neck and he assumed her quietness was due to her attempt to listen to his heartbeat.

"Even if she is protected, it won't stop Kei or anyone who cares less, for that matter." The female Ramanga stood next to him. She stared into his face and spoke within his mind.

Your blood is racing.

"I'm concerned for her safety, Anastasia. That's all."

The male's scent was nauseating.

"You know I prefer speaking than telepathy."

Anastasia nodded. "The male can't be trusted. He's a researcher."

"I know." Nathan referred to Sean. He looked at her, the old and sometimes calmed Anastasia. Her gloomy and bewitching presence still made him agitated but her awe-inspiring beauty made up for it. He trusted her, even if her nature called for her to turn on him without warning. He never forgot his status among the Deamhan who stayed with him in his home; her, Remy, and Hallie. But he

127

trusted her judgment—if he could call it that.

"He is spying on her," she stated. "I tried to read his thoughts but he blocked them from me. But her thoughts were opened to me. She isn't a researcher. What she says about looking for her mother is true."

Nathan licked his lips and blinked his eyes slowly. "Did you pick up anything about The Brotherhood coming back to Minneapolis?"

"Yes, they're making their way back to the city."

"Well, let the games begin." Nothing he could do would change the fact that old organization was coming back to the city.

"I can kill him, the researcher."

"No." Nathan folded his arms across his chest. He always contemplated what would happen if The Brotherhood came back. How would the Deamhan react? What would the vampires do?

"They'll interfere again." Anastasia read his thoughts.

"Killing Sean won't stop them from coming back," he replied. "Plus you know how I feel about killing. I don't tolerate that in my home."

Anastasia scrunched her lower lip. "Even if the female is protected and not to be touched by the Deamhan and the vampires, Kei will still try to kill her if she searches for him. You can't save her. You can't stop that."

"I know." Nathan walked toward his study room. "But I can try, Anastasia. I can try."

CHAPTER SIXTEEN

Sean and Veronica remained quiet on the drive back to Minneapolis, their eyes concentrated on the scenery rather than talking about what she planned to do. During the drive Veronica glanced over at Sean wiping the condensation from the windows.

They thanked the taxi driver for dropping them off in front of the apartment building.

Only when they stood in the foyer at Palm Oaks did Sean make his first comment.

"I don't think you can trust him."

"Coming from someone who I thought I could trust? Really, Sean?" Veronica walked up the stairs and he followed. They reached the front door of her apartment.

"Veronica, I don't know how many times I have to say sorry."

"As many times as it takes." She fumbled with her keys.

"I'm sorry then." Sean shrugged his shoulders. "I'm sorry. I'm sorry." He dropped to his knees. "I'm sorry. I'm sorry."

"Get up." Veronica shook her head. She watched him stand to his feet. She couldn't stay pissed off at him forever, even though she didn't mind the feeling. She knew eventually she'd have to get over it. Sean risked his position in the organization just by telling her and going with her to Blind Bluff Manor.

"Veronica, I mean it. I'm sorry."

"I know." She exhaled. "But you have to understand where I'm coming from, Sean."

"I do."

"So you know why I have to go to Dark Sepulcher . . . alone."

He looked at her uncertainly. Veronica didn't know either, but she wasn't ready to give up, just yet. She anxiously wanted to meet with Nathan again to find out what more information he knew. They heard Murphy's door slowly open.

"Hey, Veronica." Murphy's eyes moved to Sean. "Hey, man, what's up?"

"Hey, Murphy." Veronica managed to find the right key, gently placing it into the lock.

"Are you still up for tonight?" He opened his door further.

Veronica had forgotten again.

She caught herself, careful not to trip over any words she was about to exert. He stood in his doorway, revealing his new look. He had cut his black hair short into a buzz cut. He straightened his silver silk shirt and swiped the lint off his ironed blue jeans. His dark dress shoes gleamed in the dim light of the hallway. He looked like a corporate hedgehog than anything.

"Tonight." Veronica nodded. She turned the key, unlocking the door and watching Sean, who wasn't worried about her predicament, walk into the living room.

"Yeah, I'm still up for tonight. Um, what time did we agree on?"

"We didn't really agree on a time. Maybe seven or eight, or whenever you're ready?" Murphy smiled back. "It's only about a quarter to five, but I like to get ready early, anyway."

"All right." She stepped into the apartment. "I'll be over at seven."

"Cool, see ya then."

She slowly closed the door and turned back to Sean. He sat on her couch with his hands nestled behind his head.

"That guy likes you." His snippy comment followed his quick giggle. "Do you like him?"

"I can't believe I almost forgot again." She walked over to the couch.

"Well I can." He moved over, making room for her to sit. "We just came from Nathan's, Veronica. The last thing on your mind would be some date with a college weirdo."

"He's not weird." She defended him. "Well, not really. He's kinda cute."

"No, he's weird," he repeated. "Oh come on, the guy seems to always know when you come home. Every time you take out your keys to get into your apartment, he's right there, opening his door, trying to make conversation. That's a weirdo." Sean smiled. "Or a stalker."

"That's not funny." She jokingly slapped him on his arm.

"I'm not trying to be funny. I'm just stating the obvious facts."

He placed his arm around her and carefully kissed her forehead. "Are you gonna go?"

"Yeah."

"You sure?"

"Yeah, I need a break."

"Well, I'll be here when you get back. I might even raid your kitchen, if I manage to gather enough energy to do so." He leaned his head back, staring at the ceiling. "If you want, you can call me or message me if your date ends up being horrific."

Veronica jokingly slapped him again, on his chest, making him flinch. "You're bad." She looked up at him as he sniggered.

"Yeah, I know, Veronica." The smile disappeared from his face, replaced by a worried stare. "Yeah, I know." He swallowed. "If you want, I can also email Kenneth and lie and let him know that you've turned your search toward the sanctuary fires."

Veronica smiled briefly at Sean's attempt to mend their friendship. This time she didn't think twice about trusting him. She hoped, for his sake, that he'd follow through.

"Yeah, that'd work," she replied. "That should get them off your back for a day or so."

Sean nodded. "I was supposed to check in a hotel instead of staying here. I think they're onto me already."

* * * *

Sean remained on the couch with his head tilted to the ceiling. He couldn't sleep, nor did he want to. There was too much commotion occurring on the street below. Groups of drunken teens walked by Palm Oaks, screaming at one another in mid conversation. The noise of a police siren in the distance was followed by the blaring horn of a fire truck.

When the noises finally subsided, the apartment went silent. He didn't bother to turn on the television or browse the internet. He had to do something to make things right between himself and Veronica. He didn't know what that was, just yet. He knew how to start it. He could explain everything to her from here on out; no lies. But fearing what The Brotherhood would do to him stopped him. It was a no-no to disobey rules, and it meant being ejected from the organization. Or worse. Sure, he was told of researchers who disappeared after being caught but he assumed they were kicked out after being reprimanded. But what if something worse had happened to them? It was a question that plagued his mind.

His cell phone buzzed, and he instantly sprung to his feet. His phone beeped with an incoming text message from Kenneth. The message read "Bar 69" followed by x's and o's. He was not prepared.

Sean pulled out a small piece of paper from his briefcase and scribbled one simple line, just enough so that Veronica would finally know the truth. He wanted to write more, to tell her that if he didn't return or didn't contact her in a few days, then something horrible had happened to him. He didn't expect any sympathy from her, and he also wasn't expecting her to forgive him that easily.

He grabbed his briefcase, his laptop, and his jacket. He looked around Veronica's apartment for a sharp wooden object, thinking maybe she had an extra stake hidden underneath the couch cushions. Unable to find anything, he grabbed a knife from the kitchen and without looking back, he left her apartment and walked down the street toward the bar.

During his walk, he played the upcoming scenario in his mind. He expected Kenneth to be at the bar, with researchers in tow. Kenneth would question why he refused to obey Mr. Austin's orders by escorting Veronica to Blind Bluff Manor, by refusing to leave her apartment and check into the Gathewait Hotel, and obtaining more documents. Then Kenneth would blurt out what part of The Brotherhood oath Sean had broken, to be taken off his assignment, the researchers would surround him, and escort him back to their hotel to be processed before being put on a plane back to San Diego. But Sean already decided that he wasn't going to go willingly, which would make the meeting less than joyous.

Breaking The Brotherhood oath was the lowest level any researcher could achieve. However, it was also the easiest thing to accomplish as a researcher. Just by saying "no" meant risking any advancement in the organization. Sean knew at an early age that he'd break at least the oath, "to follow and obey the commands of your superiors under all costs," but what sane human being would follow any orders so blindly?

Question authority. That was one law that he held dear to his heart.

Sean also didn't understand why Kenneth chose the bar rather than their hotel room for this meeting. A bar wasn't a typical Brotherhood meeting place, especially in a city teeming with Deamhan. Sean reached into the pocket of his jeans to double check the knife. The dull blade ran against his fingers but he hoped it wouldn't fail him if he needed it for protection. He crossed the street at a busy intersection, near a group of teenagers at a bus shelter, frolicking on their skateboards. He passed them and whispered a muted greeting but they didn't answer back.

He approached the bar and slowly reached for the door handle. He opened the door, hearing the sound of a football game blaring over the muted sound of music coming from the juke box. Stacked chairs lined the walls of the empty bar. His nose caught the weak odor of old beer. Near the back bar, he heard pool balls clashing together and Kenneth's voice welcoming him in.

Kenneth's smile grew wide and it made Sean uneasy. His attire consisted of a black trench coat, black turtle neck sweater, and black pants—trademark clothing for field researchers. Sean quickly and cautiously scanned the area, expecting that Veronica's father sent researchers with him, but he didn't see anyone else around except for the bartender watching a football game on television.

"Your outfit just screams Brotherhood." Sean stood next to the pool table.

Kenneth glanced over his clothing. He grabbed a pool stick and reached for a stack of quarters neatly placed on the edge of the pool table. "I just finished a game. You want in?"

Sean sneered. Even in a city filled with Deamhan, Kenneth's demeanor gave off an odor of self-worthiness. The way he carried himself, the way he smiled, the way he popped the quarters into the slots on the side of the pool table, the way he positioned the balls in the triangle—it annoyed Sean. He didn't see why Mr. Austin placed trust in a person whose only care in the world evolved around sucking up to superiors to move ahead in the world and who wore different shades of black clothing, to emphasis his status as a researcher.

"I didn't expect you to come to Minneapolis so soon."

"It wasn't the plan. But a few inconsistencies and issues surrounding your assignment worried Mr. Austin at the last minute." Kenneth smiled at the position of the triangle on the pool table. He removed the triangle and tossed it to the side. "Like taking his daughter to Blind Bluff Manor."

Sean swallowed hard. "Like I told Mr. Austin before I left. His daughter isn't easy to influence."

"And like Mr. Austin said, that's where your expertise comes into play," Kenneth rudely replied back.

"How long did you think she'd believe the whole 'sanctuary fires might be the problem for everything' scenario?" Sean responded. "The girl's smarter than that."

Kenneth sharpened his pool stick and took aim. "Yes, but she's also determined and easy to influence." He released his grip and Sean watched the balls swirl around the table with one ball heading toward the right corner pocket. "That's why you were chosen for this assignment, Sean," Kenneth explained as he walked around the pool table. "And it was a simple assignment really."

"You call this an assignment?"

"Yes, I do." Kenneth walked around Sean to the other side of the table and positioned himself for the next shot. "As a Brotherhood member, it's not your call to question." He took aim again and watched another ball ease its way into the side pocket. "You do the job that's assigned to you."

"I didn't want this job or the assignment."

Kenneth placed the pool stick on the table. "This game is boring. I don't see why anyone likes pool." He looked up at Sean. "Tell me, what did Nathan Tiernan tell you when you went to Blind Bluff Manor?"

Sean paused. They knew about Nathan and his sanctuary. If he told Kenneth everything, it would jeopardize Veronica's search and he didn't want to fail her again. He had to choose his next words carefully.

Sean let out an annoying sigh. "Nothing we didn't already knew."

"Are you lying to me, Sean?" Kenneth shook his head. "Because lying to your new Region Leader is strictly forbidden and goes against the oath you took years ago."

Sean breathed in deeply. "Like I said. Nothing we didn't already knew."

Kenneth shrugged and continued his assault. "Mr. Austin is not happy with your poor and miserable performance. You've failed him, your sisters, and brothers in The Brotherhood. Not to mention, you were given the simple task to check into the hotel on Hennepin Avenue and you decided to ignore that and still stay at her apartment." He clapped his hands together. "I'm afraid, Sean that your mission will end here and now. You are ordered to go back to San Diego where you will be reprimanded in front of a Brotherhood court of your peers, who will then decide on what punishment to give you."

"Bullshit," Sean hastily replied. "I'm not going anywhere." The snippy remark quickly wiped the grin from Kenneth's face.

"Are you choosing to disobey Mr. Austin's orders again?" Kenneth asked sternly.

"She needs me here and she wants me here. I'm not leaving, Kenneth."

A devilish smiled appeared on Kenneth's face as he walked toward Sean. "Be careful, Sean."

Sean felt Kenneth's hot breath on his skin and said, "She knows about Lucius." He watched Kenneth's brow shrink and his eyes squint. "And she knows about Kei and how her father was involved in Lucius' disappearance."

Kenneth huffed. "You are stupid to believe the stories of a defected researcher."

"I'm out of The Brotherhood. I'm done." Sean turned to walk away. "And you can tell Mr. Austin that I refuse to be a lab rat for The Brotherhood." His heart began to pace and he placed his hands in his pocket, rubbing over the small knife's blade. He turned and walked toward the door, smiling. Pressure lifted slightly from his chest, and for the first time in his life, he felt free to do whatever he wanted. No more rules, no more lying to Veronica, and no more kissing ass to the upper ranks of The Brotherhood. He couldn't wait to tell Veronica the news, and he couldn't wait to apologize for the false information he'd given her.

He reached for the handle on the front door when it flew open, almost slamming into his face. He felt a cold grip around his throat that held him firmly. He looked up into the face of a pale woman with reddish hair. A wide grin extended on her face from cheek to cheek. With force, she pushed him back and tightened her grip.

Sean grabbed the knife in his pocket and yanked it out. He swung at her, and she grabbed onto his wrist. Pain shot through his hand, and he quickly dropped the knife to the ground. He felt the grip around his throat tighten. He heard Kenneth's execrable laughter behind him. The red haired woman lifted him with ease and slammed his body onto the pool table. A burning sensation shot through Sean's back and he screamed, feeling each and every pool ball digging into his back. The bartender turned to look and quickly lowered the volume on his television.

"You're not going anywhere." Kenneth leaned over Sean.

Sean looked into the woman's dancing green eyes that slowly transformed into the color black. Her grin didn't reveal the sharp teeth of a Ramanga, yet her strength matched that of a Deamhan.

"Let me go!" Sean said in between exasperated breaths but the Deamhan woman didn't budge.

"Shut up," the female Deamhan said in a whisper.

Sean attempted to raise himself, but the woman forced him back. His skin underneath her grasp began to grow numb and Sean struggled again to break free. The tingling sensation extended to his face and to his shoulders. His arms and his legs went limp, and his eyelids grew heavy.

"I need him alive." Kenneth turned to the Deamhan woman. "Not dead."

Suddenly the numbing ceased. She was a Lugat Deamhan, just like Lucius.

"Hey." They heard the bartender's voice behind them. The woman slowly released her grip from Sean's neck and turned around.

"Get the fuck out of here before I call the cops," he threatened. Sean watched helplessly as the woman reached for a pool stick and without any effort, she thrust the end into the bartender's stomach. His eyes bulged, and he wrapped his arm around the pool stick. Blood poured from his mouth, and he struggled to stay on his feet before falling to the floor.

Sean raised himself from the pool table, watching the bartender's final movements in shock. Afterwards, the female Deamhan kicked the corpse.

"What? You're going to kill me now?" Sean slowly backed away from her. She spun back around in Deamhan speed, reaching for him but when Kenneth quickly raised his hand, she stopped in mid movement.

"For your own safety, Sean, I suggest you don't fight." Kenneth straightened his jacket. He stepped over the bartender's body and walked toward the door.

The Lugat pushed Sean forward and he slowly followed Kenneth. His eyes wandered, looking for anything he could use to escape. At the same time, he struggled with keeping his thoughts hidden.

What Nathan said to him about The Brotherhood working with the Deamhan came back to him. Deamhan didn't work for humans. They hated The Brotherhood. Yet, here was a Lugat, following Kenneth's orders. What more was The Brotherhood hiding from researchers like himself, who were trained to not trust the Deamhan *ever*?

"You will take care of the body?" Kenneth spoke to the woman as he slowly opened the door.

She nodded.

"Oh and don't kill him," Kenneth added. "Mr. Austin needs him alive."

135

CHAPTER SEVENTEEN

The Surge restaurant proudly held the title "Best Seafood" restaurant in Minneapolis. Customers chose their crabs from an elongated fish tank set up in the foyer of the building. Seafood wasn't Veronica's first choice, but she couldn't persuade Murphy from not going.

Murphy told her it was the best place in Minneapolis to eat. Besides seafood, they had the best salads, lobsters, clam chowder, and buffalo wings on this side of the Mississippi.

But during dinner her mind wandered. She no longer wanted to wait or talk. The thought of meeting Nathan at Dark Sepulcher excited her to the point that she became restless. Going back also meant that Lambert would bombard her with more meddling questions about The Brotherhood and her father.

Murphy rambled about his family again, his interests, and his life. His father was a retired electrician living comfortably off his 401K in Pennsylvania. His brother was married with two kids and worked at a law firm in Florida. However, when he spoke about his mother, Veronica couldn't help notice that she retired as a teacher and died just recently after a three year battle with ovarian cancer. Before, after they'd left Dark Sepulcher days ago, he told her she was a receptionist.

She didn't question his mistake but she kept note of it. After dinner he drove her home and told her about his uncle Charlie who won the lottery and spent his winnings on Star Trek collector items and old vintage wear from the 1920s.

Once in her apartment, she felt relieved, but her disburden was short lived when she saw Sean's note.

In a scribbled line he wrote: "If not back, don't worry about me."

Sean had taken all his belongings, only leaving the files he'd stolen from The Brotherhood. Confused and angry about why he'd left, she suspected that The Brotherhood coming back to Minneapolis had something to do with it. She tossed the note in the trash and walked back to her couch. She gathered The Brotherhood papers in a pile and waited for the night.

When night finally came, she headed for Dark Sepulcher.

The bouncer immediately recognized her before she approached the door.

136

He didn't bother to check her ID. Instead he stepped aside to let her in. The cashier nodded at her and pointed to the black curtains.

Again Veronica found the club crammed full with Deamhan, vampires, and humans. The way the crowds danced in harmonic rhythms to the music reminded her of ancient Dionysian cults. She straightened her black blouse and her dark blue jeans and walked toward the back.

Out of nowhere she heard a male voice inside her head call out to her.

To her right she saw Remy sitting in a maroon-colored booth with a dark haired female. The female took a sip from her glass and giggled while his cold hand gently rubbed the side of her face. His brown eyes didn't blink while he stared at Veronica. He wrapped his right hand around the dark curls in the female's hair.

"You actually came." Remy moved to the outer edge of the booth. He stood up, straightening his long, black shirt that he wore with his black jeans. He swiped his brown hair back. "I didn't think you had it in you to come back." He spoke loud enough over the music for Veronica to hear. "But here you are." He approached her. "And my, my, don't you look lovely."

Veronica blocked her thoughts. "I'm here." She cradled The Brotherhood files, in hopes that he wouldn't notice them, but he did.

"You brought presents?" he asked.

The female in the booth let out a whimper and Remy quickly turned around. "I'll deal with you in a minute." He then turned back to Veronica.

"Don't let me disturb you from your dinner." Veronica turned.

Remy's cold hand clasped onto her wrists, halting her in her tracks. "Nonsense." He raised his hand to her cheek. "She's just a little midnight snack."

Veronica removed his hand. She turned around but Alexis now stood in her way. Her sudden entrance stunned Veronica, making her feel caught in the middle . . . just like last time.

"Welcome back." Alexis placed her hands on her hips and her eyes darted to Remy. "I hope this little flea didn't frighten you."

Veronica stepped aside. If they wanted to see who could out stare each other, they could do so without her standing in the way.

"This feels familiar." Remy smiled. "Just like the first time you came to Dark Sepulcher, Veronica, except that Alexis isn't forcing her sluttish persuasion."

"Yes, but this time you're not part of the conversation." Alexis pointed to the dark haired female sitting in the booth. "And this time, Deamhan, make sure you dispose of your food in a more disguised manner."

Remy laughed gently, then nodded. "Tell Lambert not to worry. I won't place that burden on his vampire bodyguards this time."

Alexis waved at Veronica to follow her to the door and up the stairs to Lambert's quarters.

This time the walk felt shorter to Veronica. She didn't pay much attention to the stairs and the hallway. Instead her fingertips tingled at the mere thought of meeting Nathan and Lambert. When Alexis opened the door she saw them sitting across from each other on couches centered in the middle of the room.

She cautiously walked in. When Alexis slammed the door shut behind her, she jumped at the noise.

Lambert slowly motioned for Veronica to sit next to him. To Veronica, he looked more relaxed than the last time. She believed that whatever Nathan said to him before she arrived calmed him enough to tolerate her. Still gripping The Brotherhood papers, she sat next to Nathan.

"I see you came prepared." Lambert placed his hand over his chest. He wore his brown hair in his signature ponytail. His mouth remained opened, stuck in mid-sentence. The room fell into a moment of silence. Nathan uncrossed his legs and glanced at her with a smile of encouragement.

Lambert pushed the bowl of grapes sitting on the coffee table toward her.

"No, thank you," Veronica said. She dropped her guard, losing her concentration. Vampires couldn't read human thoughts, not as easily as Deamhan could. She relaxed.

"I'm glad you were able to make it safely," Nathan said. His conservative outfit consisting of a gray casual suit with a white shirt underneath, seemed unusual to what she thought Nathan would usually wear.

"We were just discussing the differences between the Ramanga and vampires," Lambert said. "I personally believe that behavior is the major and only important difference between them. The typical Ramanga Deamhan tends to be pitiless and homicidal, while vampires tend to have a much calmer way of feeding. What do you think, Veronica?"

Veronica shrugged, uninterested in his question. To her, the Ramanga and the vampire were pitiless and homicidal; their names being the only difference.

Nathan slowly slouched back into the couch, revisiting his comfortable position.

Lambert continued. "And you can kill a vampire easier than you can kill a Deamhan."

"Some vampire historians claim that vampires have their age on their side," Nathan added, "and that they've existed longer on earth."

There were many types, different types of the undead that Veronica knew about. Besides vampires and the Deamhan, there were demons, half demons and even vampire and werewolf mixed breeds. But as far as she knew, The Brotherhood wasn't interested in researching their kind.

"My own maker was older than dirt when he made me vampire." Lambert crossed his hands. "She was a true beauty back then. Pity that I can only remember brief images of our time together before she abandoned me on an Italian beach."

Veronica wanted to question Lambert about his sire but that wasn't the information she wanted to know. Not yet anyway.

Lambert turned to Veronica and he spoke slowly. "What do you think?"

"I've never researched vampires," she answered. "So I don't know."

"What about your researcher friend? Perhaps he knows?"

Veronica shook her head. *Here he goes again; about Sean.* She didn't play into it.

"Veronica"—Nathan held up his hand to respond—"there's something you need to know about Sean."

"I'm sure she knows he's a researcher," Lambert interrupted.

"He's not a threat to me or to any of you." She raised her voice slightly.

"They're always a threat, my dear." Lambert snickered. "You told me you had no affiliation with The Brotherhood but your friend Sean is a member, which makes you an affiliate."

Nathan cleared his throat and Lambert stopped his attack. For the first time Veronica witnessed Lambert's respect for Nathan. Like Deamhan, vampires showed it in crazier ways (murder being one of them.)

Nathan spoke up. "I was once an affiliate, Lambert. So according to your logic, I'm a threat."

"Stop trying to turn Veronica into a harmless human," Lambert interrupted him. "You know this is vastly different."

Veronica felt her breathing increase. If Lambert already knew about Sean, what else did he know? She decided to back off from her defense. "He was my connection in The Brotherhood, Lambert, but he left. I don't know where he is now."

Nathan exhaled slowly. "Lambert is partially correct, Veronica. Your friend may not be as trustworthy as you think. He's working for your father."

Veronica didn't want to show that she already knew Sean's true reason for being in Minneapolis. She dropped the papers on the table. The bowl of grapes bounced gently to the side. She forced herself to exhale, and she looked to the floor. Her act was a lie and she was a fabulous actress.

She sifted through the paperwork page by page until she came across the documentation on Lambert. Like the other information, the heavily inundated markings made it somewhat hard to read. She skimmed through what wasn't blackened out, cursing under her breath that she should've done this before, the moment Sean gave them to her.

"Here." She tossed it into his lap. "This is what my affiliation with Sean was able to provide."

Lambert slowly lifted the paper to his line of vision and he began to read.

"Brotherhood files?" Nathan asked.

"I'm flattered. They actually have an interest in me." Lambert skimmed over the information.

"Are all of them blacked out like this?" Nathan asked.

"Yes," Lambert crudely answered for Veronica. He held one piece up close to get a better view. "This is nothing." He placed the papers back on the table.

"Should I be surprised about this?"

Veronica stared at the documents on the table, thinking. The idea that The Brotherhood somehow came back into Minneapolis devoured whatever positive thoughts she had left of Sean. They overwhelmed her. Her breathing increased, and her stomach twitched.

Lambert gently pushed the bowl of grapes closer to Nathan with his foot.

"Hungry?" He pointed to the grapes. Nathan grabbed a grape and popped it in his mouth.

"Eating is the one thing I miss about being human." A caricature smile appeared on Lambert's face, revealing his fangs. "Grapes were my favorite food to eat when I was human."

"I'm sure I wasn't invited her to talk about grapes." Veronica's bold statement silenced Lambert's fluffy thought.

Suddenly the tension overcoming the room became gut-wrenching.

She felt the blame, and it made her want to lash out, to clench her teeth and exert her anger by punching at random walls. This blame would never stop. Her thoughts gravitated to her father. He pushed Sean into spying on her, if it was true. Nothing in that organization happened without his say. Sean turned into an expendable researcher. She wasn't going to let her father win, even if she had to endure Lambert's pithy comments and his lack of trust.

"You do know you are protected." Nathan leaned over to her.

"I've heard, but I don't know what that means. What does it mean?" she questioned in an untroubled voice.

"It means that somewhere, out there, a Deamhan has claimed you," Lambert answered. "And no one can harm or kill you." He didn't stray from his skepticism or from his continuing comments. "Oh, the pressure of being related to the Midwest Region Leader." He began to mock her. "It's just enough to make me heave up the blood I devoured earlier."

"Only a Deamhan with power and age on their side could give out an order like that," Nathan added.

Veronica thought about the mysterious woman she saw at the burnt home, the van, and the two Deamhan twins. Maybe it was Kei? Apparently not every Deamhan obeyed this order. She grabbed the pieces of paper on Blind Bluff Manor and handed it over to Nathan. He accepted the paperwork and slowly went through it page by page.

"Sometimes you have to play along with Lambert's comments." Nathan witticism appeared to finally cease the tension.

"Yes, yes, yes, ignore poor miserable Lambert." Lambert motioned Nathan's remark away by flicking his wrist. "I'm the vampire who doesn't know anything, even if I've been around longer than most."

"My old friend," Nathan replied. "Your advice is always appreciated and needed."

"Well, my advice for Veronica is to give up her search," Lambert said. "Go back to your father and forget coming to Minneapolis."

Veronica remained quiet and listened.

"It doesn't help that you're the daughter of a man in a high position in The Brotherhood." Lambert shook his head. "It's a stamp of disapproval. And now you want to find Kei? Oh, how the turns keep turning."

"It's crossed my mind," Veronica replied. "Unlike you, I'm not scared of him."

"You say that now." Lambert laughed openly.

"My mother was assigned to research Lucius. She went missing when he went missing. Lucius sired Kei and Kei is involved in his sire's disappearance. Why wouldn't I *not* try to find him?"

"Maybe because he's a psychopath?" Lambert answered. "Kei hosts what the Deamhan call a Congregation almost every weekend," Lambert said. "Savage Deamhan fuck fests and feeding sessions mixed with dead and dying humans. If you find the location of his Congregation, you will find him." He smiled deviously. "But humans are never invited, unless they're the main course."

The concept was farfetched. She'd heard about Deamhan Congregations from Sean and other members in The Brotherhood. They were meetings, held in a secret location. It was one of the rarest times when you could find different Deamhan types socializing together without any bloodshed. Ancient Deamhan used these Congregations to go over The Dictum or to call a Decretum. Some Deamhan either sired their loyal minions or killed their un-loyal minions in these meetings. Whatever the case, humans definitely weren't allowed.

"You can't go, Veronica." Lambert turned to Nathan with an enervated look. "And you shouldn't encourage her." He pointed at Nathan. "Your oddball ideas are going to get her killed."

"I'm protected, right?" Veronica replied.

"Yes, but again, that does not mean that every Deamhan will respect that," Nathan answered. "For example, you and Sean were followed to Blind Bluff Manor by a human. By the time I realized that, the human had disappeared. With news of your arrival spreading, any Deamhan with a grudge sees this as an opportunity to get their revenge on The Brotherhood."

Veronica leaned her cheek against her right hand. "There is a woman I've seen twice following me. Once when I first came back here and just recently at the new fire in south Minneapolis."

"A minion." Lambert looked at Nathan. "Probably Kei's minion. Seriously, Nathan," he complained, "you're going to get her killed."

"Lambert," Nathan said, attempting to calm him.

"No, no, Nathan." Lambert stood up from his seat. "I've known you for a long time. You are the only human that I trust. But if you decide to help her, even I can't protect you from the Deamhan who want her dead."

"I wouldn't want you to, Lambert," Nathan replied. "But I understand and respect your decision." He looked to Veronica. "And that's why I brought you here, Veronica. I could've told you this at my own home, but I felt doing it here, in this protected environment, was best."

Veronica squinted. She didn't know what Nathan referred to but she let him continue.

"I understand your need to search for your mother, but you have to understand that you're heading into dangerous territory. You have to think this over carefully, Veronica."

"Is that what you invited me here for?" Veronica reached into her pocket, pulling out her cell phone. "To tell me that I should stop looking?" She watched Nathan and Lambert stare at each other for a moment.

"No one can protect you here, even the Deamhan that claimed you," Nathan continued. "If you go looking for Kei, you're going to get killed."

"I'm not going to just leave," Veronica replied.

"You might not have a choice, my dear," Lambert said.

Veronica flipped her phone open, glaring at the time. She felt her body tense. First Sean, now Nathan. She didn't care what Lambert thought about the situation, but she expected Nathan to at least understand.

"I'm not going to stay where I'm not wanted." Veronica closed her phone and she stood up. "Thank you, Nathan."

"You shouldn't be out there by yourself." Nathan stood up from his seat.

"I'm not some weak girl who can't take care of herself." Veronica ignored Nathan's statement. "I'm not leaving Minneapolis until I find out what happened to my mother."

Nathan looked at Lambert, who sighed and slowly stood up in his chair.

"Fine," Lambert sighed. "But I'm not bringing in any more drama to my dance floor. Having her in my club is enough." He slowly walked over to his miniature bar.

"Veronica, at least stay here until morning," Nathan said.

"I'm fine." Without warning, Veronica promptly headed for the door. She had better things to do than listen to Lambert talk about grapes and complain to her. She needed to know where Sean had run off to. Second, she had to find Kei. Kei was her ticket to Lucius. She sprinted down the hallway, down the stairs and out to the main room.

She walked through the club passing by Remy's booth but he was no longer there. The air grew hot and her desire to be in Dark Sepulcher completely diminished. She stopped and stared at the entryway. Nathan was right about one thing. It wasn't safe for her to be out on the streets at this time of night. But her desire to leave the club clouded her judgment. She couldn't think about what might happen. Like her mother, she had to be brave. She felt Lambert and Nathan staring down at her from above, and she took no notice. She walked toward the entrance and headed outside.

The wind picked up tremendously, scattering trash along the pavement. She turned the corner and walked down the desolate street; her pace slowed. A glaze of frost covered the front windows of the parked cars; overfilled garbage cans sat on the sidewalk, moving slightly left and right from the wind. She heard police sirens in the distance and the sound of a screeching car. The smell of urine fumigated her nose. Her body shivered and goose bumps appeared on her forearms.

Veronica reached for her phone but stopped herself. Why leave Dark Sepulcher just like that? She told herself nothing would get in her way, but she didn't think her own feelings could threaten her search. Both Lambert and Nathan knew more; maybe something that could help her.

She crossed the empty street, turning around to head back to Dark Sepulcher when a cold hand quickly covered her mouth. She felt an arm wrap around her stomach, pulling her from the street to a nearby alley. She struggled against this force, dropping her phone. She kicked her feet and tried to scream. Suddenly the strong force tossed her against the brick wall and she fell to the ground, landing on broken bottles and trash. She felt the sharp stings in her forearm from the embedded fragments of glass shards. Dizziness overcame her and she looked up, struggling to concentrate on who had thrown her like a rag doll.

Someone giggled.

Brandy flicked back her long brown hair, revealing a face that Veronica was all too familiar with. She recognized her immediately as one of the two Deamhan twins who attacked her in the bathroom at Dark Sepulcher a few nights ago. A jagged scar extended from the left top of her forehead, over her closed right eye and to the lower right portion of her jaw. From the indentation, she no longer had a right eye.

"I just love it when I run across a free meal." Brandy slowly knelt down next to Veronica and tilted her head slightly.

Veronica slowly stood up in shock, using the wall for leverage.

"Do you like it?" She pointed to her scar, giggling again. She raised herself up, and the left corner of her mouth slowly curled in a malicious smile. "Well, you should like it." She took a couple of steps back.

Veronica's eyes scoured the dirtied ground for anything she could use against her as a weapon. Brandy jumped forward and Veronica slid back against the wall, feeling a warm trickle of blood draining from her forehead and down the side of her face. Brandy slightly covered her mouth and giggled again. She reached out with her hand and attempted to touch Veronica's face. Her eyes began to twitch, and soon she busted out into a calm whistle.

"Please." Veronica found herself gasping and stuttering.

Brandy wiped the blood from her face. A small throb of pain pierced Veronica's forehead. Veronica searched for the wound and when she found it, she discovered that it was deep and bleeding profusely.

"She killed her." Brandy leaned up against the wall next to her with the same dark and mischievous look her eyes. "That Deamhan bitch killed my sister to save you that night and gave me this nice, little scar." Again, she pointed to the scar on her face. "And these." She revealed her palms covered in rippled and jagged scar tissue.

Veronica didn't know who Brandy referred to. "Please." Veronica felt the corner of the wall against her back.

"Please what?" Brandy grabbed Veronica's wrists, pinning both of them to the wall. "I'm gonna rip you apart." She slightly opened her thin lips. In a slow, shocking appearance, her teeth extended to three times the normal size. They were now sharp and materialized into the pointy teeth of a Ramanga. She moved her arms above her head and re-grasped Veronica's wrists with one hand while the other forced Veronica's head to the side.

"I'm going to drain you into a pretty corpse." Brandy's raspy voice frightened Veronica. "And if you survive, I'm going to do to you what she did to my sister."

"I don't know who you're talking about." Veronica tried unsuccessfully to pull her arms free. Brandy slammed her against the wall again, and Veronica lost her breath for a second. She grabbed Veronica's hair and yanked, throwing whatever strands she managed to tear from Veronica's scalp. Her strength was superior. She moved Veronica as if she weighed absolutely nothing.

"Or I could sire you," Brandy whispered. Veronica flinched, feeling her sharp teeth sinking into her neck. The pressure of her blood being sucked was excruciating. Veronica struggled and scratched, drawing blood from her attacker's face. Her fighting did little, and Brandy refused to let her go. She felt her arms being the first part of her body to succumb. Her strength soon followed, and her legs buckled from under her. She became weaker, paralyzed, and on the verge of passing out.

In an instant, Brandy stopped and loosened her grip. She stared down the alleyway. She cringed, looking back at Veronica then back down the dark alleyway.

"I knew that bitch would come." Brandy released Veronica. Veronica fell, landing on the right side of her body. She had little energy to look up at what made Brandy release her. Her blurred vision made it hard for her to see the shadowy figure at the end of the alleyway. Brandy snarled at the dark figure that didn't respond. It took a step forward and again there was silence.

"Why did you kill her?" Brandy shouted at the figure as it took another step forward. "You were her sire!"

The figure didn't respond. Instead it disappeared in a blurred image only to suddenly reappear feet from them. Veronica heard Brandy gawk as she and the figure began to scuffle, throwing each other into the brick walls. Veronica attempted to raise her body and catch a better glimpse of this Deamhan squabble, but she fell back to the floor. The fight moved too quickly for the human eye to see. They streaked back and forth, crashing into walls and garbage cans. The fight paused long enough for Veronica to witness the dark figure; a female, with her hands on the side of the Brandy's neck. The figure twisted.

Snap!

Brandy's body went limp and the female moved the head aside and gracefully sunk her teeth into the base of Brandy's neck. A considerable amount of blood spurted from the wound followed by the gentle suckling as the figure drank. Veronica focused her eyes. She'd seen this figure before.

The victorious Deamhan leaned her head back, vivaciously licking the remaining blood from her lips. Veronica panted, and her heart pumped frantically.

The woman turned her attention toward her. The white portions of her eyes were exorbitantly blood shot red, and her Ramanga teeth began to retreat to the size of normal teeth. Splotches of blood covered her face and dripped from the ends of her dark hair. The dark figure was the woman at Nathan's sanctuary.

Veronica struggled to keep her eyes open, but it seemed impossible. Slowly her eyelids grew heavy and she drifted into darkness.

CHAPTER EIGHTEEN

Veronica slowly opened her eyes.

Her hazy vision didn't clear after she blinked a few times. When it came into focus, it triggered her nightmarish attack in the alley.

She recalled the vivid attack and her rescue by the Deamhan woman she and Sean had seen in Blind Bluff Manor.

Sean!

She lifted her head from two satin pillows. Still attempting to focus her sight, she raised her body slowly, placing her feet on the edge of the bed. She touched her neck and felt the two puncture wounds covered by a cotton bandage.

A cold breeze blew in from a paned window covered with maroon drapes. She shivered and rushed across the room and closed the window, watching the movements of the drapes slowly come to a stop.

Maroon wallpaper with gold etched designs of baby dragons covered the walls from the ceiling to the floor. A small chandelier with four electric candles hung from the ceiling. An old Captain's chair (also decorated with gold dragon designs) and a Japanese soju screen sat across the room in the corner. On the Captain's chair rested a black shirt and large black pants that Veronica immediately dressed herself in.

She stood in front of a long mirror, leaning against the wall next to the soju screen. She peeled back the bandage, viewing the puncture wounds on her neck. She moaned in relief, but this was far from over. She needed to find out how she got here and where "here" was.

She pulled on the handle to the only door in the room but it didn't budge. She heard small footsteps of someone pacing back and forth outside the door. She heard a click and the door swung gently open.

No one was there.

She looked behind her and jumped, bemused to find an African American teenage girl. The girl stared back at her with arms crossed. Her brown eyes slowly studied Veronica from head to toe. Dressed in tight fitting black jeans and a white tank top, she brushed her shoulder length dreadlocks over her shoulders.

"So, you're the human everyone's talking about."

Veronica stepped back. At first she feared the teen, suspecting her to be a Deamhan. But wasn't it against their Dictum to sire someone at that age?

"I was told that." The girl tapped the side of her head. "I can hear you, y'know."

Veronica caught herself and covered her mouth (not like it was talking that placed her in her predicament.)

"I'm Hallie by the way." The Deamhan teen plopped onto Veronica's bed. She rubbed her fingers over the cover's smooth fabric. "You hungry? I can make you something."

Veronica respectfully declined. "Where am I?"

"Blind Bluff Manor."

She breathed a sigh of relief, now knowing she was in Blind Bluff Manor and astonished to see that Remy and the mysterious woman weren't the only Deamhan in the sanctuary.

"How did I get here?"

"Are you sure you aren't hungry?" she asked again, ignoring Veronica's question. "I make a mean peanut butter and jelly sandwich."

"No, I'm fine. Where's Nathan?"

"Damn, you're needy." Again, Hallie ignored Veronica's question. She stood up and began to straighten the black sheets. "He's in his study."

* * * *

Dim chandeliers, separated every fifty feet or so on the ceiling with electric candles, gave an almost eerie glow to the hallway. Veronica couldn't help but notice the decorative artifacts sealed behind unbreakable glass coffins and embedded in small square crevasses in the walls. Scrolls, still tightened and rolled in their ancient fit; small pottery shards from ancient excavations; swords; books; paintings; personal jewelry; mummified insects and mummified Egyptian cats filled the crevasses. All of it reminded Veronica of her mother, and that still she felt nowhere near close in solving her disappearance.

She continued to the closed doors ahead with paned windows tinted to keep the sunlight out. She turned the corner, viewing the edge of a huge staircase. She looked back to see if Hallie had followed her. Satisfied, Veronica descended down the stairs. What she saw amazed her. The steep staircase covered with a thick red carpet led to the first floor and to a huge exhibit; a collection that possibly rivaled that of Historical Museums. An artistic painting of an Italian city covered the wall, and it blended with a scenic route of an ancient Roman road.

At the bottom of the stairs to her left, a bright white light materialized from Nathan's study. She saw Hallie standing in front of the fireplace and the portrait of Queen Elizabeth. She moved quickly. Veronica walked past the Roman statues and approached the room quietly, again noticing the large, shaded lamps sat in the corners and the granite ceiling. Nathan sat near the fireplace on a leather couch. Across from him was the mysterious Deamhan woman who saved her in the alley.

They both turned, watching as Veronica entered the room. The woman's eyes remained glued on Veronica. She wore a long, black dress with dark hair twirled into a tight bun fixed on the back of her head. A black scarf wrapped around her neck with its excess laying across her right shoulder. Her dark brown eyes, which helped her intimidating stare, remained fixed on Veronica. She looked to be an ancient Deamhan who had seen her share of brutality. Veronica quickly turned back to Nathan, who stood up from his chair and smiled.

"Hallie told me you weren't hungry," Nathan said.

Veronica nodded.

"It's good to see that you're doing well."

"How long have I been out?" Veronica leaned against the wall, still feeling the Deamhan's tantalizing stare from her peripheral.

"Overnight," Nathan answered. "You're lucky that Anastasia found you in time." Nathan looked over to the woman, who slowly turned her attention to him.

Anastasia. Veronica rubbed the bandage on her neck. "Thank you."

Anastasia didn't respond.

"I feel like I bruised a couple of ribs." Veronica rubbed the side of her body. "Who was she, the one that attacked me?"

"She was one of the Hartley sisters. I believe you met her older sister before." Nathan stood up from his chair. "They frequented Dark Sepulcher, but that's all past now."

Veronica remembered what the Deamhan said before her fangs burrowed in her neck. She had a history with Anastasia, a history that Veronica became curious about.

"They attacked you earlier, and it was also Anastasia who thwarted them off that time."

Veronica looked back to Anastasia who now stared straight ahead at the wall.

Even while Anastasia sat, Veronica could easily tell she was taller than her. She didn't care what motivated the Deamhan woman to save her both times, but only thought about the idea of being protected—and she knew it wasn't stereotypical behavior of the Deamhan. She began to wonder if living in a sanctuary with a human had anything to do with Anastasia's human-like judgment.

"Your cell phone was destroyed in the attack," Nathan continued. "Anastasia managed to salvage what she could."

"Thank you." Veronica thanked the Deamhan. Anastasia remained quiet.

"Veronica, you have to understand the importance of Sean's activities," Nathan said, "and how his relationship with you has caused Lambert to lose his trust."

"I understand," Veronica interrupted him. "I'm completely aware of it."

"Are you?" Anastasia's comment caused Nathan and Veronica to turn their attention to her. Suddenly Veronica heard Anastasia's voice inside her head.

Don't confuse my act of kindness to be in your favor.

"Yes." Veronica immediately recounted her thought about Anastasia. "It's just not stereotypical of a Deamhan to—" She quickly glanced at Anastasia whose eyes now locked onto Nathan.

"This sanctuary isn't a stereotypical sanctuary," Nathan said. "But here it is."

Veronica made a mental note. There had to be a reason behind why Nathan chose to have Deamhan in his home. But that would have to wait. She wanted to get back to Palm Oaks and now.

"I have to get back to my apartment," Veronica said.

"I don't think that's a wise thing to do."

"Well, I can't stay here forever. I'm not afraid, Nathan, I know the dangers."

Hallie yawned. "That's what all the humans say." She tapped the mantel on the fireplace. "Until they get attacked again."

"You're still a little weak, and your apartment is not a safe place to be," Nathan said.

Neither was being in a house with Deamhan, but Veronica saw no choice. Anastasia's cold stare made her feel unwelcomed. She felt no one, not even Nathan, trusted her.

"There's no place in Minneapolis that's safe for me," Veronica responded.

"Of course." He reluctantly agreed. He rose from his chair and walked over to the other side of the room and reached for his phone. "Are you sure, Veronica?"

Veronica nodded and she watched him dial a number and place the phone to his ear. She continued to lean against the wall and she waited. The sound of the wood crackling in the fireplace became the only prevalent noise in the room. She looked at Hallie, catching the teen's blank stare. Her eyes grew stark like Anastasia. Again, Veronica felt the presence of not being wanted in Blind Bluff Manor.

"I've called for a taxi." Nathan hung up the phone. Veronica sighed, hearing Nathan's words break the awkward silence in the room. "Hallie, would you excuse us."

"Doesn't matter. I can hear you anyway." This time she tapped her ear. "You know, that's what Deamhan do."

Anastasia's head abruptly turned to Hallie and their eyes locked. Veronica didn't know why they stared each other down. But Anastasia won and Hallie huffed.

"I never get to have fun around here." She stormed out of the room.

"Sorry about that." Nathan slowly walked over to Veronica. "Hallie is a new Deamhan, just recently turned. Anastasia found her just outside of Minneapolis, on a farm, devouring the remains of a family. She's still getting used to her new life as a Metusba."

Veronica followed Nathan out of the study and to the foyer.

"The cab should be here soon, Veronica."

"I'd like to wait outside, if that's okay?"

Nathan nodded and unlocked the front door. He opened it slowly, and Veronica stepped out into the cool air. Small patches of ice stippled the mansion's long driveway. It glittered in the moonlight. In the western horizon the sun had just set and the remaining orange and yellow hues covered the lower half of the sky. Reflection from the recent sun set helped showcase the open areas of land surrounding Blind Bluff Manor. Even the frozen pond in front couldn't escape its beauty.

"Why a sanctuary?" Veronica questioned.

Nathan closed the door behind him and walked past her. "Blind Bluff Manor was never meant to be a sanctuary." He bent forward, picking up a small reddish pebble from the ground. He examined it before tossing it to join the other gravel on the road. "It was a place to store my research, a place where I could still observe the Deamhan without interfering."

"Why not leave Minneapolis and go to a bigger city that has a large amount of Deamhan like New York or Los Angeles? Why Minneapolis?"

"I'm not devoted to one area, Veronica," he replied. "I do have other homes in different cities."

"Other sanctuaries?"

"This is my only sanctuary."

"You must do a lot of research."

He nodded. "When I have the time." Using the railing as support, he carefully stepped down the steps and onto the driveway. "As I've mentioned before, my parents were once members. You understand how growing up in a family with history in The Brotherhood can become complicated. Unlike you, I actually loved participating in the exploration of the Deamhan. The more time I spent learning the ropes, the more I began to notice the true reason behind the organization and I felt as if I understood the Deamhan a little more."

They walked across the road and to a small, one lane path that crisscrossed through his entire front driveway.

"I knew that deciding to stay in Minnesota after the Chapter disbanded was a risky move but I didn't want to go back to California, not with them. Why would I? They had kicked my family out of the organization therefore I was out as well." He continued with his spiel. "Being here is what fuels me, and I'm lucky to have found this home to suit my needs. It was built as a farm home in the late 1800s. I remodeled it, added some new rooms, and called it Blind Bluff Manor, after a small cabin getaway my parents had in the forests near Portland, Oregon." They passed a small wooden bench covered with a thick blanket of snow.

Veronica became exceedingly curious about why any Deamhan would come to a human, besides the desire to feed. She also wanted to know what eventually happened to his parents but that was a question for another day. She lowered her voice. "How did you manage to get Deamhan staying here? Aren't you scared they're going to turn on you?"

"No. There isn't a reason to," he answered. "They came to me on their own."

Veronica felt her body shiver again while she struggled to maintain her warmth.

"At Dark Sepulcher, you said the woman following you was a minion," he added. Veronica nodded. "I think maybe she is a researcher." She didn't want to speculate that the minion belonged to Kei, but he was the only Deamhan that had any reason to be interested in her.

"Well researchers are easier to find than minions and I doubt she's a researcher," Nathan answered. "But I honestly don't know. Nowadays, minions are everywhere. They're dangerous than their owners in certain situations."

"I guess this whole me-being-protected thing, doesn't apply to them?"

"It applies," Nathan explained. "Only if their Deamhan owners want it to. There are many Deamhan in the city. Either they are loyal to Kei or they hate him." Nathan pointed to his left wrist. "Kei sends out his minions, and they're willing to do whatever for him." He pretended to draw an image on his wrist. "Many of them have a brand or a tattoo that signals that they belong to him."

Watching Nathan draw his imaginary tattoo signaled something in Veronica's brain. It only took seconds to realize she'd seen it before.

She didn't want to believe it. *Not him, it couldn't be.*

"You've seen it?" Nathan questioned.

She nodded, still trying to mentally establish the image.

"Sean?"

"No," she quickly answered. She came to a grisly realization. The scenario, the egregious signs that she ignored . . . She felt mindless to find out only now. Sean *did* mention Murphy's quirky behavior and how he was always there when she left or came back to her apartment."What is it, Veronica?"

"It's not Sean. It's someone else."

"Who?"

"I have to get back to my apartment." Veronica looked at Nathan. "Now."

"Is it someone you know?"

They heard the rough noise of a car engine in the near distance. Nathan hurried back to the front porch. He pressed a button on his voice box to open the gate.

"Anastasia could accompany you." Nathan raised his voice. "You're still weak from your attack."

"I just need to make sure Sean's not there." Veronica didn't trouble herself with the possibility of her apartment swarming with minions belonging to Kei. They watched the yellow taxi make its way down the gravel road and slowly come to a stop.

151

"Who?"

"Sean," Veronica answered. "I just need to make sure he's okay."

"Veronica—"

"I have to make sure." Veronica's mind began to race. Any possibility that Murphy was responsible for Sean's disappearance—it troubled her and it made her mind jump to sordid thoughts.

"Veronica, you shouldn't go back to your apartment alone," Nathan suggested again. "Let Anastasia go with you. She can protect you."

"Would she?" Veronica doubted.

"Yes she would." Nathan searched through the pockets and pulled out a small cell phone. "If you find Sean, you both should come back and stay here for the night." He handed her the phone. "Are you sure you want to go by yourself?"

"No." She wasn't sure of anything, except for finding Sean. The consequences of going back alone, especially with Murphy being a minion and Sean working for The Brotherhood, didn't cross her mind. The taxi pulled up in front of the door, and she quickly jumped in, not looking back at Nathan as the car drove down the gravel road.

* * * *

Nathan sighed, knowing that there was nothing he could do but let her go on her own. When the taxi was out of distance, he turned back, seeing Anastasia standing in the doorway.

"She shouldn't have left on her own," he said solemnly.

Barefoot, Anastasia stepped on the snow and it crushed beneath her feet. "The snow is rough today." Her soft voice carried in the air. She looked at her feet. A brief gust of cool wind lifted her long black dress. "I want to explore it." She stepped forward and she tilted her head slightly. "Would you like me to follow her instead?"

"I've never asked you to do anything that you don't want to do." He looked at her. "However, I am asking you to do this."

"You can't make me do anything I don't want to do." Anastasia adjusted the red scarf around her neck.

"Of course." He waited for Anastasia's next move. Living with Deamhan long enough, he quickly learned that haste wasn't a viable Deamhan trait. But Anastasia wasn't like any Deamhan he knew or researched about. Somehow, over centuries, she relearned trust and loyalty. After hearing about Lucius' disappearance, she arrived in Minneapolis and made her way to Blind Bluff Manor, thinking that The Brotherhood, Nathan specifically, was behind it. With her hands wrapped around Nathan's throat and her fangs extended, Nathan opened his mind to her in trust and as a favor, she spared his life.

Besides sensing resentment for her own kind and The Brotherhood, Nathan also saw her loyalty for Lucius. She would lay down her life for him without a thought and she hated Kei as much as most Deamhan hated him. However, she didn't have the following to kill him but she had the age and strength. Since then, she remained at Blind Bluff Manor, carefully observing Kei and his followers from a distance. She was the first Deamhan to live in his home and the only Deamhan Nathan trusted at that time.

"She's in danger, Anastasia."

"She's a hardheaded human," Anastasia replied. "But, if I do follow her, you know what I might have to do."

Nathan nodded.

"There will be killing involved." A faint smile appeared on Anastasia's face.

"I know."

She took two steps and in Deamhan speed she ran down the gravel road, disappearing from Nathan's sight.

CHAPTER NINETEEN

The taxi pulled up in front of Palm Oaks.

Veronica handed the driver a hundred dollars, convincing him to stick around while she went in. She unlocked the front door of the building and slowly walked in, looking up at the stairs leading to the second floor. The smell of home cooked spaghetti lingered in the hallway. She heard a muffled cry of a baby coming from an apartment down the hall.

The smell of a tobacco pipe stung her nose.

The sound of footsteps shuffling across the floor echoed above her. Veronica slowly climbed the stairs, carefully pacing her steps to avoid making any noise. She stopped when she reached the second floor, watching two men in black trench coats walk from her apartment. They passed by her without a glance and descended down the stairs.

Veronica needed just one sign and seeing their signature researcher trademark dress: black trench coats, and dark clothing, she knew they had arrived. She approached the front door of her apartment quietly, her eyes drifting back and forth to Murphy's front door. She expected him to rush out, grabbing her and pulling her from the hallway before she made a sound but it didn't happen.

Mixed voices coming from men and women seeped through the slightly opened front door. Cautiously, she pushed it further open.

Her couch, overturned with the cushions on the floor, sat next to her broken coffee table. They moved the television next to the bookcase in the corner of the living room. Researchers stood in her kitchen, her living room, her bedroom, and her bathroom, tearing apart her belongings. They didn't block her from entering her own apartment, and they didn't acknowledge her presence. They moved aside while she entered in openmouthed wonder, stepping over broken pieces of glass and shredded pieces of paper.

They packed her things in medium sized boxes, labeling them and sealing them shut. They emptied out the cupboards in her kitchen, packing away her dishes, her microwave, and her coffee maker. Coffee grounds covered the counters and the kitchen floor, along with a mixture of milk and orange juice. The smell of a smoking pipe stifled the air.

154

"What the hell are you doing?" Veronica screamed above the noise.

All movement immediately stopped.

They silently looked at her.

"Veronica Austin." Kenneth walked from her bedroom.

Veronica swiped back her hair. "Kenneth?" She couldn't believe it! Of course, she knew about what she called his "cockriding" all the way to the top in The Brotherhood, and how he became her father's closest confidant. But for some reason she didn't expect him to be in Minneapolis as Region Leader.

And to think. She actually had a crush on him at one time.

"Veronica, it's good to see you're okay." He pointed to her neck. "Were you attacked?"

She covered up her bruise with her hand. "Doesn't matter. What're you doing here?"

"I've come to take you back to San Diego."

She held up her hand, giving herself only a brief moment to understand what was happening around her. "I'm not going back." She pushed him aside and walked toward her bedroom. Veronica kicked the foam on the floor from her path, finding the picture of her and her mother lying on the floor. Her mattress, now inundated with slash marks, leaned up against the bedroom wall.

She turned around and slapped Kenneth across his face. "You and your friends have five seconds to leave my apartment. Now." She grabbed a suitcase from her closet and began to pack whatever she could find: shirts, shoes, jeans, underwear, bras. She walked into her bathroom, grabbing any necessary toiletries.

She felt him still close behind her, following her. He spoke again in a tone that could only be described as a line taken from The Brotherhood's manual.

"By order of Marcel Alvaro, Head Master of The Brotherhood, and Samuel Austin, President of the Midwest Division of The Brotherhood, you are to be taken back to San Diego where you will undergo evaluation according to the laws of The Brotherhood set forth by its founding fathers; Chapter Seven, Rules, Regulations, and Conduct of members."

"I'm not a member of your shit organization." She tossed the picture on top of the clothing, closing and latching the suitcase. "Now, are you going to leave my apartment or am I going to have to call the police?" She felt her eyes beginning to tear and her body shaking uncontrollably.

He moved in close to her and lowered his voice. "I don't give a flying fuck if you come willingly or if you don't. Hell, I don't care if you stay here and end up like your mother." His eyes narrowed. "But you will not fuck this up for me. Just because you're Mr. Austin's spoiled daughter doesn't mean you're going to do what you want."

Undeterred, Veronica smiled impishly. "Where is he?"

"Where's who?" Kenneth questioned.

"Sean. Where's Sean?"

"Don't know."

"Don't play any bullshit games with me. I know that my father sent him here to spy on me. I know everything. Where is he and what did you do to him?"

Kenneth straightened his black trench coat.

Veronica walked around him and out to her living room. The researchers invading her apartment looked fairly young and new to the organization with their clean trench coats and pressed white shirts. She glanced around at the new Minnesota Chapter of The Brotherhood and cringed at the sound of her father's voice calling her name from across the room.

She dropped her suitcase. The researchers stopped their movements and stood straight in their stance like programmed puppets. Veronica looked over her shoulder, seeing her father standing in the doorway next to her overturned couch.

He drummed his fingers on its soft surface while examining the interior of her apartment. Kenneth brought a chair from the kitchen and placed it next to him. He then helped Mr. Austin take off his trench coat and Veronica's father slowly lowered himself in the chair.

He puffed on the pipe in his mouth, placing his cane across his lap. "How are you?" His cool and collected voice sounded odd to her.

Veronica swallowed the warm spit collecting in her mouth. She already knew why he was there. For the first time since coming back to Minnesota, she felt defeated and she wanted to get as far away as possible from him.

She walked toward the door and her father called out to her, telling her to stop.

Veronica slowly turned around. She expected the next words to spew from his mouth would be intertwined with lies and deceit. She had nothing to say to him.

"What did you to to Sean?" She watched her father continue to puff on his pipe. Never in a hurry, he always took his sweet time when it came to answering questions that he didn't want to answer. It made Veronica miss her mother even more. Her mother consoled her and never kept secrets. Her father was the total opposite.

"We sent Sean back to San Diego."

"So, you did send him here to spy on me?" Veronica bit her lower lip.

"Sean did what he was trained to do." Her father spoke slowly.

Veronica grabbed her suitcase from the floor. "You son of a bitch." She clenched her teeth.

"Veronica, you must understand. This isn't about you or about me. It's about The Brotherhood."

"Yeah, Father." She mocked. "It's always about The Brotherhood." Veronica squeezed the handle of her suitcase.

"Your mother knew that. I knew that," Mr. Austin continued. "Coming back here, trying to stir up old dirt won't bring her back."

"She isn't dead, Dad," Veronica replied. "And this would've never happened if you didn't play God with our lives." She shook her head. "The Deamhan don't want you here. I don't want you here and I'm not going back. You can't make me."

Mr. Austin licked his lips and he looked to Kenneth for a brief second before replying. "I promise, Veronica. If you come back to San Diego, I'll tell you everything I know."

"I have nothing more to say to you." She walked out of her apartment and hurried down the stairs.

She pushed open the front door of the building. The taxi was gone. She placed her suitcase on the pavement and searched for the phone Nathan had given her. Her fingers shook uncontrollably as her body filled up with adrenaline. She tried hard to speed dial his number, ignoring the sound of footsteps slowly approaching her.

She tried to contain her tears. How stupid, she thought. *Even if they knew where Sean was, they'd never tell me.*

"Veronica?"

Veronica stopped and turned around. Murphy stood feet from her, dressed comfortably in a black sweater and white shorts.

Immediately, she felt her adrenal glands beginning to react in overtime. She took a step back, startled and on alert. "Get away from me, Murphy."

"What's wrong?" He took a step forward, and she took another step back to keep her distance. His eyes drifted to the side of her neck and to the bandage. She quickly covered it with her hand, trying to avoid his attention.

"Are you okay, Veronica? What happened?"

"You," Veronica said. "You happened."

"Who're those people in your apartment?" He took another step closer to her.

"Don't come any closer."

He grabbed her by the wrist. "I'm afraid I can't do that." He smiled. She slapped him across the face, causing him to release his grip. He pushed her onto the cold concrete. Her suitcase opened, spilling her belongings onto the pavement.

"Where do you think you're going?" His gaze concentrated on her.

Veronica's first reaction wasn't to scream. Instead, she kicked as hard as she could, striking him in the groin. He hunched over and she kicked him again, her foot connecting with his nose.

Murphy screamed and covered his face. A stream of blood rushed from underneath his hands and down his sweater. Veronica stood up and instantly took off down the street.

"I didn't want it to come to this!" Murphy wiped his nose with the back of his hand.

She heard his harsh foot stomps behind her and she looked back. In his left hand he held a small lead pipe and the entire lower half of his face and his right hand was covered in blood.

Her breath expelled in a puff of white mist as she ran down the sidewalk. She slipped once on a patch of ice, almost losing her footing. Behind her, she heard Murphy scream her name in a blood curdling voice that drowned out the noise from his sprinting footsteps.

"Where you gonna run to?" he yelled. "You have nowhere else to go, Veronica."

She leaped over a snow pile on the edge of the road and continued down the street, not knowing what direction she was headed.

She tried to speed dial Nathan's number again as she ran around the corner and toward a park. She opened her mouth to scream for help, hoping that someone would hear her. But her attempt was frivolous. The streets were empty, and she was alone.

Before she finished speed dialing Nathan's number, Murphy threw himself on top of her, pulling her down into the cold frothiness of the snow. She struggled to push him off her as he dug his elbow into her back and pushed her face into the frigid snow.

Veronica's face went numb, and she could no longer breathe. He grabbed her hair, lifted her head, and she gasped for air.

"Get off me!" She forced herself to choke out the words. He dropped his pipe and muscled her body onto her back. He then pinned her arms to the ground.

"Stop fighting," he said. "You're only making it worse." She continued to struggle, but he increased his hold. "If you stop, I'll take you to Sean."

She stopped instantly, staring into his eyes. The blood on his face began to drip, landing on her forehead.

"Good girl." He loosened his grip. "Good girl." He removed his hands from her wrists but remained on top of her. "I don't want to harm you. I'm only here to watch you."

"Where's Sean?" Veronica felt her wrists throb in pain.

"Sean is preoccupied." He smiled. Veronica lashed out at him again, swinging her fists in a rage. He easily pinned her down again. "Relax!" he yelled.

"If you fucking hurt him!"

"You'll do what?" He leaned forward, smiling. "You can't do anything. You see, Veronica, I'm up here." He raised his hand, above his head. "And you're down there." He pressed his hand into the snow.

"Get off me!"

"Y'know, I was just starting to like you, too." His eyes scanned her chest. "Such a waste."

"Who sent you? Kei?"

He moved his face closer to her, stopping within inches from her mouth.

"They offered me immortality," he whispered. "Do you know what that means, Veronica?"

Veronica struggled, but he pushed her wrists further into the snow.

"No more humanity, no more living in this shit world as a human. Immortality as a Lugat."

"You're crazy." Veronica grunted. "You can't trust them."

He grabbed his pipe again and lifted himself off her. He glared down at her, taking a moment to speak again. "If you run from me again, I'll cut off your fucking head and give it to him as a gift."

Veronica remained on her back, frozen in fear. She wanted to call Nathan, but it was impossible. He squinted with the look of a mechanical deviant. She knew she was going to die, right there, in the park.

An unusual clicking noise broke their conversation. Then silence. Murphy looked over his shoulder.

They heard a quick, loud noise.

Murphy dropped to his knees next to Veronica, clutching his lower stomach. She lifted her body, staring at a sudden rush of blood coming from a dime size hole in his abdomen. Veronica's eyes moved to a woman wearing a thick blue winter jacket with blonde hair. She lowered her 9mm, placing it into her purse, and she walked over to Murphy. It took only moments for Veronica to realize that she'd seen the woman before, at the burnt sanctuary home.

Veronica slowly stood up and watched the familiar woman gently kick Murphy onto his side with tip of her boot. She then knelt down next to him and began to search his body. Still alive, he moaned in pain with his body curled into a fetal position. The woman reached her hand under his sweater and to his shorts. She then proceeded to search his sneakers.

Veronica wiped the snow from her clothes, still flabbergasted. The snow underneath Murphy's body began to turn red, soaked with blood. He moaned again, and she pulled back the sweater on his left arm, revealing his tattoo.

"They usually don't get branded anymore." The woman didn't look at Veronica. She remained attentive on Murphy. "It makes them harder to find." She stood up, readjusting her blue jacket. Veronica wiped the water and wet snow from the cell phone.

"Veronica, I'm not here to harm you," she said. "But you must trust me and listen to me."

"I'm not falling for that." Veronica took a couple of steps back from her. "Not anymore."

"If his markings are what I think they are, then you're in serious danger."

Veronica stopped. The realization of being close to death finally struck her. The Deamhan twins and the van, that was nothing compared to what Murphy might have done to her. The palms of her hands were sweaty in the cold winter wind, and her legs began to feel weak and unstable. The woman didn't move. Instead, her blue eyes drifted to the body then back to Veronica.

"Are you from The Brotherhood?" Veronica coldly asked her.

"No, I'm not a researcher."

"You're a minion?"

She nodded. "Yes, I'm a minion. My name is Jessica."

"Who is your master?"

Before Jessica could reply, Veronica felt a cold rush of wind behind her. In an instant, she saw Jessica on the ground with an unknown assailant straddling her. Gripping Jessica by the neck, the assailant's moves were quick. A Deamhan.

Veronica reached for Murphy's pipe, still keeping her eyes on Jessica and her attacker. The assailant's black cap and the fabric of a long black dress flipped around during the struggle, hiding the assailant's identity from Veronica's view.

Veronica raised her hand in preparation to strike, when the assailant turned and faced her.

It was Anastasia who glared back with black pupils and her fangs extended. Her face was blotched with chunks of snow, and the sight frightened Veronica to the point that she dropped the pipe. She didn't have the time to think twice. If she didn't do anything, Anastasia was going to kill the woman who had just saved her life. There wasn't any time to explain to Anastasia. Veronica opened her mind and consciously invited Anastasia to read.

Anastasia accepted the invitation.

The front part of Veronica's brain began to burn. She closed her eyes. A feeling of extra weight overcame her senses. It wasn't like the time Remy read her thoughts. This pain was prominent, almost to the point of being insufferable.

Suddenly Anastasia pulled out from Veronica's thoughts and she raised herself from the ground, allowing Jessica to slide a couple of inches away from them. Jessica placed her hands on her chest, trying to catch her breath while staring wide-eyed at Anastasia. She then pushed back the sleeves of her jacket, revealing her minion marking on her left wrist.

"You know the marking, Anastasia. I belong to her."

Anastasia removed her cap, and her dark hair fell to her shoulders. Her eyes studied the marking before she spoke. "Selene." Her teeth retracted and her eyes slowly reverted back to its normal color.

Jessica stood to her feet, wiping the wet snow from her ruffled jacket. She kept her left arm exposed, giving Veronica a better view of her marking.

Her brand looked roughly the same as Murphy's except the letters were vastly different. They were darker, and the calligraphy wasn't modern but created in a penmanship from years past. For Veronica, they were unreadable, but for Anastasia it revealed the woman's master.

"I belong to Selene." Jessica regained her posture. She turned her attention to Murphy. "He belongs to Kei."

"I know." Anastasia tilted her head, staring at him. She quickly looked back at her.

"Selene has protected Veronica," Jessica said.

"Who's Selene?" Veronica looked at Anastasia, who didn't respond to her.

"Obviously Kei has no intention of respecting Selene's order, so he sent this minion." Jessica pointed to Murphy.

"He said he has Sean." Veronica turned to Anastasia but she shook her head.

"Unlikely," Anastasia replied. "The Brotherhood has your friend."

Jessica held out her hand to Veronica. "I came here to get you and take you to Selene's sanctuary. We need to go now."

"But I don't know who Selene is." Veronica stared at the snow on the ground and the numerous footprints they'd all made in it.

"Selene is the oldest Deamhan in the city as of now," Jessica replied. "Older than Anastasia and like Kei, Lucius is her maker."

Anastasia glared at Jessica. "Older doesn't mean you can trust her." She mocked her.

"She'll have Selene's protection." Jessica turned to Veronica. "You're not as old and as strong as her, Anastasia. You can't control Kei."

"She can't control him either," Anastasia said. "If she could, Kei would be dead and Lucius would still be here." She turned back to face them.

Jessica returned her attention to Veronica. "Veronica, Selene knows a lot about your mother." Jessica wiped the remaining snow from her forehead.

"What does she know?" Veronica began to push her for answers.

"It's not my place to ask her what she knows." Jessica shrugged. "But when you arrive safely, I'm sure she'll tell you everything." She held out her hand again. "But we need to leave, now."

Veronica looked at Anastasia who still remained with her back to them, then at Jessica. Something wasn't right. She could sense the hostility from Anastasia when it came to Selene. "I don't know if Selene can tell me what I want to know. I know Nathan can."

Jessica nodded. "Selene did warn me that it'd be difficult to get you to come with me." She reached into her pocket and pulled out a white envelope and tossed it at Anastasia. "That is for Nathan from Selene."

Anastasia examined the envelope. It was bare except for Nathan's name written in small handwriting in the upper left hand corner.

Jessica turned to look at Murphy. "He can't stay here." She looked back at Anastasia.

"You shot him, you dispose of him." Anastasia turned to walk away.

"The Dictum forbids this." Jessica's brazen remark did little affect. Anastasia continued walking. Veronica watched puffs of mist exhale from the woman's mouth.

"Anastasia!" Jessica now screamed after her. Anastasia continued to walk away, only halting in her tracks when Jessica screamed again. "Your sire Lucia didn't teach you this?"

In Deamhan speed, Anastasia ran back to them and in seconds she stood standing face to face with Jessica.

"I could easily kill you and leave you right here with him." Anastasia's eyes were stark cold and her body was rigid.

161

Shaken, Jessica took a step back from her. "I belong to Selene."

"I don't fear Selene or any Deamhan human."

Jessica readjusted her position and she now stood up straight, trying to hide her fear. "Selene told me stories about you, Anastasia," she whispered. "You'd be surprised what I know about you and what you can and won't do."

"You don't know anything about me." Anastasia moved in closer and her fangs slowly dropped.

"Selene isn't your enemy. You both want the same thing. You both want justice for Lucius. He is her true sire." Jessica's voice was shaky.

Slowly Anastasia stepped away, but her eyes continued to glare at Jessica.

Jessica breathed in deeply before speaking again. "There's a small lake that way." She pointed to her right. "You can kill Murphy and get rid of him over there."

Anastasia didn't reply. Instead she approached Murphy, lifted him from the ground and she placed his body over her shoulder.

"Fucking bitch." Murphy's curse had no effect on the conversation.

Jessica then turned to Veronica. "Veronica, we have to leave now."

"I'm going back to Blind Bluff Manor." Veronica shook her head. "Tell Selene that I do appreciate her protection, but I feel safer with people I know."

"I'll tell her." Defeated, Jessica slowly nodded. "Selene knew your mother and promised her that you'd always be protected." Jessica placed her hands in her pocket. "She is just making sure she lives up to her end."

Before Veronica had a chance to speak, Jessica turned and walked away.

Selene knew my mother?

Veronica looked back and watched as Jessica zipped up her jacket and covered her neck with a scarf. She briskly crossed the street and disappeared around the corner.

Anastasia stopped walking and turned to face Veronica. "This way." She began to walk the opposite way from the lake.

Veronica followed Anastasia out of the park.

CHAPTER TWENTY

Anastasia dumped Murphy in the backseat of a parked black Oldsmobile hidden in an alleyway nearby. Reluctantly, Veronica climbed into the vehicle on the passenger side. Anastasia started the car and pressed her foot firmly on the gas. The tires screeched and they took off.

Anastasia drove violently, swerving in and out of traffic. She kept only her right hand on the wheel and she rolled down the drive side window. Cold wind blew into the car. Veronica shivered. There was no way she could ask Anastasia to roll up the window.

Veronica looked around in the car at the interior. It was spotless; no dust on the dashboard, no garbage on the floor of the car. The rear view mirror was missing and so was the passenger side mat for the floor. Other than that (and the fact that there was a cassette player, instead of a CD player) the car looked in pristine condition.

Murphy moaned and several times he cursed under his breath. Veronica wondered what Anastasia planned to do with him if he survived the trip to Blind Bluff Manor since she didn't finish him off at the park. She turned around to look in the back seat. The leather seats were covered with blood.

Murphy looked up at her. "Fucking bitch," he whispered.

Veronica turned back around, looking at Anastasia from the corner of her left eye. Anastasia's look contained distain, and was unimpressed by Murphy's constant spiel. Every so often she adjusted her hand on the steering wheel or she brushed back her bangs from her face. Even when Murphy's moans turned into screams, she didn't look in the back seat to see if he was stabilizing or slowly dying.

Veronica kept quiet for the rest of the ride. They sped down the streets and past the orange tinted lights. Away from Minneapolis, the roads became dark and the stars were visible in the clear sky.

They reached Blind Bluff Manor before midnight. Anastasia drove up to the front stairs where Nathan waited in the front doorway, dressed in a white night robe that extended slightly below his knees. Before Veronica closed the passenger door, Anastasia sped off and disappeared behind the home with Murphy still in the back seat. Exhausted, Veronica slowly walked up to Nathan. He placed his arm around her and helped her into his home. He walked her into his study, which was warm from the fireplace. She sat, and he poured her a cup of tea.

"Are you hurt?" He sat across from her in another chair.

"No, I'm alright. Thanks." She sipped the hot tea. "My father is in Minneapolis. I guess he's helping set up the new Chapter."

"Anastasia told me about Selene's minion and the note."

Veronica jerked her head back, surprised. "When?"

"She told me in my thoughts," Nathan answered. "I didn't know Selene was in Minneapolis."

"You know her?"

"Yes, I know her," Nathan replied. "But I didn't know that she had her minion follow you."

"Or that Selene promised my mother that she'd protect me," Veronica added. "Who is she?" It bothered Veronica that she wasn't able to know more about the promise Selene made to her mother. She felt the lack of distrust pointing directly at her and infiltrating the air around her. Part of her wished she'd gone with Jessica.

"Selene is a very old Deamhan, older than the majority of Deamhan living today."

"Jessica, her minion, mentioned that," Veronica replied. "But who is she? I felt like Anastasia doesn't like her."

"No, Anastasia doesn't, but that's a story for another day," Nathan answered. "Selene was sired by Lucius in the late 1700s. From what I remember, her human family and clan were slaughtered by a rival clan and she was saved by Lucius who sired her. She was a brutal Deamhan according to old research documents. She slaughtered human and Deamhan alike. However, she was loyal to Lucius, like Anastasia is loyal to Lucius now."

"But Anastasia isn't a Lugat. Why is she loyal to him?"

Nathan tapped Veronica on her shoulder, signaling her that he was finished answering her questions. There was so much to learn and Veronica wanted to know all of it. Instead, he changed the subject back to her father.

"They won't come for you here, Veronica." As he continued to speak, Veronica didn't hear a word while she contemplated her next move. His words were clouded, but his offer for her to stay in Blind Bluff Manor while everything blew over was free from any intrusion.

She agreed, but on one condition.

"Murphy," she said. "What's Anastasia going to do with him?"

Nathan looked to the floor of his study for a moment before looking back up at Veronica.

He avoided the question. "You must be tired. I'll take you up to your room."

She agreed and decided to leave her questions for tomorrow.

She followed him out of his study and they walked to the den just in time to see Anastasia walking through the front door, closing it behind her. She stood off to the side, her eyes fixed on Nathan and her hands firmly on her hips.

Anastasia placed the note in Nathan's hand. He thanked her, and with Veronica in tow, they headed up the stairs.

Down the hall they turned right and walked down another hallway. Veronica didn't recognize this part of the sanctuary. It wasn't the same hallway from earlier. The windows weren't blocked from the sun. In fact, they weren't covered with curtains of any kind. She looked out, viewing the back yard of his home and the dark sky and the full moon. This wing of his home, his mansion, was his own personal space. The walls were bare and lacked any detail. The hallway contained plenty of low dimmed lights spaced feet apart.

"What did she look like?" Nathan said to Veronica.

She snapped back into reality. "Who?"

"Jessica, Selene's minion who gave Anastasia the note." He referred to the note. "What did she look like?"

Veronica described every detail she could remember about her, down to the way she reacted when Anastasia confronted her. Nathan nodded while she spoke and at the end of the hallway, he stopped and faced a brown door.

"This is your room." He pulled out a ring of keys and began to unlock the door. He opened and motioned for her to walk in.

The room was bare except for a queen size bed with white sheets, two standard size pillows and a black comforter to her right. A huge window sat opposite the other side of the bed covered in thin see-through white curtains. In one corner was a make-up counter with a table mirror and a cushioned chair. Unsure of this new environment, Veronica took her time to look around.

Nathan walked in after her, standing partially in the doorway. "I hope this room suits you."

She looked around another time before finally facing him. "I'll manage." Who was she fooling? She missed her apartment, she missed her personal things, and most importantly, she missed Sean. It didn't matter what room Nathan chose for her; she wasn't going to get any sleep with these worried thoughts on her mind.

"If you need anything, please let me know," he assured. "You can find your way back to my study?"

"If I have to." Veronica nodded. He stepped out, closing the door behind him. She walked over to the bed, falling into it and letting her body sink into the cushioned layers. She needed to familiarize herself with this room and her new living conditions. She was going to be here for a long time.

CHAPTER TWENTY-ONE

Veronica spent the following week relaxing in Nathan's sanctuary. Nathan gave her complete access to his late father's Deamhan research, and his own research. She ransacked complete historical documents, learning everything she could on Lucius and Kei.

She pushed The Brotherhood's resurgence in Minneapolis to the back of her mind. Worried about Sean, she assumed that her father had taken him back to San Diego where he'd be reprimanded with disobeying orders. It wasn't the end of the world for him. She knew plenty of researchers in her past who were reprimanded. Plus he was safer in San Diego anyway. But she couldn't help but think about Murphy. Even though he tried to kill her, he was still human and Anastasia had him alone, locked up in the basement for her heinous pleasure.

She didn't understand how Nathan wasn't affected by Anastasia's actions. He rarely left Blind Bluff Manor, opting to conduct his business by phone in his private study. Veronica didn't question who he was talking to or where his information came from. She assumed his connection was within The Brotherhood because he knew their every little detail. The new Chapter had set up shop in downtown Minneapolis, only blocks from Dark Sepulcher under the disguise of a local bookstore. The researchers, including Kenneth, were seen frequently on the streets during the day and at night. However, her father had already left the city.

When Veronica finally saw Anastasia, she was with Nathan in his study usually during the early hours of the morning. Her responses were fierce and quick to his questions. There was a friendship between both of them, a Ramanga and a human, that was more than just living in the same sanctuary. It was deeper than that, much deeper, and Veronica remained confused by it.

In a bigger library on the second floor, Veronica occasionally ran into Hallie but still kept her distance from the Deamhan teen. That soon changed when Hallie began to open up to her. Hallie acted like a normal teenager; staying in her room, blasting techno music from huge stereo speakers Nathan had bought her. Sometimes she played video games and when she got bored, she'd run down the hallway, yelling at the top of her lungs that she wanted to leave the manor. One night, just after sunset, Hallie stood in the doorway of Veronica's room, secretly watching her.

"Don't you get tired of reading all the time?"

Hallie's remark startled Veronica who jumped from her chair. She watched as Hallie skipped over to her bed and purposely fell face first into the mattress. She then rolled onto her back and pulled out her iPod from her pocket.

"No, not really," Veronica replied.

"Reading is so boring though," Hallie said. "Unless it's like gossip magazines and stuff."

Veronica closed her book and she turned her undivided attention to her. "You haven't read a good book."

"What you're reading aren't books. They're researcher manuals." Hallie pointed to the leather bound book in Veronica's possession. "Nathan told me about those. I wonder if I'm like, all old and stuff, will I get a human to follow me around and write about me?"

"It's possible."

"Well it won't happen now. I can't even leave this place." She stared at the ceiling. "I'm like a fucking prisoner." She turned to Veronica. "I had way more freedom as a human."

Veronica knew a little about Anastasia and Remy, but she knew almost nothing about Hallie. She grabbed a pen and her notebook from the desk drawer and started to write. "Let's start by telling me your name."

Hallie raised herself from Veronica's bed. "Seriously?"

Veronica nodded. "We can start off with your name, a little about your history, like if you attended high school when you were human."

Hallie's face beamed with curiosity and she moved to the edge of the bed with her elbows resting on her legs. "Okay. My name is Hallie Martensen."

"Is Hallie your human name or Deamhan name?"

"What?"

"Some Deamhan choose to get another name after they're sired. It's like a sign of rebirth."

"I like my name when I was human and I like it now," Hallie answered. "It's not my real name though. I don't know my real parents. I was adopted."

Veronica jotted down her name in her notebook and she continued. "How old are you?"

Hallie rolled her eyes. "Human or Deamhan years?"

"Both."

"Well, I was sixteen when I was turned. That was a few months ago."

"Do you know who turned you?"

"Nope and nor do I care," she replied.

Veronica paused. "You don't know who sired you?"

Hallie shrugged. "It was at a rave. All I remember is taking the best pills in my life there. I was with my best friend and I lost her in the crowd." Hallie closed her eyes in thought. "Then I met this boy and his friends and they gave me more pills. I just remember being outside, under the stars drinking, then when I woke up, I was covered in dirt and it was dark." She opened her eyes, which had turned from brown to the Deamhan trait of black. "I dug myself out of the ground and there was no one around. I was alone. I didn't even know where I was and how long I'd been there. I was hungry and I felt strangely strong." She stood up from the bed. "I could hear everything around me and people in the distance. I walked down the freeway, trying to find my way home. Before I reached my house, I saw a cop and I told him I was lost. But before he could help me, I had this urge to eat him." Her eyebrows shifted. "It scared me, so I ran. And that's when Anastasia found me."

"And she took you back here?"

Hallie laughed. "Not at first. She attacked me!" Her eyes lit up. "She dragged me into an alley, saying she was going to kill me, and that I was too young to be sired, and she kept questioning me about who did this to me but I didn't know anything. After begging her to not kill me, she stopped. When she took me to Blind Bluff Manor I met Nathan and he talked to me for hours. That's when I knew what happened to me and that I could never go back to my human family."

"You've only been a Deamhan for a few months?"

"Yeah, and it sucks," Hallie replied. "Oh my God, I just want to get the fuck out of here; just once!" She pouted. "I miss my friends, I miss my family. I even miss high school."

Veronica scribbled vicariously in her notepad. "So, why can't you go out?"

"Cause Anastasia always brings me back. I hate her so much. I can't do anything around here without her watching me," Hallie said. "Once, I got past the front gate before she dragged me back, threatening me with her fucking sharp teeth. I'd call the cops but . . . ." She trailed off.

"But what?"

"Who'd believe me?" Hallie sighed. "Forever is a long freaking time to be here. I mean, how am I supposed to learn about what I am if they keep me prisoner?"

"It's not safe out there, especially for a young Deamhan."

"Yeah, whatever. I don't care about Deamhan or other supernatural crap. I just want to get out of here." She stood up. "Anastasia gets to eat whoever she wants. Why can't I eat whoever I want?" Grinning, Hallie licked her lips. "The closest I got to tasting a human was with that guy she's been playing around with in the basement."

"Murphy?"

Hallie nodded. "Yeah, right before she . . ."

"What? Right before 'she' what?"

Hallie shook her head. "Never mind." She got up from Veronica's bed and turned to walk out of the room.

"Did she kill him?"

Hallie stopped and looked over her shoulder. "I'll show ya."

Veronica followed her down the hallway and down the stairs. They crept past Nathan, who sat in his study, reading, and then headed to a wooden door in the hallway near the back door of the manor.

"She's down there with him." Hallie smiled.

"He's still alive?"

"If you want to call it that." Hallie hesitated. "I used to go down there during the day when Anastasia's asleep."

The tiny hairs on the back of Veronica's neck stood up followed by a small gust of wind and the smell of expensive cologne. She immediately turned around and jumped, bumping against the door and creating a loud thud. Remy stood with his brown eyes scanning her.

"Now, now Veronica," he said as he leaned against the wall. "That would be prying." This time Veronica forced herself to not back away. Unlike their first encounter, Remy's appearance wasn't intimidating. Dressed in a sleek black shirt with tight fitting blue jeans, he towered slightly over her. His brown hair was pulled back into a ponytail, just like the last time she saw him.

"Shouldn't you be doing something angst related right now?" Remy questioned Hallie.

Hallie held out her hand. "Where's my cigs?"

Remy looked at Veronica and smiled. His eyes were hollow giving her mixed signals. "Kids these days." He reached into the pockets of his jeans and pulled out an unopened pack of cigarettes. "Always want, want, want, but never give, give, give."

Hallie snatched the pack from his grasp.

"Now, off you go." He patted Hallie on her head. "Move along now."

Hallie gave him an evil eye before heading back up the stairs.

Remy leaned against the wall, continuing to gawk at Veronica. It made her uneasy and she looked away. She tried her best to ignore his intimidating and somewhat attractive stare by hiding her thoughts.

He smiled. "What can I say? I'm good with kids."

She brushed off his remark and she began to fidget with the knob handle on the basement door.

"She's been playing with Murphy for about a week now," he continued. "She's trying to get into that little brain of his. Gotta give that human credit; he's stronger than he looks."

Veronica tried pushing her weight against the door but it didn't budge.

"So, Miss Austin. We never did finish that conversation."

"What conversation?"

"Oh you know. The one where you blocked your thoughts, then ran off at the sight of me feeding." He pouted. "You didn't even say goodbye."

"Look, I'm not some whore who'll fall for your tricks." Veronica faced him with her back to the door. "I know who you are and what you can do, so don't try to insult my intelligence."

In Deamhan speed, Remy placed his hand on the door near her head. "And that's why you fascinate me. You're like no other researcher I've ever encountered," he whispered. "Plus you smell so good."

"I'm not a researcher."

His comments didn't faze her. She moved his hand away and returned back to the door. The deadened noise from the other side became louder.

"What's she doing down there?" Veronica probed.

"Questioning the human about Kei." He moved in closer to Veronica. "Anastasia is a weird one. She's what you call *old school*. She does things her way."

"Open the door," Veronica said.

"A little demanding, aren't we?"

"I want to go down there."

"I don't think she'd appreciate that," Remy replied.

Veronica turned back around. "I have a few questions of my own for Murphy."

His eyes drifted to her chest. "If you ask nicely."

Veronica folded her hands, covering her breasts.

Remy grabbed the knob and with his Deamhan strength, he yanked the door open. The door splintered and the metallic lock flew past his head, landing on the floor.

He stepped away and gracefully bowed. "Done." He smiled.

The space was dark and Veronica reached her arms out to the side, sliding her palms against the cold concrete wall. Remy watched her while she proceeded down the steps cautiously, trying to not make a noise (she was sure that Anastasia knew someone was lurking on the top steps) and at the same time trying not to fall.

Reaching the bottom steps, Veronica smelled the stringent scent of a damp basement. A candle with a flickering flame gave off an eerie glow. She swallowed and walked alongside the concrete wall. She felt herself step on a soft object, but she continued forward. Her foot stepped onto a lower portion of the floor and she lost her footing. She tumbled forward slightly and caught herself, but not in time to feel her hip brush against another table. The table shifted and a small box filled with debris fell to the floor.

She felt a brush of wind, and in front of her she saw Anastasia's face outlined in the dark.

At first Anastasia didn't say anything. Instead her eyes darted to Remy who smiled briefly.

"She wanted a tour, Anastasia," he replied.

Anastasia reached out to the side and flicked on the light switch. The room lit up. Ropes and chains hung on the opposite end of the wall. The floor was spotless and the area opened. Veronica saw Murphy, naked and chained against the far end of the wall. She watched as Anastasia walk over to him. Small tiny cuts covered his chest and his legs. His mouth was swollen and his teeth were covered with blood.

Veronica also noticed something else; something that jolted her. His skin showed no signs of being shot and wounded. His brown eyes were now dark. He had the eyes of a Deamhan.

Upon seeing her, Murphy began to struggle in Deamhan speed. He moved rapidly in accelerated convulsions; too fast for her eyes to focus on. Her head tingled as if someone attempted to scour her thoughts. She immediately blocked them. He smiled at her but his lips were too swollen to form the shape.

Anastasia swiped Murphy across the face with the back of her hand, and the tingling sensation in Veronica's brain immediately stopped.

"What did you do to him?" Veronica asked Anastasia.

"You can see for yourself," Remy, who stood behind Veronica, answered.

Anastasia hit him again with a closed fist. His head plopped to the side and he turned back, giving her an evil look. Anastasia sired him. She had made him a Ramanga and Veronica wanted to know why.

Murphy tilted his head back and laughed, revealing his new fangs. Veronica walked over to him, stopping within a safe distance.

"I gave him what he wanted," Anastasia said.

"Oh," Murphy replied. "And what is that?"

"Immortality."

"As a fucking Ramanga?" He laughed sarcastically and this time Anastasia aimed her punch for his stomach. He bent over in pain and she grabbed him by the hair to lift his head.

Anastasia's actions surprised Veronica, yet it wasn't enough to cease her questioning. Like Anastasia, she also wanted to know where his master was. "Where's Kei?"

Blood dripped from the corners of his mouth. "Like I fucking told her," he spurted. "Fuck off."

"Where is he, Murphy?" Veronica asked again.

"Your mother is long dead." Murphy huffed between his words. "And so is your fucking researcher friend. Kei drained him dry. You should have heard him cry for his life. It was beautiful."

"Don't bother asking. He doesn't know anything about your mother," Anastasia said as she walked to the back of the room and later returned with a small butane blowtorch in hand. She turned the knob and Murphy stiffened. A blast of hot fire exploded from the barrel and he screamed.

Veronica quickly looked away from the torture. She found herself disgusted, but she couldn't bring herself to tell Anastasia to stop.

"And he doesn't know where Kei is." Anastasia turned the knob and the flame extinguished.

"If he doesn't know anything then why are you still torturing him?" Veronica asked.

Anastasia placed the blowtorch on the ground and she viewed the dark splotches of burnt skin covering Murphy's chest heal themselves. "Because I *can*, human."

Murphy puffed. "He'll come for you both." He continued his threat. "Kei will come for me and he'll make you his bitch." He looked at Anastasia and chuckled. "And he'll drain you dry."

"Kei isn't coming for you." Anastasia walked to a nearby table and grabbed a wrought iron poker. She calmly approached Murphy and quickly jabbed the metal piece into his stomach. He screamed in pain, and she held onto the knob and began to twist.

"Now this is the Anastasia I know." Remy's mouth opened and he began to rub his forearms.

Veronica saw his excitement in Anastasia's torture. He enjoyed it. She turned away, disgusted at the horrific display. She never imagined being an eye witness to a Deamhan torturing another Deamhan. It was like nothing she'd read in researcher manuals and books about the Deamhan.

Anastasia tilted her head to the side in amusement at Murphy's screams of pain. "He's no longer your master. I am." She placed her hand on his shoulder and raised his body upright. "And you, my dear Ramanga, I have for eternity."

172

CHAPTER TWENTY-TWO

Veronica walked through the front yard of the sanctuary, observing the frozen pond and the trail that circled through it. Dressed in a winter jacket that Nathan provided for her, she went exploring, staring at the stars in the sky and the thin clouds hovering in front of the moon. Her thoughts circled around Anastasia's continuing torture of Murphy and what he blurted out to her. She didn't believe a word Murphy said. However, the thought of Kei coming to Blind Bluff Manor to rescue his servant was still a possibility.

With Murphy being sent to watch her closely, it only meant that Kei knew she was in Minneapolis. She wasn't afraid. In fact, she wanted Kei to find her. Maybe he'd tell her about her mother or Lucius. Either way, she couldn't just stay in Blind Bluff Manor and do nothing. Her search had to continue, regardless if it put her back on a dangerous path.

Veronica prayed in front of the small frozen pond. She wasn't overly religious and her parents never forced religion on her. There was always the notion of good and bad; something that allowed Deamhan to live in this world, and for her mother to be taken by it. If anyone deserved life beyond death, it was her mother.

Her hair swayed at the cold rush of air and she no longer felt alone. The change of environment didn't startle her. It was either Anastasia or Remy who now stood next to her.

"Every Deamhan can smell each other." Anastasia spoke slowly.

Above, the clouds began to break and the moon finally showed off its glistening tint, adding dark shadows to the bushes and the trees below.

"I smelled them with you outside the door." Anastasia slightly turned to look at her with disturbing eyes. Her dark hair was loose and it fell over her shoulders. She wore a long black dress, which flapped in the wind. "Don't think what I'm doing to Murphy is because of you." Before Veronica replied, Anastasia spoke again. "It's not."

"I don't think you're doing it for me," Veronica replied. "You're torturing him for your own amusement. That's what Deamhan do, right?"

"You know the answer, why question?" Anastasia took a couple of steps forward. "You were taught that all Deamhan are evil and you believe Deamhan killed your mother."

"You were evil enough to save me from the Deamhan sisters," Veronica said. She saw Anastasia's shoulders jump slightly as she laughed under her breath.

"I've been trailing Branda and her sister for years," she said. "I sired them and I released them. It just so happened that they were in the city when I arrived and that they attacked you when they weren't supposed to." Startled at what Anastasia just told her, Veronica looked away. It was the opposite of what Deamhan did; saving a human over another Deamhan they'd sired. A slight breeze blew through the courtyard and Veronica felt the wind underneath her jacket. She noticed Anastasia looking up at the sky with her eyes fixed on the moon.

"Selene is the one who placed the protection on me," Veronica said. "And you don't like her so why did you follow it?"

"I'm not stupid," Anastasia answered. "I've lived for a long time to realize that sometimes, you have to obey the rules to survive."

Anastasia continued to gaze at the moon. "I was alive when men worshipped the moon and the stars were thought to be gods. I know humans and Deamhan better than you could imagine. I've seen what happens when our kind becomes uncontrollable and how humans react. I lived through the rules of the Malleus Maleficarium, the Plagues, and humans reacting to the dangers Deamhan have placed upon them. I've witnessed tortures, hangings, murders and deaths in the name of your god and superstitions, researcher."

"I'm not a researcher." Veronica watched Anastasia move in closer to her with her eyes now tearing into her soul. Veronica looked down but found herself looking back at her. What Remy said about her was right. She fit the type who did what she wanted. Veronica didn't know if she could trust her.

"I've killed plenty of researchers." Anastasia returned her gaze to the moon when she continued. "One more would be nothing to me." The atmosphere became thick and almost unbearable for Veronica. She found it extremely difficult to breathe. Anastasia's warning seemed self-explanatory enough. She didn't like her and didn't trust her.

"So saving me from Murphy? What was that?"

Anastasia lifted her head to the sky. "Mercy for Nathan." Suddenly her eyes darted back and forth and they narrowed. She became completely transfixed on their surroundings. Something wasn't right.

"What is it?" Veronica whispered.

"Q-quiet," Anastasia stuttered in the continuation of her dark lecture. "And remain still—" She stopped again in mid-sentence, but this time she sniffed the air. She took off in Deamhan speed back to the manor, leaving Veronica alone.

Veronica ran after her through the front door and stopped in the den. Pictures on the hallway's walls were crooked. The table cloths on the small tables were scrunched, and a broken vase lay on the floor. She continued down the hallway, following the clues that Anastasia had come down that way and out the back.

When she reached the backyard she saw Nathan, dressed in a brown robe with his smoking pipe in his hand, standing near the small empty garden, leaning against one of the many beautiful marble statues in the yard. Standing next to him was a woman with red hair braided into a long ponytail, dressed in a fitting red dress with Jessica standing next to her. Veronica looked to her right, seeing Anastasia with fists clenched and her eyes glaring at them with Remy and Hallie only a few feet away.

The red haired woman slowly turned around, followed by Nathan. Her face was rough, her cheekbones sharp, and her lips thin. Her bright, green eyes were bright and penetrated through Veronica. She was Deamhan.

"Yes, I am Deamhan," the woman answered Veronica's thoughts in a thick accent. "You look just like your mother."

Fascinated with her appearance, Veronica didn't reply. *This woman; she's Selene!* Her presence awed her.

Selene held out her hand. "I'm Selene. I'm the one that called for your protection."

"A pointless call," Anastasia said.

Selene licked her lips. "Anastasia, I see your pessimistic mindset hasn't changed over the centuries."

Jessica nodded briefly at Veronica, acknowledging her presence. She looked different from the last time Veronica laid eyes on her. She could clearly see her face and she stood with her posture erect.

"Veronica, I grew concerned that you didn't accompany my minion to my sanctuary," Selene said. "I wanted to come to you personally and introduce myself to you."

Concerned? Veronica didn't believe any Deamhan would be concerned for the safety of a human, not even Anastasia (who she still didn't believe saved her at the mercy of Nathan.) "Do you know what happened to my mother?" Veronica didn't waste any time.

Selene shook her head. "No, I don't. But I do believe I know what happened to Lucius who your mother followed."

"You've known all this time, and you didn't do anything?" Anastasia questioned. "He's your sire."

"And he is Kei's sire as well."

"You're older and stronger than Kei."

"Yes, but Kei has thousands of Deamhan who'll follow him into death. He has support that I don't have."

Veronica sighed and looked away.

"I promised Lucius I would look after you and your mother, Veronica," she continued. "I failed once. I won't fail again."

Veronica thought little of Selene's excuse. There had to be more. Why would Lucius care enough about a researcher following him?

"You can't rush into battle with Kei," Selene continued. "Especially when Ancient Deamhan refuse to interfere in the affairs here."

Anastasia rolled her eyes.

"Anastasia, why do you seem so repulsed by my visit?"

"Repulsed?" Anastasia stepped out from the shadows.

"Angry?" Selene searched for the right word to say.

"Maybe I seem repulsed because your excuses are disheveled," Anastasia replied. "Or maybe I seem angry because you decide to do nothing about Kei. I've never trusted you, Selene, even in the past and even now."

Anastasia's hostility for Selene seemed more than just Selene's visit with Nathan. They had a history. Anastasia's disrespect to Selene was so intense that even the air felt heavy. But instead of arguing with Anastasia, Selene remained calm.

"What do you suggest I do against Kei?" Selene asked. "I've called for a Decretum. Like you, I also want to see him dead."

"But unlike you, I've done something about it besides calling for a Decretum," Anastasia answered. Veronica first heard about a Decretum from Sean, who was unsure about its main purpose. It was a calling for Deamhan to hunt and track down other Deamhan. No researcher had ever been involved in it nor was around when it occurred.

"You have his minion." Selene nodded. "If it makes you feel better, Anastasia, what do you suggest that I do?" Veronica and Nathan turned to Anastasia, waiting for her reply.

Anastasia turned her body slightly away from Selene. "No talk. No Decretum."

Nathan didn't seem the slightest bit affected by Anastasia's hostility. He remained quiet, choosing to watch and listen instead of speaking.

"I won't argue with you on that," Selene said. "But even you know that we have to follow The Dictum before going,—as the humans say, commando."

"You are the oldest Deamhan in the city for now, Selene." Anastasia raised her voice. "Lucius is gone. You are his replacement, regardless of what Kei and his followers believe. Do what Ancients are supposed to do; maintain order."

Anastasia started to walk back into the house. "Or are you scared?" Anastasia stopped and looked back at her. Their silence and staring competition allowed Nathan and Veronica to glance back at both of them, curious about what they were doing.

Unexpectedly, Selene moved in a blur and in a second she stood face to face with Anastasia. Anastasia didn't budge but her sharp Ramanga teeth dropped quickly from her gums. Her brown eyes gradually changed as if they were filled with dark liquid, completely engulfing the white of her eyes. Selene's eyes also changed and while they stared at each other, Remy moved in quickly and he gently separated them.

"Ladies, this confrontation will get us nowhere," he said with his eyes also dark and voided of white. "Even though I love seeing a good hair pulling fight, may I suggest that we get to the bottom of what's happening in the city, find Lucius, and kill Kei."

Anastasia's teeth retracted and her eyes returned back to normal.

Selene stepped back and when her eyes turned back to its normal color of green, she spoke. "I want to see this minion that you have."

Anastasia turned back and disappeared into the house without responding. Nathan held out his hand as a welcoming gesture for Selene to enter Blind Bluff Manor. Selene motioned for Jessica to follow her, and without a moment of hesitation, she was trailing behind her and into Nathan's home.

Selene walked through the back door, and once inside the hallway leading to the basement, she paused at the crooked pictures on the wall. She rubbed the picture frame of one of them, a landscape painting with a scene of a riverbed and rocks. Another picture of a woman wearing a white bodice with an elegant dress with a scoop neckline also caught her eye.

They walked down the very same steps Veronica traveled to reach the basement. Selene raised her hand, and Jessica stopped before reaching the top step. She stood to the side and watched Veronica descend down the stairs.

Murphy was still chained to the wall, unaware of Selene's grand appearance. His head was drooped forward, and a small pool of blood collected near his feet. His previous wounds had already healed.

Selene approached him but not once did she concern herself with the various torture devices hanging from the wall. She placed her hand underneath his chin and she lifted his head. His left eye was swollen, but his right eye fluttered and opened slowly.

"You sired him?" She looked over her shoulder, staring at Anastasia who stood next to the chains hanging from the basement wall. Veronica watched as Selene examined him from head to toe.

"Wake up, minion," she whispered. "We need to talk." She removed her hand from underneath his chin, watching his head go limp and his body lean forward. "Centuries passed and you still choose torture." She referred to the state of Murphy's body. The expression on her face turned to concern. "But siring him, that is a twist, even for you, Anastasia." Selene scanned the room, her eyes glancing over the chains next to Anastasia.

Veronica found herself unable to keep her eyes off Selene. *This woman, this Deamhan, made a promise to protect me.* Veronica wanted to know why. What was so dangerous, what was so important to her mother that she trusted Lucius to protect her daughter? The questions had to wait. Now wasn't the time. She needed to find out what thoughts hid in Murphy's brain.

"Kei is having a Congregation, soon." Selene looked back at Murphy. "It's the perfect time to confront him." She placed both of her hands on the right and left side of Murphy's head. "He's weak enough to probe."

Veronica wanted to know why this wasn't done in the first place. The older the Deamhan, the more powerful they were. Selene didn't need to fear Kei. Her thoughts about Selene were loud enough for Selene to glance back at her and smile.

"A Dictum needs willing Deamhan to enforce it. If the younger Deamhan see that us older Deamhan standing against Kei, they will choose survival. Alone, I'm weaker than he is. But with older Deamhan standing at my side, I will be a force to be reckoned with," Selene answered, reading Veronica's thoughts. She turned back to Murphy and she closed her eyes. Murphy's head shot back abruptly. He started to squirm, trying to get away from Selene.

"I tried reading his thoughts, Selene and it didn't work," Anastasia said.

"Of course it wouldn't," Selene replied back. "Even at five hundred years old, Anastasia, you're too young to break through placed barriers."

Selene made contact. The room hushed. Even Anastasia looked interested. She removed herself from the cold walls of the basement, paying close attention. Murphy's body stopped squirming, and he was caught under Selene's spell. Veronica heard soft footsteps coming down the steps. Hallie stood quietly on the bottom step and watched.

A small trickle of blood poured out from Murphy's left ear, and suddenly his body began to shake violently. Selene released her grip and took a couple of steps back, slowly shaking her head.

"Impossible," Selene whispered. Her expression changed from astonishment to absolute rage mixed with fear.

"I told you," Anastasia confirmed.

"No, I was able to get through. It's dark magic. They used dark magic to place Lucius in Limbo."

"Dark magic?" Veronica had heard about dark magic from her father, but like many other things he said to her, she didn't believe it. It was demonic, evil, and practically unstable magic used for harming, torturing, and killing. The Brotherhood never explored the effects of black magic used by Deamhan and researchers.

Limbo was another part of the Deamhan that remained a mystery. Veronica remembered reading about it a few times when she was younger. It was a magical state, a place where Deamhan couldn't escape. No one knew how it came to be and how those placed in Limbo could escape it. If Kei did use dark magic and Limbo to get rid of Lucius, then the possibility of her mother also being placed in Limbo seemed all too real. It was a saddened thought but Veronica felt relieved to know that her mother could still be alive.

Murphy began to laugh. "He told me about you, Selene." Blood dripped from the corners of his mouth.

Selene made eye contact with Murphy. "And what did he say?"

"The first human to be sired by Lucius. A killer of Deamhan and human. You taught him everything he needed to know about being a Lugat."

"So then, you know what I'm going to do to you." Selene's eyes searched the room until they locked onto a piece of wood sitting upright near the back room. In Deamhan speed she rushed over to it, grabbed it, and returned to Murphy. She placed her left hand around his neck and lifted his head and placed the wood over his heart.

"No, don't. Please." His body tensed up, and his laughing ceased.

Before Veronica knew what Selene was doing to Murphy, it was too late. Slowly she embedded the piece of wood into his skin. Murphy's skin turned from a pale hue to a rusted color and it began to sink over his cheekbones and his neck. He gasped once and fell silent while his eyes shriveled into nothing.

Eventually the skin around his face began to flake and fall over. The discoloration traveled over his chest, to his arms and to his legs and eventually to his head. Selene released him and watched as his arms turned into a mixture of thick dust and blood as it dropped to the ground. His legs followed in the evaporation process until there was nothing left but a puddle of dust and blood.

Selene licked her lips in sudden blessedness. Her black eyes returned to its normal state to stare at the dust floating through the air.

Suddenly and abruptly without a word, Selene quickly ascended up the steps, followed by Jessica.

Anastasia crossed her arms in front of her chest and glowered at Selene.

Veronica hurried up the steps, hearing Nathan closely behind her. Selene stood in the foyer and motioned for Jessica to open the front door.

"What did you see?" Veronica's question strangely surprised Selene.

"She saw Limbo," Remy answered. "It's enough to make even the most oldest of Deamhan shake in their boots."

Selene shot Remy a quick glance then she spoke. "The state of Limbo is unknown, even for Deamhan." She looked at Nathan. "Thank you for your hospitality."

Nathan placed his hands on Veronica's shoulders, halting her from moving forward.

"You are most welcome, Selene." He smiled at Selene. Jessica held the door open, and the cold winter air circled through the foyer, carrying snowflakes.

"Is it possible that my mother is there with Lucius?" Veronica asked.

"I don't know." Selene stepped out into the cold air, and Jessica closed the door behind them. Nathan lowered his hands from Veronica's shoulder.

"She must have seen something to scare her to leave so quickly like that," Veronica replied.

They heard Anastasia's faint footsteps walking up the basement steps. She stood in the entranceway and upon hearing Veronica's questions, she quickly answered. "I know where Lucius is. I saw what Selene saw."

They remained quiet as they listened to Anastasia describe seeing Kei dressed in a long silk robe, sitting on a large black throne in front of a huge panned window with several minions, including Murphy, surrounding him.

Dressed in a black leather jacket with matching pants and boots, he sported dark rimmed sunglasses and he wore his brown hair slicked to the back. While the minions worshipped his every being, he remained relaxed and Anastasia sensed his strong cocky demeanor.

The images changed to Murphy, naked in a king size bed with satin sheets. He lay on his stomach, moaning in pleasure and in pain, and Kei was lying on top of him, entering him from behind. All around them were the corpses of human males, some dead and some dying, strewn about like unwanted waste. The image overlapped another picture of an old and abandoned farmhouse in the middle of a cornfield. It tilted to the side, the wood bleached from years of prolonged sunlight. A huge cliff near the edge of the field had a small stream that ran through it. Old and twisted corn stalks filled the surrounding fields. Darkness oozed from a cave near the fields. When Selene had tried piercing through the cave, the images suddenly stopped, leaving the feeling and the odor of Lucius on the tip of Anastasia's tongue.

While Selene fed from Murphy, he could no longer hide the images implanted. Selene was right about the feeling of dark magic and Lucius being in Limbo.

However, none of the images described Limbo and both Anastasia and Selene couldn't sense anything about Veronica's mother.

"I don't know why Selene was so hesitant to continue," Anastasia said. "She probably fears the dark magic." Before Veronica could ask why, Nathan interrupted.

"There isn't enough information about Limbo to understand what it truly is," he exclaimed. "Deamhan and researcher alike have heard of it but there isn't anyone alive who has experienced it." His question left more answers.

"The cave is located south from here," Anastasia replied. "About fifty miles in Steele County."

With this new information, Veronica was ready to travel to the cave Anastasia described. Black magic or no magic, it didn't matter.

"It isn't going to be easy." A voice from above caught their attention. Remy leaned on the railing, looking down at them gathered below. How long he'd been up there, listening to their conversation, no one knew except for Anastasia.

"There's a reason why Selene left as fast as she did."

"And why is that?" Veronica asked.

A wide grin appeared on Remy's face. "That's Amenirdis territory."

Veronica looked to Nathan whose eyes widened. She saw Anastasia's body stiffen and her lips slowly crunched together. Feeling kept out of the loop, she spoke up. "Who is Amenirdis?"

"Oh just the only oldest living Deamhan in the world." Remy approached the stairs and descended slowly, gliding his hands along the railing. "And a strong practitioner of dark magic."

He held his head high, like a king admired by his subjects, and when he reached the bottom stair, he stopped and lowered himself unexpectedly to sit.

"But she's dead," Anastasia responded.

"Don't lie to the poor girl, Ana." Remy smiled. "She's not dead."

"In The Brotherhood we were taught that she was killed centuries ago." Nathan leaned against the walls and folded his arms across his chest. "She was the only Deamhan who could trap humans and Deamhan in Limbo but not without a price." He looked to Remy. "How do you know she's still alive?"

"Because Deamhan like her, don't die easily." Remy examined his fingernails in a cool and calm manner. "She's more than just one of us. She's old, older than all of us, Lucius, Selene, and Kei. Older than all the Ancients that live now." He looked at Veronica. "No one alive has seen her. She doesn't show herself. Instead she has three immortal human girls endowed with magic do her dirty work for her."

Yet another powerful Deamhan entered her search, and Veronica wiped her face with her hand, taking in a deep breath.

"She's the whore of dark magic." Remy looked up at Nathan in a cold and calculated smile. "She's the Queen of Limbo. If you want anyone to suffer that fate, she's the one to go to." He stood up. "I also saw what Anastasia saw. I could smell Amenirdis' scent. It was so strong, it lingered over Murphy's thoughts."

"You've met her before?" Nathan's face filled with disbelief.

"I've met her immortal humans." Remy paused in thought. "My ego is still recovering."

"The last time I heard, she was in Europe," said Anastasia. "If she is alive and she traveled to Minnesota, it would only be because of one thing."

"To put someone in Limbo," Remy answered. They stared at each other for what felt like minutes.

Finally Anastasia spoke up. "We're no match for Amenirdis. Even her human servants are stronger than all of us."

"So sorry, sweat pea." Remy looked to Veronica.

"So that's it?" Veronica replied.

Nathan rubbed his chin in thought. "If she is the one who did this to Lucius, then there may not be anything that we *can* do. And if Remy is working for her or with her, he is also too strong as well." He walked toward his study. Veronica watched Anastasia walk down the back hallway and out to the backyard. She found herself alone with Remy still snickering at her. She contemplated her next move.

"I admire your persistence, Veronica," Remy said to her. "But this isn't one area you'd want to venture in."

Veronica sighed. Not only did she have to deal with Kei but now Amenirdis, a Deamhan she'd never heard before until now and supposedly a Deamhan old and strong enough to scare Selene, her protector.

Hallie raised her hand slightly. "If you go, Veronica, I'll go with you."

Remy laughed under his breath. "You can't protect her. You've never been past the front gates as a Deamhan."

Hallie lowered her chin into her chest and stewed. "At least I have the balls to go."

Veronica straightened her hair and she reached out her hand to Hallie. "Let's go."

"Wait." Remy stood in front of her. "You can't seriously think about going there, tonight."

"Why not?" Veronica walked around him and she headed for the front door with Hallie following her.

Again Remy moved in front of her and he slowly licked his lips. "You humans and kids are so alike; so naïve and eager for the thrill." He opened the front door. "Before we go, I need to make a quick stop."

Veronica looked at him, seeing the devilish spark in his eye.

CHAPTER TWENTY-THREE

Everything around Remy, Hallie, and Veronica moved rapidly as if it existed in its own realm. The stars streaked in the sky, and the lights from the city combined their glow. They moved faster than Veronica thought anyone or anything could move.

Remy tightly held onto her as he moved in Deamhan speed into downtown Minneapolis with Hallie close behind. They zigzagged around buses, cars and pedestrians walking down the street. Veronica felt her stomach churn, and throughout the whole wild ride, she closed her eyes, fearing if she'd open up, the images would add to her nausea.

The smell of car exhaust filled her nose, and she felt Remy slowing down, finally coming to a stop. Before leaving Blind Bluff Manor, he told her his speed would affect her. She didn't know what that meant until she found herself on the verge of vomiting. He brought up the idea of driving, but Veronica wanted to get to the cave before Selene changed her mind and decided to find Amenirdis. Plus Remy made it clear that he wasn't going to be caught in the middle of no man's land during sunrise. He then mentioned something that would help her control the traveling aversion. Something that humans drank to experience what it felt like to be a Deamhan, minus the immortality; something that she had consumed before. Sensual Appetite.

She opened her eyes. They stopped near the University of Minnesota. A snow plow drove by, pushing excess snow from the street onto the curb. Remy let go of her arm and watched Veronica slowly recover to her senses.

"Fucking epic!" Hallie cheered. "Wow, I can always run like that?"

"Keep your voice down," Remy hushed her. "I don't want him to know we're coming."

They stood in front of a white two level home with a waist-high wooden fence with a shoveled sidewalk. A small sign which read "Welcome to Our Home" was staked in the front yard. From the outside, the home looked nothing like a sanctuary.

"You've had Sensual Appetite before right?" Remy questioned Veronica.

Veronica nodded and tried to rid the memory of the taste from her mouth.

She didn't want to think of the repulsing experience.

Remy stopped in front of the steps, staring at the straw welcome mat in front of the door. He looked up and began to glance at the home like he'd never seen it before.

"Is something wrong?" Veronica quietly asked.

He continued to observe. "New paint job." He tapped on the siding of the house. He peeked through the darkened windows of the home and the white window shades that covered them on the inside. The house was completely dark with no movement. Veronica waited for Remy, who turned the knob and opened the door.

Veronica remained where she stood, then she cautiously followed Remy and Hallie into the home, hoping their presence was enough to ward off any danger they might encounter. Three men sat on a couch in the living room, facing a television. The first one who saw them enter immediately grabbed the remote and turned it off. He raised himself from the couch, nervous, and stared back at them. Veronica stood behind Remy, seeing the fear in their eyes.

Veronica assumed they were all minions and they belonged to someone. From the back room, another group appeared from the hallway and stopped where they stood. Used cups, old newspapers, and various other trash littered the floor. The yellow stained walls, also peppered with holes, contributed to Veronica's stereotype of what a Deamhan sanctuary outside of Nathan's looked like. The repugnant air filled their nostrils. Two piles of dust and blood forming the shape of two bodies, lay next to the television stand. The light fixture in the living room dangled from the ceiling by a cord severed at its base.

"Disgusting."

Remy took one slow glance around the room and took a step forward.

"Smells like rotten fish." Hallie covered her nose. A mouse ran in front of her and she jumped. "Fucking gross."

Veronica watched two female children standing near the staircase. One of them, who looked fairly young, held a small tattered doll in her hand, and the other stood in front, blocking the other from her gaze.

"Where is he?" Remy asked them. A male minion pointed up the stairs. Remy glanced over the two piles of dust. "His work?"

The male nodded.

They headed up the stairs to the second floor of the sanctuary, which looked just as filthy as downstairs. Cardboard boxes crowded the hallways, some damaged from water dripping from the ceiling. The floor creaked as they walked. A cockroach ran in front of Remy, and he crushed it with his foot without interrupting his stride. An intricate cobweb spun above them from the left side of the wall to the right.

This couldn't be the Deamhan The Brotherhood spoke about. They weren't the harbingers of death and destruction anymore. They were squatters and out of control vagrants. These minions and their Deamhan masters seemed too busy dwelling in their own filth to concentrate on someone as puny as herself. Somehow, along in their history, they lost their spine-chilling image. It was sanctuaries like these that were being destroyed and burnt to the ground. Veronica began to think that maybe it wasn't such a bad thing after all.

"It's the last door on the left." Remy pointed. They came upon the door and without warning, Remy forcefully pushed on it. The door cracked, separating from its hinges and crashed to the floor.

A female and a male, both naked and startled from the noise, raised themselves from their bed. The female immediately covered her breasts and her crotch with her hands, and the short statured male, smiled at the appearance of Remy.

"Hey, Ollie." Remy moved to the right side of the bed and Hallie moved to the other. The male laughed and raised himself up. Fully naked, he walked over to a pile of clothes stacked in the corner of the room. Veronica peered into the room, watching him dress himself in a faded shirt which read "Drunk on Duty" and white soiled shorts. An odor of sex lingered in the air. She wrinkled her nose at the appearance of this Deamhan who didn't seem to care who watched him parade around unclothed.

"Still fucking your food instead of eating it, Ollie?" Remy briefly looked at the startled female.

Ollie smoothed back his short brown hair and shrugged his shoulders. "Best of both worlds." His speech staggered with a prominent lisp. He whistled at the woman and harshly told her to beat it. She scurried out of the room with her head hung low. Now fully dressed, Ollie sat back on his bed and pulled a pack of cigarettes from underneath his pillow. He glanced at Remy before he lit his cigarette.

"You don't knock anymore?" He inhaled.

"I've never knocked," Remy responded back. Ollie's eye focused on Veronica.

"She's a cutie," he muttered. "But I'm not buying today. Come back tomorrow."

"She's not for sale." Remy brushed aside dirt particles from the bed. He sat down and crossed his legs. "I need some."

"Need what?"

"Sensual Appetite, you twit."

Ollie inhaled again but delayed in exhaling. "Don't have any," he replied, "I sell that shit like hotcakes. I get a new batch in tomorrow."

Remy reached out and yanked the cigarette from Ollie's hand. He crushed it in his grip and tossed it back into his lap. His reaction made Ollie jump slightly.

"Jeez, you didn't have to do that," he whined. Remy kneeled beside the bed, pulling out a small wooden box with a small lock from underneath. He placed it on the bed and yanked the lock and tossed the broken pieces on the floor.

"That's my personal stash." Ollie stood up. The box was filled with small glass vials stacked gently next to each other. The liquid contained in these vials varied from orange to blue to bright red.

"What's that?" Hallie questioned.

"Human blood in a bottle, manufactured by Deamhan for Deamhan. It's like heroin for our kind," Remy answered. "It's made so that any Deamhan can devour it and experience the taste of a meal, with additives added."

"I'll pass." Hallie's nose scrunched.

"That isn't cheap, y'know." Ollie inhaled.

"How much?" Remy held the small vial between his thumb and forefinger, examining the reddish bubbly fluid.

"Five hundred," Ollie replied. "And I'm being generous."

"Oh, Ollie." Remy grabbed the liquid. "You're funny, did I ever tell you that?" He tossed the vial to Veronica. Remy patted the bed and stood up. "It was nice seeing you, Ollie." He walked toward the door.

"You can't take that!" Ollie rushed after him.

Remy turned around. "Why not?"

"I'll be short, and my supplier will kill me."

Remy snickered and patted the top of Ollie's head. "Well, that's your problem."

"C'mon, Remy. My supplier isn't going to sit well with this."

"I wouldn't worry about your supplier." Remy watched Veronica put the vial in her pocket. "I'd be more worried about Anastasia. She knows you're selling."

They walked out of the room.

* * * *

"It's better than a taxi." Remy opened the vial.

They stood on the corner down the street from the sanctuary. The cold affected Veronica and she began to shiver. The coat Remy gave her off his back helped a little, but she wasn't sure if it was going to help her while traveling in Deamhan speed.

The Deamhan felt the cold, but it was nowhere near the way a human felt it. The human heart worked harder at maintaining body temperature. As far as she knew, they didn't have a body temperature nor did their heart beat at all.

Remy sniffed the liquid and handed the vial to Veronica.

"Are you sure?" She hesitated.

"You can't continue to travel in our speed. Your heart can't take it," he replied. "But this will help you tolerate it."

Veronica glanced at the vial then looked up at them. *For mother,* she thought to herself. She dreaded tasting the same icky taste when she first had Sensual Appetite. She also feared what this amount would do to her. The drink she was given in Dark Sepulcher was mixed with alcohol, but this wasn't mixed with anything.

186

She closed her eyes and tilted her head back, feeling the warm liquid ooze down her throat. She dropped the bottle, and it shattered on the pavement. Immediately she felt the effects of the drink. Her sight became blurred, and it was a challenge just to keep her eyelids from closing shut. Her head became too heavy to lift. She felt the cold of Remy's palm against hers.

"Whatever happens"— he pulled Veronica closer to her— "don't let go."

Veronica grasped him tightly and closed her eyes, hearing the wind rush in her ears. Her hair flew uncontrollably, and her legs no longer touched the ground. She felt dizzy while they constantly moved. Her body jerked to the left and to the right and the cold breeze blew down her shirt.

They traveled in Deamhan speed.

For a moment, she felt a part of their world. She attempted to squeeze Remy harder, afraid of what'd happen if she let go. She heard the frequent stomps of his feet hitting the ground and he was in mid-air again, taking uncanny strides; strides unfathomable for a human.

This experience felt nothing like she'd felt before and nothing she'd ever feel again. Their speed increased, and the wind's cold chills brushed against her skin. She had no fear and no pain. Only the feeling of floating and a sense that she was invincible.

CHAPTER TWENTY-FOUR

They came to a sudden halt, and Veronica felt her body jerk forward. She attempted to open her eyes, but her eyelids remained closed. Pressure throughout her body increased and she fell to the floor, feeling the liquid expel from her mouth.

Remy straightened his clothes. "It's breath-taking, isn't it?"

Their surroundings matched exactly what Anastasia described. They saw the tilted abandoned shack with its broken windows. Dead cornstalks dotted the landscape along with patches of snow and dirt.

Veronica remained on the pavement, moaning in pain. Hallie bent over to help her but Remy stopped Hallie.

"I got her." He placed his arms around her waist and lifted her to her feet. "Don't pass out on me now," he whispered as he placed her right arm over his shoulders. They slowly walked into the cornfield, heading toward the stream.

Veronica felt her stomach twisting and knotting. She felt as if her body was on its last breath and her blood boiled inside her veins. In between her moans she heard Remy talking to Hallie. He found it odd that his Deamhan hearing couldn't pick up any animal noises around them. They heard nothing; no bird overhead, no wolves in the distant. The silence, except for the snow crunching beneath their feet, became overbearing.

Thick clouds blanketed the sky, blocking the stars and hiding any warning of sunrise. Eventually Veronica gathered enough strength to finally open her eyes. They continued walking through pine trees and through leafless bushes.

"This place reminds me of Oregon." Veronica overheard Remy.

"When did you live in Oregon?" Hallie asked him.

"A long time ago."

The sound of running water ahead broke the silence and Remy slowed his pace. He moved Veronica's strands of hair from her face. "I think she's okay." He slowly set her on her feet.

Hallie waved her hand in front of Veronica's face. "You okay?"

Veronica wiped the droplets of bile from her chin. "Yeah, I'm fine." She stood up straight. "Let's keep going."

"Are you sure?" Remy questioned again. "We can go back if you're not feeling well."

"I'm fine," Veronica replied again. "Let's go."

"Just like a champ," Remy said.

They approached a steep creek bed, cloaking a small half frozen stream. Hallie skipped over it and immediately slipped, falling on her back. The wind picked up briefly and Hallie lifted her eyes, seeing Anastasia, dressed in black pants, black shirt, with her hair blowing in the wind, standing in front of her.

A look of enjoyment ebbed from Hallie's face. "I'm not going back and you can't make me!" She stood up. "Remy invited me along."

Remy stepped over the stream and he helped Veronica by letting her use him as support as she crossed. "I knew you'd come sooner or later." He smiled at Anastasia. "You could never resist the temptation to play with fire." He wiped his forehead.

Anastasia looked at Veronica, watching her erratic breathing. "You shouldn't have brought her here."

"Oh lighten up." Remy smiled. "She wanted to come."

Anastasia sniffed the air briefly. "Sensual Appetite?"

"It was the only way to transport her without hurting her, and you know that," Remy stated. Veronica moaned slightly, feeling the cold arctic wind cutting at her face.

"She'll slow us down," Anastasia said.

"Carry her if you want then." Remy continued through the bushes followed by Hallie and Veronica.

They headed north, carefully stepping over tree stumps. Drops of water from icicles above landed on Veronica's forehead and she wiped them away. She pushed low tree branches from her path, and she saw Anastasia easily lift a huge branch out of their way.

"How far is it?" Hallie began to complain.

"It's not like you're cold out here," Remy replied.

"I'm not. I just don't understand why any Deamhan would live out this far. I mean, how does she eat?"

"She doesn't."

"What do you mean 'she doesn't'?"

"If she isn't dead as I was led to believe, then Amenirdis is the oldest living Deamhan on the planet." Anastasia interrupted the conversation. "She needs little sustenance, if any."

"So if I get to live as long as her, then I wouldn't have to eat?" Hallie asked.

"You won't get to live as long as her," Anastasia replied. "Before I was even sired, Amenirdis was legendary. She was a powerful and nearly indestructible Deamhan who was worshipped as a goddess."

"I'd always thought she was merely a fairytale," Remy added. "Something Deamhan sires would say to scare us new ones in line."

"No one alive knows what she looks like." Anastasia quickly turned to Remy. "Your thoughts are demented Remy. Why are you looking forward to encountering her when you almost died the last time you both met?"

Remy stopped in his tracks. "Who invited you into my thoughts?" He smiled devilishly.

Anastasia moved in closer, standing inches from him. "Answer my question."

Veronica watched their standoff, waiting to see who'd be the first to attack. But no fists flew. Instead, Remy placed his hands in his pockets and he continued to smile.

"What can I say? She excites me," he replied.

Anastasia glared into his eyes.

"Guys, shouldn't we be moving?" Hallie whispered. "Dawn is only a few hours away."

Remy's eyebrows lifted. "Yes, we should."

They continued their journey. Veronica hoped they'd reach the cave before her fingers froze. She feared getting frostbite and her toes began to feel numb. While walking, Anastasia continued her story to Hallie about Amenirdis. According to Anastasia's story, Amenirdis had no sides and no boundaries. She cared little for right or wrong. Those who respected her as a goddess, Lucius included, feared her. Anastasia found it ironic that no one knew her of origins, except for the fact that she was the oldest Ancient and she practiced Dark Magic. No one knew what Deamhan type she was or how she became the Queen of Limbo (even the creation of Limbo remained an obscure thought.) The main ideas surrounding Amenirdis was that she was all powerful, all knowing, and a Deamhan that you did not cross.

Ahead, Anastasia noticed a small overhang of rocks and an entrance to a cave. She lifted her head slightly, trying to inhale any scent in the air.

"I don't smell anything," she said.

Remy sniffed and he too shook his head. Hallie even tried and she came up empty.

"Just tree sap and fish." Anastasia adjusted her eyes to look into the cave. "Even my eye sight won't allow me to look in there. It's too dark."

"Dark magic," Remy suggested. "Must mean we're here."

"Hallie, wait here with Veronica." Anastasia moved forward but Veronica stepped in front of her.

"I'm not staying out here." Veronica's stern approach caused Anastasia to snarl.

Remy snickered. "Anastasia, she's going in there, no matter how sharp your canines are."

Veronica stepped over a splintered branch and she approached the cave. She swallowed her fear hard enough to feel her throat throb. This was it. This was the reason she came to Minneapolis.

A group of bats flew over her. The sound of their wings flapping uncontrollably didn't startle her. When she took her first step into the cave, the area somehow suddenly came to life. The interior lit up and Veronica could now see the rocky cropping ahead of them.

The sandy dirt floor, littered with bat droppings, made Veronica pause for a quick second. A square rock sat in the middle of the cave and on top of it, a small lit candle flickered. But the cave was extremely bright and Veronica couldn't understand how one small flame could give off so much light. Boulders lazily stacked upon one another blocked the end of the cave.

She turned back, watching Anastasia, Hallie, and Remy enter the cave cautiously. For Deamhan, they seemed more scared than she was. But if what Anastasia said was true, they had more to fear than she did.

"Hello?" Veronica called out in a trembling curious voice. She waited for a reply yet instead she heard the soft footsteps of Anastasia behind her.

Anastasia sniffed the air again. "Stale and empty," she said to herself as she walked forward.

Suddenly the figure of a bald woman, dressed in a white flowing gown materialized from the side of the cave. Three other female figures dressed and looking exactly the same, manifested from the back and the right wall. They looked young; barely teenagers. They had to be Amenirdis' minions, the ones that Remy mentioned back in Blind Bluff Manor. Their appearance startled Veronica and she wondered why someone as powerful as Amenirdis needed humans to do her bidding in the first place.

This time Anastasia made the approach. "We're here for Amenirdis." Anastasia lowered herself onto her knees followed by Remy, who forced Hallie to follow. Witnessing this, Veronica followed their behavior.

The triplets didn't speak. Instead, they remained still with their shiny, soft looking immaculate skin. They stood near the rock, and one of them blew out the candle.

The cave went dark, but their robes pulsated in the darkness. Veronica stood up and she stepped back. The power exerting from them was staggering and just enough to make Veronica rethink coming to the cave in the first place.

"We seek Amenirdis' wisdom." Anastasia remained on her knees with her head lowered. "Is she here?"

The triplets turned their white hollowed eyes in Veronica's direction.

"She is everywhere," the third triplet replied.

"Offspring of Lucia," the first triplet said. "Amenirdis knows why you're here."

Anastasia stood to her feet. "I no longer consider myself her offspring. The last time I was called that was centuries ago and that human priest didn't live to see another day. Is Amenirdis here?"

"She's here," the second triplet replied. Anastasia looked around and behind her, seeing nothing to indicate that Amenirdis was in the cave.

Simultaneously, the triplets looked in Veronica's direction. "Humans are not allowed here." They spoke in unison.

"Look who's talking." Remy stood to his feet. "Since when did Amenirdis rely on her minions to speak for her?"

Wind rushed past them and all of a sudden Remy found himself on his knees again. His eyes rolled to the back of his head and his body convulsed. Hallie jumped up in Deamhan speed and she screamed, jolting out of the cave and disappearing into the cold night.

Veronica saw that Anastasia was also taken back. Her fangs dropped and she barked.

"Offspring of Julian Endor," the first triplet said with her eyes still glued on Veronica. "Did you not learn your lesson the last time we let you go with your life?"

Remy gripped at his throat and his body flew back into the cave wall. His hands contorted and his head shook violently.

"We didn't come to fight," Anastasia quickly offered. "We came for Lucius. We aren't foolish enough to challenge Amenirdis."

"Please," Veronica begged.

The first triplet raised her hand. "You aren't allowed to speak."

Suddenly Remy fell face first into the dirt floor. Seconds later he lifted his body, using the wall as leverage. His dark, pupil free eyes reverted back to normal.

"I guess not." He stepped forward and fell again, but Anastasia caught him in mid-air. She gently laid him back against the wall.

"Humans aren't allowed in Deamhan affairs," the first triplet said again.

Veronica stepped forward. She chose her words carefully, realizing that if they had that much power to harm Remy, they could do much worse to her. "Please, can I speak?"

The first triplet lowered her hand. "No, you cannot."

Veronica looked to Anastasia.

"The human came here to seek Amenirdis' wisdom regarding her mother."

"Her human mother is not our concern."

"Yes, but her human mother was with Lucius who was placed in Limbo by Amenirdis. I came here seeking Lucius' whereabouts and to plead with your master to free him from Limbo."

"While your strength and determination is admired —" the second triplet started.

"No human is allowed here." The third triplet finished the sentence.

"It's against—" the first triplet continued and then fell silent.

"The rules," the third triplet concluded.

"She speaks through you, but I don't want to speak with you. I want to speak to Amenirdis," Anastasia insisted. "I want to know what she did with Lucius."

The triplets turned to one another. Anastasia glanced at Veronica, who remained assertive, staring at the triplets ahead. Again she risked unknown determination. The triplets could do to her what they did to Remy or Amenirdis might appear and kill them where they stood. If it came down to a confrontation, she hoped that Anastasia was strong enough to hold them off until she escaped.

"Why are you helping this human?" The first twin asked, looking at Anastasia but she was hesitant to answer.

"What makes this human different, offspring of Lucia?" The third twin continued the questioning.

This time Anastasia replied. "Does it matter? You already know what I'm going to say. You know the real reason I'm here."

"Yes, but does the human know why you traveled to this domain?"

Suddenly a strong force slammed into Veronica and she saw Anastasia's thoughts thanks to the Sensual Appetite she devoured earlier. Pictures of her human life as a farmer's daughter in the late 1500's England and her strict Catholic parents appeared in crisp images. She saw Anastasia's maker; a dark haired woman who laughed like a jackal while watching Anastasia, drained of blood, lying helplessly in a bale of hay. Then the images of death and murder. A group of robed men, staking Anastasia and placing her in a metal coffin. That was soon followed by the image of a man who Veronica somehow knew to be Lucius, freeing Anastasia from death. Veronica sensed Anastasia's strong loyalty to Lucius. She would do anything for him. In Minneapolis she stood by his side. The images changed and Veronica saw through Anastasia's eyes when she confronted Branda and Brandy in the bathroom at Dark Sepulcher.

Veronica's eyes watered. The information became overwhelming and she wanted the projections to stop but they continued. She sensed Anastasia's regret and hatred for her own sire and being made a Ramanga. She felt that Anastasia wasn't bounded by human emotions, but she strongly wanted to be. Somewhere, inside her Ramanga soul, hid the sympathetic, caring and loving farmer's daughter by the human name of Auerelia who desperately wanted to help Veronica, not the iniquitous Anastasia who wanted to bathe in human blood.

Then the image of Nathan, surrounded in white light gave off a sense of relief. Veronica felt Anastasia's respect and admiration for him, even though the Deamhan part of her wanted to rip his throat out. She saw Anastasia in her room at Dark Sepulcher, pacing back and forth in Deamhan speed, ripping her hair out from its roots just to watch it grow back again. She then saw Anastasia watching Nathan from a distance in his study, glaring at his mannerisms and hoping to copy them to perfection one day. She longed for her humanity and she fought her dark desires and urges and in her brain, she repeatedly told herself that she would do anything to protect Nathan from harm.

Anastasia envied Veronica's humanity.

"Lucius must be freed from Limbo," Anastasia demanded.

The pain stopped and Veronica opened her eyes. The feeling of remorse engulfed her.

Anastasia quickly looked over her shoulder, past Remy and at the dark entrance of the cave. The smell of Selene circled in her nose just in time to see Selene walking toward them from the shadows with Hallie close behind her. She made no attempt to hide her approach. Frost covered the top of her reddish hair, glistening in the darkness of the cave. Her eyelids were also covered in frozen perspiration, and she wiped them with the back of her hand, clearing almost all of it away.

She kneeled and lowered her head. "I come as a servant of Amenirdis," she announced humbly. "And as the offspring of Lucius."

The triplets nodded and Selene stood to her feet.

"Offspring of Lucius," the third triplet said. "You also seek Lucius?"

"Yes, and I implore you to free him," Selene replied. "Kei had no right to seek Amenirdis' help in placing Lucius in Limbo."

"Her favor—" the first triplet started.

"Does not come without a price," the third triplet finished.

"And what price is that?" Anastasia argued back.

"A price that only Amenirdis knows," the second triplet answered.

Selene looked to Anastasia. "I accept the price," she stated.

"As do I," Anastasia also said.

"Only one must accept the price," the second triplet said.

Veronica swallowed and she gathered her wits to speak. "And my mother?"

"Quiet!" Anastasia looked back at her. "You aren't allowed to speak."

"She should be allowed," Selene replied. "She came with the same reason we're here. Being human shouldn't hold any weight in that."

The first triplet raised her hand. "Will you accept the price offspring of Lucius?"

Selene nodded but suddenly Anastasia stood in front of her. "No, *I* will accept the price."

"You have no right!" Selene quickly grabbed Anastasia by her arm and she tossed her aside. Anastasia landed on her feet and in breakneck speed she launched herself at Selene. The triplets intervened and with a quick swipe of their hand, Anastasia found herself pushed against the cave walls.

"Offspring of Lucius has accepted the price." The triplets spoke in unison. "The deal has been made." Their clothing became brighter, illuminating the surrounding area. They watched as the effulgent light blasted into Selene, turning even brighter. Veronica covered her eyes, followed by Remy, Hallie and Anastasia, who found the light too strong for their Deamhan eyes. The glow seeped between the cracks of Veronica's fingers, and even when she closed her eyes, the darkness illuminated, making it impossible to block it. The light gravitated, and the intensity of it decreased until darkness overcame the room and the small candle reappeared, kindling on the surface of a rock.

Veronica cautiously opened her eyes.

The triplets were gone. In their place, lying on the floor in front of the huge rock, was the body of Lucius.

His long light brown hair gracefully lay across his chest, covering his nipples and part of his stomach. His distorted skin looked like leather; a sign that he hadn't fed in a long time. His eyes were closed and his lips were partially opened. Anastasia rushed over to him and she knelt over his ravaged body.

Veronica saw that Selene was also lying on the ground. She slowly stood to her feet, wiping the dirt from her clothing. She looked at her hands then she felt her face. Her eyes riffled through the cave and when she made contact with Veronica, she smiled.

"That was easier than I thought." Remy watched as Anastasia turned Lucius' body on its side. When she gently touched the side of his cold face, Lucius opened his hazel eyes.

"Lucius," Anastasia whispered.

Lucius' eyes jumped to Veronica. Anastasia turned around, seeing the effect of Lucius' return in Veronica's watered eyes. Tears began to stream down her face, and her mouth quivered. Yet a hint of anger hid behind her sorrow. She still held onto the thought that her mother would reappear with him.

Anastasia gently placed her hands under Lucius' body and she lifted him to his feet. He slightly opened his eyes, letting out a grunt when he felt the hardened soil underneath his feet.

"What was the deal you made, Selene?" Remy asked.

"I don't know and I don't care." Selene approached Lucius. "My beloved, my sire. Welcome back."

Lucius turned his head slowly to look at her.

"Am I the only one who cares about this deal?" Remy spoke again. "Any deal made with Amenirdis can't be good."

Ignoring Remy's statement, Selene whispered softly into Lucius' ear. "Kei will suffer for what he's done to you. And you will be there to witness his death."

Lucius looked up at Veronica, and in his eyes she saw his strength slowly regaining. Without notice, he pushed both Anastasia and Selene violently away. He took a step toward Veronica then stopped, trying to focus his eyes on her. He held out his wrinkled hand and spoke only one word; Caroline.

"She is not Caroline." Selene jumped to her feet. "She is her daughter."

Sensing an opportunity, Veronica spoke. "Do you know what happened to my mother?"

Lucius calmly lowered his hand. In a gust of wind he ran past her and toward the entryway of the cave knocking Remy and Hallie against the rock wall, disappearing from their sight.

CHAPTER TWENTY-FIVE

Veronica heard Nathan's footsteps pacing back and forth in the foyer of Blind Bluff Manor. She stood near the window, watching a black limousine drive up the path and stop in front of the door.

Since the night of Lucius' release from Limbo, everything in and around the sanctuary came to a complete stop. Veronica could barely sleep and her appetite was close to nonexistent. As far as she was aware, no one else knew about Lucius' release and Selene wanted to keep it that way. After Lucius ran from the cave, Anastasia followed and had tried looking for him, but his scent became lost among the vampires and Deamhan in the city.

Veronica also became intrigued with Anastasia after the fiasco. She knew exactly what thoughts Anastasia kept hidden. They weren't normal thoughts for a Ramanga, but it proved to Veronica that underneath the Deamhan persona, Anastasia still had human tendencies. She decided to keep what she knew to herself but it made her view Anastasia in a whole new light.

A few days passed and Veronica grew impatient. Selene promised that she would keep in touch but she'd sent no word after the night in the cave. When she finally sent word, it wasn't on the location of Lucius but an invitation to a Congregation that Kei was throwing.

"She's here," Nathan announced to Veronica. He walked to the front door and turned the knob. "Are you sure you want to go, Veronica?"

Veronica waited before nodding her head.

Nathan opened the door, standing face to face with the human limousine driver.

Before she left the sanctuary, Nathan whispered in her ear telling her that she had nothing to worry about. Veronica let out a sigh and closed her eyes, picturing an image of her mother in the dark, looking back at her.

"This is for you, Mom," she whispered as she exited the sanctuary into the cold air. The driver followed her and made his way around to the back passenger door. Veronica approached the limo cautiously, staring at her image in the car window.

The driver opened the door and Veronica caught a glimpse of Selene, who motioned for her to get in. Veronica glanced back at Nathan before entering the limo. She gave him a soft smile as she climbed into the back seat.

Once inside, she smelled lavender. Small wine glasses were stacked near the floor, next to the opposite door. The cushions, made of velvet material, gave the limo an elegant almost expensive look.

"It's good to see you." Selene wore a red, short dress with red high heels. Her red hair sat on the top of her head in a neatly formed bun.

Veronica turned around and found herself looking into the eyes of an attractive male dressed in a tuxedo. Like all of The Deamhan, his light brown eyes were pupil free and his smooth, pale skin lacked any blemishes. His short, dark brown hair contrasted, fooling her eyes into seeing his skin glow under the light in the limo. Veronica felt totally underdressed.

The Deamhan male sipped on his wine in small gulps then he smiled. "I have the pleasure of two women." His body was average and his square face seemed too big for his body. The body of a female with ratted brown hair sat next to him, slouched in her seat with her shredded mini skirt raised high above her hips, showing her red silky underwear. Small puncture wounds covered her neck, arms, and her stomach.

"Just push her onto the floor," the Deamhan male suggested to Veronica. The limo driver walked around the back end of the limo. He sat in the front seat and started the engine. The male grabbed Veronica's hand and brought it up to his mouth, kissing it.

"She's beautiful." His mouth slightly opened while he gawked at her.

"She's under my protection," Selene replied. Veronica jerked forward as the limo proceeded to move. The Deamhan male moved aside, making enough room for Veronica to sit. She had no choice but to sit next to the corpse.

"She must be a piece of work." He snickered and dropped Veronica's hand. "Pity."

"Silvanus, I wouldn't have your driver drive all the way out here for just a meal."

"Meal?" He looked at Veronica. "More like a snack to me."

Selene smiled briefly. "Don't make me regret inviting you all the way out to Minneapolis for this."

"I wouldn't miss this for the world."

The limo drove through the front gates of Blind Bluff Manor and continued down the road.

Silvanus pouted. "Italy was getting boring anyway. It's not like it used to be. I remember when you could get a good, virgin meal for half the price. You'd think the bigger the human population, the more abundant the food." He reached under his jacket and pulled out a metallic flask. "But they all have diseases, their blood is just dreaded awful and you can't just toss them in an alley without finding their murder featured on the ten o'clock news."

"It's called adapting."

"Well, the Deamhan in this city sure aren't adapting. It's like a Bacchanalia festival every night here with Kei leading the young Deamhan astray . . . poor bastards." He smiled. "Don't get me wrong. I'll take a Bacchanalia festival any day, but not with that inbred throwing the party." He unscrewed the lid and took a sip. "And I thought the French were bad. Even the blood is horrid here." His face shriveled at the taste of the liquid.

Veronica had heard about the ancient Roman festival celebrating the god of wine. Adapted from the Greeks and their festival for Dionysus, the festivals had drunken humans, letting go of their humanity, and losing themselves to chaos and free will. It wasn't her area of expertise, but from Silvanus' interest in the subject, he appeared to be fond of them.

She remained quiet, watching the two Deamhan in conversation. Like many Deamhan she encountered in her search, she'd never heard of Silvanus until this night.

He placed the flask back into his jacket. "Why can't I find one poor soul who doesn't put crap into his or her own blood stream?"

Veronica continued to look out the tinted windows at the darkened scenery. She wanted the car ride to be as quick as possible. The car turned the corner, and the female body fell over just inches away from her feet.

"Get rid of it," Selene demanded.

Silvanus chuckled and he picked up the body, clumsily placing it on his lap. "Don't give me the whole 'I'm an Ancient and I should follow the Dictum' routine. It gets old."

Selene sighed. "Just get rid of it."

Silvanus looked at the body. Without answering, he opened his door and pushed it onto the street. Veronica heard a huge thump as the body hit the ground and rolled onto the pavement. Silvanus closed the door and resumed his comfortable position.

"There. Happy?"

Selene looked back, watching the dead body roll into the bushes on the side of the road. "This isn't about being happy, Silvanus, this is about following the rules."

"The Dictum, yes, I know," Silvanus said while rolling his eyes. "The Dictum . . . everything is about 'The Dictum' to you." He looked back at Veronica. "Excuse Selene, she's very adamant about our laws. Just like her sire." He leaned back in his seat, focusing now on Selene. "So, where is Lucius? From what I heard, he hasn't been seen since his release."

Selene didn't answer.

"You lost him? Already?" Silvanus thought for a moment. "You can't sense him?"

Veronica quickly looked at Selene.

"No." Selene ignored Veronica's gaze.

"Do you think he's dead?" Silvanus quizzed.

"No, I would've felt his death," she quickly replied. "He's alive, out there."

"You know, my dear, Lucius is the first known Deamhan to have been freed from Limbo"—Silvanus rubbed his hands together in thought— "there is a good reason that Amenirdis decided to let him go and it wasn't out of the goodness in her shriveled heart."

Selene positioned herself on her right side and she gazed out at the scenery. "Whatever the price, I'm willing to pay."

Silvanus rubbed his hands together in glee. "I can't wait to see what that price is!" He studied Veronica. "So this human is important to Lucius?"

"Yes," Selene answered. "Very much so."

Veronica cleared her throat and decided to speak. "Lucius will be there? At the Congregation?"

"I communicated with him but he didn't reply," Selene answered. "I don't know if he'll show up."

"Why wouldn't he?" Silvanus smiled. "No one misses out on a Congregation, and from what I've heard, Kei knows how to throw them." Silvanus sighed in exuberance. "Haven't been to one of those in centuries."

"I'm only bringing you because Amenirdis failed to tell you about your mother," Selene said to Veronica. "If what we know is true, then Kei was the last person to see your mother. I will force the information from him."

"Not before I get a little private time with him." Silvanus grabbed onto his lapel triumphantly. "I owe that bastard a beating or two." He placed his hand on Selene's thigh."Indeed, Silvanus."

"And after I rip his head off and devour his blood, you can thank me later by throwing some praise my way."

Selene tilted her head. "When Kei is nothing but dust and blood, then we can all rejoice."

CHAPTER TWENTY-SIX

The limo arrived in the warehouse district, located in what once was the thriving center of the city. Extraordinary in their day, the tall, now gutted brick buildings had a history filled with competing businesses, factories and living spaces. Buildings like the one used for Kei's macabre parties, still had their use.

They exited the limo. Veronica stayed close to Selene, following her to the front door guarded by two large male bodyguards dressed in long, black robes with expressionless masks. The masks resembled the legendary Moai; frozen forever but still guarding their sacred space.

When Silvanus reached the door, one of the bodyguards greeted him by name. However, they stood still with no intention of moving aside.

Selene looked to Silvanus, who smirked. "Out of my way," she demanded. The bodyguards remained in their position.

"Kei gave strict orders barring you from his Congregation ma'am."

"You heard her," Silvanus interrupted the bodyguard. "And I suggest you listen to her and step aside."

"I'm sorry, sir, but we have to follow Kei's orders."

Selene easily pushed the bodyguards aside, showing her brute strength. "Tell him I don't listen to his orders, especially when they come from the mouths of human bodyguards."

Veronica waited for the bodyguards' reactions, but they did nothing. Instead they stared as Selene pushed open the front door and proceeded inside.

"After you," Silvanus said chivalrously to Veronica.

They walked ahead, seeing a flight of stairs leading to a lower level. They reached the bottom platform and two more human bodyguards also wearing masks, stood in front of another door. They didn't question Selene, nor did they say anything. They voluntarily stepped aside and opened the door allowing them to walk through.

Bright flashing lights blinded them, giving Veronica only seconds to adjust her eyes. The room, filled with Deamhan socializing and loud, thumping music, filled the once gutted out space in the basement of the building. The smell of dampness, clove cigarettes, and cologne filled the air. Bright purple, white and red couches packed with seated Deamhan, dressed extravagantly, lined the peeled and chipped paint walls. Chandeliers and numerous disco balls hung from the ceiling, along with flashing strobe lights. The packed dance floor soon filled with the onset of a new song.

"Wow, this is a change," Silvanus said to Selene.

"This is *his* doing," Selene muttered.

"Oh, live a little, Selene. You can at least pretend to fit in."

"I don't want to pretend," she replied, her voice filled with anger.

They walked through the crowd. Veronica made every effort to stay as close to them as possible. They approached a long table, covered in black satin positioned on a black stage. Two chalices sat on the opposite ends of the table, and she saw three huge wooden chairs, decorated with blue, red, and black jewels. One chair, bigger than the rest, caught Veronica's attention. Kei sat there, probably to bask in his immoral debauchery. But who else was allowed to sit at the table?

Veronica froze in her steps, horrified at what she saw ahead of her.

A grotesque set up of five naked men hung a couple of feet in the air over a huge cauldron. A rope fastened to a large metal hook was wrapped around their wrists. Around the cauldron five more naked female victims with their mouths gagged and their wrists tied, sat on the floor. Veronica covered her mouth in shock and turned away, hearing their muffled cries and moans. A part of her wanted to run, to find help. She forced her body to turn back around.

"Stay calm," Selene whispered to her.

Her suggestion seemed ill. Veronica couldn't understand how she could remain calm while staring at something this barbaric. She wanted to help but she couldn't risk it. She wiped her face, clearing out any hint that was distressing and she placed the victims out of her mind.

A Deamhan woman and man holding hands approached Selene. "What a nice specimen." The woman's eyes danced at Veronica's appearance. "Is she yours for the evening or are you going to share?"

Veronica moved behind Selene in an attempt to hide her from the Deamhan's prying eyes.

Selene's eyes fiercely locked onto the two Deamhan. "Choose your next words wisely."

The couple looked at each other and the male laughed. "Excuse us, then. You could've just said no."

Selene immediately reached out, grabbing the male by his neck. In a quick blur, Silvanus jumped onto the female.

Veronica found their accelerated speed to be confounding and horrid; something she could never get used to. Silvanus had the female by the neck and he pinned her to the floor. She hissed and squirmed, showing sharp Ramanga fangs. Silvanus looked up at Veronica, smiling with his eyes widening in a cold, hungry stare and his fangs protruding in a wrathful angle.

Selene also had the male pinned to the ground. "I am Selene, offspring of Lucius and an Ancient. You Deamhan show no respect."

The male retracted his fangs and his eyes widened.

"And I am Silvanus, offspring of Anora and also an Ancient. But I don't really care about your respect. " He violently sunk his teeth into the soft tissue of the female's neck and he closed his eyes as he began to drink, suckling like a baby feeding from its mother's breast. The woman's quivering ceased slowly, coming to a final stop as the sucking paralyzed her. After he finished her off, Silvanus licked the excess blood from his lips and motioned for Selene to release the male. Selene released his grip and the male tried to crawl away, but in moments, Silvanus was on top of him and he sank his teeth into his neck. He finished his meal and stood up, wiping a small trail of blood sliding down the corner of his mouth. Their act went unnoticed.

"You aren't hungry?" Silvanus looked back at Selene.

"No," she answered calmly.

Veronica felt herself wanting to vomit. Silvanus regained his posture and stared at her. His skin tone slowly turned from pale to a darker shade as the fresh Deamhan blood worked its way through his veins. The two bodies slowly began to dissipate, turning into an outline of brown sand and finally into a pile of dust and blood.

"Did you have to kill them?" Veronica somehow found the nerve and bravery to ask.

Silvanus smiled. "No."

"His scent was all around them," a voice behind them stated. They turned around to see Lambert dressed in a bright white dress suit and black silk tie with polished shoes that gleamed under the falsified lights. His appearance rocked Veronica who'd thought she'd seen the last of him when she left Dark Sepulcher a while ago.

"They smelled like Kei." Lambert looked at Selene. "Correct me if I'm wrong, Selene."

"Yes, they smelled like him."

Lambert looked at Veronica. "Veronica, happy that you were able to make it." He held a chalice in his hand.

"What are you doing here?" Veronica asked, straightening her posture.

"I invited him," Selene answered. She stepped closer to Lambert. She was taller than him, yet her presence did little to intimidate him.

He smiled, unbothered by her threatening stance. "Yes, Selene and I go way back. Plus I couldn't miss this for the world."

Silvanus held out his hand to Lambert. "We haven't formally been introduced, vampire."

"And tonight is no different." Lambert turned around and slyly walked away.

Silvanus stared at his hand. "Vampires can be so supercilious."

"Yes we can." Lambert looked over his shoulder. "However, we can also be helpful." He walked onto the stage and stood in front of the long table.

They followed him cautiously and Silvanus walked around the table, examining one of the two chalices on it. He slowly seated himself in a chair and peered into the chalice, smiling. "Very comfy," he said, squirming around in the chair. He looked out to the dance floor. "This is a nice view."

"But this is a better view." Lambert pointed to the cauldron spectacle Veronica saw earlier.

Silvanus looked at the human victims. "I have to agree with you. That is a better view." He picked up his chalice in rejoice and placed it back on the table.

Veronica turned around, staring at the crowds of Deamhan enjoying their environment. She sensed Selene's agitation. She didn't care for anything mildly associated with Kei. To Selene, this wasn't what the Deamhan were about. The modern, out in the open, careless environment wasn't what the older Deamhan like Lucius, Silvanus, and Selene wanted.

"I didn't invite you here to gloat about the best views, Lambert." Selene placed her hands on her hips.

"Yes, yes." Lambert waved her worries away with a flick of his wrist. "My vampires are outside, waiting on my command. All you have to do is tell me when."

The music died down and the crowd began to hush.

"Come with me." Selene gripped Veronica by her arm and she led her off the stage and to the side with Silvanus following behind them. It grew quiet in the large room. The human victims silenced their cries. Suddenly a door creaked open from the far back of the room and footsteps approached the crowd in an eerie silence.

Throughout the crowd the name "Kei" floated in the air like an arcane name. Veronica looked back at Selene, who remained stern and unmoved by the crowd's actions.

Veronica unfolded her arms and began to rub her fingers into her sweaty palms. A weird image of what Kei looked like flashed in her mind. He had to be tall, broody, and unafraid. He had to have a stare that could gaze through her soul. She heard the faint footsteps coming from behind the stage, and she turned to look at the Deamhan who last saw her mother alive.

A man of average stature casually walked toward the table. He wasn't lavishly dressed like many of his attendees. Instead he wore a black leather jacket with blue jeans and a faded white shirt. His greasy, brown hair was slicked back; his jaw round, and his sunken eyes accentuated his prominent brow. He held a half-smoked cigarette in one hand and a can of beer in the other.

His appearance caught everyone by surprise, even Selene, who remained still yet alert. To Veronica, Kei didn't represent the image of someone who could take down Lucius. He looked assimilated into human culture and society; like an anti-Deamhan representation. Kei inhaled his cigarette and took a sip from his beer. He gulped the last of it and crunched the can, tossing it over his shoulder. The clinking noise of it hitting the floor acted like the bell, beginning round one in what was to be the fight for control of the city.

Kei raised his hands and everyone in the room went quiet. His display of control was unfathomable.

"Welcome," he said in a loud, commanding voice. The crowd repeated their welcome back to him. He glanced at everyone in the room before he climbed the stairs onto the stage. He slowly walked over to the jeweled chair and he sat, kicking his feet onto the table. He inhaled and flicked the ash of his cigarette onto the floor.

"I have to find better bodyguards." His steel cold eyes turned to Selene and Silvanus. "And you brought *that*?" He pointed at Veronica. Veronica felt the piercing glare of the crowd and she slightly turned her head to look behind her, nervous that at any moment a Deamhan would rush from the crowd to attack her.

"It's been decades, Kei," Selene said.

"Not long enough," he replied back. "Why are you here anyway? I don't remember inviting you."

The eerie silence of the crowd became more uncomfortable by the minute. Veronica gulped and closed her eyes. She felt the tingling sensation start in her head and she immediately reopened her mind. He tried to read her. This time she had no intention of hiding her thoughts from anyone.

"You know what happened to my mother, you son of a bitch!" Veronica lashed out at him. The burning sensation stopped and he cocked his head to the side with a defined smirk on his face.

He leaned back in his chair with his eyes locked onto Veronica. "Silence your minion, Selene," he said coldly.

"I'm not her minion." Veronica wasn't ready to silence herself. Kei flicked the cigarette toward Veronica, landing just inches in front of her on the floor.

Suddenly the crowd began to mumble and a voice within the crowd spoke out.

"Kill her!"

The mumbling continued, growing louder. Kei raised his hands for quiet. "No one touches her." A wide grin appeared on his face. "She's mine."

"She's protected," Selene bellowed.

Kei laughed. "In my city, I determine who's protected and who's not." He raised his chalice to the crowd and they cheered. "I don't give a flying fuck about your protection." Kei turned his head slightly to the right, glaring at Silvanus. "You think bringing another Ancient"—he then looked to Lambert— "and a vampire here to plot against me, would actually work? I own this city and every Deamhan in it."

"Lucius is head Deamhan in Minneapolis," Selene replied. "Not you."

"And where is our beloved maker?" Kei jokingly looked around the room. "He isn't here. Oh yeah, that's right. He's dead." The Deamhan in the crowd laughed at his comment.

"You never were the brightest one, Kei," Selene responded.

"True, but I was his favorite." Kei clapped his hands. From the back of the stage, two scantily dressed females appeared. They rushed to his aid, removing the chalices from the table. These minions hurried over to the cauldron and dipped the chalices in the blood collecting below the human bodies.

"But before I allow my followers to tear you both apart slowly"—Kei stood up from his seat—"you'll watch me torture, maim, and kill your human." He then raised his chalice in the air. "A toast!" Everyone in the crowd raised their chalices in the air. "To our species. To our survival. Let no one, human, vampire or Ancient, stand in our way!" They devoured their drinks from their chalices in unison. Kei wiped a small trickle of blood from the corner of his mouth and smiled wickedly.

His eyes flickered and he dropped his chalice. "Now." He opened his eyes and his pupils disappeared and his eyes turned stark black. "It's time to eat."

"I'm declaring a Decretum against you and your followers," Selene stated loudly. Again, the crowd laughed.

"This is my city, Selene," Kei replied back belligerently. "And these Deamhan are my brothers and sisters." He held his arms out to the crowd in response to the crowd's cheering. "We're tired of Ancients telling us what to do. We're tired of rules and laws."

Veronica looked to Selene, waiting for her next move.

"The only way you could get rid of Lucius was to ban him with dark magic," Selene said forcefully.

Kei non-caringly shrugged. "So fucking what," he replied.

"Kill her!" a female voice from the crowd blurted out.

"In time, brothers and sisters." Kei waved.

"Lucius loved you like a father loves his son." Selene stepped forward trying to keep a dialogue going. "And you repay him back by betraying him!"

"His mistake." Kei mused, as he began to pick at his fingernails in deviance and utter disrespect.

Veronica clearly saw the problem that Selene, Silvanus, and even Lambert saw in Kei. How could Lucius sire someone as defiant as that? He didn't care about anyone but himself. While he assimilated himself into human society he managed to perfect what the Deamhan were truly like. The Deamhan in the crowd; Ramanga, Metusba, Lamia, and Lugat, latched onto every word that came from his mouth. He was their God.

Finally he looked at Selene. "You didn't even exist until you came rolling into my city." He looked back at the crowd. "Ask them. You don't exist, but I *do*. I exist."

"Yeah, you're really famous," Veronica said in a sarcastic tone. "You're the child who wasn't strong enough to kill your own sire."

"She can't protect you from me, human. No one can," Kei said in a lowered voice. He clapped his hands again, and the front door behind the crowd opened. A trail of naked humans entered, walking in a single line toward the stage. Their wrists were tied together with rope, and they each wore a dog chain around their neck that kept them connected to one another. They passed through the slithering crowd, and when they reached the stage they stopped and turned around.

They treated humans like cattle, being led out for slaughter. Just pieces of meat, chained together like wild animals.

The sight didn't bother Selene, nor did it bother anyone in the venue, besides Veronica. A massive curdling scream came from Kei's mouth and the crowd moved in unison, toward the innocent victims to devour.

"It's time to feast!" Kei yelled out to the crowd. He then pointed to Selene. "Kill her and the Ancient. Leave the vampire and the human for me."

Just then the front door opened unexpectedly.

Everyone turned around and watched the body of one of the bouncers fall, landing in the doorway. No one said anything and Kei, confused about the cause of the commotion, walked around the table to get a better look.

His eyes slowly bulged and he remained dazed, watching Lucius slowly walk through the door. Veronica saw that Lucius now looked fully re-energized. He wore a long blue shirt and saggy black jeans. He swiped back his hair. His eyes were solid black.

Veronica turned to look at Silvanus and Selene. Their eyes danced at the sight of him. The assault was about to begin.

"Now, Lambert!" Selene called out.

Silvanus jumped onto the stage and he pushed the long table forward. It slid across the stage, stopping only inches from the front of the crowd. The chalices flew across the floor, and many in the front of the crowd jumped, caught off guard by the sudden movement.

"Kill them!" Kei screamed. "Kill them all!"

For seconds no one in the room moved at the sight of Lucius. Veronica then felt Selene's hand wrap around her wrist, and in moments she found herself in a corner of the room.

"Stay hidden," Selene whispered to her. Veronica nodded, mute and dumbfounded. Selene ran back into the crowd. In the distance Veronica saw Lucius, cutting through the horde in ease, slashing whoever stood in his way. He paid little attention to the chained humans huddled together on the floor.

The windows shattered as several vampires jumped through the broken glass and began to attack the Deamhan crowd.

Selene moved toward Kei, but he proved to be just as fast. They blurred together as they fought, smashing against the table and chairs around them. Silvanus moved in, but a female Deamhan lunged at him stopping his attack. He wrapped his hand around her neck and twisted with force, detaching her head from her body.

A brief gust of wind blew Veronica back. She covered her eyes for a moment. Suddenly, she felt cold hands wrap around her neck. A male Deamhan pushed her to the ground. She opened her mouth to scream, but he immediately placed his mouth over her own and he began to feed.

The man suddenly jerked and let go, glancing at a piece of wood sticking out from his chest. Anastasia stood behind him. She pushed the Deamhan to the side and helped Veronica to her feet.

"A Lamia," Anastasia said in a monotone voice. The sound of flesh being ripped open grabbed her attention, and Anastasia quickly turned around to watch Lucius, covered in blood from head to toe. His hair, once washed, now dripped with clots of blood and dust. A male Deamhan stood on his knees in front of Lucius, begging for his life. Lucius raised his right arm slowly and swiped with his nails across the Deamhan's throat. Another man tried to run past Lucius but he was caught and killed within seconds.

Lucius opened his mouth and screamed. The high pitched echo vibrated and drowned out the screams coming from the other Deamhan in the room. It shook the window panes and made the disco balls sway back and forth on the ceiling. It also rattled the chalices on the ground.

Near the back of the room, Veronica saw a group of Kei's followers attempting to dive through the windows to safety. Those who were still alive ran for the exits but were cornered off by Lambert's vampires who guarded the doors. Another Deamhan dressed in a black tuxedo dropped to his knees in front of Lucius and began to caress his feet. Lucius kicked him aside and continued forward.

Anastasia jumped on stage to join Selene against Kei. Kei quickly darted across the stage, passing Lambert. He jumped over the cauldron, his foot skidding across its edge. The cauldron fell, pouring its bloody contents on the floor.

"You'll pay for what you did, Kei." Selene launched herself toward him, pushing Kei onto his back. Kei pushed her off and in Deamhan speed he barreled toward the back of the room.

Silvanus followed in pursuit but stopped unexpectedly.

"You're letting him escape?" Lambert screamed out to him.

Silvanus looked over his shoulder at Lucius. "Lucius is letting him escape."

"You want him to run?" Anastasia asked in disbelief while watching Lucius finish off his last victim.

The room filled with an eerie silence.

Veronica stepped out of the corner to watch Lucius lifting a Deamhan in the air by his throat. A loud crunching sound followed, and the victim's body went limp. He dropped the Deamhan to the floor.

"Lucius?" Anastasia approached him. "Why let Kei run?"

Lucius held up his hand and Anastasia immediately stopped her questioning. The chained humans still cowered in their small huddle in the corner but their presence was ignored. Lucius slowly walked by them, stepping through the pool of blood and up to the stage. The bodies of dying Deamhan were strewn around the room. The smell of blood ravaged the air.

Selene examined the long scratches and fight wounds over her forearms and watched them slowly heal. "Why did you stop Silvanus from catching Kei?"

Veronica cautiously took a couple of steps forward and covered her nose and mouth with her hands. She too became curious as to why Lucius would mentally tell Silvanus to stop his attack.

Lucius didn't speak. He slowly walked along the stage and he looked to the ceiling then to the back of the room at the remaining vampires who waited for Lambert's command. "It's not always about revenge . . . not yet."

"This is revenge," Selene replied. "For what he did to you!"

"Selene." Lucius motioned for her to approach him. She stepped up to him and he placed his hand on the back of her head. "Don't carry my hate for me." He then motioned for Anastasia to also approach him.

"Let us do this for you." Anastasia walked over to him.

Lucius shook his head. "No, you won't."

Veronica looked at Lucius. She wanted to ask, and she wanted to know, what had really happened to her mother. Yet she remained afraid. She watched Lucius gently kiss Anastasia on her forehead followed by Selene. She understood somewhat why her mother researched him. He seemed different than any Deamhan. Besides his age and his attractiveness, he also showed the human trait of compassion.

Thoughts about her mother filled her mind and she didn't bother to block them. Picking up on these thoughts Lucius turned to face her. "I will speak to her alone."

The vampires left the room followed by Lambert. Silvanus disappeared from Veronica's eyesight in an instant. Anastasia hesitated but also left. Selene bit her lower lip before she walked out of the room.

"You look just like your mother." Lucius motioned for Veronica to come up on the stage.

Veronica haltingly stepped forward, stopping just inches from the stage. She gathered her thoughts and she took a deep breath. She climbed the steps and she walked over to him.

"My mother researched you and followed you," she said in a hushed whisper. Her nose caught the iron scent of blood still dripping from Lucius' clothing.

"I remember your mother."

"What happened to her?" Veronica asked in a shaky voice. She felt her eyes beginning to tear and she looked away for a moment. She didn't want him to see her crying.

"I will show you." He placed his arms on her shoulders.

She felt her head beginning to tingle, and before she could stop him from piercing her thoughts, it was too late. She braced herself for the pain, but it never came.

She then heard his voice in her mind.

I loved your mother.

Loved? A Deamhan couldn't love? Impossible. Yet she wanted to know more.

What happened to her? She thought.

He opened his mind and she began to see his thoughts and memories.

They were brief and skipped frantically from scene to scene. Veronica saw her mother smiling and laughing. The scene changed and she now saw her mother standing on the shores of the Mississippi River, the moonlight glistening off the dark waters.

It changed again. She saw her from a distance, the same way Lucius saw her, cautiously walking alone down a dark alleyway. Veronica sensed her panic and she smelled her lilac perfume. Something or someone was following her.

Suddenly Lucius stood behind her mother and he placed his hand on her shoulder. She turned around and whispered his name.

He lifted her in his arms, staring into her eyes and wiped the sweat from her forehead. A sense of compassion overcame him, and he stood silent and confused. For the first time in centuries, he was beginning to love again.

He fed her, making it as quickly and painless as possible. When she was barely on the edge of death he cut himself on his forearm and he placed his wound close to her mouth. He then dragged her further into an alley and placed her body on the wet concrete, watching his blood beginning to turn her.

But something happened. Lucius grew weak and Veronica felt it. His senses grew numb and he failed to detect them as they came from all sides; behind, in front, and above. He struggled against them but the humans dressed in black trench coats managed to hold him down. Their smell was strong and reeked of The Brotherhood. They were there to take him but they didn't expect Veronica's mother to be in the alley with him.

Kei stood over her, glancing at Lucius' new creation. His hair was much longer then. He mocked his sire and he leaned over Veronica's mother and gently placed his mouth over her own.

Veronica pushed herself away from Lucius' thoughts. She took a step back, leaning against the wall for support. She didn't want him to continue, she didn't want to see anymore. She knew what happened next.

Her eyes slowly filled with tears and she felt her feet falter under her. She couldn't comprehend that Lucius had tried to sire her own mother. She feared her mother lost everything that made her human, especially the ability to love Veronica as her own flesh and blood, but Kei made sure there was no time for that. He killed her right there, in that alley. They both killed her. They were all responsible.

"You both killed her!" Veronica cried, holding her face in her hands. She felt his thoughts pushing again, but she turned her head. Nothing he could say or show would make up for what they both did.

Her mother was gone, truly gone.

Veronica held her head low in silence.

EPILOGUE

The office was small and confined. Frost covered the corners of the glass windows due to the Minnesota winter. Nothing on the outside of the building signaled that The Brotherhood had set up shop in this location except for Anastasia's keen sense of smell.

Anastasia described it to Veronica as a bland odor mixed with human blood, deodorant, and surprisingly, ink and coffee. The aroma tingled her nose, like a sneeze that had not manifested itself yet. It was milder than the other smells of Deamhan, vampires, and demons. It was also more pleasurable to inhale.

The front door was unlocked, and it didn't take much force for Veronica to push it open. The sound of bells clinging echoed through the front room signaling their entry. The waiting area was vacant. The red carpet brightened from underneath them and a huge welcome sign nailed to the wall, surrounded by scenic pictures of Minnesota, seemed almost too much to bear. Veronica's eyes glowered over the room.

The office looked different the time of her mother.

Near the receptionist desk, a group of young researchers gathered around a computer, but their attention now focused on them.

"Lambs for the slaughter," Anastasia uttered under her breath.

The researchers reacted to their sudden appearance by remaining quiet. Two males standing next to each other appeared less timid than the female, whose eyes reverted past Veronica and at Anastasia.

Veronica saw Kenneth seated at a gray desk behind them. She recognized him immediately and cleared her throat to get his attention.

He looked up from his desk and smiled. He straightened his white buttoned shirt and khaki slacks and slowly stood up from his feet. Looking more like a businessman than a researcher, he approached her and held out his hand.

"Veronica."

Her eyes scanned him from head to toe. She still couldn't grasp the fact that he was now Region Leader of the Midwest Division. It made her sick, and she wanted nothing more than for Anastasia to rip his throat out. But she wasn't here for that. She just wanted to give her father a message.

"You're going to get them killed." Veronica pointed to the researchers.

Kenneth lowered his hand. "I don't think that concerns you." His eyes drifted to Anastasia, who stood a step behind Veronica. Anastasia kept herself busy by slowly opening her mouth, with her fangs extended as she took in the scent of the humans around her.

"Don't you think you're disrespecting your mother's image?" He returned his attention toward Veronica. "You're now running around with them. You're living with *them*."

Veronica turned her head slightly to the researchers. Their posture now changed. They stood erect with their shoulders back and head slightly tilted up. They masked their fear by their non-fearful stance, yet in their eyes, Veronica still saw their fear of Anastasia.

"My father disrespected my mother's image." Veronica continued to stare at the researchers. "But I'm not here to argue about that."

"Well, why are you here?"

"I have a message for my father." Veronica cleared her throat. "Tell him I know."

"Know?" Kenneth questioned. "Know what?"

"Tell him." She took a deep breath. "I'll never forgive him for what The Brotherhood did to my mother."

"Your mother over stepped her bounds," Kenneth replied. "She knew the risks that came with the job."

Anastasia rushed forward, grabbing Kenneth by his collar. Veronica jumped slightly at her unexpected movement, and the researchers gasped. Anastasia slammed him onto his desk, pinning him by his shoulders. She leaned over him with her mouth opened and her fangs fully extended.

"And what about Lucius?" She sniffed his face then growled ferociously.

"You don't scare me," Kenneth replied.

Anastasia cocked her head to the side. "I sense different." Her teeth slowly retracted. She let go of his collar and slowly backed away from him.

"Tell my father to not come looking for me," Veronica said. She turned and walked back to the front door.

"You're turning your back on your family." Kenneth rubbed his throat and lifted himself from his desk. "Like it or not, we're your family, Veronica. Not those Deamhan."

Veronica opened the front door and waited to hear the bells clink before she spoke again. "Goodbye, Kenneth." She headed out into the subzero winds of Minnesota, followed by Anastasia.

* * * *

Kenneth stood to his feet and straightened his shirt. His hands trembled slightly, and he took a deep breath, trying to relax his body. He looked at the researchers, who remained still in their position. Now their eyes were on him and his next movement.

"Get back to work," he blurted out. He placed his hands on his hips and took another deep breath. "I'm going in the back," he said. "If they come back, ring for help."

He headed toward the back room. He continued to catch his breath, realizing how close he had been to death. It felt exhilarating.

Kenneth stopped in front of a black door and wiped the sweat from his brow. He looked himself over again, making sure that his clothing wasn't scrunched or ripped. He lifted his arms to check if the sweat under his armpits moistened his shirt. He knocked gently and turned the knob, pushing the door open.

Samuel Austin sat on a two seat leather couch with his legs crossed and his pipe dangling from the right corner of his mouth. He exchanged a warm smile with Kenneth, but upon noticing the sweat dripping down his forehead, his smile changed to concern.

"You had company?" Mr. Austin asked slowly.

A half-cocked smile appeared on Kenneth's face. He walked over to a long desk, waving off any assumption of his encounter. He didn't want the old man to worry. Instead, he wanted Mr. Austin to feel comfortable with his decision of making him Region Leader of the Midwest Division.

"Just your daughter, sir." Kenneth leaned against the edge of the desk. He began to fiddle around with the cluttered objects: pens, pieces of papers, a stapler. His jumpy behavior drew Mr. Austin to grab onto the edge of the couch and lift himself slowly to his feet.

Mr. Austin raised his hand before Kenneth could move to assist him. He then grabbed his cane and puffed on his pipe before walking toward him.

"Did she come to talk to me?" he asked.

"Just a warning, sir." Kenneth folded his hands in front of his chest. "If you ask me, your daughter is all words. She brought that Deamhan with her too, just to make it look like she meant business."

"Well." Mr. Austin puffed. "Obviously she got her point across." He referred to Kenneth's rattling behavior.

Mr. Austin walked to a large five-shelf bookcase at the opposite end of the wall. He remained quiet, examining the books stacked neatly against one another. Every book significant to The Brotherhood rested on the top two shelves while anything else less important, magazines and personal reading books, rested on the remaining shelves.

"How long is this going to go on for?" Kenneth asked. He felt the question escaping his lips was wrong, and he immediately wanted to recant.

"Plans have changed, Kenneth." Mr. Austin continued to admire the bookshelf. "I've told you that you have to be flexible if you eventually want to lead this organization."

Kenneth remained unsure but nodded anyway, trusting Mr. Austin's plan—

whatever it was. He didn't know the intricate details, but he knew just enough.

"But your daughter, sir." Kenneth froze in his reply.

"My daughter is like her mother." Mr. Austin turned to face him. "Never backing down, never accepting the answers to her questions."

A female giggle exploded from the corner of the room.

Kenneth stood up. He hadn't seen her before, and she seemed to appear out of nowhere.

He watched Selene standing in the corner, partially hidden in the shadows. Kenneth wasn't sure how long she'd been standing there, watching him ease his nervousness. Mr. Austin didn't flinch when she giggled, nor did he seem surprised by her interruption. Her tight hip-hugging jeans revealed her flat and smooth midsection. Her red hair nestled comfortably on her shoulders and slightly covered the outline of her breasts. She was barefoot, and her toes were painted with bright pink nail polish. She walked out of the shadows, moving her hips from side to side, her lips puckered and her eyes fixed on Kenneth. It was enough to make any man, Deamhan or human, swoon. He also noticed that something was different about her. She looked renewed since the last time he'd seen her.

Kenneth's infatuation with her first grew when she pinned Sean on the pool table at the bar located just down the street from Veronica's apartment. That was a sight to see. He liked her style. She was cunning, and neither Lucius nor any of those damned Deamhan knew what she was truly up to.

But he did.

"He's lusting after me." She stood next to Mr. Austin, still keeping her licentious eyes at Kenneth.

"No." Kenneth wiped his mind free from his thoughts.

"You worry too much." She flipped her long red hair to her back. "The plan worked. Kei is out of the way."

"But Lucius is not in Limbo anymore," Kenneth added. "Thanks to you."

"A last minute decision that I had to make." Selene shrugged her shoulders innocently. She wrapped her arm around Mr. Austin and smiled. "Besides, Lucius isn't as strong as he used to be," she said uncaringly. "Don't worry about him. He'll be too busy trying to kill Kei to know what's really going on."

"How is breaking him free going to help us secure our spot in this city?" Kenneth asked. "The Deamhan have no choice but to obey me now," Selene answered. "I am the Ancient here. Don't worry about Lucius. He'll be too busy running trying to finish Kei off."

Kenneth nodded unsurely and watched Mr. Austin nod to Selene's statement. Getting Kei dethroned was part of the plan. In his departure, Selene would take his place. Kenneth knew that the alliance between The Brotherhood and Selene would grow cold as soon as she thought she didn't need them anymore. Kenneth wasn't sure why Mr. Austin wanted to grow another Deamhan alliance.

"Why so uncertain?" Selene snickered. "Are you frightened, Kenneth?"

"No, I just don't like how it turned out." Kenneth shrugged off his worries. "And what was the deal you made with Amenirdis to free him?"

Selene lifted her hand from Mr. Austin's shoulders. She slowly walked over to him and placed her cold hands on his chest. "It's okay to admit that you're afraid," she whispered in his right ear.

"I'm just cautious." Startled, Kenneth moved away from her.

"I'm also curious on the deal you made with Amenirdis." Mr. Austin grabbed firmly on the tip of his cane. "She is like no other Deamhan The Brotherhood has faced since its beginning."

"You both need to relax." Selene gently rubbed Kenneth's shoulders. "The deal doesn't concern you or The Brotherhood." She sat on the edge of his desk and she crossed her legs. "Kei broke his deal he made to Amenirdis. So believe me when I say that if Lucius doesn't catch him, she will."

Kenneth nodded but still remained cautious. He couldn't explain the difference he saw in Selene that made any sense. Even her disposition; the way she replied regarding Lucius and Kei, seemed as if she didn't care.

She was hiding something.

Mr. Austin stomped his cane on the ground to gather their attention. "We've managed to restart the Minnesota Chapter along with protecting my daughter to the best of our ability." He puffed on his pipe and released the smoke in a long exalted breath. "Regardless of the change of plans, we're on the right path." He looked to Kenneth. "We need to start phase two."

Kenneth nodded.

Mr. Austin turned his attention to Selene. "Believe me when I say this, Selene. Any Deamhan that attempts to harm my daughter will be met with brute force. Nothing, and I mean nothing, is going to happen to my baby girl."

~end~

Author Bio

Isaiyan Morrison was born and raised in Minnesota. She moved to San Diego, California while in the Navy. After serving four years of active duty, she moved to Los Angeles.

After a few years, she moved back to Minnesota where she started to pursue her dream to be an author.

Her novel *Deamhan*, is the first book in the Deamhan series.

She now resides in Texas with her two cats, a pit bull dog, and two guinea pigs.

Made in the USA
Charleston, SC
21 February 2014